W9-AQF-140

THE ARBOGAST CASE

THE ARBOGAST CASE

THOMAS HETTCHE

TRANSLATED BY ELIZABETH GAFFNEY

FARRAR, STRAUS AND GIROUX / NEW YORK

Farrar, Straus and Giroux
19 Union Square West, New York 10003

Copyright © 2001 by DuMont Literatur und Kunst Verlag GmbH and Co. KG, Cologne (Germany)
Translation copyright © 2003 by Elizabeth Gaffney
All rights reserved
Distributed in Canada by Douglas & McIntyre Ltd.
Printed in the United States of America
Originally published in 2001 by DuMont Buchverlag, Germany, as *Der Fall Arbogast*
Published in the United States by Farrar, Straus and Giroux
First American edition, 2003

Library of Congress Cataloging-in-Publication Data
Hettche, Thomas.
[Fall Arbogast. English]
The Arbogast case / Thomas Hettche ; translated by Elizabeth Gaffney.
p. cm.
ISBN 0-374-13812-5 (alk. paper)
I. Gaffney, Elizabeth. II. Title.

PT2668.E866F3713 2003
833'.914—dc21

2003004825

Designed by Jonathan D. Lippincott

www.fsgbooks.com

1 2 3 4 5 6 7 8 9 10

THE ARBOGAST CASE

1

She laughed as if she had just discovered something and turned back to look at him. Drawn to her laugh, he let the two sides of the swing doors slide slowly across his open palms before gently releasing them. There was almost no sound as the doors closed behind him and he stepped out into the evening twilight and her laughter. Afterward, he always remembered the quiet of that moment and the way the cool, smooth wood of the doors had brushed across his palms, almost as if he were being nudged forward. That was when it started. But when he pictured her face, later on, he couldn't really say what it was that had captivated him.

" 'When angels go abroad . . . ,' " she began, but didn't finish the sentence. As he stood there, she reached out and touched his forearm to suggest that he turn around. "Look, there."

It was almost painful, the way her touch drew the tension from his skin. He already knew the bar was called the Angel; he also knew, as he turned back to look at the yellow neon sign, that they would sleep together. All day long, he hadn't been sure, but now he could taste it on his tongue as certainly as if he held a smooth pebble in his mouth. He spit it into his hand, ashamed of it, and stuck it in his pocket. In those days, out in the country, there weren't many neon signs, and this sign's glow had seemed very faint until the end of the summer's day. There were no cars on the road that ran past the bar, and it was quiet except for the buzzing of the neon tubes. They stood there in the yellow light for a moment; he felt her hand on his arm and let it fall, then grasped her around the waist and touched the resilient synthetic fabric of her dress for the first time. She slid into his embrace as if into a coat, but then suddenly she wasn't as energetic anymore. She shivered; she needed someone to warm her up.

" 'When angels go abroad . . . the heavens smile,' " he whispered into her ear, finishing her phrase.

The way they went to his car, it was as if they'd known each other a long time. He was struck by her silence as he opened her door and closed it carefully behind her. The whole afternoon, she'd chattered and told him stories. He hesitated briefly, looking back down the road they'd traveled together. He'd pulled over at the railway overpass outside of Grangat on the way to Gottsweiher and asked if he could give her a lift. "Sure," she'd said, and only then asked where he was heading. In fact, he was on his way to Freiburg, for business, but he'd told her he was just out for a drive. She wasn't from around there, was she? he'd asked. No, Berlin. Ah, he thought—one of the refugees from the East. Did she live in Ringsheim, in the camp, then? She'd nodded, and he'd looked at her.

She might have been in her early twenties, but he found it difficult to tell with such a delicate woman. She was just over five feet and had short, curly red hair. Her eyes were always in a squint, which might have been the sun or shortsightedness—he couldn't tell—but it gave her an air of confidence, as did her Berlin accent, which sounded unfamiliar to him. Her dress, with its round neck and short-cropped sleeves, had a pattern of green leaves on an ice blue field, and she wasn't wearing a crinoline. But she was wearing a pair of white pumps. Had she been to the Black Forest before? She shook her head. And then they'd driven off. It had been a lovely day, and not merely on account of the weather, he'd thought. The date had occurred to him just then, he later recalled: the first of September, 1953. He walked around the car, opened the door on the driver's side and got in. She was silent, but he knew that didn't make any difference.

He didn't put his hand on her knee—that would have seemed too forward—but once they were off and he'd casually shifted into third, he pressed the back of his hand lightly against her upper thigh, just as if he always kept his hand there, positioned quite carelessly on the edge of the passenger seat. She didn't pull away, nor did she reciprocate that slight pressure as the night fell irrevocably around them and they drove in silence toward Grangat. After awhile, he felt her hand on his neck and her fingers slipping inside his shirt collar, roving as far as his left armpit before they retreated, and then her fingernails and then her fingertips, grazing his carotid, all the way up to his left ear, and finally plunging down his unbuttoned shirt collar, as if helpless to resist.

"Is it far?"

"About an hour."

"Why don't we just stop somewhere along the way?"

"Do we want to do that?"

"Yes." Her voice was so close against his face that he could feel her moist breath on his skin.

As he approached a small bridge between Gutach and Hausach, he braked, took his hand from the edge of her seat to downshift and gave a little gas; she leaned toward him, put her arms around him and kissed him. On the left side of the road, just before the bridge, there was a path that led through a meadow and into the darkness. Without signaling, he took the turn and rolled down a small incline. On the right, there was a small stream and the bridge that spanned it. Some shrubbery blocked the view to the road, and a field opened up off the path. He turned off the engine and cut the headlights.

Marie pulled a pack of cigarettes from her white patent-leather purse and asked him for a light. She smoked Kurmark, but the brand didn't seem to fit her at all. The perfect blend every time—"Great flavor, and mild, too," he thought, flicking his lighter on with his left thumb and cupping his other hand around hers as he touched the flame to the tip of her cigarette. She thanked him with a nod. She wasn't all that young after all, he saw. The creases at the corners of her mouth gave her laugh a trembling quality that made him want her. She told him about herself: the war, the two children she'd left behind with her mother, the wooden barracks at the refugee camp where she lived. She barely mentioned her husband. He doubted she was lying much. Her hands were not girlish. She wasn't wearing a ring and—strange that he only noticed it now—no stockings, either.

He opened the ashtray, holding the lighter with its flame still going in the other hand. She exhaled smoke and gave another nod. He took the pack of cigarettes from her hand and lit one for himself. Then he put the lighter away and dropped the cigarettes in her lap. As if that were a challenge, she moved her purse to the floor and leaned toward him, and he kissed her. He kept close to her as she leaned back, switching the cigarette to his left hand and placing his right hand behind her neck. The glow of the cigarette seemed to float in the air between the thin white steering wheel of the Isabella and the equally white Bakelite knob of the radio, just above the ashtray, into which he then let his cigarette fall without looking. She pressed her head back against the seat cushion and his arm with all her strength. He managed to pull her up to him nevertheless, and then, when her head fell back slightly, he ran his tongue along her gums, spelling out each of her teeth.

Her lower lip quivered, which didn't surprise him—he sensed the same excitement under his own skin, as well, the way it traveled from his lips through his entire body. But just as he was registering that sensation, she freed herself from his kiss and his embrace. For a moment he thought it might all be a mistake, a misunderstanding, an imposition. Then she hurriedly stubbed out her cigarette in the ashtray, and this time it was she who softly pressed him into the upholstery and crouched over him. And as she kissed him and her hands crept back inside his shirt, he held her around the waist, then found the buttons on the side of her dress and undid them. His fingers slid across a soft charmeuse undergarment and onto her skin.

"Shall I undress?"

He nodded and pushed her dress up around her legs to her hips while she reached over her head, grasped the dress with both hands and pulled it off. Her white slip gleamed as the headlights of a passing car streamed wildly across her body and then momentarily gilded the ceiling panel of the car. In the last glimmer of light, he saw that she was looking at him.

"Should we go outside? It's still warm."

He nodded again, and she unbuttoned his shirt while he undid his pants and kicked off his shoes.

"Come on," she whispered.

There she was, standing in this incredibly shiny slip in the night-dark meadow beside the dirt path. She turned and took a few steps. She'd left her shoes behind in the car. Her skin was very pale—as is often the case with redheads, or so he'd read—as she sauntered lazily, head down, through the tall, dry grass. At one point, she stopped and, keeping her back turned to the car, took off her slip, her bra and her panties.

He came up behind her, grasped her shoulders and pressed himself against her, slipping himself between her thighs. He felt how wet she was and whispered in her ear how much he wanted her. She laughed again. Not the loud, bright laughter he knew from before, but a breathy, nearly toneless cooing, in time with the movement of her hips as she ground against him. He could still see her smiling from beneath closed lids when she turned back around for a kiss. Then they collapsed onto the ground where her underwear lay, not quite letting themselves fall so much as holding each other on the way down.

She pulled away from his embrace and lay on her belly, expectant, supporting herself with her hands, not facing him. He had a full view of her ass, caressed it there, at the crack, then took hold of her hips and turned her gently onto her back. He grasped her by the thighs and pushed into her. For a moment, he thought he sensed resistance, but then she looked straight at him, bore down and began to follow his rhythm.

He didn't kiss her, just stared at her openly and kept thrusting until he came. Afterward, he considered whether he still liked her and was glad he did. He lay quietly beside her in the grass for a while, then knelt between her legs and looked at her in the moonlight, to which his eyes had now grown accustomed. He saw her thinness for the first time, her scruffy, light pubic hair, her bony hips and shoulders. Her breasts were small and pointy, her toenails painted. There were deep circles under her eyes that he'd somehow failed to notice the entire day. Even now, he thought, I don't know her. He caressed her belly with an open hand. There was no sound but the eerie whispering of the dry grass. It had gotten distinctly chilly outside. It'll be fall soon, he thought with a faint dread.

"Let's have a cigarette," she said and sat up.

He got to his feet and reached out for her hand. She let him pull her up as she scooped up her underwear with her other hand. They walked hand in hand back to the car and sat down, leaving the Isabella's doors open like two wings spread wide. He noticed she kept her panties between her legs so as not to soil the leatherette upholstery. Then she pulled the slip over her head and he gave her a light. Once again, they said nothing while they smoked, but with her left hand she stroked his inner thigh, again and again, as if she needed to be sure of him. At last, she kissed his neck, his breast, and threw her cigarette out the passenger door. She kissed him breathlessly, as if she couldn't tear herself away from him, sucked his nipples so hard that it hurt, and he flinched. But all she had to do was smile for him to bend back down to her. This time, she bit his neck, and all the while her hand was still stroking his thigh in a strangely chaste manner that would surely have reawakened his lust, even if she hadn't used her teeth.

"I'm not done yet," she murmured into his neck.

"Neither am I."

He pushed aside her slip and bit her right nipple, and she writhed as if she were spring-loaded, as if he were winding her up, and the car seat could only just contain her. She drew her knees up against her body and sucked his neck harder and harder, as if that were the only thing that sustained her. It was like the way the parts of a tool fit together—he'd never touched anyone like that before and he couldn't let go, not of her. It was only force of will that kept him from really hurting her. Not until at some point he discovered the taste of blood in his mouth, despite his attempt at restraint, did he release her, shocked; at the same moment, her mouth detached from him, and when the tension that had bound them together was released, she slid backward, almost falling out of the car.

"Come on!" she said.

By the time he'd gotten around the car, she was lying down in the grass beside the little stream. The water here rushed quite loudly around the piers of the bridge, and the breeze was colder than it had been in the protection of the scrub. The moment he approached her, she rolled away and lay in the same position as she had before, propped up on her knees and elbows. He would never forget how warm it was when he knelt behind her and reached out to touch her sex with his open hand. He held her with both hands and pushed into her, and she relaxed at once, spine slowly collapsing into the small of her back, ass pressing into his belly, until he was in her entirely. She arched against him.

"Harder!"

"More?"

"Much harder!"

He closed his eyes.

"Then hold still."

But she didn't. She turned back to look at him and laughed her laugh again. Eyes open now, he reached for her face and grasped her hair, but she grabbed his hand and sucked two of his fingers into her mouth in a way that nearly made him come. Finally, he was holding her by the base of the neck. She squirmed momentarily out of his grip, then laid her neck in his large hand. She gripped him so strongly with her sex, it was as if she wanted to delay his climax, and it seemed to him it could go on forever, that he would never be able to come, that she, whom he'd known for barely a day, understood his body far better than he did himself.

"Look at me."

He often wondered, afterward, how much time passed before he whispered to her again, asking her to look at him—again and again.

"Please, look at me."

She didn't answer. Only when her silence had sunk in did he realize that she wasn't responding to his movements, either, hadn't been for an infinitely long moment. He stopped dead and listened, and it was completely quiet, except for the whispering grass. She was no longer holding him. She was still on her arms and knees but had collapsed into herself. He slid out of her, and she away from him. She lay there with her back to him, she who had only just been so close to him, without moving. And he felt a completely unfamiliar sensation that he often thought about later on, a kind of weariness pulling on him, heavily. A weariness so black that he—a man not otherwise fearful—was suddenly as frightened as a child. As if something that was passing over had lingered to make a demand of him. And soon enough, it really did pass. Timidly, he bent over her and begged her once more to look at him.

"Look at me!"

Then he turned her over.

2

The cemetery gardener wore faded blue work pants, a matching jacket and black rubber boots. He'd long since passed the age of retirement and walked as if he had gout. He was silent as he led the medical examiner, Dr. Dallmer, to the mortuary, which was on the property of the city cemetery, across from the railroad and adjacent to the Convent of Our Lady. Dallmer was accompanied by Dr. Bärlach, a research assistant at the Institute of Pathology at Freiburg University, whom he'd brought along to conduct the autopsy. It was after midday, but because the building was also used for wakes and funeral receptions, this was the earliest they'd been able to get access to the body, which had been brought in the night before by the police. In the anteroom of the neo-Gothic building, a diffuse blue-green light filtered through the stained-glass windowpanes. The air reeked strongly of incense and water that had been standing too long in the many great vases of flowers, an odor that was magnified when the gardener unlocked the door at the side of the altar. It opened onto a small room that was brimming, to Bärlach's amazement, with metal buckets holding countless numbers of flowers, mostly lilies and gladioli, and their aroma rose up and surrounded the men.

Dr. Dallmer, a thickset, balding older gentleman with a prominent gray mustache and gold-rimmed spectacles, did not seem the least bit surprised by the floral array. He went immediately to the small window and opened it, letting in fresh air and soft afternoon light, which illuminated the white petals of the blossoms. Even the large sink was full of flowers, and the small desk and stone examination table were covered with them, too. At the rear, resting on two wooden sawhorses, was a fresh pine coffin with the lid ajar. The two doctors quietly got to work, Dr. Dallmer wiping the desk surface dry and opening the cover of the typewriter—a Hermes Baby—on which he would type the report. Bärlach, who would be conducting the autopsy, donned a white coat over his light summer suit and laid out his dissection tools on a small tray beside the sink, then thoroughly cleaned off the stone dissection table, which was littered with flower petals and bits of earth. He was very young, not yet thirty, narrow of face but tall beneath his white coat. The gardener opened the coffin and helped the doctors lift out the nude female corpse; then they thanked him and he left.

Though both men avoided looking at the dead woman unnecessarily, they noticed how small she looked lying there on the large stone table, her eyes closed, her hands covering her sex. The medical examiner rolled a form into the typewriter; the pathologist loaded a roll of film into his Leica. Then he set the camera on its tripod and exposed the first frame. For a moment, they both seemed to be waiting for something. Then the young pathologist bent over the corpse and began.

"Autopsy report: external view of the deceased. We're looking at the body of a young woman. Age, approximately early twenties. The body is cold. Rigor mortis of the large and small joints has passed."

Bärlach paused and looked over at the medical examiner, who was a surprisingly skilled typist. Dr. Dallmer nodded and the pathologist continued.

"There are signs of livor mortis and a series of contusions running diagonally across the left flank. The hair of the scalp is dyed red and cut fairly short. The roots of the hair show the natural hair color to be blond. The eyes are closed."

Dr. Bärlach ran his hand gently across the head of the dead woman, as if to calm her, then removed a small flashlight from the breast pocket of his coat and bent over her face. Without looking, he then pulled a pair of forceps from the same pocket and used them carefully to remove an object from the eye of the corpse.

"Examination of the fold of the left eyelid reveals the presence of insect eggs. The upper lid of the left eye shows dark blue and red discoloration. The left cheek appears to be swollen. Numerous linseed-size petechial hemorrhages are present on the surface of the skin. Small hemorrhages are also present on the forehead, beneath the right eye and on the right nostril. Both earlobes are pierced, and the deceased is wearing small glass earrings, set in silver."

"Set in silver?" asked the medical examiner.

"Yes."

As he nodded, Dr. Bärlach opened the dead woman's mouth.

"The oral cavity is empty of foreign objects. The teeth are in poor condition, and the second bicuspid on the lower right is missing."

He took a picture of the corpse's head before he went on.

"On the left side of the neck, beneath the jawline, there is an upward-angled ligature mark represented by an area of contused tissue eight centimeters in length. There's another area of contused tissue, with the skin somewhat abraded, extending five centimeters from beneath the chin up to the right side of the face—an additional sign of strangulation."

"You think she was strangled?" The medical examiner had stood up and was inspecting the neck of the dead woman. "It's not very clear that that's a ligature mark."

"No, you're right. It shouldn't be stated so definitively. Will you help me turn her over?"

Together, the two doctors rolled the body onto its stomach, with Dr. Bärlach carefully holding her chin. Then Dallmer sat back down at his typewriter.

"On examination of the posterior aspect," said the pathologist, continuing his report, "surface abrasions of various dimensions are evident on the neck and the area around the shoulder blades. There is a large horizontal rust-colored welt extending ten centimeters in length across the right shoulder blade, as well as additional horizontal scratch marks and contusions of up to seven centimeters long on the posterior and lateral sides of the left buttock. The anus is notably dilated and a small amount of watery red fluid is present in the rectum.

There are tears in the transitional tissue between the epidermis and the mucosal epithelium."

"Anal sex?"

Bärlach nodded. "Looks like it. Can you give me another hand?"

The medical examiner stepped up and helped him return the cadaver to its back. The pathologist leaned over the rib cage.

"Examination of the area under the right breast, in line with the axilla, reveals a lengthwise contusion of approximately one and a quarter centimeters. Fingernail marks from the index, middle and ring fingers, as well as the fifth digit, are visible on the lateral and anterior aspects of the right breast, with the position of the index finger notably lower than the others. There are three bite marks around the left nipple, indicative of an upper and lower jaw that meet without gap. A further bite mark can be seen on the left anterior aspect of the belly, in line with the navel, and here, though here there is only a single mark from the teeth of the lower jaw, there are two separate impressions left by the upper teeth, both approximately three fingers above the iliac crest."

"My God, he was taking bites out of her."

"Looks that way." Dr. Bärlach nodded and stepped over to the desk where the medical examiner sat.

"A pervert."

For a moment, it seemed as if the pathologist was going to respond, but then he simply glanced over his shoulder at Dr. Dallmer and continued with his dictation.

"Axillary and pubic hair is consistent with the decedent's gender. The hands are well maintained, the fingernails long. Examination of the fingernails reveals no detectable sign that the deceased tried to defend herself."

He paused.

"That's that."

He turned back to look at the dead woman. His professional scrutiny had reduced her to a mere body of evidence, but now, as if for the first time, he saw the young woman lying in the midst of all those flowers whose gleaming white petals seemed to compete with her waxy skin. Her hands were no longer crossed over her groin but lay alongside her hips on the stone table, her head flopped dreamily off to one side, and her lips hung open ever so slightly. She seemed lost and very young. The pathologist noticed that Dr. Dallmer was observing him from the side of the room.

"I wonder what her name was."

Bärlach shrugged. "We should hurry," he said. "The light."

"I know."

The pathologist went silently over to the sink and lifted his scalpel from the gauze pad where he had laid out his instruments.

"Interior exam," he said.

And just as routinely as if he were beginning a game of chess with a well-rehearsed opening move, the young doctor made the Y-shaped cut with which every autopsy begins, the one that runs from the pubis to the base of the sternum, at which point it splits in two and extends to both shoulders.

"Access to the body cavities reveals a layer of subcutaneous fat one to two centimeters in depth in the chest and abdominal regions. On examination of the musculature of the chest, small bilateral petechial hemorrhages are evident at the level of the breasts. Dissection of the neck discloses further evidence of hemorrhage, particularly in the musculature directly beneath the strangulation marks. The peritoneum contains a small amount of straw-colored fluid. The loops of the large bowel are markedly distended and filled with gas. The edges of the diaphragm are symmetrical and in line with the fifth rib. The liver is situated beneath the inferior border of the rib cage. The spleen is not visible from this aspect."

Dr. Bärlach carefully laid his scalpel in a kidney-shaped basin, washed the blood from his hands and took the cartilage scissors from his medical bag. Silently, he detached the sternum and rib cage.

"Following the removal of the sternum, both lungs recede markedly into the pleural cavity. The heart is approximately the size of the decedent's fist. The pericardial sac contains a small amount of straw-colored fluid. The musculature of the heart chambers is appropriately developed, and the inner walls of the coronary arteries are smooth. The bronchia contain a viscous yellow mucus, and examination of the branches of the pulmonary artery reveal uncoagulated blood. On section, the lobes of the lungs show a marked consolidation of the parenchyma, which is free of focal lesions."

The pathologist laid the heart and lungs in two metal basins and turned to the dead woman's head.

"The appearance of the tongue is unremarkable. The mucosa of the esophagus is pale. No trauma to the dorsal wall of the pharynx is seen, but a large area of hemorrhage is visible in the tissues surrounding the right greater cornu of the hyoid bone. Inspection of the trachea reveals a reddish mucus. No significant signs of hemorrhaging are evident in the region of the trachea itself."

"Would you say this suggests she was strangled?"

"Could be, but not necessarily," muttered Bärlach as he laid open the stomach of the corpse. "No defects are evident in the gastric mucosa. The stomach contains a large quantity of chyme, consisting of small bits of meat, potato and macerated light-colored vegetable matter."

"Sunday dinner," remarked the medical examiner.

"Yes," said the pathologist. "The capsule of the spleen is smooth and glistening, and sectioning reveals the parenchyma to be red-blue in color."

As he had done with all the other organs, the pathologist now lifted the spleen carefully from the body cavity with both hands and deposited it in a steel basin, dictating while he worked.

"Both adrenal glands are normal in size and unremarkable on cross section. The liver is normal in size and has a glistening capsular surface. The gallbladder contains a small amount of greenish viscous fluid. The left kidney is surrounded by the usual layer of fat, and the capsule strips off with ease. On sectioning, there is good corticomedullary definition, and the right kidney reveals the same condition. The bladder is empty. The rectum is greatly dilated, containing blood in the inferior section and soft greenish feces in the superior."

A sharp stench now filled the room and quickly overwhelmed the sweet smell of the flowers, but the pathologist took no note of it. He moved the basins to a shelf that was otherwise used for garden implements and continued with the autopsy.

"Inside the vestibule of the vagina is a small quantity of yellowish mucus. The cervix is dilated. The fallopian tubes are soft and pale. The uterus is somewhat larger than a child's fist and has a doughy consistency. Examination of the interior wall of the uterus reveals an egg cavity and a placenta the size of a five-mark coin."

"Oh God, was she really pregnant?" Dr. Dallmer stopped typing and went over to the table.

"Not anymore," answered the pathologist. "See—there's no egg."

"An abortion?"

Dr. Bärlach stood up straight and nodded. He stretched for a moment, releasing the painful tension in his lower back, then washed his hands again and took several pictures of the organs, which he arranged in bowls on the windowsill in the fading afternoon light. Finally, he asked Dallmer to help him open the skull.

"Reflection of the scalp," continued the pathologist, once the medical examiner had resumed his seat, "reveals multiple areas of subcutaneous and subgaleate hemorrhage. On removal of the skullcap, the dura separates neatly from the arachnoid. There is no evidence of increased intercranial pressure and no fluid collection in the inner ear. The brain has a normal overall architecture and size. The demarcation of the gray matter and the subcortical and deep white matter is normal. Neither external examination nor sectioning reveals significant pathological change."

The pathologist dropped another scalpel in the kidney-shaped basin. "Well, that's it."

"And the cause of death?"

"Coming up. First, let's clean up."

After taking tissue samples for microscopic examination, Dr. Bärlach returned the organs to the body cavity and the brain to the skull and neatly sewed the body closed. Only then, while he disinfected his instruments with alcohol, did he dictate the results of his exam.

"Provisional cause of death: The findings of the autopsy reveal that the decedent had recently been pregnant. The pregnancy was one to one and a half months advanced, but the dilation of the cervix and the absence of a fetus in the uterus suggest an abortion had been attempted. Numerous signs of exterior trauma suggest that the decedent had engaged in an act of intense sexual nature, possibly perversion. Findings of anal dilation and recent trauma to the rectal mucosa further suggest this interpretation. It can be concluded that anal sex occurred. The cause of death was evidently cardiac arrest resulting from assault and battery and a weakened condition as a result of a partial abortion. A final determination of cause of death will be made following the conclusion of the microscopic examination."

As they walked outside, the gardener, who had been tending to an old grave site nearby, approached and locked the door of the mortuary behind them. In the evening twilight, Dallmer and Bärlach crossed the cemetery to the parking lot beside the Convent of Our Lady. The smell of the innumerable lilies faded slowly. As usual after an autopsy, the men were quiet and avoided eye contact with each other. They shook hands in parting in the same place where they had met each other earlier.

A corpse is a kind of secret letter, thought Bärlach, smuggled across the border of death from the prison on the other side to tell the story of the person who was only so recently still alive.

3

Hans Arbogast stepped out into the fresh morning air. On that cold January morning in 1955 it was still dark at 7:00 a.m., and the prison yard and bus were illuminated only by a single spotlight. His trial had concluded the previous afternoon, and now he was leaving the Grangat jail to be transported, according to plan, to the penitentiary in Bruchsal. It was Tuesday. Prisoners were always transferred among the state's various detention centers, jails and prisons on a Tuesday. Arbogast, who was almost six feet tall and had lost quite a few pounds in the year and a half since his arrest, now looked even bonier in his coat and scarf than he had before. He would soon be twenty-eight years old. He peered up at the night sky and saw white clouds of breath issue from his mouth. His wrists were in handcuffs, but he still wore his own clothing. From here on out, though, he would be wearing a prison uniform. He was afraid to be leaving Grangat. It's forever, he told himself again and again, unable to comprehend what that might mean. Since he had been incarcerated, time had seemed to slide by him, almost as if it weren't he who was enduring its passage. He stepped on board the bus and sat down beside the two other prisoners on the wooden bench. Although it was still too dark to see, he stared out the window. Then, as the vehicle pulled onto the highway, he closed his eyes.

The rustling of a newspaper made him open them again. The prison guard across from him was unfolding a paper. Arbogast looked curiously at the headlines. There was a picture of the president's New Year's reception for the three high commissioners. Under that was another photo taken on Adenauer's birthday. On the back page, a headline read THE SHEPPARD CASE. He noticed the tag line for an ad depicting an automobile: "The 1955 Lloyd—an all-steel body." As the guard paged through the paper, Arbogast read that according to Nobel laureate Otto Warburg, cancer, "the disease of the modern era," was caused by the "chronic inhibition of cell respiration." The page turned. The guard was holding the paper directly in front of his face. Now Arbogast saw a picture of a woman in an evening gown. He was able to make out the caption: "Gloria Vanderbilt, 30, in a stunning gown on opening night at the opera in New York, the very evening her divorce is finalized; her second marriage, to the symphony conductor Leopold Stokowski, 72, lasted ten years. She was his third wife." Outside the windows, it was growing light. Arbogast was aware that his fear had passed. He stopped reading. At nine thirty, the bus arrived at Bruchsal Penitentiary.

Shortly after ten o'clock, the prisoners were escorted by two guards into the basement and then, still in handcuffs, to the showers. In the entryway to the common bathing area, they were each handed a small, disagreeable-smelling piece of soap and a hand towel and told to undress. One of the guards waited in the hall; the other stood in his uniform by the door, beside the panel that controlled the flow of water to the fixtures. When Arbogast stepped under one of the showerheads in the great tiled room, the guard turned the water on and then, a moment later, off again.

"Soap up!"

The guard insisted that they do their hair as well, which Arbogast found unpleasant because of the odor of the soap; then the guard turned the water back on.

"Rinse!"

When it was over and Arbogast had dried himself, he was permitted to gather up his clothing, and they were led to the storage area where prisoners' effects were housed. The possessions that had been kept in a cardboard box all throughout his pretrial detention in Grangat were now turned over to a guard, who sat at a large desk in the very center of the basement room, rows of high metal shelves stacked with clothing and personal effects behind him. Two prisoners who worked there took Arbogast's civilian clothes and packed them, along with the things from the cardboard box, into a paper bag. The guard dictated the list of contents as they went in, then read it back to him, and Arbogast signed.

"Up against the wall," the guard ordered the new prisoners unceremoniously, and stepped back a few paces.

The head guard stepped around his desk and examined Arbogast from all sides. He told him to raise him arms, lower his head and open his mouth, all the while discoursing upon vermin and lice. Finally, he instructed Arbogast to turn around and bend over, and when Arbogast hesitated, the guard's voice grew louder and shriller; he talked about contraband and explained, as he examined Arbogast, that people had tried just about everything. Then Arbogast was directed to turn back around, and one of the guards brought out a powder gun. Arbogast's underarms, chest and pubic hair were dusted with a white insecticide. Finally, he was issued three pairs of gray sackcloth underwear, three pairs of gray wool socks, three shirts, a pair of boots, three sets of the blue prison uniform, and two hand towels. Every prisoner had a laundry number, and the tags were quickly sewn in by one of the prison workers. Arbogast stood before the desk at a place designated by white markings on the floor and dressed himself.

Then he was taken by the two guards to his cell in Wing Two. Though no one spoke to him beyond what was absolutely necessary, Arbogast could feel their eyes on him. All of them—guards and prisoners alike—were watching him. He strove, as always, to remain calm and not to draw attention to himself, but what he really wanted to do was scream at them to keep their eyes to themselves. At first, in Grangat, people had looked away when he maintained he was innocent, but as the trial had proceeded, they'd grown more and more shameless, as if they no longer owed him the least respect. They'd been all over him like buzzing flies. The underwear scratched his skin. You'll have to get used to that, too, he told himself.

As all this was going on, the chief public prosecutor of the Grangat district superior court was holding yet another press conference. The judgment handed down at yesterday's trial was being widely debated in the press, and many news reports in the regional papers had suggested there were grounds for a mistrial. Ferdinand Oesterle, the wiry district attorney who had come to Grangat from Karlsruhe just three years before, called for quiet. As usual, he was dressed in one of his black suits, over which he would don his robe whenever he had to go before the court.

Oesterle rebutted every implication of doubt about the completeness of the evidence introduced in the Arbogast case. "Forensic medicine and the natural sciences can now be counted among our most effective weapons in the crime-fighting arsenal," he said, and he claimed that in the Arbogast case, the use of such modern methods of analysis had led uncontrovertibly to the conviction of the accused. He concluded by mentioning that it was thanks in particular to the medical expertise of Professor Maul of the Institute of Forensic Medicine at the University of Münster that they had been able to reconstruct objectively the events that took place the night of the crime. One of the journalists asked whether it was true that the prosecutor's office had initially accepted the findings of the autopsy report, which determined the cause of death to be a heart attack, and whether their expert had used that report at trial.

"Yes, well, that's technically correct," responded Oesterle, but he added that questions about that theory had arisen almost immediately—raised by Professor Maul, an experienced forensic pathologist. As to whether Professor Maul's testimony had been somewhat unusual, Oesterle said no, absolutely not. He had no doubts about the testimony. Professor Maul had made an unbiased determination that the findings of the autopsy report were consistent with asphyxiation, although they had presented in a fashion rarely seen in general practice. Regarding the inevitable next question, whether asphyxiation had ensued from throttling or the use of a garrote, Oesterle said that could be clarified by looking at the photographs of the victim. Professor Maul had clearly established that Frau Gurth was strangled with a cord or other similar implement.

"So then where is this ominous garrote, which no one has ever seen?"

Winfried Meyer, Arbogast's lawyer, shouted his question down to the courtroom from the balcony. He was a solitary figure, sitting all alone on one of the wooden benches in the upper gallery, and the heads of the assembled journalists wheeled around to look at him. Pacing back and forth in front of the empty judges' bench, Oesterle answered swiftly.

"My dear colleagues, the fact that the murder weapon has not been found has no effect—no effect whatsoever—on the unbiased testimony of Professor Maul. Furthermore, you know very well that four refugee women have been murdered in this area. Why, it's open season on these women!"

Oesterle's voice cracked when he raised it even slightly. It had happened a couple of times during the trial. He knew this about himself and strove to keep it under control, but this last sentence was loud. He'd seen two of the past year's four victims. There hadn't been a suspect for any of those murders. Sometimes, Ferdinand Oesterle dreamed that the murderer came up to him, smiling, clapped him on the back and whispered his name into his ear. But in the dream, Oesterle always missed hearing the name because he'd already shrunk away from the man's unbearable breath.

"It's open season on these women," Oesterle repeated, quietly this time.

Meyer didn't respond. He'd collapsed the previous Saturday when he was filing his appeal with the prosecutor's office. He'd passed the incident off as the lingering effects of the flu, but he still wasn't quite right. He felt afflicted, had a strange sense of infirmity—as if there were no chance of his recovering. The thirty-year-old lawyer surveyed the journalists below. He enjoyed a reputation of being the best lawyer in Grangat, and his objection now stimulated a host of new questions from the journalists. They wrote furiously. Everywhere between the rows of chairs, there stood small checked overnight bags, umbrellas, portable typewriter cases; the express train to Karlsruhe left in the early afternoon.

"Naturally," said Oesterle, responding to one of the journalists' inquiries, "Hans Arbogast certainly could turn out to have been the perpetrator in the Krüger case. The body of Marie Gurth was found in the same location, after all. And the prosecutor's office by all means reserves the right to resume its investigation into that case. We will issue indictments when and if the situation warrants. For that matter, it's also possible that we may be dealing with the highway murderer here—the criminal who has made our roads unsafe, putting fear and terror in the path of all who travel on them."

And yet at first it had seemed that the trial would result in a conviction on a lesser charge at the most. Just a week before, when Paul Mohr of the *Badische Zeitung* had interviewed him, the young reporter and Meyer had both agreed that the worst possible outcome was manslaughter. That was what Meyer and Arbogast had pleaded to, but then everything turned out differently. Maybe things had begun to shift when Oesterle had first made that totally baseless suggestion to the court, which he now repeated. There was no reason whatever to think that Arbogast was the murderer who'd been hunting down victims on deserted highways for the past three years, but as soon as Oesterle said it, the mood in the courtroom had seemed to change. And then the mother of the accused, who had quietly given her testimony and watched the subsequent proceedings almost completely motionlessly, loudly burst into tears and had to be led from the courtroom by her daughter. There was disorder and whispering in the gallery. Meyer thought about how Arbogast had begun to hide behind him after that, how he'd used him to conceal his face from the stares of the public.

But the decisive and completely unexpected turn had come when Professor Maul gave his testimony. When the pathologist took the stand, dusk had started to fall, although the lights still hadn't been switched on. It seemed to Meyer that Professor Maul had also been aware of a change in the general mood that afternoon. The lawyer had watched from across the courtroom as the expert witness took his seat at the side bench with all of his documents, charts and visual aids. Maul's pale, fat fingers had waved like insect antennae as he described the pictures of the dead woman to the court. At first, Meyer had been quite calm, but then he realized the statements Professor Maul was making had nothing to do with the deposition. It was as if

Maul had been observing the climate in the courtroom with those slowly moving fingers of his—as if, Meyer now thought, he'd been waiting for precisely the right time to make his claim. If at first there were people who had doubted what Maul said, by the end everyone was following the pathologist's arguments. Meyer's client had sensed this and grown increasingly restless. He'd actually interrupted the witness twice, which drew a rebuke from the judge and had not helped his situation in the least.

Meyer sat with his head in his hands. He asked himself yet again if he'd been made unduly nervous by the fact that the case had drawn so much media attention, or perhaps by the unexpectedly large attendance at the trial. Had all that activity and the presence of the national press corps somehow led him to make the mistake of not calling a second forensic expert? His thoughts returned once more to the deciding moment of the trial, when he'd failed to make the appropriate motion with sufficient vehemence, been unable to show sufficient cause. Errors, he thought now, head in his hands, errors and more errors. He failed to see that not all the journalists had turned back toward the prosecutor. Paul Mohr was staring straight at him, an expression of astonishment on his face as Meyer sat motionless in the balcony of the old courtroom. Oesterle was still speaking.

"Arbogast feels comfortable with killing. The man is a sadist. Within him is a beast that devours its victims once they have grown complaisant."

When he'd spoken these words, the same ones with which he'd begun his summation the preceding Friday, Ferdinand Oesterle paused, as if listening to their imaginary echo. Meyer never took his eyes off him. He remembered the photographs of the victim all too well, and for a moment he himself almost believed the prosecutor's claims. When Katrin Arbogast had come to him and asked if he would represent her husband, his main reason for accepting the job was that he'd once been a student of her father, who'd taught math at Grangat High School. He had little experience with criminal law, had never seen anything like the pictures that documented this crime. His first thought had been, That's perverted. He had never shown Katrin or anyone else the pictures. The family already had it bad enough.

"Everything suggests that Arbogast killed Marie Gurth slowly, and that in the process he brutally battered and abused her, all the while deriving sexual excitement from her suffering. These events correspond to Arbogast's personality: He's a crude, beastly individual, with tendencies toward sadistic behavior."

Up in the gallery, Winfried Meyer pulled himself together and stood up. Oesterle followed him with his eyes. For the first time, the district attorney felt certain that the trial was really over, and a feeling of numbness began to spread slowly, coolly through his body.

Meyer descended the wooden stairs as quietly as he could and went out to his car. He had to hurry; he'd promised Hans Arbogast that he would go see him in Bruchsal that day, to discuss what there was left to do. Thinking about it, Meyer felt the peculiar weariness return. He tossed his briefcase weakly on the backseat, took off his coat and drove away. Since the war, the population of the city of Grangat had dropped to just over twenty thousand. Crossing the new Murg Bridge toward Strasbourg, he quickly left the city limits behind. For a few minutes, he drove across the river valley that opened onto the Rhine, then turned onto the highway that led through the vineyards and orchards of the Black Forest foothills, heading north toward Karlsruhe and then on to Bruchsal. The Dog's Head, Grangat's local snowcapped mountain, disappeared from his rearview mirror.

It took the lawyer just over an hour and a half to travel the sixty-odd miles, which was pretty good time, considering that the snow had begun to encroach on the band of concrete highway from both sides; the few cars on the road had carved out a single unplowed lane to travel on. A couple of big trucks and one Mercedes went by in the other direction, and he passed a couple of Bugs and a prewar-model Opel. A short time later, he arrived in Bruchsal, as had been arranged in advance by telephone. He drove past the summer palace and then out of the old city again by way of the baroque Damian Gate. The prison complex loomed up alarmingly large before him. Meyer's practice was almost entirely in civil law, and he had never before seen the high prison walls of rough limestone, their watchtowers, or the high, jutting walkways along the walls. He stopped at the gate, where two small guardhouses flanked the cobblestone ramp like sentries.

Winfried Meyer said his name into the speaker on the wall beside the gray metal door; the buzzer sounded instantly, letting him in. He stepped into a high vaulted space, and the door closed pneumatically behind him. On the right and left, steps led up to guardrooms with barred windows, and he could see guards on the other side, one of whom waved him in. He had to show his identification, open his briefcase and allow his coat to be patted down. Then one of the officers directed him to a wooden door across from the metal one. He was told to ring the bell and that someone would take him to the visitors room. Almost immediately, a bolt slid back, the peephole in the wooden door was opened, and a pair of eyes examined him. He heard the key turn, and a small gate swung open. The uniformed guard locked it behind him with a double-toothed key from a large ring and then, silently touching his finger to his cap, led Meyer down a hall some thirty yards long. There were massive wooden doors on either side and an iron gate at the far end.

"What's down that way?" asked the lawyer, pointing straight ahead.

"The prison," said the elderly, somewhat stooped guard, but then realizing how odd that answer must have sounded, he elaborated: "It's the central tower of the panopticon."

Meyer had no idea what that was. It occurred to him that he'd had no way of knowing, from outside on the ramp, what the actual shape of the prison building was behind those great walls. He was just about to start up a conversation with the officer on this topic, when the man unlocked one of the wooden doors and directed him into the visiting room.

"Arbogast is waiting for you."

4

Paul Mohr wore a gray tweed suit with knickers and a matching cap, which he straightened as he left the supreme court building. His coat and bag were still in his room, as he wouldn't be leaving for Freiburg till the afternoon. He still had plenty of time to stop in at the Silver Star, where he and most of the other journalists had spent the court recesses and virtually every evening of the preceding week's trial. But then he spotted Gesine Hofmann with her camera and tripod across the street. He'd been told that the negatives on file in the Kodak photo shop on Kreuzgasse comprised a complete illustrated history of Grangat since the First World War. Almost all of the images, excluding her own, had been taken by her father, who'd died recently. Mohr reconsidered his plan and crossed the street to say hello. They'd had occasion to get to know each other during the trial, when he needed photographs, and the two of them, who were both still under twenty, had hit it off right away. Sitting around at the Silver Star one evening, they had quickly switched over to addressing one another in the familiar.

He waited while Gesine bent over the camera, looked up to check the scene in front of her and then back into the viewfinder, snapping pictures of the exodus of people streaming from the courthouse. She told him she had to develop the film right away, and nodded smilingly when he asked if he could come along. They walked the short distance to the market square, zigzagging between the rows of stalls and vendors' stands to Kreuzgasse, directly on the other side of the square. Her mother kept the shop open whenever Gesine had an appointment or work to do in the darkroom, which was separated from the shop itself by just a curtain, though it was a thick rubber one, impermeable to light. Paul Mohr nodded hello to Mrs. Hofmann, a delicate white-haired lady who was pushing film canisters back and forth across the glass-topped counter while conversing with a gentleman of a similar age to her own. The tiny lab was lined to the ceiling with metal racks, from which the countless gray hanging folders of an old-fashioned filing system dangled like bats in a cave. Gesine put down the camera, took off her coat and donned a white smock. Then she put out the lights and switched on the small red bulb that forbade entry into the room during developing.

Paul quickly grew accustomed to the warmth generated by the chemical reactions in the room. By the time Gesine turned on the enlarger, blinding him with its bright light, he'd come to the realization he was falling in love with her. He stood there silently, close behind her, watching her. Complete blackness gave way to the bright light that shone onto the negative and indirectly lit up her face. He could see the fine downy hairs on her cheek and the glistening moisture of one of her very light green eyes.

Peering over her shoulder, he turned his attention to the image and saw the courtroom with its detailed woodwork, the chairs that the journalists sat in and, behind them, the spectators. Then there was the slightly curved judges' dais with the small fluted columns; behind that, the three judges in their black robes, three jurors on the right, three on the left. One picture showed the small pedestal against the wall behind the judges, with nothing on it, and the padded doors on either side. There was one of Jochen Gurth, the husband of the deceased, smoking and talking with Mizzi Neelsen, her friend. And naturally Hans Arbogast, hands in front of his face as he was being led away by a policeman after the verdict was returned. On the wall, an enamel plaque: BADEN DISTRICT SUPERIOR COURT, GRANGAT. Arbogast as he left the courtroom in his double-breasted jacket and plaid scarf, passing through a phalanx of spectators. Behind him, the same old police officer in his heavy jacket with its shining buttons, the star and cord insignia on his cap. In that same picture was a dark-haired young woman with braids, wearing a traditional-style jacket, staring at Arbogast in disbelief. There was an emaciated man in an army cap next to a fat one with brilliantined hair and a cigarette between his lips. Arbogast and his lawyer, Meyer, examining files at the defense table. There was Katrin, the defendant's wife. Hinrichs, from the homicide division of the Freiburg Police Department, speaking with Dr. Bärlach, who had conducted the autopsy. The district attorney, Ferdinand Oesterle, and the chief judge of the Grangat court, with the knife-sharp points of his stand-up collar in stark contrast to the velvet trim of his gown. Professor Maul in front of a diagram as he gave his testimony.

Paul Mohr recalled exactly the eerie moment when the tenor of the whole proceeding had shifted. Suddenly, in his statement, the heavyset medical examiner from Münster had uttered the word *garrote*, and what had been an accident became murder. Just thinking about it sent a shiver through him. Then came a picture of the street out in front of the court building—the same shot Gesine Hofmann had just taken, but this one was from the beginning of the trial—and he had to laugh when he noticed himself in the crowd. Gesine turned back to look at him. She was so near he could feel her breath, and for a moment he thought he might be able to kiss her. He leaned closer. She smiled and dodged him. They both looked back at the photo.

"I noticed you right off," she said quietly.

Paul Mohr nodded without quite knowing what his nod might mean. You could still clearly see traces of the war on the buildings. Many of the men wore hats or army caps and long dark coats, but there was one figure in an extremely wide-cut tan trench coat. Most of the women's hair was cut short. He couldn't forget the picture of Marie that Maul had shown the court. Suddenly, the photo lab seemed cramped.

"Do you still have that negative of the victim?"

"Yes," Gesine said with a certain impatience.

Perhaps it was in order to let Paul know she didn't want to show him the picture that her tone suddenly grew distant. As she'd explained to him, she'd taken on a quasi-official role when she'd agreed to photograph the body at the crime scene and to provide prints and enlargements for the trial. But then again, maybe it was because it seemed to her that Paul was now dodging her with this question about the picture. But he didn't seem to register the terseness of her reply.

"Would you show me that one, where they found her, again?"

Silently, she pulled a file from the hanging rack closest to the developer. She knew exactly which image he meant and slid the six-by-six negative carefully into place on the enlarger, then brought the picture into focus. In the darkness of the lab, the outlines of the image in the frame of whirring light seemed terribly close, and both Paul and Gesine felt briefly ashamed to be looking at Marie Gurth in that way.

She lay there almost as if she had nestled herself down among the leaves, thought Paul Mohr as he bent over the image of the negative. Projected on the wooden tabletop, it was like an unpainted fresco on the rough wall of church, but with the light and dark areas of the image inexplicably reversed. The dry leaves on the right side and at the top of the frame looked like a white sheet on which someone had laid Marie Gurth down to sleep. She lay on her left side, eyes closed, head snuggled down into her bed, her lips—which in the negative were almost black—open in expectation, as if in a dream. Her right arm lay across her upper body, her left hand on her right shoulder; her right hand touched her left elbow. In between, the pitch-black nakedness of one of her breasts. The near modesty of her posture only served to emphasize it all the more—she seemed to be trying to hide herself in the blackberry thicket, as if crawling under the covers. The deeply veined bright white leaves covered her navel and crotch, and it almost seemed she was about to stretch her slightly bent right leg out from under a down comforter.

For an instant, Paul thought he could see the band that Professor Maul claimed to have discovered around her neck. The black and white of the negative obediently rearranged itself in accordance with that idea. He pointed to it.

"Do you see that?"

"What?"

Paul blinked, but now, where the line had been, he saw only the grain of the wood onto which the enlarger projected the image. It's like a fresco in black and white, he thought again, and then: She doesn't seem to need anything at all, except that she looks so very cold.

"What do you think? Did he do it?"

Mohr had watched the accused man closely while Maul gave his testimony. He'd gotten the impression that Arbogast thought he was clever and had great self-control, but actually, he didn't. When the witness had accused him, he'd seemed completely paralyzed, and that quiet paralysis had fostered Paul Mohr's mistrust of Arbogast. He simply couldn't imagine that this young woman could have wanted to be made love to so violently. During the closing arguments, Arbogast had wept.

He asked Gesine again, "Did he do it?"

The photographer, standing very close to him, looked at the photograph as if she'd never seen it before. Finally, she shrugged her shoulders. Then she turned to him and smiled.

"Do you want a copy of the picture?"

Paul was surprised. He wouldn't have dared to ask her, but she must have been able to tell how much it fascinated him. That's what had turned her smile—and she was still smiling—a little sad. She'd realized that his interest in her had passed, and it was the fault of the dead woman and the picture that she'd taken on that foggy morning, freezing and exhausted, after the police had hauled her out of bed. She understood that Paul Mohr was captivated by the quiet breathlessness of the picture. He couldn't stop looking at the girl, whose dark flesh flickered in the projected negative. He nodded.

"Okay, just give me a second," said Gesine Hofmann quietly.

She turned off the lamp and, in the light of the dim red bulb, took a sheet of photo stock from a cardboard box and placed it under the enlarger. The white light flashed briefly, and its afterimage still glimmered in his eyes as she transferred the paper to the developer bath with a large pair of tongs. Then she moved it to the fixative, and a couple of minutes later she turned the lights back on. In the sudden brightness, while they waited for the chemical reaction to stop and the developing shadows to coalesce into the body of Marie Gurth, both of them avoided looking at the other.

Eventually, she lifted the picture from the bath, let it drip dry, and put it in a paper envelope for him. She pushed back the double-thick rubber curtain, and they were both momentarily glad to be free of the sour, suffocating air of the lab and back out in the open. They didn't say much. Paul urged Gesine to visit him in Freiburg the next time she was there. Gesine Hofmann wrapped her arms around her upper body, shivering, and when Paul Mohr extended his hand, she didn't take it, just nodded, smiling. He thought he could feel her eyes on his back as he walked down Kreuzgasse, heading toward the train station.

Paul Mohr was familiar with Grangat; he'd been there two years before, working as an intern for the *Badische Zeitung*, right after high school, but he hadn't been back since. Now, after the long week of the trial, he was finding it difficult to leave again. Before he went back for his suitcase, he stopped in at the Silver Star one last time to see if any of his colleagues were still around, but there were no journalists in the bar. On his way to the station, he noticed how much emptier the streets were than they had been the past few days. He remembered the rigid stare with which Winfried Meyer had followed the press conference that morning, and he suddenly felt like a stranger here—ill at ease, as if there was something about the death of Marie Gurth that afflicted this little town. The image of the girl clung to him, the way she seemed to be sleeping, dreaming under the ice-cold covers of the leaves in the blackberry thicket, and he hurried to the train station.

BODY OF WOMAN FOUND ON HIGHWAY 15 had been his headline back when it happened. UNIDENTIFIED VICTIM WAS SEXUALLY ASSAULTED. His September 5, 1953, report on the case was the first to appear in a newspaper; it was also the first article he'd published using his initials, P.M., as a byline.

> Kaltenweier. Thursday evening at approximately 7:20 p.m., a gamekeeper came across the naked body of a woman while he was hunting deer near Highway 15 between Kaltenweier and

Hohrod. The body was discovered in the vicinity of kilometer marker 7, near the turnoff to Duren, lying in a shallow pool of water and covered with brambles. Strangle marks were evident on the throat and neck, her left eye was blackened, and the right breast showed scratch wounds. According to the autopsy findings, the victim suffered a violent assault, resulting in heart failure. The case is clearly one of rape-murder. The victim also appears to have been wearing a watch, which was missing from her person.

Given the circumstances, it is assumed that the body was transported to the scene in an automobile, probably on Tuesday night, some two hours after she was murdered. None of the victim's clothes have been found as yet.

The murder victim was approximately twenty years old, five foot one and slender; she had a delicate build, a round face with high cheekbones, full lips, poor dentition, blue eyes, reddish hair, average-size ears and small, well manicured hands with long fingernails.

The homicide division of the Freiburg Police Department was at the crime scene overnight and is cooperating with the local police in the search for clues and the perpetrator. Although large areas of the adjacent woods were searched, there was no trace of the deceased's clothing. Persons with any information pertaining to this crime should contact the homicide division or any police department. The Grangat district attorney's office is offering a reward of five hundred marks to members of the general public who provide information leading to the arrest of the perpetrator.

5

The first thing Winfried Meyer noticed was the frosted-glass screens in the visiting room. It wasn't just that they deprived him of the view he expected to see; it was that they completely robbed the visitor of any sense of context—one could almost have been waiting in a doctor's office. There were no iron bars in sight, but Meyer took it for granted that they were there. The guard closed the door behind him, and another guard, one he hadn't noticed at first, who'd been sitting on a chair by the door, nodded at him. The room was furnished with a simple wooden table, positioned with the narrow end facing the door. Hans Arbogast sat on one side and there was an empty chair across from him. The overhead light was off, though it had slowly begun to grow dark.

The rattling of keys and clicking of locks that were constantly being secured behind him had put Meyer in a state of rather helpless anxiety. Arbogast was not wearing handcuffs, and Meyer reached out and shook his hand, then sat down. He leaned his briefcase up against the leg of his chair and took a look at his client. He was so unaccustomed to seeing the prison garb that he had to make an effort not to stare at Arbogast. His jacket and pants were fashioned of coarse blue twill, and the jacket had red stripes on the arms. He looks calm, thought the lawyer. The stress of the past weeks was gradually letting up, and apparently Arbogast felt the relief as well. It almost seemed to Meyer as if his client was already beginning to come to terms with the situation.

"Like my suit, do you? Red's for convicted criminals. There's also white for those who are on trial and yellow for those under pretrial detention."

"How are you doing?"

Arbogast smiled and shrugged his shoulders, as if it hardly mattered. Katrin had told him that his mother hadn't spoken since the announcement of the verdict the day before. For the past year and a half, she'd kept the restaurant going and visited him every week at the jail where he was held prior to and during the trial, acting as if nothing were wrong. The customers had stopped coming, but she had kept it together. The one time he had tried to explain to her what had happened, she cut him off and said she didn't want to hear about it.

"My wife was here earlier today," Arbogast said at last.

"And?"

"I don't know what I should say to her. She believed me up to now, and that was bad enough."

"And now?"

"Now she doesn't know what to believe. I can't hold that against her. I feel the same way."

"What do you mean by that?"

Arbogast shrugged. "Have you spoken to Professor Maul again? Do you think we could talk to him about an appeal?"

Meyer actually had called the expert witness about that at the hotel the day before, shortly after the verdict came down, and asked if they could meet. Maul had told him he saw no need for that. His voice had sounded just as deliberate and hard on the phone as it had in court. He'd noticed Maul's cold eyes and small, thin-lipped mouth when they'd first introduced themselves to each other, at the very start of the trial. But it was only on that dusky afternoon when Professor Maul had seemed to look straight into the picture of Marie Gurth that Meyer had realized just what it was those lips hungered for. The pathologist had touched the surface of the crime-scene photograph like a fish bumping up against the glass wall of its aquarium, yearning for access to that other world beyond, a world that would remain forever closed to him. What he understood was death. And it had made the quivering aliveness of Maul's fingers, as he described the way Marie Gurth died, seem all the more grotesque to Meyer.

"Just between us," Maul had said at the end of their phone call, "you don't really believe your patient is innocent?"

He had actually used the word *patient.*

"I don't think we can count on any help from Professor Maul in this."

Winfried Meyer said no more. Arbogast looked at him, waiting for him to go on, to make another suggestion, to begin developing a plan, a legal strategy, something that would justify the lawyer's sitting there and staring at him, the prisoner. But the exhaustion that had seized hold of Meyer wouldn't let go. All he could do was just look at Arbogast, examine him closely, and perhaps he would see something that told him that Hans Arbogast really wasn't the murderer of Marie Gurth.

But Arbogast didn't move. He had a strong chin that made him look almost as if he had no neck, and his lower lip protruded slightly, as if he were pouting. There was nothing youthful about his face anymore; it looked just about as coarsely hewn, as virile, as the prosecutor had described. His slightly wavy light-colored hair had been parted on the left and combed down with water. He had a receding hairline. His cheeks were hollow, accentuating the lines that ran from his nose to his mouth. When he laughed, his lips pulled back and you could see his large white teeth. He had blond eyelashes. The way he held himself was loose and hesitant, the youngest-seeming thing about him. Of course, his hands were enormous. It had often seemed to Meyer, when he sat next to Arbogast during the trial, that his hands were holding one another down.

Just looking at them, you could see the strength that Arbogast wielded, which certainly hadn't been an advantage at the trial; he'd been apprenticed to a butcher, though he'd graduated from high school and his father had wanted him to go on to university. When his father died, Hans Arbogast had been working as a long-haul truck driver. He'd used his inheritance to buy a quarry but soon thereafter he'd sold it again. He had a young son, and Meyer recalled how loving he had been with the boy on their Sunday visits. A short time before the murder, Arbogast had taken over a dealership that sold billiard tables, and he'd helped out with his parents' restaurant. Like any butcher, he was meticulous about hygiene and kept his nails trimmed very short. He strongly preferred to wear white shirts, as Meyer knew from the days of his pretrial detainment, when Meyer had frequently brought them to him.

The guard on the chair by the door cleared his throat and said something that Meyer wasn't able to understand, then cleared his throat again.

"So, are you all finished here, counselor?" the guard repeated.

Arbogast didn't react.

Meyer started and shook his head. He reached into his briefcase and pulled out a small red clothbound volume.

"Paragraph sixteen of the Penal Code," he began, quickly flipping to the passage in the book, "is titled 'Crimes and Misdemeanors Pertaining to the Taking of Life.' Section two eleven: 'The murderer shall be punished with a term of life in prison.' "

"I don't understand what you mean by that, Mr. Meyer. Are you trying to tell me I'm never getting out of here? Is that what you mean?"

"For the time being, what that means is that murder is the most reprehensible way of killing a human being. And therefore, although a lighter sentence was originally anticipated, it means you will spend the rest of your life in jail. That's what it means, nothing more. Period."

"But I haven't murdered anyone!"

Meyer knew that, of course, but his exhaustion simply wouldn't go away. It was like an overcast sky. Like this case. Maybe he hadn't made a mistake when he failed to object vehemently to Professor Maul's testimony; the man was a professor of forensic medicine at the University of Münster, after all. Suddenly, everyone had thought that Arbogast was guilty. Again and again, Meyer looked down at the small book he held open in his hands and then back up at Arbogast, who returned his gaze. Both of them seemed to have been cut loose from time. Within Meyer, there throbbed that strange, dull, monotonous weariness, which enabled him to lose track of where he was; and Arbogast himself was feeling increasingly lost. A short time ago he had still held hope that some legal maneuvers might be undertaken to help him; now he understood that the trial, which had stripped him naked day after day, was to culminate in the sentence his lawyer had just read aloud and explained to him. Arbogast smiled as if he understood him, and Winfried Meyer felt his heart gladden at that. He would have told Arbogast so, if only he hadn't been so tired.

"Please read on," said Arbogast softly, almost whispering. A thought had flashed through his mind like lightning: I'm alone. Irremediably alone. And by the profound sadness that flowed through him, he grasped for the first time the tragedy that had enveloped him and how enormous his secret hope had been that one day all of this would end.

"Just read," he said again.

And so Winfried Meyer read unceremoniously on: " 'A murderer is one who viciously, for the gratification of sexual urges, out of greed, or for any other base cause, takes the life of another person, maliciously, cruelly or by use of some means that constitutes a danger to the public.' "

"Why so complicated?"

"Because the particular reprehensibility of the deed and therefore the designation of *murder* pertain only to a crime with the specific characteristics that are set out here, by this law. We say that these conditions are sufficient to describe a death as a murder, or, to put it another way, in the presence of these conditions, section two eleven pertains—permanently and irrevocably. Conversely, in the absence of these factors, a finding of murder may not be determined."

"I see." Arbogast smiled again. "I take it that in my case the base cause for which I am supposed to have murdered Marie was the desire for sexual satisfaction."

"Not so fast!" said Meyer, carefully closing the book. As he struggled to concentrate, he repeatedly stroked the book's cover. "In the case of a sex crime, the murder may be carried out for the satisfaction of sexual urges. It may mean that sexual gratification was the reason the act of murder was committed, but it also covers cases where death is caused incidentally, in the course of a rape, or where the victim is killed so that the murderer can subsequently satisfy himself sexually on the corpse. It's of no relevance to the court whether this sexual satisfaction actually occurred. But I'm getting ahead of myself."

"How's that?"

"First of all, it's necessary to distinguish between the various characteristics of a murder. Which is to say the repugnance of the motive, the manner in which the crime was carried out and its object. The so-called base causes to which you referred, which led to yesterday's judgment against you, pertain only to the first of these groups."

"What exactly do you mean by 'base'?"

"It's quite simple: Motives are considered base when they run counter to general moral principles and are of the lowest level. For example, the bloodthirstiness of a murderer who wants to see his victim die and kills gratuitously, as a performance, out of a desire to kill or as a pastime. Or a murderer who kills for the thrill of it, or for sport. And then in cases of a combined rape and murder, the criminal is always considered to have had base motives."

Meyer had forgotten why he was even explaining all this. Was it some self-justification, or was he explaining the law to Arbogast just to torture him, or was it because he actually believed that truth had been served when the verdict was read? At any rate, he knew he needed to bring this discourse to an end.

"Murder in the second degree, which you were convicted of, has to do with the manner in which the crime was executed. A perpetrator who exploited the unsuspecting nature and defenselessness of his victim is considered to have acted with malice; he is considered brutal if he demonstrated no compassion or mercy, and if he tortured or caused psychological or physical pain for a longer duration or to a greater degree than that which would be required simply to kill his victim."

Hans Arbogast's hands remained clasped and motionless. Sometimes, when people spoke of the pain he was supposed to have caused Marie, he could once again taste her blood in his mouth. It was difficult for him to remember her face at such times, when even his own seemed to vanish.

"Mr. Meyer, I still don't see why you're explaining all this to me. What about the appeal we discussed in the courtroom? Don't we want to file a petition with the court?"

"Mr. Arbogast, I'm very sorry, but in your case section two eleven of the Penal Code, which I have been trying to clarify for you, has been applied with maximum severity."

Meyer repeatedly stroked the cover of his little red book, as if he were trying to imprint the title in his memory. Then he looked up and stared straight into Arbogast's face. He was actually smiling, which made Arbogast realize how stiff his facial expressions had been the whole time.

"Of course we will appeal, but it won't be possible right away. And now I suppose I will take my leave of you for today, Mr. Arbogast, unless you have any other questions. You seem to be doing quite well, under the circumstances. You must be aware that I have not quite been myself since my collapse at the court. I am plagued, as they say, by a strange exhaustion. I don't know if you know what that's like."

Winfried Meyer looked at his client and waited for him to nod. He had the feeling he could just sit there like that forever and look at Hans Arbogast, who would look at him with equal fixedness. But before long, Arbogast did nod, and Winfried Meyer stood up, feeling as if he had been delivered from that fate, and extended his hand.

"Good-bye, Mr. Arbogast. And chin up. It'll all work out."

Hans Arbogast silently shook his lawyer's hand and watched while the guard unlocked the door to the visiting room and Meyer left. The lawyer was thinking that as long as this inexplicable weariness was hanging over him, he really couldn't manage the trip out here to Bruchsal. He followed the jailer and eventually made his way back through the steel door and out into the twilight. While Meyer was deciding to conduct all future business with his client by mail, Hans Arbogast waited for the jailer to return and take him back to his cell. In the silence, he noticed the banging of the heating pipes in the wall behind him. Arbogast blinked. They had talked about the cinema, too. She'd seen *The Black Forest Girl* at the new film palace at Bahnhof Zoo, and she'd thought about it often since she'd been in the West, Marie had told him with a laugh. She'd really called it a film *palace*. Arbogast had never been to Berlin. "I understand," she had said. He was always going back over the same conversations, which had even then been unnecessary, a pretext, as both of them were well aware. Of course he knew the movie *The Black Forest Girl*. They had shown it in the great hall at the Three Kings Hotel. It had been advertized as the first German movie shot in color since the end of the war.

"Sonja Ziemann and Rudolf Prack."

"And Paul Hörbiger."

She hadn't asked whom he'd seen the movie with. It had occurred to him then that he was wearing his wedding ring, and that made him think about home all the sudden. His parents' restaurant and bar, the Salmon, was on Schutterwälderstrasse, where the city of Grangat faded off into the floodplain of the Rhine valley, with its countless small hamlets and tobacco fields, the open barns with rustling yellow leaves drying inside them and poplar forests growing in the marshy ground. The Vosges Mountains rose up at the horizon like the silhouette of some southern land. It was there, into the marsh, that he had taken her body in the backseat of his Isabella, when he didn't know what else to do. Right at the beginning of the movie, Sonja Ziemann won a car, a two-tone Ford Taunus Cabriolet, and drove it down the mountain road through the Black Forest to St. Blasien, where the action of the film took place. But the city walls had looked more like those of Gengenbach or St. Christoph, Arbogast thought now. He remembered perfectly the way the black hood of the Ford was arched like the keel of a boat and the oxblood color of the chassis. That car in the movie would have cost eight and a half thousand, free and clear, but it could also do a hundred kilometers an hour.

Arbogast blinked into the dimness of the visiting room and tried to remember who had told him where they'd done the exterior shots for the film, but then his thoughts were oddly drawn back to a small church he'd passed one day when he was out for a drive somewhere near Bad Peterstal—St. Mary of the Chains. And that reminded him of the Strauss House. Shortly after the war, when he was still very young, he'd traveled to Strasbourg with a friend. When they got there, they'd pushed their bikes through the streets, carrying their rucksacks on their backs. Back then, the town was still completely abandoned from the war. Many of the storefront shops in the old Renaissance buildings had been closed and boarded up, and the whole place was filthy. He remembered the carcass of a dog they had seen floating down the Rhine—the pink flesh of its belly looked swollen and its nipples were visible through thin patches in its dirty white hair. Why hadn't he driven her body to France? He thought about the fact that she'd never been to Strasbourg.

"You know the place where he paints her?" he'd asked.

With that, Marie had reached her hand across the white tablecloth and laid it on his arm. That was the first time she'd touched him. "She's wearing a traditional dress and the hat with the red pompoms, and suddenly the camera pulls back and you can see far into the valley and all across the Black Forest, and he takes her in his arms. 'What is it that you want from me? You already have someone,' she says, and he answers, 'Babs, don't you know, that's all over with.' "

"And then he sings, 'Black Forest Girls Aren't Easily Had.' "

It was the first time she'd laughed that laugh—the one he hadn't been able to forget ever since. He remembered it exactly. They had been at the Angel, and it was the first time he'd really looked at her. She wasn't the first girl he'd picked up on the road, invited for a glass of wine and convinced to join him in an hour's dalliance, nor was she a particular beauty, but there was something about her laugh he'd found disconcerting. Still laughing, she had started to hum one of the songs from the movie and then finally begun to sing it. As fond as he was of recollecting the sound of her voice, it sent a shiver through him every time he did so, for he could hear the words she'd sung ringing in his ears: *You found me once, now come back and take me with you.* Arbogast blinked and listened to what was within him. And when everything inside had fallen silent, he once again heard the banging of the pipes. His mouth was dry.

6

The barroom at the Salmon was large but low, the ceiling held up by two massive beams, the walls paneled in dark wood. The surface of the benches that ran around almost the entire circumference of the room had been polished to a glossy finish by much sitting. Long, narrow tables stood against the benches, and the middle of the room was empty. The small windows were set high and deep in the walls to protect against the possibility of flooding from the marshes, making the room appear dark, even during daylight hours. When she came in, Katrin Arbogast opened one of the windows despite the cold weather, because it was sunny out, and a shaft of light fell on the middle of the faded, almost white counter. Toys belonging to her three-year-old son lay about—blocks, a tin tractor and a small pistol that Hans had carved in prison and painted. Michael was having his afternoon nap upstairs in his bed, which stood next to her own. No one but her mother-in-law was there. They used to have many guests for lunch at midday. The Salmon was right on the main highway to the Rhine, and people had stopped in on their way from Strasbourg. Not anymore. She could feel Hans's mother watching her.

Margarethe Arbogast was sitting at the round table in the niche next to the bar, where the family usually ate. There was a crucifix on the wall above her. She was still dressed up. The first day of the trial, she had put on her black wool dress with the brooch, arranged her braided gray hair in a bun on top of her head, and begun to wait. Katrin didn't know what for. Hans's mother had made her statement that first day and then just sat in the gallery and listened. Katrin had brought her back home after she collapsed in tears in court, and now she sat and waited, as if something else was still going to happen. Katrin certainly would have liked to know what that might be. It had taken her all morning to get to Bruchsal on the train. Her husband had just come from the clothing dispensary when they brought her into the visiting room, and she would have laughed at his uniform if he hadn't looked so terribly serious in it. Although both of them wanted to, they hadn't succeeded in talking about the trial. Katrin had hoped that Hans's sister Elke would be at the Salmon today. But she came there just as seldom as she went to visit her brother.

"It's over, Mother," Katrin said without expecting a response or really knowing what she meant by that. For a moment she thought it could have been her own life she was talking about.

Katrin went into the next room and closed the heavy sliding doors behind her. This was the room where weddings had once been celebrated, as well as anniversaries and major birthdays. The room was dark and musty-smelling, with heavy curtains in front of the windows, but that hadn't mattered. One time recently, when she hadn't been able to stop talking, over and over, about what had happened, her father had angrily blurted out that she ought to just get a divorce. Katrin was twenty-three years old. Her hands nestled in the cool depressions of the door grips like small hibernating animals; but when she noticed it, she pulled them away quickly, knowing that otherwise they would quickly pick up that metallic smell. In the dim light, the old sheets with which she had covered the billiard tables seemed to be glowing. There were twelve of them, and where there were tears in the sheets, you could see small patches of green felt and, on one table, the outline of numerous balls. Whenever she came in here, she was reminded of the enthusiasm with which Hans had taken on the billiard-table dealership. It was shortly before his arrest that he'd bought this shipment of a dozen tables. He'd gotten them for a song, he'd said, and they were all supposed to have been sold within the span of a few weeks, some of them in Freiburg, which was where he'd been going when he ran into the little tramp.

It seemed to her now, after all the reflection of the past months, that she and Hans had been dreadfully young at their wedding, shortly after the monetary reform had been enacted. It had never occurred to her before how young they were—they'd known each other from school, and she'd gone out with Hans since the time boys first began to be interested in her. Even now, she couldn't imagine being with anyone else. After he was gone, in jail, she'd begun to imagine over and over the way he'd kissed the refugee woman, how he'd put his arms around her in the car that was so important to him. At first, she had wept and been unable to eat for days on end. She was barely able to take care of Michael and had spent a few weeks living back at her parents' place. There must have been others, too. He'd had so many opportunities! All that trust for nothing, she'd thought, and after that, she was less afraid. A couple months on, when the indictment still stood, she had all at once and quite easily come to the decision that she would not divorce him. As the pain of it began to recede, she felt a profound calmness. "Wait and hope, that's all we can do," Hans's mother said, and Katrin nodded.

The past year had been almost peaceful, she thought to herself now, as she pulled back the sheet from the billiard table closest to where she was standing. She remembered the night they were delivered. Katrin had protested to Hans that there was no way he could spend so much money, not to mention that they needed the room for the restaurant. He'd just smiled at her and waxed on about the virtues of the Brunswick tables. He'd stroked the felt with the flat of his hand and told her about the wood the frames were built from, how many coats of what kind of varnish, how heavy the slabs of slate were that underlay the felt, how crucial it was that the tables be absolutely level and even. He had made her touch the surface.

"You can't see the slate," he'd whispered, moving her hand across the felt, "but you can feel its weight. Can't you feel the pull of it through the fabric?"

She had nodded, really believing she could sense the presence of the stone. Then they'd kissed, a long time, and he'd pressed her against the table and touched her through her thin dress. It had been a sultry day outside, but it was cool in there. Later that night a storm had come in off the Rhine. He'd brought out a small wooden case with three balls and set them in motion, drawing countless patterns of confused lines between the felt-covered bumpers. In the darkness of the thunderstorm, the balls expended their collective energy in ricocheting and rebounding, crashing wildly against one another and into the bumpers, arcing off on tangents, and it had seemed an obscene, blasphemous game—one that both attracted and repelled her. It fairly turned her stomach, how anxiously her own gaze had followed the action on the table, striving to predict the consequences of the slightest contacts as well as the stronger collisions, projecting any number of straight paths. Even after they had given up watching them and begun kissing and caressing each other, she could hear the dull clacking of the white balls. It seemed like it would never stop. That was the last time he had touched her.

After everything she'd heard at the trial, she was glad they hadn't made love there on the billiard table on that stormy evening, and yet she was sorry, too. He had been right after all: Every time she came into this room and passed her hand across the surface of the table, it did seem to her that the stone hidden beneath the felt had been waiting for her touch.

7

The door clicked shut behind him and locked. On the right was the washbasin, on the left a locker containing a dented set of dishes and cutlery. On one side, there was a table and a bench that could be folded up against the wall. You sat on the bench, facing the door. On the opposite wall was a bed that folded away similarly. The bed frame was metal with webbing and a small side rail. There was a mattress, a pillow, two blankets. Arbogast estimated the dimensions of the cell at twelve feet deep by eight feet wide and the ceiling at nine feet, which would add up to well under a thousand cubic feet of space. The ceiling was whitewashed and the walls painted light green. The floor was tile. The surface of the plaster walls was scratched with dates and cryptic symbols. The cell regulations were posted on one wall: "The prisoner is required to rise from bed promptly at the sound of the 6:30 wake-up bell. He will wash, brush his teeth and prepare himself to receive his coffee." In the wall next to the door, there was a recessed area containing a tar-lined bucket. The window across from the door was about three feet square and set six feet high into the wall. The door was narrow, made of solid oak, with crossbeams and a ring that was connected to a bell. Next to the ring was the peephole, and beneath that, a slot which opened only from without.

At midday, a bell rang in the main guardhouse, and the head guard called out, "Food-service workers, report for duty!"

The two prisoners whose job it was fetched the large vats of food that had been brought up from the kitchen, then carried them from cell to cell. The slot opened, Arbogast held out his bowl, and a guard ladled some gray soup into it. After the meal, the mail was distributed, and Arbogast received his entry packet, as it was called, which was sent to every prisoner upon his arrival at the prison. It contained a pad of gray letter-sized paper with matching envelopes and a pencil, as well as a pamphlet entitled "Regulations Pertaining to the Communication of Prisoners with the Outside World." Arbogast was eager to write to Katrin, to begin to explain to her what he hadn't been able to say that morning, but that afternoon, when the door suddenly opened and a guard came in with a small ladder to bang at the bars of his window with a hammer, his page was still blank, except for "Dear Katrin." The officer reassured him that the mail wouldn't be collected till Sunday anyway; he didn't have to rush. If he stood on the stool, Arbogast could see a small bit of road, sky and the prison wall. The Americans had bombed Bruchsal pretty thoroughly but had left the prison undisturbed so that they could put Nazis away here after the war, or so it was said. Arbogast had heard that at the very end of the war there had been a prison revolt during which the director was killed and one of the guards had an arm ripped from his body. In the evening, they passed out bread, a small piece of margarine, some cheese and a tin bowl full of tea.

The following morning, the bell rang at half past six. Arbogast was instructed to fold up his bed and have his bucket ready. He'd barely had time to do so before the door opened and someone took away the bucket, emptied it at the end of the hall and brought it back. He was given a cup of malt coffee and a piece of bread. His tin bowl served as a plate. After his first breakfast in the Bruchsal Prison, he was instructed to sweep out his cell with the broom that stood against the wall of the toilet niche, beside the bucket. At seven thirty, it was time for the paper workers, mat weavers, net makers and all those who worked in their cells to go to the exercise yard. Arbogast was told that as long as he hadn't been called to his intake conference, he was to go along.

"Prepare to go to the yard!"

The cells were unlocked and the prisoners stepped out of their doors and into file. Arbogast look around him and nodded at the men standing next to him, but no one met his gaze. It seemed to him that the distance the others kept from him was greater than that between the rest of the prisoners. Arbogast felt afraid. It was said that there were hierarchies among prisoners, and that rapists were the most despised of all. The guard inspected the line of prisoners and commanded, "Cells one hundred to one fifteen, to the yard."

There was the thundering of footsteps on the walkway. Arbogast feared he would be trampled or shoved, but nothing like that happened. One after the other, they passed the tower, went down the stairs and out into the yard, where they were counted again by another jailer. The yard was triangular, with two sides made up by the walls of adjacent wings of the prison and the third by the outer wall. It was swarming with blue uniforms. There were guards with machine guns up on the wall and five officers in the center of the yard. The prisoners marched in a circle, two by two. Quiet conversations were held in small groups. Talking loudly, standing still and exchanging goods were all strictly forbidden. Nevertheless, Arbogast saw cigarettes and small packages being handed back and forth. He walked alone. After an hour, they were taken back to their cells. In the brief moment that they all stood waiting in front of their doors, Arbogast nodded to his neighbor, a skinny old man who turned away from him. Shortly after the doors were locked behind them, Arbogast was given a razor through the slot in his door. He had been summoned to his intake conference.

"Get a move on, Arbogast. But do a thorough job."

Hans Arbogast shaved as quickly as he could in the cold water and then sat waiting at his table for over an hour, clean-shaven. There was nothing to do, so he did nothing. His hands were folded together and he looked up at the window. When he heard footsteps and then the key in the lock, he stood up and went to the cell door, expecting to be led away somewhere. He was quite surprised when a priest walked in with his hands folded across his cassock.

"Just a moment, please," said the priest, smiling, "not so fast. They won't start without you. Before the conference, I'd like to have a little conversation, just you and I. Please, take a seat."

Arbogast sat. The cell door was relocked. The priest remained standing near the doorway.

"I'm Father Karges," he began. "And you are Hans Arbogast."

It wasn't a question, but Arbogast nodded.

"You're Catholic."

Again, it wasn't a question. Karges was in his mid-forties. His shiny reddish skin was stretched tautly from his chin and the top of his collar, and he had a wide, rather moist smile on his face. He clasped his hands as if trying to decide what to say.

"Father, I'm innocent," Arbogast blurted.

Karges seemed not to have any eyelashes, or at least they were so fine and light as to be nearly invisible, but even so, he fluttered his lids. Arbogast had to look away. He had slept badly, had been just on the edge of wakefulness all night, holding his head in his hands, pressed up against the wall, surrounded by so many strange noises. He was exhausted.

"Really. I'm innocent. I didn't kill her."

Karges nodded and smiled, then cleared his throat. He gestured with his hands toward the walls and looked more closely around the cell. "So, do you have any idea where you are?"

Arbogast shook his head. It seemed to him that the priest's hands were dancing in his cell.

"This prison was built a little over a hundred years ago, at a time when people wanted to do away with the old penal colonies and workhouses. In those days, if you can imagine it, there were vast common dormitories and workrooms where convicted felons were housed alongside orphans, all of them filthy and unkempt. In an effort to change all that, the Bruchsal Men's Penitentiary of the Grand Duchy of Baden, in which you now find yourself, was built. It was modeled on the Pentonville Penitentiary outside of London. It was the first prison on the Continent constructed according to the principle of the panopticon—a sanitary and finely tuned machine. But do you know what really made this place unique?"

Arbogast shook his head again, and Karges ran his hand across the wall by the door, as if he could sense the strength that lay behind the plaster.

"It was the first prison in Germany to introduce the incarceration of prisoners in individual cells. An act called the Regulations Pertaining to the Administration of the New Men's Penitentiary in Bruchsal, ratified on March the sixth, 1845, stipulated in paragraph one that 'each prisoner be housed in an individual cell and be restricted day and night from association with other prisoners.' Bruchsal was *the* model on which all subsequent German prisons were constructed—"

Karges put particular emphasis on the word *the* and allowed himself a pregnant pause at the end of the sentence. Arbogast couldn't begin to fathom why the priest was telling him all of this.

"The concept of keeping prisoners in isolation, which was developed by the Quakers, was a thoroughly modern innovation at the time. The purpose was twofold. On one hand, it was intended to prevent them from infecting one another with the evils of their criminality. On the other hand, the sustained and complete removal of the wrongdoer from all human community was meant to generate remorse and longing for reacceptance into the circle of law-abiding society—a remorse so great that the wrongdoer would look inward, and ultimately be able to return, chastened, to society."

Arbogast closed his eyes again. He couldn't help thinking of his lawyer, and suddenly he understood what Meyer had meant when he described his state of exhaustion. It was an exhaustion filled with words; he was so overfull of words he thought he would be ill. He rubbed his eyes with his knuckles.

"The physical realization of all these principles is what you have before you." Arbogast could hear the priest's hands sliding across the plaster.

"The prisoner was kept in his cell at all times. He not only slept there but ate there and worked there, too. When he left his cell to attend church or went into the courtyard, he wore a mask that rendered him unrecognizable to others, and he was not permitted to speak on the way there. As for the time a prisoner spent in the courtyard, he was still kept isolated—in a small wedge-shaped walled compartment of a larger circular courtyard. One of these courtyards still exists, between the first and second wings, and it was actually still in use until the end of the war. In church, the prisoners sat in separate enclosed seats, which were referred to as 'stalls' and allowed only a direct view of the pulpit. So, tell me, Arbogast, are you planning to attend church services here?"

The sound of the man's fleshy hands running over the rough plaster finally ceased. At last, he had been asked a question, and Arbogast opened his eyes with some astonishment and stood up. Karges laughed and, cocking his head a little to one side, once again clasped his hands together across his belly.

"Oh, please, sit back down. Please do sit down. What do you think—will you come to services?"

"Yes, Father, of course."

"That's excellent. I can assure you that we no longer have such individual stalls as I described. And there is a choir. Would you be interested in singing with the choir?"

Arbogast nodded.

"You say that you're innocent, Arbogast?"

Arbogast nodded again and looked intently at the priest.

"Do you know what it means that you've been sentenced to a penitentiary of this sort?" Karges folded his hands together in front of his face and touched the tips of his index fingers to his lower lip. He looked out at Arbogast over his hands and continued quietly.

"To be incarcerated in a penitentiary implies the loss of your rights as a citizen. You cannot vote. Nor are you allowed to petition the government. And do you know why that is? Because you're an outsider, Arbogast. To put it in a certain way, your body is no longer a territory of the state that has imprisoned you. You're outside. Do you understand me?"

Arbogast shook his head no.

"You're enemy terrain. And so it doesn't matter a whit if you're guilty or not. Do you understand? And do you understand who is the only one that can help you now?"

He shook his head again.

"The sole emissary, the sole intermediary in the relationship between these two enemy territories—between the state and your criminal body, that is—is me. Priests are able to go in and out of the soul, Arbogast. Do you understand me? That's our job. We can sanctify a piece of land that has been desecrated. Think about it. And while you're at it, forget about thinking that you're innocent. No one is innocent."

Arbogast nodded. Karges left, and a quarter hour later, two guards came to get him and took him to the barber, a prisoner who cut other prisoners' hair in his cell. There were three others already waiting in front of the door. Arbogast nodded at them, and they nodded back, but no one spoke to him until he was called inside.

"Well then, who are you? You're new."

Arbogast took a seat on the chair that stood in the center of the room, and the barber began cutting right away. The arms of the barber's blue jacket were rolled up to his elbows and he wore a white towel over his left forearm, like a waiter.

"Half an inch all over," he explained quickly. "Unfortunately, I have no choice in the matter."

"I'm Hans Arbogast."

But the barber said nothing more. He mutely took Arbogast's hair between his two fingers and snipped away, and Arbogast patiently allowed it to happen. The last time he'd had his hair cut was before the trial, by a proper barber who'd come to the prison in Grangat, where he was being held. Now he couldn't care less how the haircut came out.

"Arbogast?"

He looked up and into the eyes of a dark-haired man in a tweed suit, maybe thirty years old. He pulled up a chair and sat next to Arbogast.

"I'm Mr. Ihsels, the teacher here. I saw in your records that you have a high school diploma."

"Yes. I graduated in '44."

"Why didn't you ever go to college after the war?"

"My father really wanted me to, but I never liked school. I was apprenticed to a butcher."

"Your father's dead now?"

"Yes. Five years ago. He died of a heart attack."

"I'm sorry to hear that. I want you to know that if you're interested, you can continue your education from here. Either with practical training of some sort or by taking college courses through the mail. We also have language classes, and there's a library, which is under the care of Mr. Millhöfer and now contains some ten thousand volumes. They're all nicely wrapped in brown paper, and you can take out a new one every week on your library card."

"All finished!" said the barber.

"Come with me," said the teacher, taking Arbogast's arm and helping him up from the chair. "Your next stop is the doctor." He smilingly brushed a few stray hairs from Arbogast's shoulders and took his leave of the barber, saying, "Looks good, Richard!"

The two guards who had brought Arbogast there were still outside the door, and now they took him to the doctor's office. The exam room and the infirmary were both located in the central tower building. Arbogast was beginning to grow accustomed to the rhythms of the jailers: walk a short distance, then stand there and wait for some door to be unlocked, then a few more steps forward and wait again for the door to be locked behind you, then forward. Out in front of the infirmary, there were several other new arrivals. After a while, their names were called and they had to undress and then continue to wait there unclothed until they were called up to the desk, where two guards sat with the prisoners' files and an open filing cabinet containing the intake exam forms.

"Hello." The doctor in his white coat swiveled around on his desk chair to face him. "I'm Dr. Endres."

Arbogast couldn't help thinking back to the time when he'd worked at the slaughterhouse and how he had sometimes stroked the hindquarter of one of the dead calves hanging on the meat hooks, how he'd run his hand across the soft fur, the fine swirls of black and white, before he took the carcass down.

"Take a deep breath."

The doctor palpated his groin.

"Now pull back your foreskin."

8

That afternoon, Arbogast was brought to the warden's office for his intake conference, and once again he had to wait at the door until another new arrival had had his turn. On his way out, the other man told Arbogast he could go in. A desk of highly polished mahogany veneer sat at an angle in the center of the great round room, which was on the third floor of the central tower of the prison building. The desk was bare except for a pendulum clock under a bell jar. In front of the desk lay a light brown sisal mat with a dark red border of the sort that was made by the prisoners there.

"Right there, please." The warden pointed to the mat and Arbogast went and stood on it. He didn't know what to do with his hands and finally clasped them behind his back. He'd expected the warden to be an older man, certainly not this young or thin. His bony shoulders stood out beneath his light brown cardigan. Beneath that, he wore a white shirt and dark brown tie.

"Well now, Arbogast, what we need to do is come up with a plan for you. That's to say, we must consider what you will do with yourself during the years you spend here. Do you understand?"

Arbogast nodded.

"I take it you've already spoken with Mr. Ihsels and Father Karges. You will certainly also come to know Mr. Millhöfer, the other teacher here at the prison, as well as Dr. Endres's assistant, Dr. Frege. Presumably, you won't have much to do with Father Ohlmann, since you're a Catholic. By the way, I am Warden Mehring."

"Yes."

Arbogast didn't know what else to say.

"Yes indeed. Now, for your information: Most of the employees at this facility, excluding the administrative and managerial staff, with whom you're not likely to have much contact, are guards. The security staff of the Bruchsal Penitentiary consists of exactly twenty head guards, eighteen lieutenant guards, twelve regular guards and twenty-four assistant guards. Would you like to say something?"

Arbogast shook his head.

"It would seem the best course of action to me, Arbogast, not to put you into a common cell with others, at least for the time being. You see, rapists and murderers are not very well liked here."

"I'm innocent, Warden."

"Be that as it may, I think it would be best this way. Not that you have anything to fear—your security is guaranteed. We won't let anything happen to you. It's just that, well—how to put this?—you shouldn't expect a great deal of sympathy from your fellow prisoners, if you see what I mean."

"Yes."

"And if anything does come up, simply let someone know."

"I'll do that."

"And you are in agreement with the plan of solitary confinement?"

"Yes."

"I hear you would like to attend church services?"

"Yes."

"And classes?"

"Yes."

"Good. And what sort of work would you like to do? You'll have to choose from one of the jobs that can be done in your cell."

"I don't know."

"Either bags or bottles would be all right, I'd think. That's either gluing paper bags together or weaving wicker baskets around bottles."

"Yes, that's fine."

"Well, which one? Bags or bottles? How about bottles?"

"Yes, sure."

Arbogast nodded. The warden stared at him silently for a moment before dismissing him. While he was being brought back to his cell, Arbogast thought about whether the warden had been looking for some sign in him that would speak of the crime he'd been convicted of committing. Everyone looked at him. It was evening, and he was glad.

9

From the outside, the walls of the Bruchsal Penitentiary gave the impression of a fortress—eighteen feet of rough limestone blocks topped with battlements and watchtowers—without ever allowing the visitor to see the prison itself or its four wings of red sandstone. Four of the towers had chimneys from oil-burning stoves and windows from which one could look out onto the surrounding terrain. Before shooting, the sentries were obliged to give some warning. This might mean a warning shot into the air or a shouted command such as "*Stop or I'll shoot*." Under every cell's window, the cell number was painted on a white rectangle. In the center, there was a tall crenellated tower, octagonal, just like the outer walls, with high arched windows. The top floor was devoted to the chapel. The whole place had massive stone walls; only the cell doors were of wood. The exterior walkways that led to the individual cells were constructed of the same sort of cast iron as the central spiral staircase that descended through the tower. The wings were separated from the central part of the main building by iron gates. On every level, there was a sink with hot water located adjacent to the gates. Hans Arbogast's cell was located in Wing Two, and between Wing Three and Wing Four lay the courtyard where the prisoners took their exercise.

At night, beams from the spotlights of the guards who kept watch along the outer wall shone in through his window like weak moonlight, filtered by the double bars. The light wasn't bright enough to give shape to the objects in the room or throw shadows, but it permeated the room without warmth or dimension and made the bedsheets glimmer. It was as if there were grains of light caught beneath his lids, and unless something had happened during the day to fill his head and help him ignore the restlessness of his body, it was enough to keep sleep at bay all night. Most days, nothing happened, and so Hans Arbogast just lay there, awake. During the day, the cell doors were locked, and at night, they were double-bolted. He listened to the dogs' constant barking outside and the ceaseless footsteps of the guards going up and down the walkways. Sometimes the spy hole in his door opened and someone peered in. There were twelve German shepherds at the facility. Their kennels were near the kitchen garden, and at night they were put out on leads attached to long lines that ran parallel to the prison walls. The sound of the rings gliding along the steel wire reminded Arbogast of a cold wind blowing in from the sea in the evening, rushing over jagged rocks still damp from the tide.

He quickly lost his sense of time, and soon Arbogast no longer even perceived the passing of the days. He tried to recall everything he could from his past, to bring some of the smells and flavors from that time to this empty life. He hadn't fought in the war and hadn't traveled much, just that one trip to Strasbourg, a weekend outing he'd made to Hamburg in his first car in 1951, and his honeymoon on Mainau Island in Lake Constance. But he vividly remembered the maps his teachers had from time to time unrolled and hung on the map stand in school. The Neander Thal, the Limes, the Acropolis, a medieval castle, the Battle of Tannenberg, Germany's borders in 1937, the imperial powers and their colonies. Hans Arbogast lay with one hand under his head and the other rubbing his chest and belly, remembering and quietly speaking place-names to himself: Kamchatka, Timbuktu, southwest Germany, Macao, the Cape of Good Hope, Tangiers, the Silk Road, Irkutsk, the Bering Sea, the Amazon, the Congo, the Danube Delta, Australia, St. Joseph's Colony, Tahiti, the Galápagos, the Panama Canal. He rolled over on the narrow mattress and faced the wall. He pressed the back of his hand to the cool plaster. It always reminded him of the first time he'd touched her skin. But he couldn't bear it for long and rolled over onto his back again.

As he described to his wife, he soon began to feel that the space in his head was growing ever smaller. After his hopes of imminent release had faded, he found that the world within him shrank. Like a suffocating man desperate for larger lungs and more oxygen, he wished for more memories, more of a past. Everything was tired and worn, every picture flat, and every sound seemed to echo, and even those sensations were ebbing. Eventually, that feeling, too, passed away, and it no longer even seemed to him that his memory was shrinking: Everything was simply at a standstill; everything stayed the same. At some point, his lawyer, Meyer, informed him that the high court had denied his appeal. "With this decision, Mr. Arbogast, the judgment against you becomes final." That was maybe three years in. All that was left to him was her. Slowly, deeply, he breathed her in. At the trial, the pathologist had said that her hair wasn't really red—it had been dyed "Titian red." But it had seemed to him when they were smoking together in his car that even the downy hairs on her arms had glowed red, and her eyelashes, too, for a moment at least, when the late afternoon sun had fallen across her face at the restaurant where they'd eaten, a place called Over the Falls.

It was a long time since he'd been able to masturbate to the image of her face; the idea of doing it sickened him now, as did reimagining their lovemaking. Even before the trial began, he had blocked out, to the extent that it was possible, all memory of her lying dead in his arms. But after all he'd heard said about himself and about her, and, above all, after he'd seen those photographs of her dead body, it became completely impossible for him to touch himself while he thought about her. Ever since he first saw them, those pictures had kept the memory of her and, inseparable from that, her death fresh in his mind.

One time he tried to use the pictures to show Meyer the ways in which death had altered and disfigured her body, but the lawyer hadn't understood what he meant. He thought the young lady looked quite normal, he'd said.

"But I don't even recognize that girl!" he'd protested.

"What exactly do you mean by that?"

Silently, Arbogast had bent over the photograph. But the more he'd tried to make clear to the lawyer that death had left certain marks on her body, the less understanding the lawyer seemed to have for him.

After that, he gave up trying describe to anyone what it was like, the moment she died. He'd been observed for several weeks at the Freiburg University Psychiatric Clinic, but he hadn't even told the doctor, Professor Kasimir, about the self-loathing he'd felt that night as he held her dead body in his arms. Later on, the memory of her kisses and her touch had returned to him, as if in consolation, and in all the ensuing years, they had never failed him. It was as if Marie had given herself over to him in the moment of her death. On the nights that she came to him, and she came nearly every night, he never touched himself. He was convinced that he could never make love to a real woman again, though, considering his life sentence, that was more or less irrelevant. In exchange, I get to have sex with death, he thought, smiling into the wall. Only very rarely did he imagine his wife in some position or other, or another girl from his past, or the two whores he'd had in St. Pauli that time, and then he would quickly masturbate.

10

"How are you?"

"Fine."

Arbogast nodded at Katrin. She was sitting across from him at the glossy painted wooden table. A guard waited by the door. Behind her, the frosted-glass windowpane glowed white. Visitors to the prison were required to request each meeting in writing, and the prisoner had to be granted permission for the visit by the warden's office. Katrin tried to come as often as was allowed, which was every two weeks, but because there was no way of telling in advance if the prisoner had been granted the permission for the visit, sometimes she came in vain. Arbogast himself never knew he was getting a visit until the visitor was there. He was soon able to predict what she'd be wearing when she did come, though. The knitted jacket under her coat in winter. In summer she favored her white blouse and tended to leave off the jacket.

He watched her breathing, and as the years passed, he began to feel he would prefer it if she just didn't talk. His eyes took in the lines in her face and the way she crossed her naked forearms on the surface of the table. He observed the way she blinked and swallowed. He took note of changes in the way she wore her hair and makeup and thought he could see her aging; he noticed that she never bought new jewelry. He could hardly ever recall the past he'd had with her anymore, but when she was there with him, he could. The way he'd fallen in love with her shortly before graduation, their afternoons at the old quarry, the night they'd spent out in the reeds, their wedding, how it had been when she was pregnant with Michael. He looked at her baldly, watched her breathe. There was no way she could have known it, but when he returned to his cell, he took his renewed memories back with him into the solitude, like provisions. Most often, however, she interrupted his silent contemplations too quickly in order to tell him how things were going with Michael or his mother, what had happened at the Salmon lately, how the money was holding up and various bits of gossip about some neighbor or other. Katrin had always been the one to keep his world in order, and it seemed she was determined to continue doing so, even now that it wasn't actually his world anymore.

He would dearly have loved to tell her about Marie. About the way she died, though he would have left that for later, and about the strange feeling he'd had for this woman he barely knew. Arbogast had never mentioned his other affairs to Katrin—he was always having affairs—but that night as he drove home, he didn't know if he'd be able to keep this secret. It was only when he'd set down Marie's white handbag on the night table right next to where Katrin was sleeping that he realized he'd even brought it with him, and that he'd done it precisely in order to give Katrin a sign of this other world he'd inhabited since Marie first lay dead in his arms. He watched Katrin's breathing. He was still in that other world. She had never asked him about Marie.

"I wish you would write me longer letters."

He shook his head apologetically. While he was being held in Grangat, she'd spent a lot of time with him, and often brought Michael with her. They would simply play with him till the visit was over. Now she came less often and wanted him to write to her. But he couldn't think of anything to say. Endearments and promises didn't sound any better with constant repetition, especially when there was no shared life to make them feel new. Arbogast knew that the other prisoners felt the same way. People talked about it in the yard. They told one another stories and traded tobacco for drawings to put in their letters. Some of them could paint and were able to fill the pages wordlessly. A couple of times, Arbogast had given his pages to an old guy in Wing One, who had drawn a new border to go around those same old words. Once it was a portrait that looked a good deal like him, another time a drawing of the Salmon, which he'd conjured up based on Arbogast's descriptions exchanged during the exercise period in the yard.

It was easy for Katrin. She wrote to him of what happened to her during the day.

"It makes me so happy," she started up again, "when you write about what you do during the day and what you think about."

She reached for his hand, and for a moment he was shocked to feel her touch. The guard looked away. Now and then, she had even kissed him good-bye without his getting in trouble for it. He pulled his hand away from her. Sometimes he thought about her warm skin and how much she had changed in the time they'd known each other. How soft her belly had become after giving birth and how she used to cross her legs around his hips and press herself against him with her eyes closed. They didn't talk about what it was like to live without being touched, and he didn't dare ask if she had taken up with someone else. Or if she still loved him.

After the first few years, Arbogast's relationship with Michael, who had been three when he was arrested, began to change. Whereas at the beginning they had played in the visiting room, once the boy saw his father in the prison uniform, their closeness seemed to fade increasingly away. Katrin still brought him, but the boy grew bored easily. After he started school, and then grammar school, he often just stood there in front of Arbogast and stared at him. He no longer tolerated being hugged.

"That scratches!"

"Oh, come on, don't be like that."

"I don't want to, Papa. Let go of me. That scratches!"

At some point, it was only Katrin who came, alone.

11

"There's something creepy about you," she said quietly when he asked her what she thought of him. Katrin looked at him.

"You were just gone. There was this handbag that smelled of a strange perfume, and you were gone. I had the handbag and the car in which you had picked up that little tramp, and nothing more. You were just gone!"

Arbogast nodded and looked at the floor.

Katrin couldn't speak, she was crying so hard. She squeezed her eyes shut for a moment. "You didn't even tell me you were going to the police."

"I know."

"Have you had a lot of others?"

He didn't look at her. She waited. They had gone over this so many times. Everything had been said—and yet nothing was clear.

"What did you think about when we had sex?"

Arbogast shook his head.

"Was I boring?"

"No, of course not."

"How did you touch her?"

Arbogast shook his head more forcefully and said nothing.

"Won't you at least talk to me, after all of this!" she shouted.

But he said nothing, and so she left.

In the evening there was sausage and bread. The next morning coffee and bread, as usual. For lunch, a noodle soup and plum pancakes. For dinner, jellied meat, roasted potatoes and beet salad. On

Wednesday it was barley soup, boiled spinach with bacon and mashed potatoes for lunch, then rice pudding and apple compote in the evening. Thursday lunch was potato soup and raisin cake with baked fruit for dessert, and for dinner, herring in tomato sauce, boiled potatoes and tea. Friday, oatmeal gruel, fish cakes and parsley potatoes at midday, and in the evening noodles with tomato sauce. Then came the weekend, which meant they got two hours a day in the yard. On Saturday there was gruel in the morning and then beans and salted potatoes with sauce for lunch. In the afternoon, a ten-minute shower; in the evening, a film, which was projected onto a screen that was set up in the hall of the First Wing. The prisoners sat crowded closely together on the benches and waited for the projector to begin whirring. *The Woodsman of the Silver Forest*.

Sunday morning before church there was sweet cocoa and bread with honey. The prisoners filed silently upstairs to the church, where six guards stood on duty by the door. When the organ started up, they took off their hats. The high walls of the pews still had something of the feel of the stalls Karges had described in which the prisoners had once been separated from one another. As soon as the choir started singing, the men began to whisper and to trade tobacco, cigarettes and dime novels. The priest entered from a separate balcony that led to the pulpit. For lunch on Sunday, there was mushroom soup and then schnitzel with yellow beets and potatoes. Chocolate pudding for dessert. In the evening, just like every Sunday evening, they had sausages, bread and coffee. Katrin looked at him. Sometimes his silence put her into such a rage that she could barely stand it in the little visitor's room.

"Your mother's not well."

"Why doesn't she visit me?"

"She's not doing well."

"What's wrong?"

"What's *wrong*?" It's his fault, Katrin thought; everything is his fault—and with that thought, her rage faded and she grew completely calm.

"How's Micha doing in school?" he asked.

"Fine."

Arbogast nodded. He was acting just like he understood what was going on in the outside world, Katrin thought. But she was thinking, as she often did when she came there, that, in fact, he understood nothing, nothing at all.

He was thinking about how much of his daily quota he still had to do. Every morning after returning from the exercise yard, thirty potbellied wine bottles were brought to his cell, and he had to weave the basketry around them. The prison worker who delivered them was another lifer, like Arbogast. In the beginning, he always used to sing some song about Chianti wine as he set the load of bottles down, but then at some point he'd left off with it. At first, Arbogast really had to weave rushes around the foot of the bottle, but later it was just a piece of plastic that he wrapped with wicker. With his left hand, he turned the bottle; with his right, he paid out the strand of wicker. He was paid three cents per piece and then, later on, as much as four cents. The cell door was unbolted and Father Karges entered.

"Mr. Arbogast?"

12

Katrin's hand moved back and forth across the white surface of the wooden table. She cleared her throat and avoided looking at Arbogast. It was October 1960. At this time of year, she always thought back to that fall. He'd been in prison for seven years. She had a job lined up in Freiburg for the following year, and in January she and Michael would be moving there, renting an apartment in a postwar building. Everything was going to change. The wood of the table was cracked and rough beneath the paint. She knew his face, knew the way he was looking at her now. She had seen his face change with every visit she'd made, and the less they talked to each other, the better she'd learned to read his features. It wasn't hard. After just two or three years, she'd begun to see how it was collapsing. She didn't want to look at him now.

"Do you understand what I'm saying?" she asked him quietly without opening her eyes. "I want a divorce."

At first, she hadn't understood why his gaze made her feel so uncomfortable. But then one day, she'd gone to the priest for counsel, and he'd told her about the purpose of solitary confinement and the way it used to be at Bruchsal in the olden days, and she'd begun to understand what was happening to Hans. Karges had told her about how the prisoners once had to wear leather masks whenever they left their cells, and the image of those leather-clad faces stuck with her. It seemed to her as if Hans had a mask that he only took off just before he came into the visitor's room; it seemed as if he had no skin of his own anymore. You could see in his features everything he felt, and they were growing increasingly disturbed with the passage of the years. She thought she could read his every thought from his face—at first, mostly rage and sorrow, which followed each other in quick succession, as with a child, but then with the passage of time, these gave way to desolation and emptiness, which seemed to her to go deeper than just his eyes or his mouth. They pervaded his very laugh, his eyelids, the deep creases in his cheeks, governed the way he held his head.

"Yes, I understand what you said."

His voice was the worst of all. In a strange way, being in that cell had robbed his voice of its volume. He'd described the cell to her in all its details many times, and she was jealous of it, the same way she was jealous of his memories of Marie Gurth, which, Katrin was certain, had never loosed their hold on him. Now, at last, she made eye contact with him. She took one long last look at him, and then she put out her hand and took her leave.

Later, he tried to calculate how much time had passed between that moment and the next time he saw her, which was at the courthouse in Bruchsal, but he couldn't. He knew it must have been sometime around the beginning of the following year, but to him, even that contact seemed like nothing more than a continuation of her absence. Time is passing, he'd thought, and put out his hand to her.

The Bruchsal civil court was quite close to the prison, but nonetheless, he had been transported the short distance in a car, under the watch of two guards. Over his prison uniform he wore a light coat that one of his jailers had given him. His name was called by the court, and he spotted Katrin as soon as he entered the small courtroom. He didn't know her lawyer, but he'd already seen Winfried Meyer in the hall. Meyer had clapped him on the shoulder and said how good it was to see him. Now the lawyer sat down beside him. Katrin had come with both of her parents. They saw him in the gallery, which was otherwise empty of people, but when he nodded to them, they looked away. He'd been looking forward to seeing Michael, but the boy wasn't there. Arbogast barely listened to the questions he was asked and mechanically gave the information that was requested of him. Katrin had a new way of doing her hair. It was pulled back and piled high on her head, which made her face look unfamiliar. The way she turned and spoke quietly with her rather pale young lawyer was strange to him, too. One of the prison guards, a man whom he had known for years now, sat behind him, and from time to time Arbogast looked back to check that he was still there. The old man would nod at him.

Fortunately, the procedure didn't take long. After it was over, Meyer promised that he would visit him again soon, then said goodbye. Arbogast nodded. He was about to go over to Katrin and her parents—he had suddenly realized he would never see her again—but before he could do so, the lawyer took his arm and nodded to the guards. Then Katrin was gone, and he was taken back to the prison in the paddy wagon. The first thing Arbogast did when he got back to his cell was to open up the newspaper. He'd taken out a subscription to the *Grangat Daily*. As usual, a few passages had been rendered illegible by the censor's blue ink. Arbogast was incapable of thinking about what had just happened. He briefly recalled the moment when Katrin had told him she wanted a divorce, but he couldn't remember when that had been. He flipped through the pages of the tabloid without reading them. His only thought, as he ran his hands over the blue censored patches, was that he didn't want to subscribe to the paper anymore.

13

Winfried Meyer wrote the address on the front of the large mailing envelope. He remembered his last meeting with Arbogast, on the occasion of his divorce. He could hear his secretary talking on the phone in the next room but couldn't make out what she was saying. The office still smelled of fresh paint, although it was six months now since the renovation. On the side table stood a vase of pine boughs decorated with Christmas ornaments. It was December 12, 1962. The envelope was heavy—it contained all the materials pertaining to the Arbogast case—and as soon as he handed it over to his secretary, the case would be closed forever.

He had appealed the court's denial of his first petition to retry the case, and that morning he'd received word that this last appeal had also been denied.

> Dear Mr. Arbogast,
>
> After much effort, I had succeeded in getting two new expert witnesses, both of whom were prepared to contest the fateful testimony of Professor Maul.

Winfried Meyer enclosed along with the letter copies of the statements by the new expert witnesses he'd gotten to review the case. The first one was from a forensic pathologist from Munich called Dr. Landrum, and it was unequivocal. "The accused has stated," wrote Landrum, "that at some point during the abnormal sex act, Miss Gurth suddenly collapsed and her heart stopped beating. The perpetrator had no way of expecting such an outcome." "That's the decisive point," Meyer had explained to his client. "You had no way of knowing what would happen that night."

But what really had happened that night? The lawyer thought back to the trial, now seven years ago, and what he recalled above all else were the photographic enlargements of the girl in the blackberry thicket that Professor Maul had shown to the court. Arbogast had never spoken of what he experienced that night, and Meyer had never dared to ask. He'd often been struck by the notion that the trial might have gone differently if only he'd been able to understand his client better. Meyer slid the second witness's statement into the envelope, as well. It was from Dr. Neumann, the director of the Institute for Forensic Medicine at the University Hospital of Vienna. Meyer had visited him there two years before and convinced him to serve as a witness. It had been difficult to get the materials from the police and the prosecutor's office for the witnesses to examine. He was initially told that they were not available to the public, then that the files had already been sent out, then that the photos were too fragile. Everywhere he sensed a reluctance to take up the matter of Arbogast again, which was only made clearer by Neumann's statement: "It is not possible to determine medically whether the cause of death in this case was the rape. It is clear that a sexual encounter took place, subsequent to blows and throttling that left the victim unable to defend herself. The available evidence is not, however, sufficient to prove death by strangulation in a court of law."

When he had received this report, he'd gone to see Arbogast one last time. After explaining the legal issues to him, he'd told Arbogast not to get his hopes up, but he said he did think that there was a chance of success for his petition for a retrial. It would go to the second criminal division of the district supreme court. He remembered vividly how Arbogast had simply nodded and said nothing. It was a bright, sunny day, and the frosted windows of the visitor's room were illuminated from without. There was something creepy about Arbogast. It was six months since the court had denied his appeal on the basis that the new experts had no evidence superior to that which had been available to Maul. Meyer had written to Arbogast: "This doesn't mean that there are no new findings in the new testimony, but rather that technically, in the strict legal sense of section 359 of the Criminal Code, a case may only be reopened when new evidence has come to light. The court is not convinced there is sufficient evidence at this time."

Meyer had immediately appealed this ruling and submitted the statements of the two new witnesses, but now the circuit court in Karlesruhe had denied that, too. "I do not know what further service I can be of to you," Meyer wrote now. "We have exhausted all avenues available to you through the criminal justice system." At the end of the letter, the lawyer said he hoped Arbogast would understand that he did not have time to bring the enclosed files to Bruchsal personally. Hans Arbogast nodded, as if Meyer was speaking directly to him, and replaced the letter in the envelope with the rest of the papers. Then he continued what he had been doing before—painting the little wooden figurines that were standing before him on the table. They were hollow, with places to set incense in the bottom and holes in the ends of their clay pipes through which the smoke would rise. Nearby, there were small bottles of paint, rags, paintbrushes and a bowl of turpentine. The whole cell was permeated with the smell, as it always was at Christmastime, when the prisoners earned extra money by making crafts for the Christmas fairs. In winter, they also received three rings of sausage each, donated from a butcher shop. When it was cold out, the sausage would keep a long time on the windowsill, inside the bars. On Christmas Eve, there would be apples and nuts, given to them by the clergy of the surrounding parishes, and on the first day of Christmas, a roast with potatoes and vegetables, and chocolate pudding for dessert, just like every year.

In recent years, they always seemed to be making some new craft object at the prison. *Sputnik* was the men's name for the bundles of bent wire wrapped up in rubber bands that some of them swallowed. It was common for the number of self-inflicted injuries to pick up around Christmas as men sought to get themselves a few days in the infirmary. When the rubber bands were dissolved by the stomach acid, the wires perforated the stomach wall. The prisoner would cough up blood. The idea of that pain pleased Arbogast. In half an hour, the lights would go out. As he was putting the lids back on the paint jars, he suddenly felt afraid of the dark for the first time. He felt that weak. Then he opened his window, letting in the cold night air and the sounds of the prison: the dogs, the voices calling from window to window, the footsteps of the guards on the metal walkways. Someone above him was tapping on the heating pipe with a spoon. At some point, he heard the bell. The prison sheltered him, as it always did, and he knew that nothing could happen to him there within its great high rooms. The prison's four wings were conjoined, like the rays of a star, at the central watchtower, and each quadrant of 102 cells was watched over by a single guard, 3 rows of 17 cells on each side of each wing. The lights went out and he folded his bed down from the wall in darkness, as usual. He was thinking that each cell was suspended from one of the walls of the inner courtyards like a single cell of a honeycomb, and that if not for the narrow cast-iron walkways that connected them, each would be isolated and unreachable. We are all alone, thought Arbogast, and, oddly enough, that thought didn't disturb him in the least—on the contrary, it seemed to leech away his fear completely.

14

In the early part of the following year—it was January 1963—an incident took place. Someone jostled someone else on the walkway that led to the cells. Afterward, it wasn't clear who had picked the fight, but at any rate, Arbogast, who was otherwise unobtrusive, had reacted with uncharacteristic violence. He senselessly attacked one of the other prisoners, and the guard who was escorting them was unable to separate the two men. An alarm was raised, and three other guards came running from the tower, but by the time they were able to pry Arbogast, who was a head taller than any of the guards, off of him, the man was in pretty awful shape. It was clear that Arbogast would have to do ten days in the detention block.

It was the first time he had ever been punished. The detention cell was located in one of the towers. It was an empty room with stucco walls. There was no bed or table, just a cement platform to lie on. He was given two blankets and a bucket, nothing more. The tiny window was set high up in the wall and could be sealed up with metal shutters so no sounds emanating from the cell were audible outside. At the door of the cell, he had been compelled to strip off his prison uniform. He was naked when they locked him in, with what was known as a "stiff shirt" in his hand—a garment made of fabric so tough it could not be torn and used to hang oneself. He was fed tea and bread. The first couple days he didn't mind. He inspected the many lewd drawings on the walls. Directly above the sleeping platform was a coarsely rendered, fairly sizable drawing of a woman with her thighs spread wide, revealing outsized labia. Beneath it was the word *cunt* and an arrow pointing between her legs. Beneath the window, almost as if it were pointing up at it, was an enormous phallus. There were names, dates, obscenities. Some of the writing was in Italian and some in the Cyrillic alphabet. Everywhere there were numbers, years, time served: *Ten years, Fifteen years*. And *In three days, I'll be free!*

Marie had whispered something in his ear once, and on his third day in the detention block, he realized he'd forgotten what it was. He could still feel her warm breath on his ear, her cheek on his, her hand on his upper arm, but he didn't know what she'd said anymore. No matter how many times he tried to make her repeat it to him, she held her silence. That was when he began to be afraid, afraid that he would forget everything. That women would be nothing but the faces he sometimes saw on the strips of newsprint that had served him as toilet paper these past eight years. Suddenly he was certain that he would be there forever. He tried not to think at all, and to prevent himself from forgetting even more, to avoid any thought of Marie. On the fifth day, he remembered how they'd lain in the grass and she'd told him of Berlin. Of the unbearably hot summer in the bombed-out building where she'd gazed into the night sky from a sprung mattress with the stuffing coming out and let herself be kissed for the first time.

"No, I've never made it to Berlin. Do you think you want to go back?"

She did. She didn't think she could stand it where she was much longer. If only her husband could get some work in Berlin.

"But then we'd never see each other again."

She laughed. "But today," she'd said—she was there today, wasn't she?

"Kiss me."

The concrete wasn't very hard. He used his fingernails to scrape her name into its surface, very closely spaced. *Marie*. Then he masturbated, and he was surprised to realize how long it had been since he'd done that. He didn't know how long. One time, he chewed his bread into a warm, soft paste and used it to seal his mouth closed. He spat his tea into the air above his head and let it rain down upon him. For a long time, he lay on his back and tapped a particular spot on his stomach, somewhat above his navel, and felt certain that if he ceased to do so, he would go blind. The tapping continued for days, it seemed. He thought in time with the tapping of his fingers: Don't stop, don't stop. But when he realized that, he had already stopped without even noticing he'd done so. For a moment, he was alarmed to find that he really was blind; then he noticed he could still see. Her eyes looked at him, at such times, the same way they had back then, when she'd lain in his arms, but he couldn't remember what color they were. He wept at that. He had just finished scratching a box around her name, *Marie*, when the door opened.

When Arbogast got back to his cell, he heard his neighbors knocking out signals on the walls, and when he went to the window, someone called out to him, saying that he should lie on the floor by the heating pipe; from there he could tell the others what it had been like. But no one had ever wanted to talk to him before, and he had no desire to tell them anything. The teacher had told him that lifers could request a musical instrument or keep a parakeet in their cells. Arbogast didn't want a parakeet. The following weekend, he wrote a letter to Professor Maul at the University of Münster and begged him not to let him die in prison. He was innocent, after all.

Maul wrote the following note in the margin of the letter: "No interest. File."

15

"When a person's mother dies," began Karges after a brief hello, "it's as if one had lost one's bearings—or so a French poet once said."

"What are you saying? What do you mean, Father? My mother?"

Karges stood in the doorway with his lips pressed to his folded hands and nodded.

"I'm sorry, Arbogast. She died yesterday."

That was August 1963. The priest watched the prisoner closely. Arbogast, who had been standing under the window, went over to the table and then to the bed. He undid the catch and folded the mattress down, which was forbidden during the day. It was as if he had been rehearsing this subversive act for years. He sat down on the bed, his hands between his legs, and stared in front of him. Karges began to talk.

"You're one of a kind now, Arbogast. What I mean by that is, now that that which formed you is no more, nothing about you can be improved upon. All your scratches, flaws, defects are yours for good now. Now you are finally responsible for yourself. There's no second round anymore, if all this seemed to be just the trial run and you were holding out for the real thing. That's what we all think, after all, when we refuse to stand behind what we have done."

Karges waited for Arbogast's reaction, but Arbogast just stared straight out in front of him. Karges considered whether to insist that Arbogast fold up his bed, just to try to get him to look at him, but he decided against it.

"Atonement is threefold, Arbogast. First there's contrition, which you must feel within yourself. Then comes confession, in which you openly attest to your guilt. Finally, there is the release from guilt: the satisfaction. But of these three, the most important is confession, for only once you have acknowledged your wrongdoing, can God forgive you. And only then can I speak the words *Ego te absolvo*. Believe me, Arbogast, now is the time."

"But there's nothing for me to confess," mumbled Arbogast almost reflexively, without looking up. "I'm innocent."

"Even those who remain silent, who will not speak, the higher powers will eventually bring to confession. Believe me. The very silence becomes eloquent; it becomes a self-reproach. It's as if there exists something within us that protests against this refusal to express our strongest emotions, as if this denial gives rise to a counterimpulse toward an unconscious admission of guilt."

Now, at last, Arbogast met the priest's gaze. "Father?"

"Arbogast?"

"Can I go to her?"

"Yes. You may attend the burial. The day after tomorrow."

Karges nodded, hesitating briefly over whether to push the prisoner further to extract the redeeming confession that Karges was certain waited within him. But at last he decided to leave it for now, knocked on the door and was let out.

Arbogast watched the door being bolted shut behind him. It seemed to him that as the lock snapped shut, the barometric pressure in the room rose to an unbearable level, and he leapt up to open the window. Warm summer air poured in along with voices from the courtyard and the metallic chirping of the larks that were perched in the fields nearby. After the divorce, his mother had written him to say she could understand what Katrin had done. And that she and his father had always had a good marriage. With the exception of his father's death, what Hans had done was the most terrible thing ever to happen to her, she wrote; she could not comprehend how a person could bear such terrible guilt. Arbogast had nodded at each sentence when he read the letter, just as if she were sitting there in front of him, rebuking him. Whenever he'd done something forbidden as a boy, he knew he had only to wait like this, until she'd said her piece, and afterward everything would be all right again. And so he held her letter in his hands and nodded at every word. But when he got to the end of the page, the voice that he heard in his head simply stopped. It was silent. Arbogast remembered vividly what that had felt like. It was just silent; nothing happened. After some time, he had folded the letter up and slowly put it back in its envelope. Now he listened to the larks singing outside and looked out at the fields of stubble.

About noon, two days later, two guards and a driver took Arbogast to Grangat. That morning, he'd been taken down to the cellar and reissued his civilian clothes. The suit smelled of mothballs and dust. It had been January when he was transferred to Bruchsal, and the suit was far too warm for the August heat. One didn't feel it so much behind the thick prison walls, but in the patrol car it was unbearable. The sweat had soaked through his shirt before they got to Grangat. During the entire drive, Arbogast didn't say a word, just looked out the windows. He was taking in the new-model cars on the road, which were strange to him. When they got to the city, he barely recognized the streets. Next to the old brick buildings of the light industrial area, there were now vast flat-roofed boxes and gas stations with colorful illuminated signs. He had hoped he might see someone he knew, but none of the faces was familiar.

There was a little time yet before the burial, and he asked if they could take him by the Salmon briefly. The driver nodded and let Arbogast tell him the way. As he directed the driver through Grangat—the route wasn't too much of a detour—his heart began to thump in his chest and his hands grew clammy. The car pulled over and he got out with the two guards, but he hesitated for as long as he could at the threshold of the restaurant, pretending he was looking around. In the absence of the wind from the car window, the heat overwhelmed him again and sweat poured down his back. He reached in and loosened the shirt collar beneath his jacket, trying to move a little air across his skin. Nothing about the old building with its exposed wooden beams seemed to have changed, though it was over ten years since he had been there. The exterior did look a little shabby, though, in comparison to the freshly painted houses on either side. The street had been widened and resurfaced, and the front yard with its picket fence had disappeared beneath the asphalt along with the old cobblestone pavement. Carefully, Arbogast stepped into the entry, walked past the empty coat hooks in the hall and into the bar, where it seemed to him to be even hotter and very humid.

Arbogast didn't know whom he might see, but he thought perhaps it would be Elke, his younger sister, with whom he hadn't spoken since his arrest. All through the trial, she had sat beside their mother and looked away whenever he tried to catch her eye. She'd never visited him in jail, and after she failed to respond to two letters, he'd stopped writing her. The guards waited at the door. Arbogast was just loosening his tie and undoing the top button of his shirt—he'd worn it last on the day of the verdict against him—when Katrin stepped into the room from the kitchen. He'd heard that even after the divorce and her move to Freiburg, she'd continued to take care of his mother, but, oddly enough, he hadn't expected to meet her here. He turned back with some alarm to look at the two guards, as if they might tell him what to do, but they didn't respond. Katrin took him in with a quick look, and he was still able to tell just what she was thinking. She was thinking about the day they'd bought that suit together, and when he saw that, he thought of it, too. She smiled, and he extended his hand to her as she untied the apron she was wearing over her black dress. But she pulled him gently to her and hugged him. He withdrew from the embrace awkwardly. They still hadn't spoken a word. He took a couple of steps into the big room.

"It's hot," he said, pulling at his stiff collar. It chafed his neck.

"Yes."

She took off the apron and put it aside, continuing to peer at him.

"It's all just like before."

She shook her head. "Everything's being sold."

"Really?"

"Really."

He nodded. The smell of the place was so familiar to him—he sniffed the air like a dog, taking it in—and it was as if he'd only left there just that morning to go turn himself in to the police, rather than more than ten years ago. Soon it would be yet another year since that September day when he had met Marie. As he'd lain awake the previous night, he'd wondered whether his mother's death was his fault, too. Naturally, they would be selling everything. His mother had had to close the bar shortly after his arrest, because the customers stopped coming. Arbogast stood in place and turned back to look at the guards, still waiting in the doorway.

"Would you like a beer?" Katrin asked, like the tavernkeeper she was once supposed to have been.

The guards both nodded and took the bottles she offered them from the refrigerator behind the bar. Arbogast didn't know if his mother had believed him when he said he didn't do it. He had always put off asking her that till the next visit, and then the next time he would put it off again. Now he would never be able to ask. But actually he knew that for his mother, it hadn't really been about whether he'd done it—it was what had happened to her life, the way it stood still and never resumed. He remembered the way she had sat in the milky light of the visitor's room, her head slightly bowed, seeming to listen to the banging of the heating pipes, never looking up at him even once. That must have been the last time she came. And now he would never meet her gaze again, thought Arbogast.

"Where's Michael?"

"At Elke's. She's bringing him to the cemetery."

"So how's he doing?"

"I think he grows taller every day."

Arbogast nodded.

"Why doesn't he ever write me?"

"I tell him to, but how can I help it if he doesn't want to?"

Arbogast nodded again.

"Is there someone interested in the property?"

"Yes. No one you would know."

"Well, do whatever you think's best."

"The lawyer will write you with the offer as soon as we have it. But it may all happen rather quickly."

"Then maybe I should take a look around before it's too late."

"Yes, why don't you do that."

The room that he had filled up with billiard tables, back then, was empty. Katrin had managed to sell all twelve of them shortly after his trial, though below market price. You could still see scratches in the wooden floorboards from when they'd brought them in and taken them out again. The window curtains were drawn and it was dim in the room until the guards came in and propped open the doors so that they could keep their eyes on him. Sunlight fell on the long table that Katrin had set up in the center of the room for the funeral reception and covered with a tablecloth, just the way they used to do. Arbogast recognized the old blue-and-white coffee service and the silverware that they had brought out only on Sundays and holidays. He let his hand trail across the tablecloth and carefully straightened a cake server with his fingertip.

"Can you come by afterward?" asked Katrin from the doorway.

"No, I have to go back." He shook his head and then looked closely around him at the old room.

"There is something I'd like to take back with me, though," said Arbogast when he came across a box beneath one of the windowsills. Beside the box, there were dead flies and cobwebs and a small stack of beer coasters. The guards waited by the door while he carefully brushed the dust from the light beechwood case and brass hinges.

"And what would that be?" asked Katrin as he came back out of the dark hall, heading toward the door.

"My billiard balls," Arbogast said, and handed the case to the prison guards so they could inspect it.

Katrin didn't respond, but he could see from her look that she remembered how much his billiard balls had meant to him. She smiled at him and he looked away. When they all drove to the cemetery, he was amazed to see Katrin behind the wheel of a light blue VW Bug. He didn't even know when she'd gotten her license. Throughout the entire trip to the mortuary chapel of the cemetery—the same place he knew they had once brought Marie Gurth's body—he held the case of billiard balls on his lap.

The guards waited at the door of the small chapel. The bright summer light set the stained-glass windows ablaze with color. Arbogast could feel the stares against his back as he stepped forward to the open casket and then, without looking at anyone, sat down in the first row and bowed his head. It was cool in there. His mother's face was half-sunk into a soft white satin pillow and so emaciated and strange to him, he hardly knew her. The coffin was surrounded by flowers and wreaths. She never wore lipstick, he thought, and the sorrow welled up in him to his eyeballs. When he looked up, he noticed that there were several children peering at him with undisguised curiosity. None of them was familiar to him. Eventually, their parents scolded them and they quit staring. He knew almost all of the adults without even having to look at their faces, and the ones he didn't know he was able to identify by whom they were sitting next to. Eventually, the small door at the altar opened and a young priest stepped forward. While the congregation sang, Arbogast sat with the billiard case on his lap and opened the lid. He looked at the balls for a long time. There in the blue velvet were nestled three balls, one black and two of such a bright, creamy whiteness that he couldn't help but think of the palest shade of skin.

16

Early in 1964, the head warden summoned Arbogast to see him. It was the second time since he'd been at Bruchsal that he'd entered that office. To start with, Mehring asked how Arbogast was doing, after all that time. Hans Arbogast told him he felt fine. But he quickly discovered why the warden had really wanted to see him: It had to do with the new steel and concrete workhouse that had been built alongside the prison walls. The various workshops were being relocated to the new facility.

"First of all, this is going to bring about considerable improvement in the working conditions. As you know, the work areas have always been located on the top floors of each of the four wings and on the basement level. But the one thing we really want to do away with is solitary work in the cells."

Arbogast was stunned when he grasped what Mehring was suggesting. He desperately tried to think of what he should say. He did not want to work communally with the other prisoners. Hadn't the entire prison been designed precisely to keep the prisoners to themselves?

"In recent years, we've had a number of protests against cell work." Mehring saw the fear in Arbogast's face. "It's not a problem for you, is it?"

"No, of course not."

"Good, I'm glad to hear it. Tell me, how long have you been here now?"

"Nine years, Warden. And before that two years in pretrial detention in Grangat. Why?"

"Nine years. That's a long time."

Mehring looked hard at him for a moment. He had known too many prisoners not to understand exactly what was going on inside Arbogast: He feared nothing so much as change. The cell had become his shell. And now there was a possibility there wouldn't be cells anymore.

"Times are changing, Arbogast," he said slowly, holding the prisoner's gaze. "Times are changing."

Arbogast nodded. He had no idea what the warden meant.

"So you haven't had any problems with the other prisoners?"

It was odd how long it had been since Arbogast had feared that someone would do something to him. The very idea was funny to him. He had to smile. He knew that at some point early on during his time here, he'd begun to tell people he was innocent. He'd said it over and over again, every time someone shoved him or insulted him in the exercise yard, and the one time when he'd been jostled on the stairs. Eventually, it had stopped without his even noticing when. But nonetheless, he had never begun talking to the other inmates. On the contrary: He'd noticed at some point that when he had to speak, it came out as just a whisper, and he'd begun to fear he would lose his voice entirely. After just a few sentences, his throat would become sore, and the constant feeling that he needed to cough further deterred him from speaking. Even after the doctor had reassured him that a person couldn't lose the ability to speak simply through lack of practice, he sometimes still worried that he'd find himself unable to respond when someone talked to him in the yard.

"And what are you smiling about right now?"

"I don't know. I'm innocent."

"Good, I'm glad to hear it."

The warden wasn't sure if he ought to be concerned about Arbogast or not; perhaps he was just strange. Aside from his collapse after his mother died and the ten days he'd spent in detention, there had been no other problems with him. That suggested normal progress. Most of the lifers experienced their first bout of rage when they were seven or eight years in, some a little sooner. After that, they either went crazy or calmed down. He didn't think Arbogast was crazy.

"All right, then, I'll have you transferred to Wing Four, with the mat makers, tomorrow, and you can get started at the workshop there the day after. Your days are going to have a little more variety, Arbogast. Are you all right with that?"

"Yes, of course."

Arbogast nodded and was taken back to his cell. He found it difficult to leave his cell the next morning. Aside from three days in the infirmary and the ten days in the detention block, he'd spent the last nine years of his life there. During the night, he tried to fix firmly in his memory the array of sounds that had become, over the years, the true place where he dwelled. He'd gradually come to rely on and find security in the exact number of steps it took the guards to get from the central tower to his cell door, in the sound of the old man in the cell next door rattling his tin dishes and utensils, even though they'd never spoken, in the banging of the heating pipes.

After that, the days were different. After breakfast, Arbogast went to work with the others. They waited in front of their cells for the various workshop foremen to come and pick up their crews each morning. There was roll call, and then they marched to the stairs, went down the spiral staircase to the cellar and then walked from there through an underground passage to the new building, where the workshops and the kitchen were located. The mat-making facility was on the fourth floor. They used sisal and coconut fiber to make rugs and floor mats for cars. There was also an upholstery shop, a basket-making workshop, a saddlery, a locksmith's, a shoemaker's, a cabinet-maker's, a printing shop and a laundry. In the cellar was the bakery. At a quarter to twelve, Arbogast returned to his cell for lunch, and at twelve-thirty it was back to work. The period in the exercise yard was now from three-thirty to four-thirty, and lockdown was at five. A few days after his move, Arbogast was standing beneath the window of his new cell and scrutinizing, centimeter by centimeter, the strange drawings, scribblings and carvings that he had not made on the wall. He was trying to read them, as if they were a letter written to him, when the door was unlocked and the teacher came in.

"Good evening, Arbogast," he said in a friendly way and gestured for the guard to close the door behind him. He sat down on the bench, facing Arbogast. "I wanted to see how things are going for you in the new cell."

"Fine thanks." Arbogast leaned against the wall beneath the window and crossed his arms.

"And the work?"

"It's fine."

"And your colleagues? No problems?"

"No, no one's given me any trouble."

He was left alone, and no one minded if he walked up and joined in a conversation.

"That's terrific. Sounds like everything's going as well as can be expected."

"But I'm innocent," said Arbogast. "I don't belong here."

The teacher nodded. "I've been wanting to talk to you about that, Arbogast. I've thought a lot about the letter that you sent to Professor Maul some time ago. Perhaps it would be a good idea to try something like that again."

"What are you suggesting, Mr. Ihsels?"

"Things aren't the same as they once were, Arbogast," the teacher said. "The mood of the criminal justice system has shifted. People are actually talking about reforming the Penal Code. And in the last few years, a couple of enormous miscarriages of justice have been overturned. I brought you an article you might be interested in."

Ihsels pulled a newspaper clipping out of the inner pocket of his jacket, then patted his breast pocket and extracted a folded-up slip of paper. He put them both on the table. "I've also got an address for you. I think it would make sense for you to write to this person and describe the details of your case."

"Thank you, Mr. Ihsels," said Arbogast as the teacher knocked on the door and was let out.

"Just don't say where you got the name! Good night, Arbogast."

That very night, after reading the long newspaper article on the Brühne case—in which the author excoriated the actions of the court in the severest language—Abrogast wrote to Fritz Sarrazin, the director of the German League for Human Rights: "If your interest in challenging the justice system extends beyond pompous noisemaking to the desire to actually help a wrongfully convicted man, you will take on my case."

17

Fritz Sarrazin let the five-by-eight sheet of brown paper drop and looked out at the mountains. The year was ending with wet weather. Down in the valley, the lake flashed under the force of the driving rain. There were few cars on the highway. The Castello del Monte, as he called his house in his correspondence, was situated in such a manner that no one could drive south through Lugano without being seen by Fritz Sarrazin.

"The man's done eleven years in prison for a murder he claims he didn't commit. We'll see. I still haven't received a single letter from a convict who admitted his crime. If you listen to them, they're all innocent."

He wished Sue would say something. He glanced over the breakfast table at his wife's uncombed blond hair; then her head disappeared once again behind her newspaper. He followed the neckline of her bathrobe, which hung open from her shoulders, framing her torso above the table. He could see one breast, looking drowsy and so soft, it made her seem younger than her thirty years. It was hard to believe she was thirty. He thought about how they would go down into Bissone that evening, like every other, just as twilight fell, to get the afternoon mail and then go for a drink at the Albergo Palma.

The man was in Bruchsal. Sarrazin knew Bruchsal. His glance fell thoughtfully on the breakfast table, and this time his eye was caught by the brightly colored front cover of *Der Spiegel* that had arrived that morning. December 29, 1965. "Behavioral Science: Man and His Instincts." The cover illustration depicted a naked couple, the woman with her back to the camera, the man holding a goose in front of his genitals. Presumably, the reference was to the behavioral scientist Lorenz's well-known study of the gray goose. They each had an electrode attached to one leg, and the wires led to the ears of another woman, whose wide-open eyes stared into space. Her brown hair melded into a sort of cloud, from which a rocket with the symbols of the Soviet Union and the United States on its tail fins was being launched. Behind the rocket, there was a large red pair of female lips, and above it, so that the rocket's tip aimed right between the large breasts, a woman's torso in blue.

The signature in the lower right corner of the image read Kapitzke, which reminded him of a Henry Jaeger novel that described the conditions at the Bruchsal penitentiary; the novel's hero was called Labitzke. In two days, it would be New Year's Eve. Sarrazin opened the magazine and tried to read.

Adenauer had finally stepped down from his post as leader of the party. Chancellor Ludwig Erhard was quoted as saying, "Many of the problems that went unsolved in the first fourteen years have persisted during my brief tenure or have yet to be fully addressed." Someone named Professor Josef Nöcker opined that Mexico City's elevation above sea level did not imply a greater risk of fatalities at the Olympic Games.

Sarrazin broke off from his reading.

"I was at Bruchsal once."

"Were you? Why?" Sue didn't look up from her paper.

"I went to see the cell where Carl Hau was held."

"Hmm."

"It was ghastly to imagine that Hau spent seventeen years there in isolation."

Sarrazin continued flipping the pages. In one article he noticed a photo of an athlete, Heidi Biebl, who reminded him of Sue. It was mostly the wide, almost completely straight line of her eyebrows. Sue kept the marble-topped radiator cover under the picture window covered with countless potted houseplants. Now Sarrazin moved a few of them away, sat down there and rubbed his wife's leg. His hand traced from where her legs were crossed all the way down to the ankle. He knocked off her slipper and began rubbing her foot. Finally, she met his eye, and he shifted his caresses to her inner thigh and upward. Her soft skin was still warm with sleep.

"Do you know the story of Carl Hau?"

He kissed her knee and she shook her head no, laughing.

"Tell me."

"The story of Dr. Carl Hau was one of the strangest and most mysterious criminal cases before World War One. The actual facts of the case are that one evening the widow of medical privy councilor Dr. Molitor of Baden-Baden was summoned by telephone to the post office to pick up a receipt she'd forgotten when she had sent a telegram. She was a wealthy woman who lived in a luxurious villa and played an important role in the social life of the city. She was accompanied on the errand by her daughter Olga, but on the way to the post office, she was shot at close range."

"Naturally, the phone call was a setup."

"Naturally. The maid thought she had recognized the voice of the caller as that of Carl Hau. Now, take a guess who Carl Hau was."

"Who?"

"The husband of Olga's sister, Lina."

"Aha! Did he have an alibi?"

"Yes and no. He was in London with his wife and child at the time of the murder."

"I don't get it."

"Or really, he *had* been in London. But according to his deposition, while he was there, he received a telegram from his employers, the Standard Oil Company, instructing him to travel to Berlin. Then when he was under way to Calais, he decided to go to Frankfurt instead, and he sent his wife a telegram from there, informing her that the business meeting had been changed. At a Frankfurt barbershop, he got himself a false beard, and he had a wig that he'd brought with him dyed to match it. The day of the murder, he put them on and took the train to Baden-Baden. But he attracted attention because of the false beard and was even seen near the crime scene shortly before the murder."

"That sounds pretty simple. He was arrested?"

"Yes—in London. He had returned immediately. He was put into pretrial detention in Karlsruhe, where the trial was held."

"What about his wife?"

"At first, his wife insisted that he was innocent. But Carl Hau proved either unwilling or unable to explain his peculiar behavior, and shortly before the trial, she declared that she, too, was now convinced that her husband was guilty of murdering her mother. But the thought of this was unbearable to her—she couldn't stand the fact that the whole world would be talking about her family as soon as the trial began. She drowned herself in Lake Pfäffiker."

"Oh dear."

"Meanwhile, Hau still wouldn't talk. His attorney visited him and said that unless he explained himself, even he would have to come to the conclusion that Hau was the killer. Hau told him, 'Fine, you can go ahead and think I'm guilty; you can base your defense on it. But I didn't do it.' "

"What an odd character. What else is known about him?"

"He was the son of a bank president and grew up without a mother, neglected by his father. He began to live a dissolute existence as early as high school, when he got himself infected with syphilis. He met the Molitor family on Corsica, where he had gone on a doctor's recommendation to recover after suffering from a hemorrhage. Initially, the family was strongly opposed to a union between the two young people, and so Carl and Lina ran off to Switzerland together. When they had used up all the money Lina had in the bank, the two of them decided to commit suicide together. Carl Hau managed to fire a shot into his lover's chest, but apparently he didn't have the guts to turn the weapon on himself. He was never held responsible for the shooting. Quite to the contrary, the two of them were quickly married off to suppress the scandal.

"Carl Hau went on to complete his law degree in Washington, D.C., and found a job as private secretary to the general consulate of the Ottoman Empire in Washington. He traveled frequently to Constantinople and subsequently did legal work for several companies there. He continued to lead an extravagant lifestyle, which he was able to sustain thanks only to the financial resources of his wife."

"In other words, he was pretty dissolute."

"We can say one thing for certain about Hau: He was odd. But that in itself is not a motive for killing his mother-in-law."

"But all the circumstantial evidence pointed to it."

"At any rate, Hau continued to protest that he was not the murderer throughout the jury trial, which began during a heat wave in Karlsruhe in the summer of 1907. He would admit only to those details of his activity that could be proven, and there were no witnesses to the crucial half hour in which the murder was committed."

"But the circumstantial evidence!"

"Perhaps. But on the other hand, there was something a bit too transparently obvious about the whole situation with the fake telegram, the beard and the wig. It's hard to believe that a man of Hau's intelligence could have thought he'd be able to deceive anyone that way. It all drew far too much attention to itself. And it didn't fit with Hau's behavior in court."

"So there was some secret."

"Perhaps. At any rate, over the course of the trial, his refusal to give any information about why he was in Baden-Baden, wearing such a costume, or to explain various other events that took place in the time leading up to the murder, such as uncashed checks and the mysterious telegrams—all of this actually began to make him seem oddly credible. It was somehow too obvious that the suspicion had fallen on this cultivated man, and seemed possible that his silence might be concealing something greater, which he would never reveal, even if it cost him his head."

"So what happened at the trial?"

"At first, it seemed quite promising to establish a motive of jealousy."

"Aha."

"Yes, perhaps Frau Molitor had been summoned to the post office so that her daughter Olga would be left alone at home."

"You mean that Hau wanted his mother-in-law out of the house so he could see Olga."

"Exactly."

"A tryst."

"Or maybe the opposite: He wanted to shoot Olga because she wouldn't return his love—or had ceased to."

"Or maybe he did it for the inheritance."

"So, you can imagine that the excitement at the trial was enormous. Most of the spectators were quite taken with Hau's calm, resolute demeanor, not to mention his suspected unspoken love for Olga. Every day, there were more people at the courthouse. On the day of the verdict, there were demonstrations and the police were called in. Thousands of protesters laid siege to the courthouse and two battalions of armed soldiers had to be brought in for crowd control. They stood there with weapons drawn until two a.m., just to keep the masses at bay. Finally, at two a.m., the verdict was handed down: Hau was declared guilty of the murder of Mrs. Molitor. The DA argued for the death penalty, and the court concurred."

"And?"

"A few weeks later, the grand duke of Baden commuted Hau's sentence. Instead of the death penalty, he was sentenced to life in prison."

"Thus Bruchsal."

"Yes, precisely. He was sent to Bruchsal. He served seventeen years there in solitary confinement. Then in 1924, he was released on the condition that he refrain from making any contact with Olga Molitor, who had since changed her name and moved to Switzerland, and from engaging in sensational publicity to do with the trial. He swiftly dispensed with the second condition. The following year, two books were brought out by the Berlin publishing house Ullstein—*Sentenced to Death: The Story of My Trial* and *Lifer: What I've Seen and Suffered.* As a result, his parole was revoked and a new warrant was issued for his arrest, but Hau fled to Italy, where he took his own life in 1926."

"No!"

"Yes."

Fritz Sarrazin was silent for a moment. The letter from Bruchsal had made him restless. He enjoyed a reputation for being a man who acted swiftly, and he often told the story of his own premature birth: He'd arrived three weeks early, on February 9, 1897, on a railway car of the Orient Express while his parents were on their way home from a trip to Constantinople. The question now was just what he ought to do about this letter.

His last project had been the Brühne case, and when the secret Nazi past of President Lübke had come to light, he had publicly and vehemently spoken out against the German justice system. He took pleasure in giving guests tours of his archives and showing them the bound volumes containing his articles, essays, pamphlets and reports. The scion of a side branch of the prominent Sarrazin family and son of a hotelier from Geneva, Sarrazin had begun his working life as a legal reporter in Frankfurt, Berlin and Vienna before World War I, while he was at the university studying criminal justice and art history. He'd spent the war in South America, working as a consultant for the Brazil office of Mercedes-Benz, among other jobs. Then Henri Nannen of *Der Stern* had hired him, and after that he had been one of the chief correspondents at the Munich *Abendzeitung*. But it had been years now since he'd moved to Switzerland and taken up writing novels.

Fritz Sarrazin was a small, placid-seeming man, who kept his rather long white hair combed severely back. He generally wore a pair of prominent horn-rimmed glasses with large lenses, and the eyes that peered out through them were even now so extraordinarily alert that people sometimes misread him as being naïve. He had a preference for light-colored linen suits and bow ties. Oddly enough, it was only when he reread Hans Arbogast's letter that evening that he noticed the name Heinrich Maul. Maul was a person he was already familiar with.

And so it would come to pass that later that evening Fritz Sarrazin made his decision and sat down to write a letter to Dr. Ansgar Klein, the highly regarded Frankfurt criminal defense lawyer. Klein had been part of the team that had gotten the Rohrbach case reopened. He enclosed Hans Arbogast's letter and then wrote a brief card to Arbogast thanking him for his confidence and wishing him a happy New Year. He would take both pieces of mail to the post office the following day, the last day of 1965, and drop them off at the counter before they closed. Soon enough, that strange air of expectation would fall over the small town of Tessin, which lay shrouded by the thin drizzle, but just then the place seemed to be even sleepier than usual.

Sarrazin now cleared his throat, looked over at Sue for a moment, and continued.

"I was in Bruchsal in the late twenties, and I went to see the cell. I tell you, it's a ghastly place. That a person should spend so many years alone like that, with just the table, the bed, the chair—and a window too high up to look out of."

"And that's where this guy who wrote to you today is doing his time?"

Sarrazin didn't respond. He looked down at the road that connected the Mediterranean to northern Europe. The rain had let up.

"Do you want to hear your horoscope?" asked Sue after a while.

"Hmm."

"Okay, here it is: Aquarius. *La luna vi è propizia, ma state attenti a fare sempre una cosa per volta.*"

He watched her lips form the words almost completely without accent. And the slight stammer that remained seemed to be there only to remind him of the way she'd spoken when he first met her. It was at a seminar he'd been invited to give in the United States, on the West Coast. Every Tuesday at eleven o'clock, he'd held forth for an hour in a large room with windows that opened onto the sea, and the light brought a glow to her face that he couldn't turn away from. Every morning, dolphins had leapt from the waves quite close to shore.

18

"Arbogast, you've got a visitor."

It was a late afternoon, somewhere in the beginning of February 1966, when Hans Arbogast was taken to the visitor's room. It had been a long time since he'd had a visitor, and since no one had informed him anyone would be coming, he had no idea who it could be. He wondered about it the whole way there.

Dr. Klein was nervous, too. It was like that every time he met a new client, and he smiled to himself about it. As often in this situation, he thought about how, as a teenager, he had desperately tried to make his British pen pal forget about the political disturbances going on in Germany by striking a certain tone in his letters—the same one that was used like a magical charm in his parents' house to ward off the threats of the real world. He'd managed to keep the letters safe in a tin box throughout the war. The correspondence had ended in 1938 with empty expressions of farewell, because of the war. He thought about the letters, but he had no idea where they were anymore. It had been a different time. He'd often thought that if he had children, he'd send them to study in America. But the truth was, he had no children, and it was two years since the last woman had moved out. He tugged gingerly on the sleeves of his white shirt until his favorite cuff links just peeked out from his jacket. They were flat stones of amber encircled by thin gold bands, and one of the stones contained a tiny mosquito.

When Arbogast was brought in, he stood up immediately and extended his hand. The lawyer was rather tall and gaunt. The few hairs left to him were cropped short. His smile was thin but appealing. He was quite an attractive man, Hans Arbogast thought when he first looked at him. Arbogast cleared his throat. He hoped his voice would not fail him.

"Please allow me to introduce myself. Dr. Ansgar Klein, criminal defense lawyer."

19

Just then in Tessin, another of the powerful storms that were common at that time of year was moving through the valley. By midday, the storm had turned the lake so dark, one might have thought it was night. Fritz Sarrazin tromped up through the garden and hurried into the house. He closed the door to the veranda carefully behind him. When he first stepped into the living room, it was so dim, he could barely see anything. The house was completely quiet except for the sound of the rain beating against the glass. He wiped the rain from his forehead and wondered where Sue could be. Then he spotted her. She was standing quite close to him, although almost entirely hidden in the folds of the green-and-gold brocade drapes. She receded farther into them at the sound of an extended thunder crack that rolled through the valley, echoing, coming ever closer and then fading away in the direction of Lugano. She didn't look at him until the air was almost quiet again.

"It's not going to get us," he said, seeking, as usual, to calm her fears.

She kept close to the sheltering form of the drapes as she moved toward him, then finally traded in their protection for that of his cool shoulder. He secretly knew that her fear existed primarily to foster his sense of manliness, and yet he enjoyed it.

"Have you spoken with the lawyer yet?"

"No, not yet. Why?"

"I'm curious to hear what he thinks of Arbogast."

"I think he's seeing him today. Why are you so interested?"

"I keep thinking about that girl, the one called Maria."

"It's Marie, Marie Gurth."

"Do you think he did it?"

Sarrazin thought for a moment. Somehow, he had never asked himself that question quite so directly.

Finally, with hesitation, he said, "I don't think so." Above all, it had been a feeling he had that led him to get involved in Arbogast's case. "No, I really don't think so."

"Why not?"

Fritz Sarrazin shrugged his shoulders. He knew why Sue was asking. He'd had all the press clippings about the trial sent to him from the archives at the *Münchner Abendzeitung* and had shown them to her earlier in the day. The file, which was probably still lying on the dining room table, contained a photograph of the victim that made it look as if she was snuggling down among the branches of a blackberry thicket. Sue's hand was resting on his stomach, as if she were controlling his breath.

"What would that be like, to die while having sex?"

It felt to Fritz Sarrazin as if a cold kiss had brushed his lips. He briefly entertained the thought in earnest: What it would be like to be holding Sue and suddenly feel her sag beneath him? A single inadvertent movement, that's all it would take, and her gaze could turn away from him forever. His hand on her neck, her head in his hand, going slack in a way it never had in life. The silence of her skin. All secrets sealed for once and all, he thought, not knowing which he meant. Only his own breath from that time on. Would he stop making love to her then, at that moment? Would he stay by her, stand guard while her body cooled? Sarrazin shook off the thought with another shrug of his shoulders.

"Do you think they'll reopen an investigation into what really happened that night?" asked Sue.

Sarrazin paused and then said, "It's incredibly difficult to get to the point where they retry a case. The justice system tends to take offense at the implications of such an attempt—i.e., that the truth might not have been served by the original proceedings."

"So are you saying that Klein has no chance of succeeding?"

"I'm not saying that. He got a new trial in the Rohrbach case. And he won it. What he has to do is come up with new evidence that would have been likely to affect the verdict if it had been produced at the first trial. If he can make a plausible case for that, he'll be granted a new trial."

The storm raged on for a long time. The thunder continued to rumble through the valley and the rain pelted the window, the echoes of both sounds reverberating as if the two forces were locked in some battle in the sky above the house. Sue stroked Sarrazin's belly. Sarrazin struggled not to think about death—neither the girl's nor his own, which was often on his mind lately, and above all he tried not to think about Sue dying in his arms, at his hand.

"I think I would vomit," he said at last.

"What?"

"If you suddenly died while we were making love."

"Why would you vomit?"

"Out of loneliness."

20

Dr. Klein had recently started driving a white Mercedes 300. The thing he liked most about it were the tail fins. It was an automatic, with the shift at the steering wheel, and Klein enjoyed the fact that its 160-horsepower engine could get the car up to a hundred miles an hour without showing the slightest strain. With the power of attorney that Arbogast had given him, he drove directly from the prison back to Grangat to take a look at the trial records at the DA's office. While he was there, he also asked where he might be able to find Arbogast's first lawyer. He was directed to the rathskeller where Meyer usually went for lunch at that time of day.

Klein walked the short distance to the market square. A flight of wide steps led down to the vaulted cellar, which was only lightly populated. Narrow bands of light shone through the small windows, illuminating swirling dust motes and landing across a few of the white tablecloths. At one of the tables sat a man about forty years old. Klein introduced himself and asked if he was Winfried Meyer. Chewing, the man nodded and gestured for him to take a seat.

Of course he had believed that Arbogast was innocent, he said. And he still did. Under his heavy lids, Meyer's eyes were alert and he looked closely at Ansgar Klein. He gestured to a waiter, requested another glass and filled it from the carafe of red wine on the table. Klein asked him why he hadn't done anything further after his appeal was turned down. Meyer smiled and raised his glass.

"My dear colleague! You know quite well how difficult it is to get a retrial. I did everything I could, really."

Klein nodded.

"Please don't misunderstand me. I think it's a scandal that Hans Arbogast is sitting in jail today on account of that appalling piece of expert testimony delivered in 1955. But on the other hand, if we insisted on taking every case beyond the limits of the appeal system, if we demanded a new trial in every case, well, the justice system would collapse."

Klein nodded again. Without a doubt, Meyer was correct. A verdict was handed down on the basis of the authority of the law and the reliability of the trial process. This meant every trial that was reopened called the authority of the court into doubt. The question was, How many such challenges could the system withstand?

"As a lawyer, you surely understand that a verdict must be accepted as final. I can live with the decisions of the justice system to that extent."

Ansgar Klein wasn't sure any longer if it even made sense to ask this man the questions he had prepared. Meyer's vivid eyes returned to his face again and again as he ate. But Klein held his silence, wondering instead what it would be like to work as a lawyer in a small town like this, year in, year out. He looked at Meyer's plate. Boiled meatballs and dumplings in caper sauce. He gathered himself together.

"Could you tell me why you so rarely visited your client?"

Meyer just looked at him and blinked, pondering that one.

"Never mind," said Klein, suddenly turning gruff. He stood up. "It's my case now, and I would ask only that you refrain from giving statements about Hans Arbogast in the future."

Ansgar Klein turned back to look at the table once more as he climbed up the steps of the restaurant. In the strip of light from the window, he saw Meyer's eyes gleam, and he was glad to be leaving that gaze behind. It was with a sense of relief that he went next to the offices of the *Grangater Tageblatt* and requested to have copies of all their coverage of the first trial sent up from the archives. He had skipped lunch, and so he dined early at his hotel, the Palm Garden, and soon retired to his room, where he laid out all his files on the case on one side of the double bed, only half of which he would be needing for himself. He stayed up late reading through the material. Even after he had finally switched off the light, the details of the case seemed to swirl through his mind, along with thoughts of how Arbogast's wife had felt, the opinions of the press and the lawyers, the DA's closing statement, the opinions of all those who had known Arbogast. When all the other voices had finally quieted down, one final image stayed with him—a sketchy vision of how Arbogast had held her in his arms and her being dead. What had Arbogast felt in that moment? Klein wondered, and in the quiet ensuing from that question, sleep came over him.

21

The following morning at 10:00 a.m., Klein was back at Bruchsal. While he waited for his client, he thought about their conversation from the day before. In retrospect, he wondered about Arbogast's grave demeanor, the strangely unapproachable quality he seemed to radiate. Even given the present situation, he would have expected the son of a restaurateur to be a bit friendlier, more gregarious. But there was something chilly about him, thought Klein as he took out the files from the first trial. When Hans Arbogast entered the visitor's room, the table was entirely covered with papers, and Ansgar Klein looked up at him as if he weren't quite sure at first who it was he had before him. The prisoner took a seat and nodded at the lawyer.

"It happened right before the federal elections, didn't it?" Klein began.

Arbogast shrugged and said nothing. The lawyer was looking at him harder today than he had the day before. Nothing in his face appeared to move at all.

"Did you vote for Adenauer?"

Arbogast took a long time clearing his throat. "I didn't vote at all that Sunday," he said at last. His voice was thick.

"You turned yourself in to the police on Monday, the seventh of September, 1953?"

"Exactly."

"I understand—you had other worries that weekend. But we need to clear a few things up. At first, you said only that you had picked her up on the highway on September first and then let her off again after having bought her pocketbook from her for your wife. You were still claiming that you'd barely had anything to do with Frau Gurth. Later you testified that she had died in your presence. Finally, you explained that she had died at your hand, although you had not intended this."

"Yes."

"And then you subsequently repudiated this confession, saying it had been coerced."

"Yes."

"You had a police record. When you worked as a butcher's apprentice, you were said to have been gratuitously brutal in your treatment of the cows and calves. I read in the *Badische Zeitung* of January thirteenth, 1955, 'From the indictment filed by the district attorney, Arbogast appears to be a sadist and a compulsive personality.' "

"I didn't kill Marie Gurth. And I'm not a sadist."

"Back then, Professor Maul drew a pretty graphic picture of how he believed the crime took place."

"We were making love, and then all of a sudden she was dead. That's the truth."

Hans Arbogast noticed the scratchy feeling in his throat had diminished.

"But you yourself said it: 'It must have happened, then—it's horrible. I must have cut off her air.' When you said 'cut off her air,' didn't you mean that you'd strangled her?"

"No, not at all, but I had been holding her neck."

"And just suffocated her by accident?"

"No. I don't know."

"The psychologist, Professor Kasimir, who observed you for six weeks, didn't believe you. He agreed with Dr. Maul's findings. He testified that you knew exactly what you'd done but tried to conceal it and lied about it quite intentionally—all of which he found consistent with certain psychological symptoms."

"I'm not guilty."

"There's also Dr. Schwarz from the Grangat Ministry of Health, who examined you. Here's what he said: 'A. killed Mrs. G. slowly, and in the process brutally battered and sexually abused her. Such behavior is characteristic of A.'s personality. It has already been determined that A. is a coarse and brutal man with tendencies toward sadism. It is certain that he violated her bestially, tormented her and was himself aroused by her sufferings. He deposited the body in the same area where the body of another murder victim, Fräulein Neumeier, was found after having been abused in a similar fashion.' Did you kill Fräulein Neumeier, too?"

"No, of course not. Nothing ever came of the investigation they began during the trial."

"And yet Professor Kasimir said he observed an abrupt change in your demeanor every time the name of Barbara Neumeier was mentioned. I quote: 'He grew restless and began to breathe heavily.' Why were you panting, Mr. Arbogast?"

"I have no idea if I was breathing heavily when the professor mentioned Fräulein Neumeier. But that was a big thing back then, the highway murderer, and suddenly everyone was saying it was me."

"In his summation, the district attorney spoke of your moral degeneracy. You used your intelligence, he said, to further a purpose more brutal than any animal's. It could be stated with utter certainty that you were one of the worst sexual predators ever known to plague Baden with your loathsome presence. You executed your sexual assault and murder according to a grisly, sadistic plan, whereby you would kill your victim only once you had rendered her entirely defenseless."

For a moment, Hans Arbogast felt sure that he couldn't move his legs. But in fact, there was nowhere he could have gone. There was only that one route back to his cell, which someone would eventually lead him down once the lawyer left him. There's no point, he thought, and had to laugh at the very idea of the hope he'd expressed in his letter to Fritz Sarrazin. He thought of the last letter his lawyer, Meyer, had sent him, and he thought of Father Karges. Arbogast shook his head, smiling. In the end, the priest would be vindicated: guilty. Arbogast looked past Dr. Klein to the glowing white of the frosted window. Today, you could see the shadows of the bars falling across it. He stared blinking into the whiteness for a while. Outside it was a clear, sunny winter day.

"So you don't believe me," he said quietly. Then he looked at the lawyer and smiled. "Then why are you here, Dr. Klein?"

The lawyer was completely surprised by his client's reaction. He couldn't fathom why he was smiling. But he did get his first glimpse of the extent to which Abogast was doubly incarcerated—inside the prison, but also inside himself. What's beneath the surface? he wondered. Was Arbogast right that he didn't believe him? Ansgar Klein pushed his papers together and carefully, slowly put them back into his briefcase before responding to Arbogast.

"In the judge's decision there's a sentence that goes like this: 'And thus meticulous medical and legal analysis has generated from the photographs of the murdered woman and our knowledge of the perpetrator a picture of a crime that indeed had no witnesses other than the murderer and his victim.' That's practically poetry, don't you think, Mr. Arbogast? Only you know what happened that September first."

Ansgar Klein stood up and nodded to the guard sitting on the chair by the door. Then he reached out his hand to Arbogast and smiled his thin smile, a smile his client would have to get used to.

"But as to your question: You're wrong. I do believe you, Mr. Arbogast."

22

Arbogast put down the razor on the edge of the sink, wiped his face dry with the hand towel and stroked his cheeks as he examined his face in the small metal mirror. Men mark the cycles of their adult lives by the changes in the growth of their beards. By the time the hairs eventually become hard and stiff, the skin has lost its youth. Arbogast traced the lines in his cheeks with his thumb and forefinger. Sometimes he asked himself what in the world it would be like to kiss someone with that mouth.

As always, when he got to thinking about what would happen if he were ever let out of prison, he thought of his car. The Isabella had been his dream car. In 1952, he'd done a business deal that went well and immediately gone out and bought it, utterly without hesitation. He realized now that he'd always felt its purchase was a bit premature, that he'd had no right to that car at that time. In 1961, when he'd heard that the automaker, the Borgward company, had gone under, it had ruptured his false sense that everything would stay the same while he was in prison. It had brought him to the realization that time was passing and, indeed, that soon enough nothing would be the way he remembered it anymore. For example, the Borgward dealership where he'd bought his car wasn't there anymore. Nobody talked about that make of car any longer. But the ads for new-model BMWs that he saw in the *Grangater Tageblatt* continued to look strange to him. It made him feel better to think of his Isabella sitting in a garage, well oiled, with the cover pulled over it.

It's time, he thought. He had been called from the mat workshop to meet with Dr. Klein, and as he was led away from the visitors' room, back down the hall and into the cellar of the central tower to return to his labors, he allowed himself for just one defiant moment to imagine being a free man again. As he worked, he couldn't stop thinking about the conversation with Dr. Klein, trying to come up with some sign, some reason or other that he should trust the man. Back in his cell, before lunch came, he got out Fritz Sarrazin's letter once again. He tried to imagine Sarrazin. He recalled the way Dr. Klein had looked at him. Outside on the walkways, there was the usual midday clatter of coming and going. Then lunch came, and it grew quiet. In an hour, he would be taken back to the workshop again. He sat at the table, unable to eat.

It was a long time since he had noticed how quiet it could get in that place; now it came to him in a flash, and for a moment it seemed surprising to him that the door of his cell was locked. He felt sick to his stomach. And there, once again, was Marie, while they were smoking and waiting for their lust to reawaken, tracing the engraved metal logo in the center of the dashboard—*Isabella*—with the pinkie finger of her left hand, letting the ash of the cigarette that dangled from her lips grow long. He had bent down to her then and kissed her armpits, and the ash had trembled and fallen. She had laughed. He had asked her a question. Her face was very close to his, lit up with that smile which had made him so happy. And she had talked. She spoke softly of Berlin and her escape with her husband, of the children she'd left behind with her mother-in-law and how much she missed them, of life in the refugee camp.

All he'd known about refugees until then came from what he'd read in the paper or stories he'd heard about people who were put up in other families' homes after the war. He'd never been to the refugee camp in Ringsheim. She kissed him on the cheek and spoke so quietly he could barely understand what she was saying, her lips so close they formed the words tenderly against his skin, her moist breath caressing his eye. It was a typical Labor Service camp from the war—prefab barracks that were simply screwed together on-site. The long, narrow rows of tin buildings had housed an antiaircraft battery till the end of the war. Each room had one window in front and one in back and a small kitchen garden by the door for vegetables and potatoes. The gardens were flooded by the rains every fall. The wooden floors sagged. The latrine was ten minutes away. You could hear every noise your neighbors made. She told him how, when her husband was in Grangat at work, she would sit there completely still for hours on end, just hoping that people would think she wasn't at home. And for a couple of hours, no one would come in, no one would call her name, and no one would knock on the door or rap on the window, whose bunting curtains she kept pulled tightly closed.

Her voice was even and almost without intonation, as if she were discussing something unimportant. She made it sound like she was quite detached from the life at the camp, as if she hardly cared. Nothing was important to her but his embrace, and her eagerness for his lips reawakened his lust. When he asked her at last why she had decided to leave East Berlin, she just shrugged and butted her forehead against his cheek like an animal wanting to be stroked. Why hadn't she looked for a job? Still she said nothing. But then he had been in a rush to get out of the car and back in her arms, and he'd stubbed out his half-smoked cigarette in the ashtray. He had kissed her mouth just one more time after that, when it was dead. Because of that nonchalance, he thought now, and wasn't sure if it was true. He remembered how he'd held her head in his two hands after the muscles had gone slack. He rose, went over to the toilet, dumped his lunch in the bowl, and pulled the chain to flush it. It was two years now since they'd installed plumbing in the cells.

Arbogast considered whether he was going to vomit, and whether Klein would help him. The curiosity in the lawyer's eyes was no different from what he'd seen in so many others over the years. He took a pack of cigarettes and his matches from the shelf above the table. Her cold mouth, the dream. Arbogast smoked and waited. He fell asleep shortly before midnight, at just the same time that Fritz Sarrazin boarded a train in Basel, on his way from Lugano to Frankfurt.

The writer had reserved a berth in the first-class sleeping car. Once he made sure that his luggage was taken care of, he walked back to the dining car, where all the lights were dimmed except for the small lamps on the tables. At the galley end of the car, a single waiter sat reading. Sarrazin took a seat at one of the tables—he could see evidence of the long evening on the tablecloth—and the waiter looked up from his illustrated paper and came over to him.

"Good evening."

"Good evening. Is it still possible to get something to eat?"

"I'm sorry, but the kitchen is closed."

"Could I get some red wine?"

"Certainly."

"Wonderful. A half bottle please. And maybe a few olives and prosciutto if that's possible?"

Sarrazin hadn't eaten dinner, just a sandwich at a bar in Lugano when Sue had brought him to the station.

"I'm sorry, just olives."

The gold tassels on the little red lamp shades trembled in rhythm with the movement of the train over the rails, bringing the circle of yellow light that fell on the tablecloth strangely to life. It was dark by the window, and outside he could see the mountains they were crossing. They came threateningly close to the window whenever the train slowed down to take a tight curve—rocky slopes, dwarfed vegetation, stone supporting walls with moss growing in the mortar. Once, as they emerged from one of the countless tunnels, there was a mountain stream rushing by just inches from his windowpane. He peered out the window without seeing anything, just eating fat, juicy black olives cured in oil and garlic. The waiter had said they were from Sicily. Whenever the car went over a section of rough rails, Sarrazin would reach instinctively for his wineglass and pick it up without even having to look at it. Then he would take a sip.

He wasn't really thinking. It was more that various feelings rose and fell within him, among them the anticipation of meeting Ansgar Klein; but the longer he sat and drank, the more aware he became of a background level of anxiety that had to do with Hans Arbogast. He couldn't shake the notion that he'd gotten himself into something bigger than he'd expected by answering Arbogast's letter. Despite all the facts that had convinced him of Arbogast's innocence—or at least that the trial against the man had been insufficient to prove otherwise—there was still something unfathomable about the death of the girl, and Arbogast was inextricably bound to that. Death clung to him, thought Sarrazin, because he had been so close to it.

The carafe of wine was soon empty, what with the constant jostling of the train. He wasn't sure if he should be afraid of what would happen. Rather than ordering more wine, he got up and left. He slept deeply, undisturbed by dreams, in the wonderfully cool starched white sheets of his berth, directly above one of the axles of the train car. The porter woke him with a knock on the door and a cup of coffee a half hour before the train reached Frankfurt on the first of March, 1966.

23

"Would you like some tea?"

"Yes, please."

"What sort? I have a smoked Russian, Earl Grey, Darjeeling. Or maybe a Chinese tea?"

"Whatever you're having."

The lawyer nodded, and Fritz Sarrazin watched him take a tin box and potbellied green teapot from the sideboard. While the secretary went to fetch water, he scooped three or four spoonfuls into a small woven tea ball and set the teapot directly on an electric burner on the sideboard, explaining that the pot was made of cast iron. Sarrazin took note of the way Klein fell silent and became utterly engrossed as he handled the various kitchen implements, which seemed out of place amid the piles of papers and files, the telephone and the law books in the bookcase that spanned an entire wall. The office was located on the eighth floor of an office building and was appointed in the functional, reserved style that was fashionable at the time. When the water boiled, Klein switched off the burner and hung the tea ball inside the pot.

"How are things coming along?" Sarrazin asked, no longer able to restrain himself when Klein brought out two delicate porcelain teacups and set them on a black lacquered tray on the desk.

"What's that, the tea?" Klein smiled, removed the tea ball from the pot and poured.

Sarrazin shook his head.

"Oh . . . he's quite charming," said the lawyer with some hesitation, testing the water. And then he added, "Very serious. He looks good, I think. But you can see the time he's done, the years."

"I know what you mean."

Often, time hung over a prisoner like a shroud—you could recognize that there was a person underneath, but their expressions were completely blank. He'd seen it in every case he'd been involved with. It was as if the person himself had gradually fallen apart thanks to life in prison. Sarrazin realized that they would have to move quickly. He also knew that if Klein was convinced of Arbogast's innocence, he'd do everything possible. He nodded as the lawyer continued speaking.

"But actually, there's little I can say about him. No one will know who he really is until he's freed."

"Of course. Is that going to make it difficult to mount a defense?"

"I must say I got a powerful feeling, sitting across from Arbogast."

"Yes?"

"There was a sense in which he seemed to be withholding something. That, too, may have to do with his situation in prison, all the years he spent in solitary and the injustice of being wrongfully convicted, but there were a couple of times I felt something else—that his demeanor was at once forced and yet somehow contemptuous."

"You found something threatening about him?"

"Yes, in a way, I did find it threatening."

"But you still think he's innocent?"

"I do."

"Really?" asked Fritz Sarrazin again. He took off his watch and began slowly, methodically to wind it. It had a slim profile, a white face and gold numerals and hands.

"Yes," said Ansgar Klein for the second time. "At the very least, there were procedural errors that justify the attempt to reopen the case."

"Well, shall we get started?"

Sarrazin put the watch back on his left wrist and polished off his tea—it was dark and quite spicy. He discovered a woman's head stamped in bas relief into the porcelain at the bottom of the cup. It stared rigidly, eyelessly up at him.

"Very well." Dr. Klein took up a stack of documents. "First of all, the entire case against the then twenty-eight-year-old Hans Arbogast hinged on the testimony of Professor Heinrich Maul. Maul explained with great certainty that the marks left on Frau Gurth's corpse were unambiguous signs that she was strangled with a rope or cord after having been brutally and sadistically abused."

"But the autopsy report contradicted this."

"Exactly. And then during the trial, Dr. Bärlach, the Freiburg pathologist who'd conducted the autopsy and originally determined the cause of death to be a heart attack, suddenly agreed with Maul's interpretation."

"Why?"

"Maul was considered an infallible expert."

"But he didn't even see the body."

"No, his opinion was formed solely on the basis of enlargements of the crime-scene photos and the images taken at the autopsy. The court had the enlargements made, so the witness was looking at eighteen-by-twenty-fours, rather than the original nine-by-twelves."

"And of course all the photos were taken after the body had been transported something like twenty miles and then hidden in the underbrush. Meaning that none of the marks can be linked with any real certainty to an actual assault. They might also be attributable to the way the body was handled in transit, or have been the effect of the branches."

"Quite right. There's not a single case in the history of forensic medicine where a pathologist has dared to determine a cause of death on the basis of photographs alone."

"So why didn't the defense challenge it?"

"This is where my colleague Meyer made the error that decided the trial. Arbogast reaffirmed the veracity of his statements and told his lawyer that he could only shake his head at Professor Maul's interpretation, at which point Meyer immediately filed a motion to call an additional expert witness. But he made an error in citing his grounds for calling for this new witness; all he said was that considering how much depended on the accuracy of the testimony, it would seem advisable to have a second expert. Naturally, Professor Maul testified that he was certain of his conclusions and needed no further help from another expert. The court rejected Meyer's motion after an hour in conference, on insufficient grounds."

"My God!"

"Indeed. The defense more or less capitulated. If Meyer had even mentioned the contradictions in Maul's statements, he would have succeeded in his motion."

"But weren't the contradictions noticed only later, in the interview in *Euro-Med?*"

"No, actually you're wrong there. It came up at the trial. Even though Maul's written deposition—which, by the way, was actually prepared by his colleague Dr. Schmidt-Wulfen—didn't really question that strangulation or suffocation was the cause of death, he couldn't really prove intent. I quote: 'There is, theoretically, the possibility that Arbogast violently compelled the victim to engage in sexual intercourse with him from the start, but we can find no way of proving this theory on the basis of the materials we have examined.' Period. The defense should have pinned him down on that. But what were you saying about *Euro-Med?*"

"In 1955, within a year of the trial, Maul told an interviewer for the journal *Euro-Med* that what he saw in the photograph, a clearly visible mark left by the cord, was quite a common finding, an everyday occurrence, the sort of thing he'd seen thousands of times. He said that the photograph unmistakably showed the impression of a garrote. But in 1956, a year later, he was quoted in a volume by Kalincky-Koch called *Police and Policework* as saying, 'I pored over the photographs, picture after picture, and I'm embarrassed to say that it was only on the second day that I discovered the marks made by the garrote on the neck, below the ear.' So now all of a sudden he's saying his finding wasn't a routine one, that it was a brilliant observation. 'I must say, I brooded over those pictures for a day and a half without getting anywhere, and then in one stroke it was clear to me—I saw what I had always suspected.' "

"Yes. I think the pictures are going to be crucial for the retrial, too. Maybe we'd be able to get somewhere with Maul if we got him some new pictures."

"If there were more images than he originally saw, different angles, he could recant his testimony without losing face."

"I've already tried to get the negatives from the Grangat DA's office. You know what they told me?" Klein pulled a letter from a pile of documents.

Fritz Sarrazin bowed slightly and gestured for him to read it.

" 'Your request for access to the negatives is denied on the grounds that this material is important case evidence. It cannot be loaned out, for fear of damage.' Instead, they suggest that the police lab at the Baden-Württemberg district office could make us prints or slides of the particular images. I told them no thanks."

Fritz Sarrazin nodded. "Then we still wouldn't know what the actual film looks like."

"Exactly. Since then, I've heard from Manfred Altman, one of the top lawyers in the DA's office, that apparently the Federal Office of Criminal Investigation will allow an approved specialist to print the pictures we want."

"So now we need a photo specialist."

"Yes, and I've already started researching that. Here in Frankfurt, there's a company called Hansa Aerial Photography. They specialize in aerial work, but in addition to a couple of airplanes, they also have the most up-to-date equipment for improving the resolution of negatives. I know someone there, and I've already contacted them." Ansgar Klein was quiet for a moment. "Herr Sarrazin?"

"Yes?"

"What do you think about the violence that indisputably did take place, regardless of everything else?"

"You mean even if it wasn't murder?"

"Yes. The autopsy report described bite marks and all that, after all."

"What are you getting at?"

"Well, doesn't the fact that Arbogast had anal sex with Frau Gurth suggest a certain aggression?"

"Oh, I didn't know about that. The papers seem not to have had the stomach to mention it."

"And when you think about his build . . ."

Fritz Sarrazin looked at Dr. Klein with some puzzlement.

"What I mean is, Marie Gurth was barely five feet tall. And the documents are full of descriptions of Arbogast's 'particularly large genitalia.' "

"Really? I didn't know that either. But I still don't think so."

"Think what?"

"I don't think that's any reason for us to stop believing that he's innocent." Fritz Sarrazin hesitated. As he placed his teacup back on the table, he was aware of his rising distaste at the violent images that were growing ever more concrete in his mind's eye. "We can never know what happened between the two of them, but that's no reason to stop believing."

Ansgar Klein looked closely at Fritz Sarrazin. He'd never read any of his novels, but he was familiar with his journalistic work. Sarrazin didn't seem all that much older than he was. His white hair set off his round tanned face and his lively light eyes. He was wearing a light summer suit—much too light for Germany in March—and a white cotton shirt that was somewhat rumpled in comparison to Klein's own polyester one.

" 'The victim was dead and the only living person who knew what happened had sealed up his soul,' " he said at last.

"Excuse me?" Sarrazin was startled out of his own musings.

"That's a line from the judge's opinion. 'The victim was dead and the only living person who knew what happened had sealed up his soul.' " Klein had opened the file and was now pointing to the text with his right index finger. "It goes on: 'The court does not possess the expertise to evaluate all the facts independently and therefore must rely upon the advice of scientific experts. In this case, it has fallen largely to the expert witness's testimony to establish the chain of events. Professor Maul from Münster has told us with an astonishing degree of certainty that this death could be the result of only one thing: strangulation. The signs of strangulation on the corpse were identified with great precision. This court is convinced that the chain of events suggested by the expert witness is generally accurate.' That's what we've got to worry about."

"I'm not sure I understand what you mean."

"Do you remember the name Oesterle from the files, the DA? He thought Arbogast was guilty from the very start, the first hearing. So did Maul. So did the papers. Everyone's preconceptions supported everyone else's. Now, years later, we have to find a way to break through that phalanx. We have to get to the point where we can start talking about what really happened that night."

Fritz Sarrazin nodded and thought about the series of show trials that had taken place in the past year and been eagerly followed by the German public—the Rohrbach case, Vera Brühne and other mysterious murders, such as the Nitribitt case. He didn't think Klein would object to all the attention this would generate. The lawyer definitely enjoyed the spotlight. He thought about how Klein had used publicity to his advantage in the Rohrbach case. They sat silently and each drank another cup of tea before parting. The lawyer was going down to the courthouse, and Fritz Sarrazin headed for the Hessian Court hotel, where he had taken a room. They planned to meet there for dinner later that night.

That morning, Sarrazin had taken a cab from the train station, but now he decided to walk back through the city. The war was twenty years past, but the sense of certainty that had once made German cities thrive had not returned. Perhaps one would never again get the sense, walking through the streets of Germany, that they had always been there. Not unlike myself, thought Sarrazin, shaking his head and smiling at himself and his bourgeois nostalgia. The feeling that these town squares had always been there, that there had always been shops opening onto the squares, that there had been streets with addresses at which one could be found—all that was certainly gone forever; there was no trace left of the old downtown with its narrow alleys and wood-frame buildings. The architecture of the 1950s made buildings look like playthings; their pretty pastel colors seemed provisional in the midst of the empty lots. It was nearly midday, and the sun cast sharp shadows into the empty space.

A century before, the city wall had been taken down and replaced with trees, but all the trees were cut down and burned for heat during the war. Even some of the streets of row houses outside the greenbelt had been turned to skeletons by the war. Many crossroads and intersections were now just symbolic of where the buildings and squares had been. The train station had survived intact, though, which he had marveled at when he arrived the day before. That and the old exhibition hall, which he vaguely remembered having visited once, long ago. Directly across the street from it was the Hessian Court, a building whose architectural details lay somewhere between camouflage and concession of defeat.

But his room was pleasant and his suitcase already there, waiting for him. After a bath, Fritz Sarrazin spent the afternoon on the bed, reading through the Arbogast documents that Dr. Klein had given him. He arrived in the hotel's large dining room at the appointed time to find Ansgar Klein already there, at a window table, though the view through the gap in the heavy curtains consisted of little more than the flashing headlights of cars driving past.

They both had soup and then steak with potatoes and salad. The beef was Argentine, a delicacy that had only recently become available, thanks to deep-freezing technology and air transit. The topic of the South American steaks led them to talk about the war. Fritz Sarrazin told of his emigration to Brazil and the various positions he'd held as an industrial consultant, then of his career as a theater critic in Berlin and Vienna, which he'd long since given up. They drank a bottle of French Bordeaux with dinner and then ordered aquavit. As they raised the chilled glasses in a toast, each was thinking with surprise that he enjoyed the other man's company. They didn't discuss Arbogast at all. Afterward, they decided to move on to Jimmy's, the bar in the basement of the hotel, for a drink. They stood at the bar, watching the bartender work. His face was pockmarked and he had a long, thin neck. The voice of a black singer at the piano filled the room. She was wearing a tuxedo, her hair was brilliantined, and her lower lip trembled as she sang Gershwin tunes. Sarrazin noticed that there were many Americans in uniform in the bar, and many young girls. *Germany*, he thought to himself as he looked around. He remembered the Lufthansa planes that had continued making regular flights to Rio till the very end. This was his sort of music. Sarrazin closed his eyes and listened to her sing "I Loves You, Porgy." After a minute, he realized he was humming along and cleared his throat. He smiled at Klein.

"So I've heard there's been some unrest here at the university in Frankfurt."

"Yes, there'll be some changes," said Klein. "Thank God. You know, they're also talking a lot about reforming the Penal Code."

"What about the Soviet zone?"

Klein shrugged. "I don't know whether we should try to accommodate the East. Maybe Kiesinger was right after all. Shall we get some drinks?"

Sarrazin nodded and Klein signaled to the bartender. They both ordered whiskey on the rocks.

Klein hadn't even noticed the applause, but suddenly the singer was on break and it was quiet in the bar. He tried for a moment to imagine the silence of being in a cell, to picture how Arbogast was breathing at that very moment, how he was staring at the wall, his head resting on his arm—while the two of them stood around at a bar, drinking. He noticed that the singer had sat down at a table in the corner with three men in dark blue U.S. Air Force uniforms.

"Ansgar?"

Klein was startled to hear Sarrazin call him by his first name. But the writer raised his glass to him and smiled.

"Don't you think we should be on a first-name basis?"

The lawyer nodded his assent happily and clinked his glass with Sarrazin's. They drank to Arbogast and to setting him free from a situation in which he'd been doubly wronged—first convicted of a crime he didn't commit and then stuck away in the cell that had confined him ever since. They clinked their glasses again. Sarrazin thought of Sue. All day long, his thoughts had returned repeatedly to his wife and their house in Tessin. To that thunderstorm and death. He had tried not to think about Arbogast. Now he had the strange feeling that the prisoner was staring straight at him, across the distance.

"Fritz?"

Now he, too, was startled out of his thoughts.

"Tell me, why do you do all this?"

Sarrazin laughed. "Maybe because of the stories? I really do think they should have happy endings. Or at least the right endings, if you know what I mean."

Klein nodded. "But isn't it really a little strange to spend your time thinking up crimes?"

Sarrazin wondered what Klein wanted him to say. He pictured his office at home, the view of the valley in the morning, the way the sun slid across the corner of his typewriter like a lazy snake, casting its light on the roller and warming it.

"I'm very interested in what happens to people—especially, for example, when they have killed."

"Does that mean that you use your involvement in real cases to provide you with material for your novels?"

"Well, yes, but that's not the important thing. You know, Ansgar, the first thing I always see is someone's body. Undamaged, like the rest of us—except that who among us is undamaged? That's where the story starts. I remember it exactly: It was in Italy, late at night, fall, everything dark but for the single dim streetlight flickering in the wind out in front of a bar on a country road. Parked out front were several decommissioned army jeeps. One of them had the carcass of a wild boar tied to the grille, and there was a shotgun rack mounted behind the seats. I could sense the ancient walls of an Etruscan city somewhere above me, but all I could see was the blue sign that read SALE E TABACCHI. I went inside. The bar was being used as a storeroom. There were whole hams dangling from the ceiling, racks of newspapers behind the door, various salamis and a gigantic mortadella in a glass display case, and every sort of tobacco and cigarette available on the shelves above the register. Cleansers, toilet paper, bulbous basket-woven bottles of Chianti stacked against the counter. A chill rose up from the terrazzo tile floor."

"I don't get it."

Fritz Sarrazin gestured with his chin. "Look over there."

The singer was still talking to the three men in uniform. She laughed and drank from a long-stemmed glass. She clearly took note of who was staring at her. It looked like she had a difficult job.

"Her?"

"Yes."

Sarrazin was still looking at the black singer. She looked tired and her gaze was growing visibly less confident. The stories of people's lives are always there, he thought, just waiting to be read from their skin.

"Why are you interested in helping Arbogast?" he asked quietly, never shifting his gaze from the singer. "He's got no money. And what happened that night was undoubtedly a nasty affair, nothing glamorous about it. So is it because of the injustice that was done to Hans Arbogast? Because you believe he's innocent? Really?"

Sarrazin wondered how he could explain to Klein what he meant. He was thinking that the two of them needed to discuss what it was that so fascinated and compelled them about Arbogast. He was just about to try to do this when the singer stood up from her chair and looked over at him.

What he felt in that moment stuck with him even the following day, on the train back home. As it drew near Bruchsal, he thought about paying a visit to Arbogast, as if only the prisoner could understand the way he'd felt. It was the end of a long day, but still March the first, 1966, when he'd looked up and actually thought he saw death in the singer's eyes, just as clearly as if he'd heard someone humming a melody. He couldn't look away. The singer laughed. Her head lilted to one side like a flower on its stem. Then she bared her throat, and suddenly, out of the void, he saw something he'd never imagined before: that other throat, the dead girl's, moving the same way and just as lovely. All the men sitting with her had risen when the singer stood up, and now one of them kissed her just below her ear. She leaned her head back so far that another of the men—they were all black men—took the opportunity to run his fingers across her lips.

24

The office was located in the Iduna Building on Frankfurt's Exchange Place, and though it was just ten stories high, in the 1960s it had been one of the first office buildings to rise above the city's peaked prewar roofline. Its exterior was clad in sheets of dark blue anodized steel and the interior reflected the restrained, purely cubic architecture of the building's steel skeleton. The windows and glass doors were framed with thin bands of steel; the floors of the lobby and the stairwells were done in dark polished granite. The handrails were black vulcanized rubber. There were two narrow elevators with doors that folded when you opened them, and on each level a small urn-shaped aluminum ashtray was built into the wall between the elevator doors. There were two tenants on each floor. Beside each large glass door was a plate with the name of the company and a doorbell.

Five lawyers and their secretaries worked on the eighth floor. Dr. Klein was handling the Arbogast case alone, and he spent almost the entire spring working on the motion to reopen the case. First, he went to the Federal Police Agency in Wiesbaden with a photographic expert from Hansa Aerial Photography and had new prints made according to the expert's directions. As he and Fritz Sarrazin had discussed, he sent one set of the photographs straight to Professor Maul in Münster along with a friendly letter explaining that in the light of the enclosed photographic materials—some of which had not been introduced as evidence at the trial and some of which had now been reprinted using new and improved scientific techniques—it seemed extremely unlikely that Hans Arbogast could have strangled or suffocated Marie Gurth. He requested that Professor Maul take a look at the new materials and said he hoped the professor would now arrive at the same conclusion as the several other expert witnesses they were planning to call at the retrial of the case. Ansgar Klein signed his letter "Respectfully yours."

Klein had his secretary put together numerous copies of a dossier containing all the most important documents pertaining to the crime and the trial, including the new prints of what Klein referred to as the "discovery site." He sent out the dossier to several forensic pathologists who were possible expert witnesses and to experts in photography. He began working his press contacts, too. Among others, he talked to Henrik Tietz from *Der Spiegel*, which was published in Frankfurt. Klein was an old friend of Tietz's father, a professor of psychiatry. A short time thereafter, the young legal correspondent came over to Klein's office to take a look at the material from the trial. When he leaned back in his chair, his face receded from the circle of light cast by the desk lamp and vanished into the twilight, but he continued to ask quiet questions while Klein described the case to him.

When finally the lawyer had finished, he leaned back into the upholstered leather and wood chair. For a couple of minutes, the room was silent.

"Why do you think Maul testified as he did back then, at the trial in Grangat?" asked the reporter at last.

Klein shrugged. "I don't know. I really don't."

"How many years has it been?"

"Thirteen now."

Tietz nodded but said nothing further, and they sat in silence for another moment. Marie Gurth lay in the circle of light from the desk lamp. Perhaps it began to rain then, perhaps not. At any rate, Klein finally gave the reporter the dossier, and Tietz promised to look into it further. Klein was optimistic something would come of it. Sarrazin, too, got the impression that *Der Spiegel* might run an article about Arbogast, when Klein told him about the meeting a couple of weeks later; they were talking on the phone and Klein also told him he'd paid a visit to the firm's offices in Essen. At first, Sarrazin didn't see the point.

Klein explained that Germany's minister of justice, Dr. Heinemann, was a partner at his firm, on leave because of his public office. "Who knows? Maybe we can have some influence on the district attorney's office somehow or other. After all, they have to do what they're told, and they can't just ignore the minister of justice. He's their boss."

Sarrazin laughed. "What else have you got?"

"I've got seven experts who have agreed to testify on Arbogast's behalf."

Klein got up and walked as far around his desk as the telephone cord would allow, then stood looking out the window. It was spring now, and the weather was gradually turning warm. Outside, he heard the rattling of metal sunshades. Everywhere, the forests of the Taunus region were vibrating with green.

"How's the weather where you are?"

"Hot," said Sarrazin. "You certainly sound like you're in a good mood."

"I am. I really think that using these photogrammetric experts might work. It hits right at the heart of Maul's testimony."

Early the next morning, well before eight, while he was fixing himself a pot of the Earl Gray tea he'd bought the day before—it had been recommended as having an especially distinctive aroma—Klein received a call from Dr. Maul.

"Dr. Klein? Professor Maul here, calling from Münster."

Klein was glad the tea was already brewed when he'd picked up the phone. He said hello and took his first sip. Maul got straight to the point. His voice was a soft drawl, which surprised Klein, given the pictures he'd seen of him.

Maul began by saying he couldn't comprehend how new prints of the photographs could pose any challenge to his testimony. He was still completely convinced that Arbogast had strangled the girl. "What was her name again?" he asked.

"Marie Gurth."

"Yes, Marie."

Professor Maul paused a moment, and Klein thought he could hear him picking up the photograph. He said he stood by his original interpretation.

Klein suggested that it might be a good idea to meet, and he offered to go to Münster whenever it was convenient for the professor.

"No, no, that won't be necessary. It really doesn't seem to me that your efforts have succeeded in bringing any new information to light."

Professor Maul didn't have anything further to say, and Klein saw little to be gained from dragging the conversation out. After a few closing pleasantries, it was over.

Klein stood up and went to the window, struggling to keep the rage from boiling up within him. He looked at himself in the windowpane and smoothed his narrow tie. He was thirty-eight now and just as gangly as he'd been as a boy. He liked to wear dark, slim suits, and since his divorce, he had kept his thinning gray hair cropped short. He couldn't remember ever having been intimidated by an expert witness. Ansgar Klein loosened his tie, and the rage he'd felt from the telephone conversation with Maul slowly loosed its hold on him.

On the same day Ansgar Klein submitted a petition to Dr. Valois, the chief judge of the Criminal Division of the Grangat District Superior Court, requesting that the case against Hans Arbogast be reopened. In his petition, Klein stated that neither the court itself nor the expert witness had had a chance to examine the negatives. The enlargements had been made by an amateur; on top of which, enlargements of the two negatives that showed detailed views of the victim's neck had not even been introduced into evidence. Finally, to support the claim that these findings constituted new evidence in the sense of section 359, paragraph five of the Criminal Proceedings Code, he had the names of three doctors and four experts in the fields of photogrammetry, photographic chemistry and technical photography who were willing to testify in the case.

25

The cabinet where the television and audiovisual equipment were kept stood at the front of the conference room and was made of the same mahogany as the conference table, which could seat as many as thirty editors. Sometimes, when he'd worked long past the time the paper was put to bed, preparing material for the editorial conference the next day or rushing to cut some long article by a freelancer so it could be scheduled as soon as possible, Paul Mohr came into this room and sat for an hour, drinking whiskey from the editor in chief's well-stocked bar and watching the late news or a French movie on television. By seven o'clock, it was always pretty quiet on the third floor of the *Badische Zeitung*. Downstairs, the newsroom was still busy, but the people on the feuilleton section got to go home earlier, except perhaps for the theater editor, who sometimes came in late to type up a review of a premiere.

Later on, he would remember the moment precisely: He was watching a news-magazine show on television late that August evening in 1966 when the screen flashed the picture of a man he knew. It was a few seconds before the name of the man was mentioned, and that brought the memory back to him in all detail. But for one brief, nameless moment while he searched his memory, he had the searing feeling of being faced with something long forgotten and unexpected. He set down his glass with a tinkling of ice and craned toward the screen. Mohr didn't recognize the man until he heard the name Arbogast. Then the patter of words turned to sentences and the name appeared under the photograph. The program cut to a man Paul

Mohr didn't recognize, who was speaking to the camera: "It's simply unbelievable. A man has been sitting in prison for thirteen years and is supposed to stay there for the rest of his life, all because of one piece of expert testimony that has been repudiated by eleven international experts in the relevant fields. And as for the courts that are reviewing the experts' affidavits in connection with our petition to reopen the case, well, they won't even allow the accuracy of those affidavits to be verified."

The name Ansgar Klein appeared on the screen—presumably Arbogast's lawyer—and Paul Mohr forgot to listen any further. He was thinking about Gesine, the young photographer from Grangat. He stood up and went over to the small mirrored bar. He anticipated seeing his face in its reflection while he walked around the conference table, and he wondered if he could remember what he looked like back then well enough even to be aware of all the changes the intervening years had wrought. He bent down over the row of bottles and saw his features fractured by the mirrored tiles of the tray, which were held in place by many colored plastic pins. Paul Mohr was now thirty-two. He had just started his master's degree in Freiburg when he met Gesine, and Grangat was where he'd written his first articles. The brief report about the body of a woman found by the side of the road had been one of his first substantial pieces. He'd been an editor for two years now. He wondered whether he'd like to see Gesine Hofmann again. Maybe, he thought. He poured himself another whiskey and nodded at himself in the mirror the way he might have at a person he wasn't sure he liked.

When he looked back over at the TV, the image had changed. Professor Heinrich Maul's face appeared on the screen, and Mohr focused on the program again. He remembered quite vividly how certain he had been that the case would end in a manslaughter conviction at the most—up until the point when Professor Maul had testified. He was curious to see if the professor's opinion had changed.

"How do you feel about the idea that there should always be two expert witnesses of equal stature in jury trials?" asked the interviewer.

That had been the crucial question in the Arbogast case. For despite the gravity of the charges and certain other reasons that suggested a second expert should have been allowed, the defense lawyer's petition to call another expert to the stand had been rejected. Mohr recalled the name of the lawyer who had lost the case: Meyer.

"The danger—or shall I say the risk?—is this: that the second witness will say something different merely in order to have said something different. That doesn't necessarily mean it's right."

The camera cut back to the television studio and the photograph of Arbogast. The television commentator said it was a scandal even back then that the district attorney's office had indicted Arbogast for first-degree murder solely on the basis of an autopsy report. Worse yet was the fact that the court had handed down a decision based on a single piece of oral testimony, one that actually contradicted the findings of the autopsy. And finally, it was even more outrageous that the court was still, after more than ten years had passed, completely unwilling to reconsider what the journalist referred to as a "sham verdict," even in the face of new evidence. After all, there were international experts who had doubts about the judgment.

The commentator paused, and they cut to another interview sequence. A woman in a white coat stood in front of a two-story neoclassical brick building. She had short hair and was obviously not wearing makeup. In her right hand she held a cigarette that sometimes made its way into the frame of the camera. Paul Mohr thought she looked about forty. She said she was familiar with Professor Maul's testimony in this case from forensics journals and that she had her doubts about it. She hoped they understood that at this point, without having personally examined the evidence, she couldn't say anything more concrete. Her name flashed on the screen: *Dr. Katja Lavans*. And beneath it, *East Berlin*.

From the movements of her right arm, you could tell that she was stubbing out her cigarette. The camera reflexively followed her gesture for a moment and took in a view of a small goldfish pool, empty except for the delicate wrought-iron fish head that protruded from it. It must surely have been a fountain once, but now it was so encrusted with angry rust that it would never spit water again. Paul Mohr turned off the television. The picture shrank down to a tiny white dot in the center of the screen and vanished slowly, with a flicker. When the screen had gone completely dark, Mohr closed the doors on the television cabinet.

At the same time, Ansgar Klein was still holding the heavy ivory-colored telephone receiver to his ear. The tips of his thumb, index and middle fingers hovered over the cradle for a moment. Fritz Sarrazin had long since put down the receiver on the other end, and the attorney heard only the unvarying sound of the dial tone from the earpiece. Carefully, he set the receiver back down on the two white buttons of the cradle and felt them take up its weight from his hand. The dial tone cut off with a click and the receiver lay in its place.

It was 8:30 and the whole building was quiet, except for the small sounds of the building's aluminum facade contracting as it cooled down, the sun having set on the west side of the building an hour before. From the street, he could hear cars going past, people shouting, all the sounds of a summer evening. Ansgar Klein looked down Goethe Street, which in recent years had become known as the best shopping street in the city, toward the empty square where the Frankfurt Opera had once stood. The roofless ruin of the neoclassical building had been shored up after the war and a security fence erected around it, but it still hadn't been rebuilt. He remembered watching it burn when he was a boy.

For years now, birch saplings had been growing out of the small, empty window holes of the upper stories, and since his office had moved to its present location, he'd monitored their growth. But at that moment, he didn't notice the thin trunks struggling to stay upright on crooked roots that clung to cracks in the sandstone. It had now been three weeks since August the second, when his petition to have Hans Arbogast released from prison, pending the appeal of the case, was denied. He had cited section 360, paragraph one of the Criminal Proceedings Code, according to which a prison sentence could be suspended in the case of a petition to retry a case. He hadn't told Arbogast about the denial, since he'd expected the decision on the retrial motion itself to be handed down soon and he didn't want to upset his client unnecessarily. Now the decision had been made. The Criminal Division of the Grangat District Superior Court had rejected Klein's petition for permission to retry the case.

Ansgar Klein opened the window and a gust of hot wind hit him unexpectedly in the face.

"Shit!"

His curse mingled with the noises from the street. He closed his eyes. The heat beat against his lids. The air smelled of dust, exhaust and dying flowers. He contemplated the court's grounds for the denial: The photographic experts' testimony did indeed constitute new evidence, according to the decision, and the court recognized that his experts' technical ability to interpret the photographic materials was superior to Maul's; however, with regard to the question of who could best interpret what the marks in the photographs implied about the corpse of the victim, the court had been compelled to recognize the superior expertise of the forensic pathologist.

"Superior expertise. Shit!"

He closed the window and sat back down at the desk. He sat shivering for a while in the air-conditioned room. He would submit a formal objection to the ruling, but for now, this denial had dashed their hopes of having Arbogast set free. It seemed that the Grangat court was determined not to let the case get any further exposure. Klein wasn't sure what they should do next, and he dreaded informing his client of this development. He would go to Bruchsal first thing the next morning, and then on to Tessin, where he and Sarrazin could quietly sit down and try figure out how to proceed. Though he didn't look forward to delivering the message to him, he hoped that Arbogast hadn't been given the bad news already. He wasn't sure the man had the strength to bear it. Lately, Klein had gotten the feeling that Arbogast's connections to the world were growing ever weaker, and that his sense of reality was increasingly reliant upon the hope of being granted a new trial.

26

Katja Lavans lived near Treptower Park in East Berlin. This evening, she'd invited friends over to celebrate turning in the postdoctoral thesis that would secure her official appointment to the faculty of the institute. Her nine-year-old daughter, Ilse, was spending the night with a friend from school. Since her divorce, Katja had only very rarely had people over, and so she was even more disappointed to learn from Doris Landner, the wife of one of her colleagues, that both Doris's husband and Katja's assistant had suddenly been called to cover the night shift.

"Now there will be two empty places!"

She closed the door behind Doris. Katja had spent the entire afternoon in the kitchen and had just finished setting the table for six outside on the large veranda, which was supported by thin wrought-iron columns. Doris knew Katja wouldn't allow herself to show her disappointment any further. People who didn't know Katja well thought of her as an extremely rational woman who was indifferent about her appearance, an impression that was fostered by the way she dressed and presented herself. She possessed a boyish brashness and never wore makeup, which made the symmetrical features of her face even more noticeable and belied her age, which was thirty-eight. She kept her brown hair cut short and smoked incessantly, frequently letting a burning cigarette dangle from the corner of her mouth. She felt like lighting one up right then, in fact, but Doris set down her net shopping bags, wrapped her arms around her and kissed her on both cheeks.

"Congratulations again! So tell me, how do you feel?"

Katja looked at Doris. For a moment, she had no idea what Doris was talking about, but then she remembered, and the first thing she thought of was how she had decided to go outside for a smoke after having turned in her thesis. The Institute of Forensic Medicine was directly adjacent to the grounds of the Charité Hospital on Hannoverstrasse, and with its two enormous wings and the high wall with the wrought-iron gate, it was reminiscent of a turn-of-the-century mansion.

In front of the stairway, the scraggly remains of a boxwood hedge encircled an empty fish pool. Katja Lavans had stopped there briefly for a cigarette—Eckstein: the real thing, the right choice. All the strain of the past half year had fallen away from her at that moment. She tossed her butt into the empty pool, as usual, then wondered whose job it was to clean the pool out. She was holding a small package in her hand. Professor Weimann had left it for her in the office. Under the wrapping paper was a small black Bakelite box imprinted with the words *R.V. Deckers Medical Instruments*. Inside, nestled on a bed of white leatherette, lay a scalpel—it was precisely the sort that her father, who was also a doctor, considered the very best. Katja Lavans had taken it out and seen that her initials had been engraved on the handle.

Doris hauled her two overflowing shopping bags up onto the kitchen table and pulled out six bottles of French red wine. Doris worked as a simultaneous translator for a textile-mill collective in Biesdorf, just outside Berlin, and had excellent contacts. Katja said she didn't want to ask where she'd gotten it. Doris was amazed once again at how forgetful her friend was—they'd arranged weeks ago that she would take care of bringing the drinks. Then the bell rang, and it was Bernhard, another colleague of Katja's from the Institute. Before he even congratulated Katja, he apologized for having forgotten his gift. Doris mumbled something about having to go see about the food, then disappeared into the kitchen, leaving Katja and Bernhard alone in the stairwell. Bernhard wasn't sure if he should embrace her or not. Then, just as he'd taken a step toward her and raised his arms, Max thundered up the steps with a bunch of flowers and pushed right past him to kiss Katja on both cheeks.

She had known Bernhard since their first semester, and as she often said, he was not just a better pathologist than she was; he was also her best friend. She took both men's arms and led them out onto the veranda, then went to look for a vase. She hurried, knowing that Bernhard wouldn't speak a word to Max—he was much too shy to speak English. She quickly returned with the flowers, gathered up the extra place settings and glasses and put them on the sideboard in the living room, then assigned her guests places at the round table and lit the candles while Doris brought out the food.

They had meat loaf, beans and potatoes. The group of them often ate together, since Max, a musical-composition student from Boston who was spending a year abroad at the College of Art in West Berlin, invited himself over almost as frequently as Bernhard did. Doris liked to encourage the American to come over to the Russian sector so she could speak English with him, but Katja always ended up speaking German with Max, for the sake of Bernhard, who otherwise wouldn't be able to follow. None of the four really minded the halting nature of the resulting conversation. They asked her about her research project, "On the Use of Animal Hair as a Murder Weapon," though of course they were all already familiar with it. Her project investigated the practice, common among ancient cultures and described in early European sources, of administering small amounts of animal hair, usually cut very finely, to an intended murder victim. Katja had often told them about her research and vividly described the ulcerated stomach walls she had observed on autopsy of her experimental subjects—mice. But that evening, to celebrate the occasion of the gathering, as Bernhard put it, Katja was encouraged to read the introduction aloud. She went and got a copy of the book, freshly arrived from the offices of Grete Kaiser, Berlin, and read the first page:

" 'Only when one considers the many and various fields of knowledge for which the study of hair is important can one begin to comprehend how broad the cultural significance of hair truly is.' "

Katja Lavans was standing at the head of the table. She had to struggle not to laugh, and the three who listened to her read were doing so with grins on their faces. It was one of the first warm evenings of the year, and Katja had gotten out the silver candelabra her in-laws had given her for her wedding. The flames of the five candles were reflected many times over in the glasses on the table and cast tiny points of light onto the surface of the red wine.

Dorris nodded. "Keep going!"

" 'Zoology describes the hair of animal pelts and precisely classifies each type of animal according to the particular characteristics of its hair. We can determine the species or even the individual animal from which a particular hair has come by examining the cuticle, the cortex, the color, the pliancy, the amount of air trapped within the shaft and the texture. In human physiology and mythology, hair is of great importance, and here, of course, we are speaking primarily of the hair of the head. To preserve or increase a woman's attractiveness or a man's strength, human beings have traditionally bound or braided their hair, burned it, dyed it, greased it and washed it. Homer referred to human hair as a gift from Aphrodite. Hair loss is commonly felt to be a profound psychic blow. It is clear that hair is invested with great psychosexual meaning.' "

Max stroked Doris's hair, and she laughed. Katja waited till her friends had quieted down again before she read on.

" 'For a young woman to have her hair cut has been considered a symbol of lost honor; significantly, this sort of "lynching justice" has sometimes been carried out in cases of sexual indiscretion, a phenomenon described by writers as early as Tacitus. When the ancient Teutons lost a battle, they would cut their hair as a sign of their humiliation and disgrace.' Well," she said, putting her text down, "I think that's enough of that."

They all clapped. Then Max got up and went inside. He returned with a box, which he set on the table. It was somewhat more than a foot high and roughly cubic.

"A gift," said Doris, and Katja thanked Max with a hug before she began unwrapping it.

Finally, she was holding a dark varnished wooden box about a foot square and just four inches high. On top, there were two chrome-plated metal rods. Max seemed to find Katja's bafflement quite amusing.

"A lamp?" asked Doris after a brief silence.

"Music!" said Max, taking the device in both hands. "This is an example of the first ever electronic musical instrument, invented by the Russian physicist Lev Sergeyvich Termin."

"When was this?" asked Katja somewhat disbelievingly.

"Termin began to give demonstrations of what he then called his etherphone in 1921. He presented it at public and private audiences all around Russia, even to Lenin himself!"

"And then?" asked Katja.

"In 1927, he went to the United States. By then, he'd changed his name to Leon Theremin—apparently, the French-sounding name was chosen to lend the young scientist an air of sophistication. And his instrument became known as the theremin."

"And then he grew rich and famous."

"No, unfortunately, not at all. In 1929, he sold the patent rights, and Professor Theremin lived in the United States for the next ten years, giving lessons on the theremin. By the way, the instrument was said to be playable by anyone who could hum a tune. So that makes it exactly the right instrument for you!"

Doris laughed at this little jab at Katja's lack of musical talent. Max pointed at the box and suggested that she try it. Katja had covered her mouth with both hands and was shaking her head.

"How exactly does it work?"

"The performer simply modifies the frequency and amplitude."

"You mean the sound is created simply by altering the frequency of the sound wave?"

"You got it."

Bernhard nodded and plugged in the machine, which had just a single knob. Immediately, you could hear a quiet, even humming sound. Max grasped the machine by its wooden base and pushed it over to Katja, who was still shaking her head.

"The theremin is played by moving one's hands near the two large metal antennae. One antenna controls the volume—moving closer dampens the sound. With the other, you modulate the pitch."

Katja nodded and tentatively, as if she were moving through a darkened room, searching for the wall, reached for the metal rod. It actually seemed like she was touching something they couldn't see: the sound, which suddenly grew louder. The movement of her hand seemed to give it shape, contour. Then, as she brought her other hand toward the second antenna, the volume changed, disappearing and then coming back, rather as if it were circling the table.

"That's sort of creepy sounding," said Doris, and Katja quickly pulled her arms away.

"So what ever happened to Professor Theremin?" she asked.

"One day in 1938, a group of men in dark suits appeared at his lab in Manhattan and whisked Leon Theremin away without any explanation. Maybe he was taken back to the Soviet Union. Who knows?"

No one spoke for a moment. They were listening to the sounds from the neighboring apartments whose windows opened onto the courtyard, their eyes averted from one another. Doris had her chin in her hand and stared into the darkness. Katja was watching Max continually push his black hair out of his face. Max was large and tall, the way she imagined an American would be. She liked the way his eyes flitted about when he didn't know what to do with himself, like now, and the exaggerated gestures he would use to bring himself back to reality. Katja began pouring wine into everyone's glasses, but Max put his hand over his and smiled at her.

"Sorry, Katja, but I think I have to go," he said quietly.

She knew he had to be back in the American sector before midnight, and he rose to leave even before the others had a chance to finish the wine she'd poured. Katja walked him to the door. Max waved good-bye to her as he rushed off down the steps, his light-colored coat flapping open. When Katja returned to the veranda, Doris was just explaining how she'd gotten ahold of the wine, and Bernhard mentioned how good it was. Afterward, no one seemed to know what else to say.

At some point, Katja asked, "Do you think they really took him back to the Soviet Union?"

Doris shook her head and took a deep breath. Bernhard said nothing, then cleared his throat as if he was trying to get his voice back after a long period of silence. Finally, he quietly mentioned that he'd brought her an article he thought she might find interesting. He pulled a magazine out of a thin file folder that had been leaning up against the railing all evening. Katja knew immediately from the cover that it was an issue of the West German medical review *Euro-Med*.

"What's it about?"

"That butcher from a certain nonsocialist foreign country, the one about whom you recently spoke on television—and defended so courageously. It's an interview with the original expert witness."

"And?"

"Well, Professor Maul actually testified that he'd discovered strangulation marks solely on the basis of the photos of the body."

"Wasn't there an autopsy report?"

"Of course there was."

"Well?"

"Heart attack."

"That's impossible!"

"Nope."

Bernhard had flipped open to the interview and read: " 'The bruise mark left by the cord can be seen in the photograph and is quite a common finding, really, the sort of thing we've seen thousands of times.' "

"But you can't base expert testimony on a photograph!"

"Maul says, 'The photograph showing the mark made by the cord was absolutely clear.' "

"Is this guy nuts? How could he know the mark wasn't made postmortem?"

"Can that happen? Can bruises form after you're dead?" asked Doris.

Bernhard shrugged and yawned. Katja nodded and asked to see the interview. He gave it to her, and she began to read.

"Well, I'm going to start cleaning up," said Doris, stacking up plates. "Do you want to help, Bernhard?"

The two of them brought the dishes into the kitchen. Afterward, Katja wasn't even sure if they had said good-bye. By the time she had finished the article, the apartment had grown quiet, and only then did she notice that they were gone.

There was still a bottle of wine on the table, open and half-empty. Her glass was standing beside it, and Katja poured herself some more. She lit a cigarette and looked out at the night sky, noticing the different ways it was reflected in the dark windows of the many apartments, depending on the floor. It was growing slowly cooler. The man who had allegedly killed the girl had been sentenced to life in prison. She tried to imagine what the dead girl had looked like, in his arms, how her muscles had gone limp in his embrace, and the way he wouldn't have been able to catch her eye, because her eyes would never see again.

The worst thing for Katja was always having to look into those empty eyes. Every now and then, she imagined she could still see some tiny, very nearly extinguished glimmer deep within them. There were other times when she'd thought she could see death itself there. Katja wondered what this man, whose name she didn't know and who might be a murderer, had felt at that moment. Then she thought she heard the roar of her lion, as her husband had always referred to it, over at the zoo, and she forgot about the man whose name she didn't know was Hans Arbogast.

Instead, she was recalling her many visits to the zoo to collect samples of animal hair for her research. Every time she'd walked by the lion, he'd growled so loudly that she found herself quickening her pace. She carefully brought one finger closer to the theremin and ran it along one of the chrome-plated rods. She liked the bright whirring sound that she had created, and she concentrated on moving her hand very evenly, so she wouldn't lose it. It seemed to her that it existed somewhere in the air in front of her hand; it had a shape and a form whose contours she was exploring, rather than creating. With her other hand, she made the sound glow by increasing its volume. The whirring grew clearer. The louder it grew, the more deeply it resonated, until it seemed to Katja that a transparent membrane was growing in the flickering light, a breathing form that turned and writhed and finally darted out from under her hands.

Then the tone grew more even and began to sink very slowly beneath her, rigid and growing ever quieter, like the steel hull of a ship going down. At the end, this deep pulsating humming slowly rose back to a brighter sound that oddly resembled the lion's growl, for despite being completely technological, it, too, was a foreign, lonely presence in the night.

27

At the gate, he was told that Father Karges wanted to speak with him. Which meant Hans Arbogast had already been given the news.

"I'd prefer to see my client directly."

"The priest wanted me to tell you he would take just a brief moment of your time."

The officer directed him to a small side door in the dark archway under the gatehouse, where it was cool even at the end of the hot August day. Klein shivered as the double steel doors closed behind him.

"This way, please." The guard locked the door and allowed him to pass.

They climbed fifty-odd steps up the narrow, winding stone stairway. At the top, the lawyer waited on the small landing and the guard squeezed past him to unlock the door. A narrow hallway. On the right, Klein saw a guardroom with rifles in glass-fronted cabinets against the wall, tables and chairs where several men in uniform sat talking. At the end of the hall was a glass door. Through it, Klein could see the sky. The guard unlocked this, too, and stepped aside to let Klein pass. He gestured outside, and Klein stepped out into the open, onto the walkway along the top of the prison wall. Some ten paces further down the walk, the priest was waiting for him, his cassock flapping in the wind.

Ansgar Klein had met Karges before. He'd asked to meet with the priest in order to get a better picture of Arbogast, and they'd had a brief conversation. At that point, Karges hadn't given the impression of being especially interested in prolonging the meeting. He seemed to think that Arbogast's troubles had more to do with the fact that he'd given up going to Mass since his wife had divorced him and didn't even go to church on Christmas. Klein remembered from their first meeting how rigid and determined the priest had been in his insistence that Arbogast was guilty.

The priest was wearing sunglasses with purple lenses. He smiled and extended his hand. It was just past midday, and the light under the cloudless August sky was glaring.

"How nice that you were able to take a moment to speak with me, Mr. Klein."

Klein nodded and smiled faintly.

"I come up here onto the wall a lot. It gives one such a feeling of exaltation. This is the border. Inside and outside, if you know what I mean."

Klein nodded and looked around him, blinking. On the other side of the wall were the roofs of Bruchsal. What did Karges want from him?

"Would you like to know where your client is kept? Right over there is his cell—Wing Four, the window with the number three twelve."

Klein looked down into the yard and the red sandstone building that filled it. One of the walls was marked WING 4, and looking at the second level, more or less in the middle, he found the number 312. He saw a group of prisoners in the courtyard below, sitting in a circle around a young man in a dark suit. Two guards kept watch nearby.

"And that is Father Ohlmann, my Lutheran colleague. Bible study. Are you a Protestant?"

Klein hesitated a moment. "Yes."

"You had to think about it?"

Klein smiled. "Father, I have other things on my mind right now. The application to reopen Hans Arbogast's case has been denied."

"I know." Karges laughed, and for a moment the light struck his face in such a way that the lawyer could see the priest's cold eyes through the purple lenses of the glasses, almost as if he were looking into an aquarium.

"Have you told him already?"

"Yes."

The wind tore the words from their mouths and scattered them. What an asshole, thought Klein.

"Why?" he asked, raising his voice.

"Why not? I've always known that Arbogast was guilty. I wanted to use this opportunity to get him to come to confession."

"And? How's he doing?"

"Did you know that this boundary wall is five hundred eighty meters long? I've forgotten the exact height. In each tower, there's a guard on duty with a semiautomatic machine gun. Have you ever seen a U.S. machine gun? In the war perhaps? Oh, come on, come on! It'll only take a moment."

The priest was already heading across to the next watchtower, and Klein followed him reluctantly. When he got to the tower, Karges was already standing there, smiling, beside a wooden box near the observation window through which the guards kept watch over the yard below. The bottom of the gun case was lined with felt, and the gun was leaning up against it. Karges picked it up, chambered a round and tossed it to Klein with a laugh. In the dim light of the tower room, Klein could no longer make out the priest's eyes at all behind his purple lenses. The weapon was heavy, its wooden grip worn and smooth. Klein handed it back to him and walked outside without speaking. He headed for the gatehouse tower.

"Actually, Klein, what I wanted to say to you was something else entirely." Karges had caught up and was following close behind him. "You must try to get Arbogast to confess. Don't you agree? Only if he shows remorse can he be absolved of that girl's death."

"What did you say to him?"

The priest laughed and shook his head. "You still believe he's innocent, don't you? But that's laughable. Just look at his mouth. Take a close look at him, and then just be glad you'll never bump into him on the outside—especially considering your dislike of guns."

There was a bell beside the glass door with its metal bars, which led back into the gatehouse, and Klein had to wait for someone to let him inside. Standing there out of the wind, in the shelter of the gatehouse, it was suddenly very hot again.

"So how is he? How did he take it?"

"You'll see for yourself soon enough."

The priest was still smiling.

Finally, one of the guards came and unlocked the door. As Klein passed through, he turned back to look at Karges once more. His purple lenses now glowed softly. He smiled and waved through the barred glass as the door was relocked. Klein was in a hurry to get to Arbogast. He was surprised that he wasn't led to the visitor's room. When he inquired, he was told by a guard that Arbogast wasn't there, and he wasn't at his job, either.

"What's wrong? What's happened to him?"

The guard just stood there.

"He won't leave his cell. He's refused to eat anything since yesterday, and he won't take exercise in the yard or go to work. The warden has only held off on putting him in the punishment block because he knew you were coming today. He doesn't want to go to the infirmary, either."

"Why would he go to the infirmary? What's happened to him?"

"You'll see," said the guard, avoiding his gaze.

They crossed through the central building, climbed the circular stairs to the second story and crossed the narrow walkway to Arbogast's cell.

"The warden has requested that you try to get Arbogast to snap out of it. Otherwise, he'll be sent to the isolation cell," said the guard before unlocking the door.

Klein had never been inside a prison cell before. He stepped forward and then the guard locked the door behind him. Arbogast's bed wasn't folded against the wall as it ought to have been during the day. He lay on the mattress without a shirt on, a pillow under his neck. The first thing Klein saw was his bloody forehead. His left eyebrow looked like it had exploded and was crusted with blood, as was his hairline and the whole left side of his face. The wall Arbogast was leaning against was also bloody. He said nothing to Klein, and Klein was silent, too, as he stood with his back against the door. The room was small and suffocatingly hot. As soon as he'd entered, beads of sweat began to form on his brow and under the collar of his shirt and to run down his torso. He noticed that Arbogast didn't seem to be sweating at all.

Klein silently cursed the priest. It was his fault that Arbogast had gotten himself into this condition. His demeanor was frightening, his eyes as dead and motionless as the rest of his body. The bright white sun penetrated the open window through the countless tiny squares of the screen. There was a damp handkerchief stained with reddish splotches lying on the floor beside the bed. Under the table, a dish and bowl. The remains of some soup was spilled on the floor and flies were sitting in it. Klein breathed slowly through his mouth to avoid taking in the smells of the food and the prison itself.

Silently, he opened his briefcase and took out the decision. He handed it to Arbogast, who leaned forward lethargically and took the paper. Klein saw that his knuckles were crusted with scabs as well, as if he had beaten himself. He had no idea what to say. Arbogast sank back against the wall and read. He didn't make eye contact with the lawyer.

Arbogast cleared his throat and then began to read aloud: " 'The photographic experts' testimony does indeed constitute new evidence, and the court recognizes these experts' technical ability to interpret the photographic materials as superior to Professor Maul's. However, with regard to the question of who can best interpret what the marks in the photographs imply about the corpse of the victim, the court is compelled to recognize the superior expertise of the forensic pathologist.' "

He let the gray sheet of paper fall and then looked up at Klein. "I guess your job is over, then?"

It may well be, Klein thought sadly to himself, but he was nevertheless just as angry now to hear those sentences aloud as he had been the first time he'd read them. He couldn't understand why his objections had been dismissed. But he tried a smile.

"No, absolutely not," he said, shaking his head reassuringly. "We just have to come up with a new plan."

"Yes, I guess you do."

Arbogast didn't believe him. He closed his eyes.

Klein would have liked to talk with him, but the man was so alien to him, so removed from everything he was familiar with, that the lawyer didn't dare to ask him what had happened. Instead, he simply stood there for some time and scrutinized Arbogast. After more than thirteen years in prison, his entire being had been shaped by the cell, by his total lack of exposure to any other environment, any other clothes, any conversation with anyone unknown. Klein saw in him all the typical characteristics of a prisoner serving an extended sentence—above all, an apathy that was somehow reminiscent of the slow movements of zoo animals. It was so disconcertingly self-conscious that one could easily get the impression the prisoner didn't care about anything—until that seeming quiet cracked wide open like the scab on a wound. Klein had never been able to imagine the loneliness of a night in a cell. Even now, he wasn't sure how to talk to Arbogast. In the end, he simply urged him to go back to work, to avoid getting into trouble. Arbogast nodded, his eyes closed. Then Klein told him about his conversation with the priest. At that, Arbogast laughed and actually looked at him briefly. But the laugh quickly died away, and it once again seemed he was looking straight through the lawyer.

Klein was exhausted by the stuffy air of the cell. He would have liked to sit down, but the bench was folded up against the wall, and he didn't want to sit next to Arbogast on the bed. He saw contempt hovering around the lips of his client and couldn't help thinking of what the priest had said to him. He wondered if the priest could be right about Arbogast being guilty, and his client began to seem more frightening to him than before. The moment of the crime—if it was a crime—is locked away behind those eyes of his, thought Klein. Arbogast neither got up nor gave Klein his hand when the lawyer took his leave. Indeed, he didn't even look up when the door swung shut again.

28

Klein drove straight through to Switzerland, where he stopped for the night at a small hotel in Montreux. He ate dinner at a restaurant on the promenade overlooking Lake Geneva and stared out over the water till dark, hardly touching his glass of wine. He couldn't get his visit to the prison out of his mind. This was a crucial moment. If Arbogast gave up and lost control of himself in the wake of this disappointment, it would make it more difficult to present him as an irreproachable prisoner later on, at trial. But Klein also had to admit he was no longer sure there would be a later on for Arbogast. He had thought it would be easier to get this retrial granted, on the basis of the mistakes made by the previous defense lawyer, but perhaps his past successes had made him too casual. That twitch he thought he'd seen in Arbogast's lips made him both angry and concerned. It was a kind of message of despair that had made its way to the outside. It told of a profound pain that Klein knew he couldn't begin to imagine. But he tried to as he looked out across the lake and then again later, in bed, as a consequence of which he didn't sleep very well that sweltering August night.

The following day before noon, he pressed on toward Italy, but he took a short detour to stop at the grave of Rilke in Raron. The poet's gravestone was close to the wall of the church, under a beautiful Gothic window, and from there Klein could see all of Valais spreading out wide below him, hot under the summer sun. A bright grayish haze lay over the steep slopes. A pair of ravens flew past, squawking busily, and cruised on into the valley through which the Rhône meandered slowly, its banks eaten away on either side. But Klein couldn't think of anything besides Arbogast and the suffocating odor of his cell.

Klein crossed the Alps at Simplon and arrived in Bissone in the early afternoon. As they had arranged, Sarrazin met him at a bar on a small piazza, a place with a shady veranda and metal chairs with seats woven from bright blue, yellow and red plastic strips. But Klein hadn't counted on Sue coming along. They ordered a round of Camparis, but it took him a while to feel at ease. He showed Sarrazin the decision and the objection he had immediately written to it, and then he told him about his visit with Arbogast.

They quickly agreed that their next tactic must be to cast doubt on Professor Maul's testimony. In addition, they would step up their publicity efforts with the aim of bringing the scandal of the first trial to the attention of the public, along with the unbearable obtuseness of the court that was now impeding the reopening of the case. They didn't have great hopes for the results of an investigation begun the previous spring by the German Society for Forensic and Social Medicine—its members were clearly much too closely aligned with Professor Maul's faction to be of much use to them.

"That's why I was so delighted yesterday when I saw a television interview with Katja Lavans," said Fritz Sarrazin. "She spoke out quite vehemently against the denial of our application."

"You mean the pathologist from East Berlin?"

"Yes."

"Do you think we could get her on the telephone?"

Sarrazin nodded tentatively and smiled, as if he were already looking forward to the conversation.

"And by the way, the Hansa Aerial Photography people have recommended someone from the technical university in Zurich—Professor Kaser, a renowned specialist in photogrammetrics and geodesy."

"And *what?*"

"Geodesy." Ansgar Klein began to snicker at that. But he surprised even himself when he actually blurted out, "Geodesy! The science of measuring the earth?" Apparently the stress of the previous day and his long journey were now catching up with him.

"I could go see him," suggested Sarrazin, ordering three more Camparis from the waiter and watching closely as Klein, who was still laughing, tried to get ahold of himself. Sue was giggling quietly.

"Yes, I wanted to suggest that myself," said Klein, taking a deep breath, as if he'd just completed some difficult task.

"*Bene, Dottore*. If you make an appointment for me with Professor Kaser, I'll go up to Zurich, and while I'm there, I'll try to get Max Wyss on our side—he's the chief of the Forensic Science Service for the police department there. He's a top expert in microscopic evidence. I've met him at a couple of conferences. And I'm certain he doesn't have any connection to Professor Maul."

They toasted each other with the tall, thin Campari glasses, and then Sue asked Klein about his life when he wasn't working. Klein responded with some amusing stories about cases he'd worked on in recent years. Sue noticed it was growing cool.

"By the way, you'll have to leave your car in town—the path up to our house isn't suitable for driving."

In fact, the path was just about wide enough for a cart. Outside of town, it was very quiet and darkness had already fallen on the steep slopes of the mountain. Only occasionally, when they came in view of the lake, did the landscape seem to brighten, and Sue and Sarrazin would pause on the path so their guest could enjoy the view.

"I don't think Arbogast can hold out much longer," said the lawyer hesitantly at one of these stops. He was holding his suitcase in one hand.

Sarrazin nodded and said nothing, but the lawyer knew what he was thinking, oddly enough. He was thinking that in a certain sense it didn't matter what happened to Arbogast. They could do only what they could do. They couldn't help Arbogast at the moment, no matter what was going to happen. Sarrazin glanced in the direction Sue had gone—she was some thirty paces ahead of them now—and they continued silently, following her the rest of the way up the path.

The lawyer noticed that Sue's shoes were precisely the same shade of blue as the stripes on her brightly colored summer dress. Its skirt was puffy from the crinoline beneath it and swung out in a wide arc from her waist. Over her shoulders, she wore the pink sweater that had lain in her lap most of the afternoon. Her head was bowed, as if she were searching for something on the ground, and she proceeded up the shadowy path with calm, evenly paced steps. The forest and the scree slopes on either side were suffused with dampness and the chill of the evening.

29

Sitting on the edge of the bed, Sue caressed the white hair of his chest as if she were sifting fine white sand through her fingers at the beach. It was still quite warm in their bedroom, though the floor-to-ceiling windows stood open to let in the cool night air. The lamp from the terrace threw a cold rectangle of light onto the ceiling, making the edges of everything in the room glimmer. She felt Fritz looking at her: her back, the line of her shoulders, her breasts, which rose and fell as she stroked him. His skin was dry and soft—things she'd come to associate with old age, since she'd known him. It's late, she thought, and closed her eyes. They'd stayed out on the terrace a long time, watching the lights of cars on the road in the valley. Klein had convinced them to stay up for a while, but finally they'd left him alone with a bottle of Greco di Tuffo that had just been opened. With her eyes still closed, she felt Fritz move and, half-dreaming, imagined him tracing the lines of shadow on her thigh. She listened to the noises on the terrace, the clinking as the wine bottle was lifted from the ice bucket, the creaking of the chair, the lawyer occasionally clearing his throat.

30

Paul Mohr lived in a Freiburg neighborhood where all the streets were named after deciduous trees, and, indeed, the leaves in the narrow gardens of the row houses were just starting to fall. From his writing desk on the second story, he looked out at two fruit trees that grew close to the patio, with its large flat paving stones, and then at the medium-sized cherry tree, the tall birch in the corner, which had been there when these houses were put in, and the boxwood hedge at the edge of the yard. It was September 28, 1967, and someone was just stopping by to visit his wife. He heard the doorbell ring, steps in the hall and then voices in the living room, laughter. He opened the newspaper and read the headline: ARBOGAST CASE CLOSED AT LAST. A special committee of the German Society for Forensic and Social Medicine, which had been formed to investigate the evidence in the case, had reaffirmed the opinion of Professor Heinrich Maul, one of its members.

Mohr was surprised. Given the recent press coverage, he hadn't expected this. Ever since seeing Hans Arbogast's face on television, he'd been stumbling across brief reports about the prisoner who'd now served fourteen years. The previous week, there had even been an article in *Der Spiegel*. After reading it, he'd requested the clippings file on the case from the morgue and taken it home with him. The cardboard binder was well worn and contained a thick pack of articles, some folded, some cut out and glued to pages; most were yellowed, but a few of them were printed on that unhealthy, ageless white paper used for special editions. At the top of the pile was his own article from 1953, and he read it over once again. It gave Paul Mohr a strange feeling of embarrassment to look at these old stories, headlines and photos that had been intended for one particular day and yet lived on in the newspaper archives, sometimes being summoned forth but actually lifeless, like the undead. They were so far removed from their own time that even the advertisements were dated.

Paul Mohr read a series of pieces in the *Grangater Tageblatt*, all signed "G.J." They followed the case from Arbogast's arrest to the verdict. The first headline read ARBOGAST DENIES INTENT TO KILL. The next day it was DA SEEKS LIFE TERM. Then DEFENSE PLEADS TO MANSLAUGHTER. And finally, CIRCUMSTANTIAL EVIDENCE LEADS TO CONVICTION. There was a report about the conviction in the *Badische Zeitung*, and Franz Kehlmann had written numerous pieces for the *Stuttgarte Zeitung*, but otherwise the larger papers hadn't been very interested in the case. It was Kehlmann, a legal reporter from Grangat, who signed his articles "N.N.," who had raised the doubts about the circumstantial evidence. In 1962, before the appeal was declined, one of his headlines had read EXPERT WITNESS IN ERROR? In 1966, there was a piece covering the petition to reopen the case: WILL ARBOGAST MURDER TRIAL RETURN TO COURT? And then later that year, he'd covered the denial: NO NEW TRIAL FOR ARBOGAST.

Beginning with the denial of the petition for a new trial, Paul Mohr had noticed the name Ansgar Klein appearing in the press coverage with increasing frequency, and also that the case had begun to attract an unexpected amount of attention. In November 1966, a long article about Arbogast by Henrik Tietz had appeared in *Der Spiegel*, and the following spring there had been a second one by the same author. Shortly thereafter, a four-column piece had appeared in the *Suddeutsche Zeitung*, in which Ansgar Klein had been quoted extensively. Finally, there was a recent essay that took up an entire page in the *Münchner Abendzeitung* under the headline TURNAROUND IN ARBOGAST CASE? The author was a crime novelist named Fritz Sarrazin, and he described in detail the miscarriages of justice that had taken place and the terrible fate of Arbogast. Well done, thought Paul

Mohr. The defense had made good use of the year since their appeal was denied to generate some publicity about the case. Only now did Paul Mohr realize how important it was to generate support for Arbogast. In March, at a conference of the German Society for Forensic and Social Medicine, a panel of five professors had been convened to reassess "whether it could be definitively proven that Marie Gurth died of any other cause besides strangulation." The panel had been given access to six binders containing the most important files, the expert testimony from the first and second appeals for a new trial, a copy of the old slides from the Freiburg Criminal Investigation Unit and a set of new slides from the Federal Office of Criminal Investigation. There was a short notice in the *Stuttgarte Zeitung*, which quoted Rudolf Schieler, the minister of justice for Baden-Württemburg, as saying that he had insisted on an independent panel to consider the matter of the Arbogast case, and that he had taken a personal interest in seeing that this case was finally resolved once and for all. Now that panel had decided. The chief district attorney for the Grangat District, Manfred Altmann, had given a statement to the *Badische Zeitung*, saying that his colleagues no longer saw even the slightest grounds for reopening the case. Everything possible had been done from the point of view of both the justice system and forensic science.

Paul Mohr looked at the photo that illustrated the article. He had given it to the editor himself. Then he pushed the file of clippings to the side and took another look at the original. Back then, he had been utterly fascinated with it. He had wanted it, no matter the cost. He remembered that moment when he'd had a choice between kissing Gesine Hofmann and asking her to let him have a print of the photograph. The memory of the surprised look on her face made him smile. Marie Gurth looked as if she were sleeping on a pillow of blackberry branches, he thought.

Ansgar Klein was looking at the same picture, at the same moment, though he saw it in a different paper that had chosen the same image to illustrate its coverage of the expert panel's decision against Arbogast. He immediately placed a call to Fritz Sarrazin. Sue was in the living room and answered the phone. From his office, Fritz listened to the tone of her voice. He'd often watched her talking on the phone. She would hold her head at an angle, constantly twisting the cord in her fingers while her gaze moved across the space in front of her like the rotating beam of a lighthouse, without her actually seeing anything at all. He couldn't make out the words, but he could tell it wasn't anyone in her family—the tone of her voice was too hard to be English. But it wasn't Italian, either, which meant it wasn't one of her friends from the village. Then she called for him to come quickly, saying it was Ansgar Klein on the phone. He was startled at first, then hurried over.

"Hello, Fritz."

Sue had given him the phone, but she was still standing there beside him, looking at him as if anxious to see his reaction.

"It's awful," said Ansgar Klein without further introduction. "The panel of experts has determined that Frau Gurth died of strangulation."

"That can't be!"

Sarrazin closed his eyes and rubbed his hand over his face. He hadn't expected this. No, it didn't seem possible that after all these years, five independent experts could reaffirm that erroneous testimony. Fritz Sarrazin shook his head. Considering the way Ansgar had described Arbogast, he doubted the man would be able to deal with this latest setback. The rejection of their petition for the new trial a year ago had been bad enough. Arbogast had remained in his cell for a week straight, refusing to eat, and been punished with ten days in solitary. It had been a long time after that before Klein could even talk to him again.

"No, it can't be, but it is."

Sarrazin knew what he meant. They had long since decided how they would proceed with this case. "Will you go to see him tomorrow, then?"

"Yes."

"Should I call him, too?"

"Yes, please, it would mean a lot."

Sarrazin nodded, and they said good-bye.

Sue looked at him. He tried to see something in her eyes that wasn't completely familiar to him, but there wasn't anything. He could see that she was cold. For the first time since summer, she was wearing a sweater.

"This is a horrible development for Arbogast, isn't it?" she asked, hugging herself tightly. Sarrazin put his arms around her and they kissed. The fog rose up from the mountain, through the garden and came in the open window, bringing dampness and dark. It was late afternoon, and the light was a sickly gray that seemed about to fade out and die at any moment. Sarrazin wished it were night already so that he could switch on the lights, perhaps light a fire, and he and Sue could pretend it was winter.

Since the previous summer, when the court had declined their petition, Sarrazin had devoted most of his time to making the general public interested in Arbogast's fate. After countless interviews and articles, it seemed that the strategy had been successful. But once again, he had underestimated the power of the legal system in which Hans Arbogast was trapped. It was a machine that unceasingly manufactured the stories of people's lives. Sarrazin had a notion that this machine was driven not by the collective body of all those paragraphs of legalese, but by the countless, unfathomable relationships among the individual letters of each word. The law, as it existed today, contained all of history inside it, on many levels. He'd often thought he could hear echoes of the language used during Germany's imperial past in the current Criminal Code; in certain passages, there were also shades of the heated rhetoric from the period between the wars, when new laws had been drafted in rapid succession; then, too, there were tones of the horrible premeditated sobriety of the Nazis, who had stormed across the Penal Code, incorporating into it one reform after the next, as if the law itself were nothing more than a series of empty streets. It seemed to Sarrazin that together, all these disparate voices within the law constituted the real prison that held Arbogast captive. All the lawyers and the judges, all the witnesses and the guards alike were possessed by this cacophonous chorus. He imagined it to be like the babbling of the Pentecostalists he had once seen in the mountains near Bern when he was a child—they had fallen into a trance and spoken in tongues.

He resolved that he would get in touch with Arbogast himself, first thing the next morning, before the lawyer had a chance to get there. The prison was on lockdown for the night, at any rate. Although he knew it was a sign of his own cowardice, he decided it was more important right then to light the fire—to make sure that Sue was warm.

31

Klein didn't get to Bruchsal until late the next day, and it was already growing dark when Arbogast was taken back to his cell after the meeting with his lawyer. It was fall now, thought Arbogast, leaning his cheek against the cool wall beneath his window. The air smelled of her, just like it did every year around this time. The smell was always there, but now it was especially powerful. The lawyer had asked him why he was smiling. He'd kept quiet and shaken his head. It was a thing that couldn't be explained: Marie was everywhere. Ever since the moment he'd held her unmoving head in his hands, she had always been there. The lawyer had asked him if he would be able to deal with the panel's decision. "Yes, of course." Was there some way he could help him further? Would you please just be quiet, Arbogast had thought. Sometimes, he lay awake for a while, after the lights went out, and tried to touch himself without her noticing. He'd never been able to do it. In all the years, there had never been a touch that wasn't her touch.

"So why did you decide to leave Berlin?"

Had he really asked her that? She'd just laughed and used her finger to get the last bit of ice cream from the silver dish. He knew nothing about her. Later, in the car, she had given him a good strong neck massage, as if they'd known each other for ages. In her other hand, she'd been holding a cigarette. He closed his eyes and kissed Marie. He felt the wall against his cheek. The plaster smelled damp at night, of gypsum and mildew. "Why don't you confess, Arbogast?" asked Karges every time he visited his cell. "You must come to confession, so that you may be absolved." Arbogast just shook his head. He had asked himself time and again how he could get away from her. She ground out her cigarette in the ashtray and took his head in her hands. He lost himself in her eyes. No one had ever kissed him that way. He remembered the smell of the Isabella's plastic precisely—it had never gone away, not even faded. Her breath on his cheek. Her breath was gone. It was true: He had acted like a murderer. Earlier, when they were eating at the restaurant in Triberg, as the waiter was returning with the check, he had asked her, "Why did you leave your children behind?"

She had grown serious then, her hands in her lap, shaking her head. "That's none of your business!"

He stroked his belly. The contours of the room wavered before his eyes, just barely recognizable. Arbogast was disgusted by the act of touching himself. And he couldn't confess, either. He didn't believe there was anything further the lawyer could do for him.

32

"Charité, Institute of Forensic Medicine."

"Hello. This is Fritz Sarrazin. May I speak with Dr. Lavans, please?"

"This is she."

Sarrazin was quiet for a moment, stunned that the conversation was actually going to take place. He smiled at how anxious he was. He'd had to go through the Swiss foreign operator in Zurich. A woman's voice had warned him he would have less than an hour; then the connection would be broken off. He had waited, and then the phone rang again.

"I'll connect you now."

"Hello. I'm so glad to have gotten through to you, doctor."

"Hello."

"As I said, my name is Fritz Sarrazin, and I'm involved in the Arbogast case. I'm sure you recall it. The interview you gave when the application to reopen the case was denied was recently broadcast on Swiss television."

"Yes."

"Well, that's why I'm calling. I was very glad to hear what you had to say about the testimony of your colleague Professor Maul. I'm working with Ansgar Klein, Mr. Arbogast's lawyer, who is still seeking to have a new trial granted. And I'm calling because we'd like to ask if you would be willing to serve as an expert witness in the case."

"To counter Professor Maul's testimony, you mean?"

"Yes, of course."

"I'm not sure. First of all, I would have to have all the materials sent to me in East Berlin, and then I would have to get permission to travel to the West for the trial."

"Yes, exactly. It would have to be arranged. But you see, you could be a great help to us. Firstly, you have a stellar reputation as a forensic pathologist, even outside East Germany. But second, it's very difficult to find anyone here in the West who is willing to provide any sort of objective assessment of Professor Maul's testimony."

"Professor Maul is undoubtedly one of the leading authorities."

"Yes, he is. But anyone can make a mistake. And unfortunately, Professor Maul is not prepared to admit to having made an error. As you may know, a panel of star experts convened by the German Society for Forensic and Social Medicine recently issued a resounding reaffirmation of Professor Maul's testimony in the case."

"I see—so the situation is hopeless."

The pathologist was right, of course. Fritz Sarrazin considered what he could say in response.

"You've hit the nail on the head. But nonetheless, Hans Arbogast has now served fourteen years in prison, and we believe that he's not guilty."

"I understand. Am I right to assume that the principal question is one of postmortem bleeding?"

"Yes."

"Another question: Who was the woman?" asked Katja Lavans.

Till then, she'd been standing beside the two desks that were pushed together under the window and had pulled the telephone, which was mounted on a telescoping arm, over to the window. Now she sat down. There was a Christmas star on the windowsill, beneath the white half curtains.

"Marie Gurth," said Sarrazin. "Née Häusler, from Berlin. She had just turned twenty-five when she died."

"When did it happen?"

"September first, 1953."

"Do you know what part of Berlin she lived in?"

"Just a second—I can look that up." Sarrazin flipped through the files briefly, the telephone receiver clamped between his shoulder and chin. "In Karow," he said after a minute.

"And in the West?"

"In a refugee camp near Grangat."

"Was she married?"

"Yes. Her husband was an engineer. Their two children stayed behind with her mother in Berlin."

"How awful. And her husband?"

"Marie Gurth died on a Tuesday. On the following Saturday, September fifth, her husband showed up at the police station and stated that his wife was 'absent.' The following day, he identified the body of the dead woman as his wife's."

"Did he actually use the word *absent*?"

"That's what it says in the report. According to his statement, she had an appointment at the Grangat employment office. Afterward, she showed up at his workplace on Englerstrasse in Grangat and they went to lunch together at the cafeteria in the train station. During lunch, she told him she had hitchhiked and that the driver had invited her to go for a walk with him and go swimming in the Rhine. But she hadn't gone. Jochen Gurth said his wife was planning to hitchhike back to Ringsheim after lunch, and that she had declined his suggestion that she wait around till evening so they could take the train back together. That was the last time they saw each other."

"And why didn't he contact the police earlier?"

"His wife frequently traveled the country roads in search of work and had sometimes stayed away overnight. He became concerned only when the Stuttgart businessman with whom he imagined she was staying suddenly showed up to see her at the Ringsheim camp. But then he'd imagined that his wife must have gone back to see their children and her parents in the Soviet zone. He didn't go to the police to report her missing till he read in the paper that a woman's body had been discovered."

All of a sudden, the edge of the telephone receiver seemed to be digging sharply into Katja Lavans's ear. When he said the words *country roads*, it brought to mind the recent outing to Wörlitz with her daughter, Ilse. They had gone ice-skating and shopped at the Christmas market. There was hot mulled wine, and they had warmed themselves at small coal fires built in cast-iron basins set up between the stalls. Katja Lavans reached down the back of her turtleneck sweater and rubbed her neck, which was sore after a day of work at the microscope. Fritz Sarrazin waited silently. Outside her window, the winter-evening sky was dark orange and blue and brightly lit by the moon, which was almost full that night. She thought about home and the fresh, cold air that blew constantly into her apartment from the park at this time of year.

"What about the media coverage?"

"Just a moment." She could hear Fritz Sarrazin leafing through his papers, not reacting to her silence. "Well, the *Badische Zeitung*, for one, wrote that 'members of the press and those interested in the proceedings could easily draw the conclusion that Arbogast found a willing partner on his drive through the Black Forest.' "

"Weren't there character witnesses?"

"No, there were not. Miss Gurth's best friend was a woman named Mizzi Neelsen, who also lived at the refugee camp, and even though she was reluctant to say much, she admitted that Miss Gurth had lived a, shall we say, *carefree* existence. She dressed provocatively and went after men who had money. She had also had numerous assignations with men who picked her up hitchhiking. According to what her friend told the *Badische Zeitung*, she was quite clever about concealing her little flings from her husband."

"Mr. Sarrazin?"

"Yes?"

"Where are you calling from?"

"Why do you ask?"

"No reason. I was just curious where you lived. Are you Swiss?"

"Yes, you got it. I live in Tessin, which you probably wouldn't have heard of. It's near Bissone, north of Lake Lugano."

"Do you have a house there?"

"Yes."

Katja Lavans stood back up, and she noticed how the white fluorescent lights burned her eyes, as if they dried them out. She closed her eyes. She would have loved to pace a few steps, but the extension arm of the phone didn't move easily, and the length of the phone cord allowed her no more than a yard of play. She was amazed to realize that she hadn't smoked a cigarette during the entire conversation, and she immediately lit one.

Sarrazin looked out the window. The lake shone dully. No rain tonight, no wind. An entire village lay reflected in the water, but he couldn't recall its name.

"Why are you so interested in rape-murder cases?" she asked.

"I'm a writer."

"Oh. You write crime novels?"

"You'll laugh, but yes."

Katja Lavans did laugh, and blew smoke through her nose. "Mr. Sarrazin?"

"Yes?"

"Do you smoke?"

"No, I'm afraid I can't say that I do, Dr. Lavans. Why do you ask?"

"Just wondering. But to get back to the reason for your call . . . before I can agree to serve as a witness in your case, it will have to be determined whether the relevant materials can be sent to me here and how I would get to West Germany. I'll need to discuss it with my superior. Where will the trial be taking place, anyway—if it does?"

"In Grangat. That's in the Black Forest. I think there will be a way to make it happen."

"Very well. If that can be arranged, I would be happy to provide my expert opinion. Postmortem hemorrhaging is precisely my specialty."

"Indeed. There's just one other problem. Arbogast has no resources whatsoever, and we would be able to offer only minimal compensation for your services."

Katja Lavans smiled at how embarrassing it clearly was to Fritz Sarrazin not to be able to pay her.

"That doesn't matter," she said.

"Wonderful. Thank you very much for your time. I'll try to get back to you as soon as possible. I think the best step would be for Dr. Klein to pay you a visit and describe the case to you in greater detail. Would that be all right with you?"

"Yes, of course. That would be fine."

The pathologist nodded. As soon as they had said good-bye and hung up, she picked up the phone again and dialed. Since her divorce, whenever she had to work later than expected, she would call Frau Krawein downstairs and ask her to call her daughter to the phone for a moment. Her hours were long enough to start with, but it happened nonetheless. Ilse didn't sleep well if her mother hadn't wished her good night, and the Krawein family on the ground floor were the only ones in the building with a telephone.

"Mama?"

As usual, Ilse bombarded her with sentences. It took a while before Katja could send her back upstairs to bed without her being sad. Finally, she told her once more to sleep well, then hung up.

Only then did Katja Lavans notice that she was still standing there in the office beside the two desks that had been pushed together. Her thoughts went back to Mrs. Müller, whose case she had been working on before Fritz Sarrazin called her. Without thinking about it, she put her cigarettes and lighter in a pocket of her white coat, turned off the lights in the office and then the ones in the hall—for she knew that she was the last one there at that hour—and went down to the Chamber, which was what they called the room with the refrigerated drawers at the institute. Mrs. Müller's autopsy was set for the following morning, and the paperwork she had from the doctor who'd handled the case amounted to an admission of total bafflement. Pretty much all they knew was that the woman had been twenty-eight years old, five foot nine and 127 pounds. And that she'd suddenly started to bleed from the nose and ears. But at that point, she was already dead.

You could hear the humming of the refrigeration equipment throughout the building, but it grew steadily louder as Katja Lavans climbed downstairs to the basement level and then followed the exposed heat and water pipes that snaked in the direction of the lab. It was cold and musty-smelling down there in the tiled room, and you could hear the sound of condensed water dripping from the refrigerator onto the floor. Katja Lavans pulled the handle and the drawer slid open like a filing cabinet, then another tug and the narrow gurney rolled out toward the pathologist.

"Hello there," she said as she pulled the sheet away from the young woman's face. She was waxen in death, as if a see-through plastic tablecloth had been laid over her.

It all came down to making a final determination on the post-mortem bleeding, thought Katja Lavans. The young woman was attractive. Katja Lavans pulled back one of her lids, looked into the eye beneath and was barely able meet its gaze—it was so utterly rigid. Once again, what she really wanted to know was what it was like not to feel anything anymore, to be cold and dead.

"Now, tell me about yourself," she whispered.

33

As always, Klein took enormous pleasure in the particular moment of takeoff when the plane was rushing along the runway, every part of it vibrating in sync with the tension that built and built within himself, until suddenly everything went quiet as the force of gravity seemed to push against the motion of the plane, which lifted into the air. He kept his eyes tightly closed to make sure nothing distracted him from the sensations the takeoff worked upon his body. The Pan Am Boeing 727 was a new type of aircraft, with three jet engines, and it was only in the past year that it had replaced the propeller-driven DC-6 on this route. Not until the aircraft had reached its cruising altitude on that January day in the year 1968 and had entered the Allied air corridor through East Germany, shortly past Fulda, did the lawyer return to himself, rather as he might have at the conclusion of a movie. The stewardess, who imagined he must be feeling airsick, bent down to him and asked him in English how he was feeling. Her perfume smelled like fresh white flowers. He shook his head, smiled and asked for a Coca-Cola on ice, his thoughts having already strayed to his appointment in East Berlin. It might well be the factor that determined how much more they could do for Hans Arbogast.

Time just seemed to dwindle away on this case. It was already winter again, and he'd just learned that the district court in Karlesruhe had denied the motion he'd filed a year and a half ago, protesting the rejection of his request for a new trial. For a while, Arbogast had refused to work, to go to the courtyard or to shave, and he had barely spoken when Klein visited him. But at least he hadn't gone back to self-mutilation. Klein had had to convince him again and again that there was still hope. Finally, on a visit the previous spring, Arbogast had asked him to describe in great detail what the outside world looked like—the streets, the cars people drove, how they dressed. But that euphoria hadn't lasted long, and then for the entire summer, Arbogast had refused to see his lawyer. Sometimes, he sent Sarrazin letters decorated with pencil drawings; they were always full of references to what had happened that night with Marie Gurth. When Klein tried talking to him about it, he would say nothing. Often, when he was sitting in the visitor's room, looking at Arbogast, both of them holding their silence, Klein would think back to the initial letter Fritz Sarrazin had written him and how he'd driven directly to the prison in Bruchsal. Everything had seemed so simple then. It was always difficult to get a case reopened, and the justice system did everything it could to avoid retrial. It was just that this case had seemed so clear.

Ansgar Klein shook his head. Sometimes he wondered if it was right to continue raising Arbogast's hopes this way. It seemed that it was only Sarrazin and he who kept Arbogast in this murky state of hopelessness, year after year, senselessly perhaps. Without their efforts on his behalf, he would most likely long since have gone over to the other side. At times, Klein imagined Arbogast's cell as the portal into a world populated by nothing but memories and fantasies. The weight of it might be too much for him, the way his recollections of the past gave rise to a chain of ideas that seemed plausible, though in fact they were false. Klein remembered vividly that first visit Sarrazin had paid him in Frankfurt, when they had gone to Jimmy's, the hotel bar, and raised their glasses to Arbogast. He remembered the voice of the singer.

The court had explained its denial of the last petition by saying it was insufficient simply to provide evidence that would have made it *possible* for the court to come to a different judgment. The evidence had to *contradict* the judgment, and the new depositions supplied by Arbogast's lawyer had not done this. There was no doubt that the statements about the prints of the photographs constituted new evidence, but the court could not overlook the fact that the original judges had reached their guilty verdict on the basis of more than the photographic evidence alone. The autopsy findings had also supported the theory that the victim was strangled. That victim would now be a forty-year-old woman, thought Ansgar Klein on the taxi ride from Templehof Airport. Berlin had been in the headlines often during the past year, thanks to the ongoing student protests, and as he was driven to the hotel on Mommsenstrasse where his secretary had reserved him a room, Klein looked out at the streets with great curiosity, searching for traces of all that activity.

It was just past eleven o'clock when he arrived at the hotel, and he still had plenty of time before his 2:30 meeting with Dr. Strahl, East Germany's attorney general. He unpacked his suitcase and transferred some papers to his briefcase, then went out for a stroll down the Kurfürstendamm. He stopped for a cup of tea at the Café Kranzler and afterward went on to the Zoo Station, where he caught the S-Bahn to Friedrichstrasse. When he stepped off the train, he experienced the process of going through East German customs for the first time. At the end of it, he had five East German marks, which was the minimum exchange required for citizens of the nonsocialist economic zone, as well as a day visa and a stamp in his passport. He walked off down the dimly lit corridors and staircases and into the other part of the city.

It was almost seven years since the wall had gone up and Berlin had become, as the phrase went, a divided city. He didn't know anyone over here, and the situation seemed quite unnatural to him, which, in turn, also made it interesting—or at least that's how he'd felt in Frankfurt. He tried to orient himself in relation to Friedrichstrasse. For a second, he thought he could conjure up the smell of the stewardess's perfume, which he'd found so compelling several hours earlier, but it was impossible. As he walked along Unter den Linden, he decided that after his appointment with Dr. Strahl he would return and take a look inside a large bookstore he'd noticed on the street level of a new building near the Soviet embassy. He was still a little early. If it went badly, he figured he'd even have time to visit the Pergamon Museum afterward, since there wouldn't be anything further to discuss with Katja Lavans. He wandered slowly past the Russian guards and then up to the barricades in front of the Brandenburg Gate.

The office of the attorney general of the German Democratic Republic was located on Otto-Grotewald-Strasse. Klein tried to remember what the street used to be called. The entrance of the grandiose late-nineteenth-century building gave way onto a large courtyard. Klein was instructed to wait until someone came to take him upstairs to Dr. Strahl's office. He waited at a high doorway for several more minutes, until at last a thin man came toward him from an office at the far end of the narrow hallway. Klein hadn't even paid attention to him at first, until the man shifted a bundle of files to his left arm, extended his right hand and introduced himself.

They were barely in Dr. Strahl's office before that little show of friendliness was over. The windows on the first floor were so high, they dwarfed the room's numerous tall filing cabinets. The two men went over to a seating area—desk, conference table, chairs—that seemed to hover like a constellation in the center of the creaky, rather worn parquet floor. There was a faded light green carpet that was intended to match the thin drapes.

"What can I do for you?"

Attorney General Dr. Joseph Strahl, resistance fighter, active antifacist and dogmatic member of the Central Committee of the Party, had apparently decided not to part with the thin smile he wore on his lips. His narrow-cut light gray suit fit him perfectly. Coffee was brought, and the lawyer began to lay out his request.

He was expecting mostly to be asked why, of all people, Katja Lavans was needed to serve as an expert witness in the trial of Hans Arbogast, and to prepare himself for this, he had read her study on the use of animal hair in murder and her other research papers. Of the numerous important blood tests that were now increasingly being used to determine time and cause of death, many had been developed largely based on her research at Charité, which was widely recognized in the West. But as it turned out, Dr. Strahl was hardly concerned with that at all. It seemed only too obvious to him that an East German researcher should play a crucial role in a West German criminal trial. His questions all had to do with whether and how Ansgar Klein had made contact with Dr. Lavans and how the lawyer planned to arrange for the appearance of the witness in Grangat.

Klein struggled to formulate a plan for Katja Lavans's visit to the West off the top of his head. Finally, Dr. Strahl interrupted him. He emphasized that he couldn't make any promises, then picked up the telephone, which was attached to the side of his desk, and said that he would be only too glad to be of service to a colleague from the West.

"Put me through to the Ministry of Academic Affairs, please. The Travel Bureau. Yes, exactly."

With his eyes, he indicated to the lawyer that this would take a moment.

"Yes, Strahl here. The unit leader, please. . . . Yes, I'll wait."

Klein resisted the impulse to look at his watch. He looked at the desk set of green onyx, the fountain pen and numerous pencils sitting in a metal dish. Various stamps. An old-fashioned desk lamp with a green glass shade on one side; on the other, a stack of files in color-coded folders.

"What cadre does Comrade Dr. Lavans belong to?"

Once again, Strahl stared at Klein without speaking. Klein glanced away. Between the windows, there was a familiar portrait of Lenin in profile, standing on the bank of a river.

"Travel cadre, you say? Thank you."

Dr. Strahl hung up and smiled his thin, ever-ready smile.

It wasn't till Ansgar Klein was back out on Otto-Grotewald-Strasse that he looked at his watch. It had been less than an hour, but there wasn't enough time to go see the Pergamon Altar. The lawyer turned right and then continued straight ahead until he came to Charité Hospital.

34

Klein took in the room at a glance: high ceilings, green linoleum that had been laid over the parquet floor, roll-front cabinets flanking the door to the office. There was a sink with a mirror and a towel, and, in one corner, a Zeiss microscope with its cover. Katja Lavans rose, shook his hand, pulled a chair up to her side of the desk and invited him to take a seat.

"Cigarette?"

He declined and leaned his briefcase against the chair. She was wearing a white lab coat, a pair of forceps and a scalpel protruding from its left breast pocket. She looked younger than she had on television. He liked her short hair, and he watched her closely as she picked up an ashtray and a pack of cigarettes, tapped one free and lit it. Katja Lavans came straight to the point.

"Your partner, Mr. Sarrazin, has already explained a little bit about the case to me. I told him on the phone that I'm in principle quite willing to serve as an expert witness."

She avoided blowing smoke in his face, and he had to think about what to say next—a thing that never happened to him.

"Yes, we were very pleased to hear that. I'm certain we'll be able to work out the details. There's a great deal riding on this for us—we've been working on behalf of Hans Arbogast for years now. We need someone with the courage to face down the unified front put up by your West German colleagues. When we heard your remarks on television, we realized at once that we must contact you. You hold a position in forensic medicine at Humboldt University, in addition to your work here?"

"Yes, I've just been appointed."

"Congratulations."

"I'm also divorced."

He wondered for a moment, expressionless, how old she might be, then ventured: "So am I."

Katja Lavans ground out her cigarette. She pushed the ashtray away as she exhaled the last bit of smoke.

"Did you know that the oldest known work on forensic medicine, the book *Hsi Yuan Lu*, or *The Washing Away of Wrongs*, dates from the year 1248? A Chinese friend who was visiting told me it was still in use in China into the nineteenth century. *Hsi Yuan Lu* consists of five books: The first covers trauma and abortion; the second distinguishes the injuries caused by various tools and methods and whether they were sustained pre- or postmortem; the third book covers death by strangulation and drowning; and the remaining two deal extensively with poisons and toxicology."

"Ancient Chinese secrets, eh?"

She gave a thin smile and looked straight at him. "If you like. At any rate, the part on strangulation might be of interest with regard to your case."

Klein nodded. "So when did forensic medicine begin here in Europe?"

"Beginning of the seventeenth century. The first text on the subject is a work by Paolo Zacchia, personal physician to the Pope. Incidentally, this building was once the premiere morgue of Berlin. The back of the building faces the Dorotheenstadt cemetery, where Johannes R. Becher is buried."

"And Bert Brecht, right?"

"Yes, that's right. You must have seen the Charité Hospital's outpatient clinic—it's pretty much directly across from us—and then further up is the Natural History Museum."

Ansgar Klein nodded. "And you're going to tell me that I absolutely must visit it?"

She smiled. "Well, you really ought to see the dinosaurs."

"Maybe next time."

"Back then, this place, which was Germany's first institute of forensic medicine, was a completely modern facility. By the way, do you know what the original function of the morgue was?"

"No."

"Unclaimed bodies—and at the end of the last century, there were nearly seven hundred of them a year here in Berlin—were laid out in long rows to facilitate what they call 'identification.' "

Klein nodded.

The pathologist bent forward and flicked at a pencil on her desk blotter with her left index finger, all the while gazing directly at Klein.

"The body of a human being is a curious thing. The person retains a personality even after death. In Roman times, the corpse was consecrated into the hands of the ancestors—*diis manibus*—and the family had the only right to burial. I think that solves the problem pretty well."

"The problem being whether, after death, a person who has led an upright life becomes a mere thing?"

She nodded. "Exactly. A thing can be defined as the possession of another person or the community, which suggests that an autopsy could be construed as property damage."

"But if the corpse were still a body, then it would be bodily harm."

"Yes. For that reason, it has been decided by our high court that a corpse is not a thing that can be owned in the sense of the Civil Law Code of 1922, and it can't be inherited either—nor is it a body. So you see, it's a strange entity: Even after death, it remains on the margin between life and death."

Slowly, Katja Lavans pushed the pencil across to the opposite corner of her desk blotter. It seemed to her that he was only now, for the first time, really looking at her. She liked his gaze, as she liked his voice. Without looking up, she fished another cigarette from the pack and lit it. Only when she looked up and exhaled did he speak.

"I think you'll be getting the go-ahead in the next couple of days. Both to serve as an expert witness and for the travel clearance."

"You talked to Dr. Strahl?"

"Yes, just now. He hasn't agreed yet, but I don't see any reason there should be a problem. If you could let me know as soon as it's settled, I'll send you the complete file at once. For the time being, I've only got this set of photos with me."

Klein took out a small brown envelope that contained some of the crime-scene photos—the ones he had decided it wouldn't be too risky to carry across the border. He passed them to Katja Lavans, who spread them out on the table like playing cards.

"In cases of murder or unusual circumstance, it's basic practice for the pictures to be made from plates that are at least thirteen by eighteen, to allow for capturing minute detail and the best-possible resolution. There should be images of the victim both clothed and unclothed, front and back views."

"She was naked when she was found."

"Furthermore, a tripod should be used to get a precise vertical shot, eliminating any possibility of distortion."

"I know the pictures aren't great."

"And one should use a film or plate that can be developed for soft contrast."

She arranged and rearranged the pictures. At one point, as if she could see not the future but the past in them, she pulled the one depicting Marie Gurth in the blackberry thicket from the pile and examined it closely; then she fastidiously laid out all the pictures so that their corners met at right angles.

"Well then," she said quietly, without looking up, "shall we get started?"

Klein looked at her, nodded and remained silent for a short while, until he understood what she wanted. He cleared his throat and began.

"On the evening of September third, 1953, while he was out on a deer hunt, a gamekeeper by the name of Mechling discovered the naked corpse of a woman on a highway embankment. The naked bodies of two previous women had been found in the same vicinity, in 1949 and 1952, and, similarly to this case, the locations where those bodies were recovered were determined not to have been the sites of the murders. In this case, the Homicide Division of the Freiburg Police Department arrived on the scene the night of the discovery and searched the area, together with the local police, focusing particularly on the adjacent woods. The thirty-five-millimeter and medium-format color photographs you have before you were taken by a Grangat photographer, who was hauled out of bed for the occasion. The police report mentions signs of strangulation on the neck and throat, bruising around the left eye and scratches on the side of the right breast. At approximately two a.m. the body was transferred to a coffin and removed to the morgue at the Grangat municipal cemetery."

Klein paused, waited. Katja Lavans waited, too. Without looking up, she slid one of the photos from the outer left row of the grid, moving it somewhat toward the center. For a moment, it seemed to Klein she was humming to herself. He cleared his throat again.

"The following day, Friday, September fourth, the medical examiner, Dr. Dallmer, and Dr. Bärlach conducted the autopsy. Throughout the procedure, the pathologist used twenty-four-by-thirty-six format thirty-five-millimeter film."

"And?"

"Cause of death: heart failure secondary to assault and battery, as well as the weakened condition of the victim following an incomplete abortion."

"And the autopsy report? External, internal and microscopic examinations?"

"You'll have it all, just as soon as Dr. Strahl gives the official okay. Unfortunately, I can't send it to you until he does."

She nodded. Now she was looking at him. It would later occur to him, with some amazement, how utterly without charm her gaze was. Indeed, it seemed she was regarding him with utter detachment, memorizing precisely each line in his face. And yet there was nothing cold or unfriendly about her; on the contrary, all her movements and even the tone of her voice were girlish—childish even. She hadn't been unfriendly, but he did find the strange, childlike coldness with which she looked at him distinctly unpleasant. She asked him what he thought of Arbogast, the innocent murderer. With the impression of his last visit still vivid in his mind, Klein began to describe how much Arbogast had changed over the years. "After all this time, prison has really gotten to him," he said hesitatingly. "It's gotten under his skin. In fact, if you can imagine this, I would say that the prison has become a kind of second skin to him—all the smells and sounds of it, all the guards and inmates, all the regulations and the silence in his cell."

"You mean he's lost his mind?"

"No, I don't think so. It's more that he possesses a strange, burning, radiant energy. It's very difficult to describe. You'll be surprised when you meet him."

"Can you describe what he looks like?"

Ansgar Klein thought for a moment and shook his head. "I really can't."

"But you believe him?"

"I do—"

"But?"

"It's just that I can't imagine what he would be like outside that prison cell, which he carries with him always."

Katja Lavans nodded. Klein noticed that her hands were red around the knuckles and her cuticles shredded. He declined, with thanks, her invitation to dinner with her and her daughter.

They were standing at the top of the short staircase out in front of the institute, and she cast her gaze down toward a small dry fish pond.

"Have you ever seen the Pergamon Altar?"

"No. Why?"

She nodded but didn't answer him, then folded her arms across her chest, shivering.

"Well, see you soon, then," he said at last, and smiled at her.

"Sure, see you."

On the way back to the S-Bahn station at Friedrichstrasse, Ansgar Klein lost his sense of direction. He was on Oranienburgerstrasse, just across from the synagogue, before he realized he should have gone the other way. Getting back across the checkpoint at the border was no problem. He ate dinner on Savignyplatz, a short distance from his hotel, and went to bed early, as his plane was leaving first thing the next morning. But before he actually fell asleep, he envisioned once more the edifice of the Bode Museum, emerging like the prow of a great Spanish galleon from the haze, and all through the damp fall evening, there echoed the horrible screeching of streetcars.

35

At about the same time, Fritz Sarrazin had an appointment with Anton Kaser of the Confederate Technical College in Zurich. Their meeting was set for noon, and Sarrazin had already stopped in to see Max Wyss, the director of the Forensic Science Service of the Zurich Police Department, whom he hoped would serve as an expert in the collection of forensic evidence. Sarrazin knew him, and Wyss had quickly agreed to serve as an expert witness for free. After Sarrazin told him about the case, Wyss seemed quite optimistic, given Professor Maul's irresponsible use of the poor-quality photographs. They had parted with a firm handshake, and afterward Sarrazin spent some time wandering around the old part of the city. Finally, he ended up at the Lindenhof, watching the chess players, whose playing field, a large checkerboard paved with colored stones, was situated on the outer rim of the plaza. There was the fountain with a slender Gothic figure on a tall column. The green benches. The double staircases leading up to the Masonic temple. The small green dome of the church on Zähringerplatz in the distance. And beyond that, the technical college. The knee-high knights and castles against the green. No one spoke. Finally, Sarrazin tore himself away from the game and walked toward the lake. The plan was for him to meet up with Kaser at the lakeside resort on Utoquai.

The double row of chestnut trees that lined the road along the lakeshore was bare and as wet as the dark leaves that covered the ground all around. Warm lights shone out from the cafés in the winter gardens of the grand old hotels onto the promenade. Sarrazin had assumed that the bathing area would be closed at this time of year, but the gate leading to the small walkway was unlocked, and an old man who was sweeping the boardwalk directed him to where he would be able to find Professor Kaser. The wooden structure with its wide overhanging roofs and small towers at the corners was completely deserted, and the crevices and edges of the wooden planks were dark with damp and cold. Past the changing cabins, Sarrazin found the gate that opened onto a small bathing platform with ladders leading down into the water. On a bench near the steps going down, there lay a large white towel, and as Sarrazin walked toward it, he saw someone swimming in the otherwise almost completely placid lake—doing the crawl. The man was coming in his direction and pulling a noticeable wake behind him. The lake was so calm that day, it looked like a length of heavy fabric had been laid over it. Sarrazin didn't feel the slightest urge to come in contact with the water. He recalled one quite unpleasant occasion when he'd ventured into Lake Lugano too early in the year.

To avoid being splashed, he waited at a cautious distance from the wooden ladder until Anton Kaser had climbed all the way out of the water and wrapped himself in the white towel. His skin was dark, in some places almost blue, and he appeared to have rubbed himself with grease before his swim. Drops of water formed beads on his forehead. No, he didn't mind the cold, he told Sarrazin, and suggested that since he had to be back at the college in a short time, they simply have their conversation there. Sarrazin thanked Kaser for taking the time to see him at all. He explained that he was there because of some photographs. Kaser nodded as he used the corner of the terrycloth towel to dry between his toes.

"Your specialty is in geometrics and photogrammetry, isn't it?"

Kaser nodded again, and Sarrazin took this as an invitation to tell him in greater detail why he was there. He described the case as hinging entirely on the crime-scene photographs and the question of whether they could legitimately be used to demonstrate Arbogast's guilt, since they were the only basis for Maul's testimony. Kaser nodded.

"Our problem is this: We've already made one appeal to reopen the case, based on the argument that the photographs were insufficient evidence to serve as the sole basis for the indictment. Unfortunately, although the court acknowledged our superior technical ability with regard to the photographs themselves, when it came to who was better able to interpret the content of the photographs, the court recognized the superior authority of the forensic pathologist, Professor Maul. Lovely phrase that, isn't it? *Superior authority*."

Professor Kaser nodded again. "Here at the technical college," he said slowly, "we have developed a device for photographic analysis that is capable of far greater resolution than the human eye. It can greatly improve the ability of a human researcher to identify photographic details and brings a new level of objectivity to the analysis."

"You mean that it minimizes the chances of drawing a false conclusion from a piece of photographic evidence?"

"That is exactly why we built the Halifax M-Four."

Now it was Fritz Sarrazin who nodded. "Aren't you freezing?" he asked.

"No, I'm really not. Strange, isn't it?"

While Anton Kaser continued to dry his feet, Sarrazin nodded again and looked quietly and with satisfaction out over the lake, whose surface now appeared to him as blank and smooth as a piece of wet soap.

36

Just as Ilse was about to disappear silently into her room, as she so often did after dinner these days, the pathologist briskly pulled on her boots and coat and announced that she was going out to visit Professor Weimann.

"Oh, going to see your criminal, are you?"

Katja nodded, smiling. Ilse had known Weimann since she was a baby, and she had always called him that. In fact, he had been on the greater Berlin homicide squad from the twenties through to the end of the war, and he enjoyed telling people about it. After the war, he had been the student of, and then later the first assistant to, the privy councillor Fritz Strassmann. He had maintained an expansive collection of photographs dating from his time working on the police force, and when the institute's entire collection was lost during the war, his own was preserved and became the basis for the new photo archive that Katja Lavans had helped him develop when she was his student. Professor Strassmann had been dead for years now, and Weimann himself was long since retired. She left her apartment on Leiblstrasse and took the S-Bahn past Ostkreuz to Frankfurter Allee. From there, she walked in the direction of Bersarinstrasse. It was February, and the dry, frigid Berlin air seemed to pulsate through the wide, empty streets. Short, painfully icy gusts of wind numbed her nose, cheeks and forehead.

Professor Weimann lived in a prewar building on the corner of Matternstrasse. Now that his wife had died, Lavans wasn't invited to dinner quite as often anymore, and when she did visit him, bearing cake and ground coffee, she always dreaded seeing how much her old teacher had deteriorated. She rang the bell, waited a long time without an answer, and she was just about to leave a note on the small pad that hung from a nail on the jamb when he finally opened the door. He was clearly delighted to see her, ushered her inside and led her into the living room.

It was dreadfully cold in the hallway—he was apparently keeping just the one room heated—but even from the doorway of the living room, you could feel the hot air blasting from the floor-to-ceiling stove with its shiny dark green tiles. Weimann took a wineglass from a shelf, set it down next to his own on the low coffee table, and poured Katja Lavans a glass of red wine.

"And to what do I owe the pleasure of your visit, my dear colleague?"

Weimann was fairly drunk and looked it, sitting there in his jogging outfit. It wasn't the first time that Katja Lavans had been surprised by the fact that she didn't care—his drinking didn't affect her affection for him in the least. But she did know that with him in this state, she ought to come straight to the point. She glanced furtively around the room, thinking she saw increasing signs of neglect.

"Strangulation," she said.

"Strangulation," he repeated with a slur and raised his glass to hers in a toast. At the moment their glasses clinked, she realized what it was she wanted to know.

"What's it like? How does it feel?"

"Strangulation! Well, there are countless reports of the effects of strangulation and hanging. Most of them come from condemned men who somehow survived, suicides whose ropes broke and a few people who have experimented on themselves. The descriptions rarely mention pain; it's much more a loss of all sensation or even a feeling of pleasure accompanied by a sense of well-being, free-flowing thought and then, of course, the well-known experience of having one's life flash before one's eyes."

"Yes, but what exactly is happening at this point?"

"Yes, what exactly is happening?" Weimann chuckled and tugged on his nose. "Do you know Langreuters's experiments? You'll find this interesting. Langreuters investigated the closing of the airway during strangulation in the following manner: After the resection of the cranium and brain of a cadaver, he exposed the pharynx from inside the base of the skull, and then, in a dark room, using the light from a laryngoscope, he was able to get a sense of what happens during the various phases of strangulation."

"And?"

"First off, the position of the weapon—be it cord, garotte or the hand of the killer—is decisive. But basically, the compression of the carotid artery is the primary event. The interruption of breathing caused by the compression of the trachea is not essential. Often, the base of the tongue is pressed upward and obstructs the nasopharynx. Some more wine, my dear colleague?"

Katja Lavans was surprised to discover that she had drained her glass. She nodded.

"How does one recognize a death by strangulation?"

"But Dr. Lavans, the garotte always leaves a mark. That's second-semester stuff. Are you making fun of me?"

She was not. But she wanted to make sure—absolutely sure—she was not overlooking anything. And so she thought back to the second semester. "Where the tool of strangulation cuts most deeply, abrasion of the skin can be seen, initially as an area of light brown discoloration, then a darker patch of dried skin. The indentation caused by strangulation encircles the neck and is generally of an even depth all around. If skin folds are compressed during the act, local hemorrhaging or even bleeding may occur."

"Precisely. And Katja, please don't forget that such bleeding is almost always a sign that the strangulation took place prior to death and is thus extremely important in any criminal investigation."

Weimann busied himself with refilling their glasses, taking care not to spill the wine. Katja looked around the room again, and this time she noticed two empty bottles bulging out from behind the brocade curtains. No wonder it had taken him so long to answer the door.

"Furthermore," he said, "in cases of strangulation, the venous flow of blood away from the head is interrupted, while at the same time the arteries continue to bring blood in, resulting in an easily detectable congestion of blood in the head. The characteristic signs include tiny spots of hemorrhaging in the soft tissues of the eye sockets, under the lids and around the eyes, as well as on the cheeks and sometimes the forehead, the outer ears and the scalp."

"And on autopsy?"

"You tell me, Katja."

The way they addressed each other had changed dramatically when his wife died—it had become more familiar, but it hadn't gotten to the point of inappropriateness, yet. She looked at him, and when she tried to meet his rather shaky but well-intentioned gaze, she still saw the affection of the teacher well pleased with his student—that's what he had always been to her. She cleared her throat, and for a moment she felt as if she were still a doctoral candidate, about to stand for one of his exams.

"First of all, on autopsy of the soft tissues of the throat, one finds hemorrhaging at every layer of the musculature. Depending on the precise location of the stranglehold, there may be lesions on the structures of the pharynx, particularly at the thyroid and cricoid cartilage, but in order to make a clear determination of violent assault, it is necessary to resect the soft tissues of the throat layer by layer."

"Exactly!" he said, interrupting her, and raised his glass so suddenly that she feared he would spill his wine. "But what is the most important thing? What's the one thing one must never forget?"

She shrugged. His glass still hovered dangerously near her shirt.

"I don't know."

"You don't know, Frau Doctor?" He shook his head, apparently greatly disappointed, though this delayed his next sip by only a moment. Then he carefully placed the glass on the table before him and smiled at her. "You don't know? Then I'll tell you: The one thing you must never forget is that in cases of suffocation, the blood is still free-flowing and uncoagulated after death. Thus the autopsy of the neck must be conducted in a bloodless field. Do you hear? The drainage of the vessels is essential! You start with the dissection of the head, then go on to the chest and the peritoneum. Only once you have guaranteed that blood cannot flow into the throat area, either from above or below, do you resect the soft tissues, and only if you follow that protocol can you make an unbiased determination of hemorrhaging in the soft tissues of the throat. Otherwise, the uncoagulated blood can create a situation where it is impossible to distinguish pre- and postmortem artifacts."

Katja leaned back into the green velvet of the wide sofa and smiled. She hadn't actually seen the autopsy report yet, but now she had hope that there was a hole in it. Then she thought of the dictum that the simplest solution is always the right one.

"Professor Weimann, is it conceivable that even a gentle embrace of the neck could be fatal?"

"Oh yes. Under certain circumstances, even a very light throttling can cause sudden death; if the stranglehold stimulates the vagus nerve or the carotid sinus intensely enough, it could lead to asphyxiation and cardiac arrest. One often hears about this phenomenon, the Hering reflex, in criminal trials—usually when the perpetrator's trying to get himself off the hook. But in my experience, it happens only very rarely."

"So it's not a likely scenario?"

"Extremely unlikely. I'd never place my bet on that as a cause of death."

He dismissed even the remotest possibility with a swift flick of his left hand. Then he noticed the wine bottle was empty. It took him a few moments to absorb that fact, and Katja Lavans sat contemplating the issue at hand until he finally interrupted her thoughts.

"On the other hand, as I'm sure you're aware, it's clear that suffocation and arousal are quite closely related."

Katja wasn't quite sure what Weimann was getting at, and she shook her head.

"You're not familiar with the phenomenon of the agonal erection?"

Katja didn't move a muscle.

"Some doctor or other wrote about it after a dozen black men were hanged on Martinique. Just a moment . . . I'm sure I have the book here somewhere. Hang on. I've got to read it to you."

Weimann rose from his place beside the fire. For a moment, she thought it might be a good idea to accompany him, to make sure he didn't fall down, but he made it quite ably to the door and went out into the hall to look for the book. She could hear him go into the kitchen first and then came the sound of bottles clinking against one another, and she was somewhat reassured about his state. Clever, she thought, standing up herself and noticing that she was both tired and a little depressed, as was common for her whenever she'd spent a long time discussing death and dying. It wasn't that death had a direct effect on her—the many ways in which a person could die were too much a part of her daily work for that. But time and again, she'd felt that a coating of sorrow had somehow settled down on her unnoticed, like a fine layer of dust. It would take no more than a single thorough cleaning to clear her mood of this taint, she knew, but sometimes—especially when she was tired, like now—she was overwhelmed by the feeling that the sadness was never-ending.

She realized she was pacing back and forth on the carpet, taking enormous steps, staring at her toes, and she went over to the window, where there was a door to the balcony. In the overheated room, water vapor had condensed on the glass and dripped down into the swollen black wooden door frame, warping it. She tugged hard until it opened, then stepped outside. The balcony was on the corner of the building, overlooking the intersection of Besarinstrasse and Frankfurter Allee, and it seemed to her, standing there at the railing, that the whole city lay before her, glittering and twinkling under the brown haze of coal smog that eerily reflected its lights. Professor Weimann cleared his throat behind her.

"I found it. Listen to this."

Weimann stood beside the tiled coal stove and poured both of them more wine from a fresh bottle, holding the book in his other hand. She took in his bushy white sideburns and the tiny red and blue veins on his droopy white old man's cheeks as if for the first time; the long roots of his lower incisors were yellow from a lifetime of smoking. There was his prodigious belly bulging out from beneath the too-small warm-up jacket with its light blue arms and dark blue front, a pattern of stripes running across the chest. There were the droopy seat of his pants and his old leather slippers.

"Listen to this," he said again, and peered at her over his glasses—the same look with which he'd first won her over, just as lively and excited as ever.

" 'I proceeded to the place of execution,' writes Guyon, an army doctor on the island of Martinique, 'and saw that all of the condemned men immediately developed powerful erections at the moment of suffocation. (The men, Negroes, were all clothed in a thin white woven fabric.) Shortly thereafter, five of them urinated, and the fluid spilled on the ground. An hour after the execution, I went to the dock where the bodies of the men had been taken and found that the first nine were still in a state of half erection and that their urethras overflowed with a fluid that had wet their shirts and could only have come from the prostate. Of the last five, only two showed signs of having ejaculated.' "

37

Katja Lavans caught the last train back home. She slipped quietly into the kitchen so as not to wake Ilse. In the small built-in cabinet under the window, she found a bottle of the same wine, Blaustengler, that she'd been drinking with Weimann. She sighed and resigned herself to her fate. She had cause to celebrate. On the trip home, she had suddenly thought of *The Washing Away of Wrongs* again, in particular the section that described the distinctions between injuries sustained during life and postmortem ones. Another ancient Chinese secret, she thought.

She opened the front door of the gas stove she used both to cook on and to heat the kitchen and carefully closed the door to the kitchen, though her daughter's bedroom was all the way at the end of the long, narrow hallway—too far for her to hear her. Then she reached up to the top shelf of the kitchen cupboard, where she also kept the electric coffeepot, carefully pulled down the theremin and set it on the table. All day, she hadn't been able to stop thinking of Ansgar Klein and what he'd said about the burning, radiant energy that Arbogast wore like a second skin, thanks to his imprisonment. "I can't imagine what he would be like outside that prison cell, which he carries with him always," he'd said, and Katja Lavans had to confess to herself that she was slightly afraid of this innocent murderer. Nevertheless, once she'd plugged in the instrument and poured herself a glass of wine, she turned off the lights.

Immediately, everything in the room glowed blue in the light of the gas oven. She had spent many winter evenings in this light, and ever since she'd lived there, the quiet hissing of the stove had been the sound of warmth for her. Arbogast had been in prison for nearly fifteen years and locked away inside him was a death that seemed to have had no cause. Quietly and immovably, death left people behind. The crime was just a puzzle to be solved. I myself am invulnerable, thought Katja Lavans. She gamely raised her glass to *The Washing Away of Wrongs* before she began to play the theremin. She had still never met anyone else who played it, nor even heard anyone play, so she had no idea if she had any skill. Someone had told her that there was an old woman in Leningrad who was a theremin virtuoso and had even made records, but Katja hadn't been able to find any of them. The instrument was as lonely as the sound it produced, and perhaps it was precisely that sensation of isolation which Katja so enjoyed when she turned it on and moved her hands up and down the bars.

But at least her hands weren't alone. When she played a long time, it would begin to seem like they were something separate from her. She watched as her left hand carefully approached the antenna and slightly decreased the volume of the sound, then sharpened it, while her right hand raised and then lowered the pitch by pulling away from the second rod. Her left hand approached the first rod again, nearly extinguishing the sound, then brought it back, pulsating and demanding, then hesitating, in a duet of volume and tone. It was a game with no end, and one that Katja often used to pass the time. But she rarely succeeded in achieving her goal: the creation of a sound that seemed natural, a sound one might hear not as a voice but just a tone, without a body, without a face, something that couldn't die and wouldn't stare back at her.

38

"Bernhard? Are you there?"

Katja Lavans knocked and then, without waiting for a response, cautiously opened the office door of her former university classmate. His office was on the eighteenth floor of Charité. This was the compromise they had reached. He had asked her many times to call first before coming over, but she always forgot, and whenever she needed advice, she marched directly across the street and went to see him. She imagined that being very quiet would somehow make up for the interruptions.

"What are you doing here? It's Saturday," she said, though in fact she was relieved to find him in.

"And how's your daughter doing?" he asked, throwing the reproach back at her and pushing his dictation equipment to the side.

She noticed that the machine was a brand that came from the West. His question, laden with irony, brought to mind his two children, now seven and four years old. After her divorce, Katja had often sought refuge at Bernhard and his wife's place, something the two of them had been kind enough to refer to as "baby-sitting." It had taken her more than a year to find a way to reconstruct her life around that empty space. Now she perched on the edge of Bernhard's large, exceptionally neat desk and laid her file on his leather-edged Bayer desk blotter almost as gingerly as she had knocked before entering.

"Will you help me with something?"

Bernhard grinned.

She wouldn't have bothered him if she hadn't known that he really did like it when she brought him a new criminal case to divert himself with. Their friendship had remained close since they'd finished their studies, and now that he was married, it seemed his habit of falling miserably in love with her once annually had been broken, for the time being at least.

"It's about that expert witness who testified solely on the basis of photographic evidence."

"Professor Maul from Münster?"

She nodded. "This file is the autopsy report."

"Yes?"

"They want me to testify at the retrial. Please tell me right now what she really died of—so they'll let me go to the West?"

"Right now?" Bernhard grinned.

"Right now."

Bernhard opened up the autopsy report on Marie Gurth. As he read, and then thought about what he'd read, his smile faded. A couple of minutes later, when he began to speak, his voice was serious.

"The microscopic examination reveals that the patient had sustained tissue damage from a previous case of myocarditis and was suffering from acute myocarditis when she died."

"Yes," said Katja. "That must have weakened her already poor physical condition. Not to mention that she was pregnant."

"With regressive changes to the chorion," added Bernhard, without looking up.

"Right. Which is why they initially thought she'd had an abortion."

Bernhard set the autopsy report back down on the desk. "So what did she actually die of?"

"That's the thing—according to the autopsy, nothing." Katja flipped through the file and then read aloud: " 'Autopsy findings have revealed no naturally occurring illness that could explain Mrs. Gurth's death. Nor are the injuries discovered on Mrs. Gurth's body in any way serious enough to have caused her sudden death. The findings do at least enable us to rule out the possibility of death by violent strangulation.' "

"How is it that your man got convicted on this one?"

"Because a forensics expert insisted in his testimony before the court that she *had* been strangled."

"In direct contradiction of the autopsy report? That's absurd. I've never heard of such a thing."

"The witness was Professor Maul, and the autopsy was conducted by a young resident. That's one thing. And then there's the fact that the report does indicate signs of struggle as well as signs of, shall we say, intense arousal."

Bernhard looked at her inquiringly.

"The court spent considerable time on the question of whether Arbogast had anal sex with the dead woman. The autopsy report goes into it, as well."

"Interesting. So did he?"

Katja shrugged.

"Were there traces of sperm?"

"No, none."

"Circulatory collapse sounds like a reasonable hypothesis to me. So what can I do to help you with this?"

"Are you familiar with a book called *Hsi Yuan Lu—The Washing Away of Wrongs?*"

Bernhard looked at her uncomprehendingly.

"Professor Maul's strangulation theory is based entirely on the supposition that contusions on the neck are necessarily a sign of strangulation, because they and the underlying hemorrhage could only have been made while the victim was alive and her blood was flowing. My question to you is whether such marks could in fact also have been made postmortem and how I would prove that."

"The woman's body was moved, wasn't it?"

"Yes. And there's a passage in the autopsy report that might shed some light on it: 'No explanation has been found for the numerous small contusions and abrasions that were found in diverse locations all over the deceased's body.' "

"If you knew how she was moved, you could design an experiment to demonstrate what effects such handling would have had on the body postmortem."

"That's just what I was getting to, Bernhard. Do you think such an experiment would be recognized by the courts?"

"I would think so, definitely."

"Even in the West?"

He nodded, smiling. "I'll have to remember to tell you what you can bring me back from over there."

Katja nodded at that and left him to his work.

39

On Saturdays, there was usually no one around at the institute except whoever was on call to do the intake on new cadavers. It was quiet when Katja returned from the Charité building across the way, and as the old door swung shut behind her, the only sound was that of the humming refrigeration unit. She wouldn't have been there, either, if the pathologist on call hadn't rung her up to say that the body of a young woman had come into the morgue that morning. As she passed through the rear courtyard, she stopped and picked up two bricks from a pile of rubble beneath a stunted birch tree, then took the old freight elevator down to the Chamber. As always, the condensation from the refrigerators was plinking on the tiles somewhere, but when the fluorescent lights with their blue hum flickered on, the dripping sound seemed quieter. Katja Lavans washed the bricks in a large basin and left them there. She pulled on gloves and a mask and looked for that day's date on the bank of refrigerator drawers. She tugged on one and the gurney rolled out. She looked again and pulled out another drawer. Next, she opened the bag containing the corpse of the young woman that had just come in.

She hadn't even been dead ten hours and was still in rigor mortis. According to the tag on her foot, she was in her early forties, but to Katja Lavans, she seemed ageless and lovely. Perhaps it was because there was normally no time for her to simply look at the cadaver before she began the autopsy. *Just this once, let me not care what she died of,* she thought, and stroked the woman's short blond hair. Her face was undamaged. *She has beautiful shoulders,* thought Katja, pulling down the body bag and gently turning the cadaver on its side. Then she went over to the washbasin, wet down a white cloth towel, took one of the bricks and went back over to the body. With one hand, she lifted up the dead woman's head and carefully placed the brick beneath it, then covered the brick with the damp cloth, as if she wanted to soften the pillow. She placed the brick under the woman's neck in such a way that the edge would press against the same place where Marie Gurth's neck was marked with what Professor Maul had identified as a sign of strangulation. Carefully, she lowered the head.

The second cadaver seemed to be that of a girl, despite her age—twenty-three. She was gaunt and had dark hair. Her eyebrows grew almost together and she wore no makeup. She had died of gas inhalation five days before. Katja Lavans turned her onto her side, as well. But this time, she laid the brick under the dead woman's neck without any padding between. Then she went over to her desk at the far side of the room and sat down to wait. She would take the first pictures in three hours' time—thirteen-by-eighteens in black and white, and a set of six-by-sixes in color, too. Then another set in twelve hours. As she swiveled around on her office chair, it occurred to her that the way the two women were lying, facing each other, they seemed deeply sunken in sleep and yet somehow also aware of each other's nearness.

40

This year, too, the snow in the four courtyards melted, it grew warmer, and finally it was daylight when the wake-up bell rang at 6:30. Arbogast didn't even know if he was awake as he dressed himself with the same motions as always, washed, waited for the hole in his door to open and for his cup of malt coffee and his bread to be handed through. Then eat, sweep, leave the cell, stand muster, onward. Time had been good to him lately, and he knew all its names now. The noise of people trampling down the metal walkways was distinct from the sound of footsteps going up the narrow circular stairs, the hollow echo through the tunnel that led to the workshop building and the scuffling along the cement floor of the stairwell that led to the mat workshop on the fourth floor. The days he spent in the din of the enormous loom that wove the sisal and coco mats all had the same name; he couldn't tell them apart from one another anymore. It was sometime later that he realized he couldn't remember the names and faces of people either. He'd known them all a long time now, and people said hello to him; he talked to the other inmates, the prison workers and the guards every day, but then immediately he would forget their names. At some point in the spring of 1968, he read or heard on the radio about a plague of locusts that was making its way across northern Africa, devouring the plantations and cotton fields. It had started in Masquat, in the sheikdom of Oman, and it reminded him of a similar plague of the same kind of locust that had eaten thousands of tons of oranges and caused millions of dollars' worth of damage in the Sous Valley of Morocco in 1954, just before his imprisonment.

At 11:45, Arbogast returned to his cell, and shortly thereafter the food cart went down the walkway from cell to cell. When the window in his door opened, Arbogast held out his bowl. The prison worker handed him his mail and told him he had a visitor.

On his return trip, after doling out the lunch, the guard took Arbogast with him to the central tower, where they had to wait briefly in front of the block foreman's office. In passing, Arbogast glanced into the office and looked at the board with the cards that indicated which cells were occupied by which prisoners. He saw his own card: number 312. It was always there, in the same place, though the names on the other cards changed constantly. He was still trying to remember all the other names when the young assistant guard led him off to the visitors' room. Following the guard, it seemed to Arbogast that he suddenly saw all the worn, tattered cards swirling up in a storm around him, like a cartoon tornado, and there were the names of all the inmates written on the cards in fountain pen or ballpoint, blue or black or even dark green, by all the many block foremen and all the workers assigned to the various floors and wings, all the guards, lieutenant guards and captains, and all of them were flying and whirling around one single card—the one with his name on it—which was stuck in the center, apparently immovable, in that wooden board with its thirty-four slots for each of the thirty-four prisoners on the second floor of Wing Four of the New Bruchsal Men's Penitentiary.

Ansgar Klein looked up from the file he was reading and nodded at Arbogast, smiling. He hadn't seen him in a long time and he'd been anxious about this moment. As he had feared, it seemed his client had slipped even further into that distant world of the prison cell. Klein saw it clearly in the prisoner's gaze. Arbogast stepped forward a bit unsteadily. The dizzying vision, of which Klein had no idea, hadn't quite let go of him yet. The guard closed the door behind him and Arbogast sat down.

"I'm here because of a new application we're filing for a retrial, Mr. Arbogast," said Klein. "It's finally gotten to the point where we have something new to work with, and I want to tell you how we plan to proceed."

Klein pushed a copy of a lengthy document across the table. Arbogast had his hands in his lap, and without taking up the papers, he tilted his head to one side and read the date—June 24, 1968. His eyes picked up stray phrases the way one overhears a conversation at a neighboring table. "Petition for New Trial Submitted by Dr. Ansgar Klein, Frankfurt am Main," read Hans Arbogast, and something about "substantial new evidence in accordance with paragraph 359 of the Penal Code."

"This petition is based primarily on the various postmortem hemorrhages, Mr. Arbogast, and it attempts to introduce new facts."

Ansgar Klein spoke very intently and emphatically to his client, who was clearly having some difficulty extracting himself from his own private world. Klein had told Sarrazin two years before that he didn't think Arbogast could survive imprisonment much longer. He was now painfully aware of how Arbogast's gaze continually drifted away and how the man couldn't manage to overcome the slumped posture that seemed to be the norm for him now.

"What does *postmortem* mean?" asked Arbogast quietly, without looking at his lawyer.

"I'll get to that in just a moment."

Arbogast nodded and Klein went on: "As I said in a letter to you some time ago, it's been essential for us to secure new witnesses, as prominent as possible. I believe we've now done that. And most importantly, we've convinced a doctor named Katja Lavans, from Humbolt University in East Berlin, to testify."

"From the Soviet zone?" asked Arbogast with surprise, and looked at him with interest for the first time.

"Yes. Katja Lavans is a highly respected pathologist. You have a copy of her deposition here and can take a look at it later. Basically, Dr. Lavans makes a plausible case that Professor Maul's testimony proceeded from a false presupposition—namely, that the body had not been disturbed since the time of death. Do you understand?"

Arbogast nodded and looked intently at Klein, his interest now aroused. "You mean that Marie might not have been injured until after she was dead?"

"That's exactly what I meant by *postmortem*," said Klein. "Dr. Lavans has conducted experiments demonstrating that even several hours after death, the exertion of force on a dead body can cause bruising."

Arbogast nodded.

"The body was moved a number of times, and Dr. Lavans has proven that all the bruises and contusions could have occurred postmortem. Which fully exonerates you, Mr. Arbogast."

"I understand," mumbled Arbogast.

"And then we have another deposition—from Professor Anton Kaser from the technical college in Zurich," said Klein. Arbogast looked at him inquiringly. "That's the Confederate Technical College, the most famous university in Switzerland, Mr. Arbogast."

"So what does the Swiss professor have to say?"

"Kaser thinks Maul's testimony is appalling, considering that the photos of Marie Gurth's body show no evidence whatsoever that she was strangled with either a garrote or anything else resembling a rope. Furthermore, Dr. Kaser is the inventor of a special device for photographic analysis, which will be used to evaluate our pictures."

Arbogast nodded, but Ansgar Klein got the impression that his client saw the facts of the case as something very far removed from himself. The lawyer almost felt uncomfortable that he had to trouble him with them. He continued on, speaking more quickly.

"We also have a deposition from Max Wyss, the chief of the Forensic Science Service for the Zurich Police Department, who has been able to rule out with a great deal of certainty the possibility that Mrs. Gurth was strangled with either a cord or a wire. Finally, we have written testimony from Dr. Otto Mahlke, formerly of the Federal Office of Criminal Investigation in Wiesbaden. Dr. Mahlke comes to the same conclusion as Wyss. You ought to remember Dr. Mahlke from the first trial. He was there then, too."

Arbogast thought about it and then shook his head. Though he still appeared removed from everything the lawyer said, his gaze was alert and focused now. Ansgar Klein took a moment and searched for the right thing to say to give him hope.

"It's going to work out!" he said at last, and smiled lamely.

After all that time? Arbogast didn't respond. Nor did he say much when the lawyer asked him how he was doing. His days were the same as always. Except that when he got back to his cell, peace eluded him. He paced back and forth between the walls for hours, touching the plaster as he went, as if he was searching for a particular spot on the wall intended for some special purpose. He hummed and kept his eyes closed. Finally, he pressed his forehead against the cool plaster and scratched a pattern into it with his thumbnail. A small square and then another one beside it, barely a fingernail in width. He just kept scratching squares into the plaster until he completely forgot the passage of time, the same way he forgot the melody that he was humming over and over. Only when the little trapdoor opened and he had to pass his dishes through did he return to himself. He ate his food with a guilty conscience, as if he'd just been caught doing something forbidden.

Afterward, he took out the file and began to read the deposition of the doctor from East Berlin. One of his thumbs hurt. It was bleeding at the cuticle, and he sucked the wound as he read and licked the fine, sour-tasting plaster dust from his fingers. "Numerous experts who were involved in the trial or have subsequently become involved in the case have rightly suggested the possibility that this death was the result of sudden heart failure. Indeed, incidents of sudden death during sexual intercourse are not as rare as the layman may think." It seemed to him that Katja Lavans's statements revealed more about his own past than he could himself. All that was missing from her account was the moment of silence which still burned within him. It was the common thread that had linked every night of all the years ever since. It seemed the pathologist hadn't been able to imagine that one moment. He would have liked to know what she looked like, what sort of life she led. He couldn't imagine that there was now a wall dividing Berlin in two. Has she ever seen a picture of me? he wondered.

Summer came quickly. After work, from three to four-thirty, they went to the yard. The doors were unlocked and they lined up rank and file in front of their cells. The guard marched down the line and counted them off.

"Cells three hundred to three fifteen, march!"

The walkways rumbled as they went off through the tower and finally passed out the narrow doorway into the courtyard, where they were counted once again. The yard was a triangle of brick, with two sides formed by Wing Three and Wing Four and the base by the outer wall. On the wall were the machine guns. There were five guards in the middle of the yard. The men walked around in a circle, side by side. For years now, Arbogast's partner had been a small man with a walrus mustache, who told the same stories over and over again about growing up on his parents' farm. Arbogast had no idea why he'd been put with him or even what the man, whose name was Heinrich, was in for. Arbogast watched the other men trade cigarettes. He'd given up smoking himself. The old man from the cell next to Arbogast's cackled and let Arbogast go first when they came to the narrow tower doorway. He had been in prison for five years now for an assault and battery that had ended in the victim's death. They were counted again. At five o'clock, they were locked back in their cells.

The teacher had been coming to visit Arbogast in his cell periodically since Arbogast began correspondence courses in business. He would stop by with the study materials for the next section and stay to talk with him for a while. Arbogast closed his eyes. Late that night, he had the feeling his stomach was churning with razor blades that were slicing him to bits. This kept up for a couple of days, during which he ate nothing, and then one day in early September, he fell ill at work, and the foreman sent him to see the doctor.

Dr. Endres told him to lie on the table and palpated his belly. In the years since Arbogast's first medical exam at the prison, the chief doctor's features had only grown harder. It was as if Dr. Endres was bitterly waiting for something and had decided that he wouldn't move a muscle until it happened. The men gossiped about all the prison employees, told stories, but no one ever talked about the doctor. It looked like gastritis, the doctor said, and his assistant wrote the diagnosis down in Arbogast's file. An orderly took him back to his cell and dumped his bedclothes into a large sack while he stood waiting, then led him up to the infirmary in the tower. On the ground level, there was the reception desk, as well as a holding cell, the laundry room, the examination room and the dental clinic; upstairs, there were four infirmary rooms, two large ones with eight beds each and two smaller ones with four beds each, as well as the nurses' station, a small kitchenette and the bathroom. Arbogast stayed there ten days and afterward, for the rest of the fall, he was put on a special diet.

Dr. Endres had prescribed drops for his stomach, as needed, but the pains returned only infrequently. In early December, Arbogast read in the paper that a woman had slapped Chancellor Kiesinger and screamed at him, "*Nazi! Nazi!*" He carefully gathered up the work sheets for his correspondence course and stacked them in a neat pile on the shelf. Then he moved his stool over to the window, climbed up on it and looked out at the little bit of street, wall and sky that his view allowed. Joy crumbled in the silence, couldn't withstand it. Nor could time, thought Arbogast. Ansgar Klein had submitted his second petition to have the case retried back in the spring, and now the year was ending without anything having happened. Fear is easier to bear when it comes slowly. Once, while Arbogast was standing on his stool, getting his fill of the world outside, the door of his cell opened and Father Karges came in.

"You know, Arbogast," said the priest before the cell door was locked behind him, "from out there, your cell is just a window in Wing Four of the prison, nothing more. How long have you been here? Fifteen years? Which means that this is pretty much your entire world, is it not?"

He had a small bag in his hand, which he swung back and forth. As he did every year, Karges was distributing the gifts that the local people had put together for the prisoners.

"It says WING FOUR on the side of the wall, and your window is labeled 312. But of course you've seen that when you're exercising in the yard."

Hans Arbogast climbed down off his stool and sat on the edge of the bed because he didn't want the priest to sit there himself. He accepted the dark red bag, which was decorated with pictures of stars and candles, and opened it, although the rules said he should wait until the following day. Two apples, a pair of socks, five cigarettes, and a bar of chocolate. Karges pulled the stool up to the table and sat down. He leaned forward and peered at Arbogast.

"Are you really still innocent, Arbogast?"

Hans Arbogast bit into an apple and nodded. He was only just barely able to hide the effort required for him to withstand the priest's gaze. But he managed it. On Christmas Eve, there would be stollen and tea with rum, like every year. It was the only time they got alcohol in the entire year, if you didn't count the home brew some of the men made, but he rarely drank that. And tomorrow, as always, there would be soup with dumplings, followed by schnitzel with spinach and mashed potatoes, and chocolate pudding and real coffee for dessert. Arbogast kept his mouth shut. After another minute, Karges rose and banged on the door to be let out.

"There's one other thing: As of 1969, the Penal Code reforms will go into effect. Your civil rights will be restored to you next year. So with that in mind, I wish you a Merry Christmas, Arbogast!"

41

All night long, the beams of the spotlights shone into his cell through the grid of bars and wire mesh on his window. They lit up the ceiling and chased off sleep—just the same way now, after all the years, as they had the first night he was there. Hans Arbogast had left the window open, and he lay there now, feeling the spring air waft down on him. He listened to the barking of the German shepherds going back and forth on their running lines. At first, he didn't want to think about Marie, and when she came into his mind nonetheless, he tried to send her away. Finally, with some difficulty, he kept her face at a distance and looked at it. For some time now, the pathologist's version of that night with Marie had begun to seem more familiar to him than his own memory of reality. How had the grass smelled at the end of that summer, and what had the air smelled of? Her perfume? But when he closed his eyes, he still imagined he could smell her sex on his fingers, and once again her voice resonated with the sound of her breath. Then, as if for the first time, he was overwhelmed by the moment of silence that followed and he remembered how the cool, smooth wood of the door panel had seemed to brush against his hand in support and encouragement. Back then, he had thought it was the angel that had seemed to follow them around everywhere that day and had shown itself in the glowing sign at the restaurant. There was no doubt that that was when it all began.

Sometimes he imagined how he would look standing beside her today, with her not having aged at all. How his hands, the hands of an adult, would hold her, this woman who was still and always would be twenty-five. But since he could barely convince himself that so many women were now younger than he was, this thought didn't really hold him back, and he let himself fall into her arms. It was strange to love someone who was dead, but even more so to be dead oneself. For that was how he thought of himself: with only the walls of his cell to clothe him, dead skin upon his numb, motionless flesh. Some of the men said it was the food they were served, but he didn't believe that. It was because of time, and the stillness of it, like that night to which he returned again and again. In her silent face, which seemed to understand all about it, he saw the tenderness of her touch. He recognized her voice instantly. At first, it was a whisper, then quiet singing—he could almost make out the words. He knew what she was singing even so, of course, and waited with a smile on his lips for the words, so close against his ear. *You found me once, now come back and take me with you.*

The following morning, he was summoned from the mat workshop to take a phone call in the central office. The guard who came for him didn't know what it was about. He shrugged, took Arbogast by the shoulder and pushed him through the iron-barred gate in the cellar, which led into the central building, then let him make his own way up the winding stairway to the office.

In Frankfurt, Ansgar Klein waited for his client to come to the phone. The lawyer was extremely excited and paced back and forth in front of his desk, tugging on the telephone cord as if it were a toy. Finally, after three years, the moment had come. He rocked back and forth on his tiptoes and closed his eyes. When he heard the rustling sound of the receiver being picked up, he broke out in a smile.

"Hans Arbogast."

For a moment, the lawyer couldn't find his voice. "The retrial," Klein said at last and cleared his throat. "We have been granted a new trial. I've just received the decision from the Grangat District Superior Court."

Arbogast said nothing.

"This is Ansgar Klein calling from Frankfurt. Do you understand what I just said? Mr. Arbogast?"

Arbogast nodded. His mind was blank.

"Mr. Arbogast, can you hear me?"

"Yes," said Arbogast without intonation, and nodded again. And after another moment had passed, he added, "Thank you, Mr. Klein."

"You don't have to thank me, Arbogast. Do you know what this means?"

Hans Arbogast shook his head and looked around at the office, which he had been in only a very few times over the years. On the wall between the windows there was a bird's-eye-view watercolor of the Bruchsal prison framed behind glass. Arbogast knew the man who had painted it. The warden's secretary looked at him with curiosity.

"Arbogast?" shouted Ansgar Klein into the telephone. "You're free, Arbogast! You can leave there at once. According to the provisions of paragraph three-sixty of the Penal Code, the court has suspended your sentence."

Arbogast lowered the receiver. He seemed to want to say something to the secretary.

"Should I come pick you up?" asked Klein as Arbogast raised the receiver back to his ear. He nodded, then handed the phone to the secretary.

The warden was summoned and everyone congratulated Arbogast. The next time he was able to think, he found himself sitting on his bed, looking around him. The cell was twelve feet long by eight feet wide, the ceiling nine feet high. It contained somewhat less than a thousand cubic feet of air. The ceiling was slightly uneven. The walls were painted light green up to shoulder height, then above that, white. The floor was tiled in black and white. The view from the bed was of the sink with the polished-metal mirror and shelf unit on the wall above and the milky light green plastic shower curtain that concealed the toilet. Gradually, over the years, the prison had replaced the tar-lined buckets with toilets and upgraded the folding beds and tables that had been bolted to the floor. Arbogast remembered just how he'd felt when the new furniture arrived—rather as if he had moved house—and how it had taken him a while to feel at home again. He looked at the window and blinked. It was exactly three feet square. Beneath it, against the same wall as the bed, was his locker. The table and stool were set against the long wall, and beside the door stood the tall, narrow cast-iron radiator. The narrow oaken door was reinforced with heavy metal crossbars. On the wall near the door were the light switch and a doorbell. The door had the spy hole and the small panel that could be opened only from the outside for passing in food.

Arbogast packed up his things and waited. So much was happening out there. The French President, de Gaulle, had just resigned. The Chinese and the Russians were shooting at one another across the Ussuri River. In Northern Ireland, Catholics and Protestants were killing one another. Another Starfighter had crashed—he'd seen the picture. Supposedly, Americans would soon be landing on the moon. The previous week, a spaceship with three astronauts aboard had orbited the Earth. They came to get him that evening and returned his civilian clothing and personal effects. He held the box in his hands. Three balls lay nestled in the blue velvet—one black, the other two of such a creamy whiteness that, looking at them, one could hardly help thinking of very pale skin.

42

It was late afternoon on April 30 when the report came over the wire-service ticker in the pressroom, saying that the Arbogast case was going to retrial. That night, after having spent fourteen years there, Hans Arbogast would be released from the Bruchsal Penitentiary. For a moment, Paul Mohr considered driving over there, then decided not to, but he did stay late at the office that night to watch the television coverage of Arbogast's release, which he'd learned was going to be broadcast on Channel 3. He had an array of archive materials spread out before him on the shiny mahogany tabletop in the conference room and needed to go through them, but even with the sound off on the television, he found himself unable to concentrate. Finally, he resigned himself to it and went over to the bar to pour himself a whiskey. He would just wait and see what happened.

Naturally, he was thinking about Gesine, and as a result, he very nearly missed the beginning of the report. But then the screen showed the gate of Bruchsal Penitentiary—as they had called it in the old days—and the sight startled him from his musings. He turned up the volume. ". . . television lights and the prison spotlights of the state penal facility in Bruchsal, where Hans Arbogast has just stepped out into freedom with a large suitcase in his hands." Presumably, the footage had been taken in haste, without sound, and the reporter was commenting from offscreen. "Here is Dr. Ansgar Klein, the Frankfurt lawyer who fought for the decision to reopen the case, picking up his client. For Hans Arbogast, this can be considered a birthday present delivered one day late—he turned forty-two on April twenty-ninth.

Overjoyed at having his freedom restored, he answered questions from a horde of reporters who turned out to see his release. When asked what he had missed most during his long incarceration, Arbogast answered, 'Justice.' But even so, he never gave up the hope of being released. Arbogast went on to say that he took correspondence courses in business while he was in prison, for which he paid six hundred marks, drawn from the wages he earned working in the prison's mat workshop."

The television screen still showed Arbogast and Klein standing in front of the prison door. Mohr was shocked to see him and wondered if he himself had aged that much. He remembered how young the accused man had seemed back then. Despite the late hour, the lawyer was carrying his light-colored jacket over his arm. It's spring, thought Paul Mohr, as if he'd needed the television images to tell him that. The journalists and onlookers seemed to disappear into the darkness on either side of the spotlights. Uneasily, he examined face after face in the crowd, and at one point he imagined that he recognized Gesine with her camera. "The first thing Arbogast did upon arriving at the hotel room Dr. Klein had reserved for him was order a cup of coffee and a steak. For the time being, he's not discussing his future plans. Arbogast's wife divorced him in 1961."

When the report was over, Paul Mohr turned off the television, poured himself another whiskey and got back to work. At that same moment, in Grangat, Hans Arbogast found himself alone again. He had set the billiard case on the bedside table. His suitcase, which contained his few personal effects, letters and, above all, the photos he'd collected over the years, was standing in the small entryway that led from the hotel room proper to the hall. Arbogast was standing at the window, holding the curtains slightly aside; he couldn't get enough of looking out. The room was at the front of the hotel, and his window had a view onto the street. For a while, Arbogast had watched the journalists putting away their cameras and taking down the lights, and slowly the echoes of their voices faded away in his head. Now he was watching a lone pedestrian walk past, and he followed the man with his eyes until he disappeared from view. He was unaccustomed to wearing a shirt with a collar and found that it chafed him. He undid the top button. When he tried to concentrate on his thoughts, he couldn't do it. He sat on the bed and stroked the cool black Bakelite of the telephone receiver. This time, he resisted the temptation to pick it up. He'd already done it three times, though, and had had to apologize to the person who answered at the front desk.

"Oh, sorry. Yes, it was a mistake. Good-bye. No, really, it was nothing."

It was just knowing that there was someone out there. That he himself was allowed to leave. Arbogast let himself sink into the soft down comforter and inhaled the fresh scent of clean linen.

43

"Klein just called!" Fritz was smiling. "Arbogast has gone to bed."

Sue looked at him, waiting for more.

"He's staying at the Palm Garden Hotel, and the two of them had dinner together. Klein was telling me that Arbogast watched every bite he took with fascination—it's been so long since he saw another person eat. But he didn't say much, and then he wanted to be by himself. Klein took him up to his room, and apparently Arbogast unlocked the door very carefully, then locked it again equally carefully from within."

Sue was lying in bed, reading, with two pillows propped up behind her back. Now she put her book aside. "I'm so glad it finally worked out."

"Well, nothing's decided yet. The trial's only just about to begin. But I'd say it looks good."

Sarrazin had been reading in his study when the telephone rang. He was wearing, as he often did, a white burnoose with gold trim that he'd bought in Tangiers.

"Do you remember the time we were having breakfast and I told you about Bruchsal?"

Sue nodded. It was growing cooler out. A short time later, she was undoing a row of seemingly countless little mother-of-pearl buttons while he peered out into the night, breathing in the pungent odor of wet larch needles that pervaded the spring air.

"Is Klein going to come for a visit, to celebrate?"

"I don't think so," said Sarrazin. "At least we haven't discussed it."

Her hand darted beneath the white cotton fabric and across his stomach.

"That's too bad."

44

Hans Arbogast rang the bell and waited. He looked down at the flower beds with their profusion of yellow blossoms growing against the house on either side of the stoop. The address was Lupinenweg 4, and it was a narrow street of one-and-a-half-story row houses standing behind low brick walls. He rang again and switched his suitcase from his left hand to his right. Both these things—the suitcase and the address—had been given to him by Ansgar Klein. Everything had been arranged, including the time he was to arrive. He grew uneasy as he sensed that there was no movement coming from within the house and he rang again. Above him, small, very white spring clouds were whipping across the sky. The blueness behind them still hurt his eyes. Gusts of wind shrieked along the ridge of the roof. He rang again and switched the suitcase back to his other hand. Only when he finally heard footsteps on the stairs did he venture to place one foot on the top step. He heard the key turn in the lock of the white door and then he saw his sister's face. He stood on the small stoop in the front yard; she stood on the narrow stair that led to the upper level. They just stood there, balanced against each other, almost artistically, in a way that precluded any sort of more elaborate greeting. Then at last, instead of stepping up to hug her, Arbogast extended his hand. Elke shook it and invited him inside. They proceeded up the creaky stairs a quarter turn to a doorway on the first floor and passed through into the small hall. It was almost square and had four doors that opened onto it. Elke, his younger sister, who had grown up so much, turned back to look at him.

"Well, Hans, welcome!"

Now she smiled, and they very nearly embraced. The last time they'd seen each other was six years before, at their mother's funeral. Elke was still single. With a flick of her ring finger, she pushed a strand of hair out of her face. He didn't want to think about why she'd never visited him, not even once during his pretrial imprisonment in Grangat. She had never responded to the letters he wrote her early on. Since the divorce and the death of his mother, she was the only remaining family he had. He realized that he was afraid she might hate him.

"Kitchen, bathroom, bedroom, living room!"

Elke gestured around her and then opened the door to the larger of the apartment's rooms. It had a second door leading out onto the small balcony and was furnished with a sofa and matching coffee table, a living room cabinet, and two green velour cocktail chairs with spindly legs. The cabinet was from the Salmon, as were the picture hanging on the wall above the sofa—a landscape—and the tablecloth. There was no television in sight.

"This will be your bedroom."

He nodded awkwardly. "Wonderful. And thank you very much."

"But of course. There was no question about it. Would you like a coffee?"

He nodded again. They drank coffee from the service that he remembered from his childhood, and later, when it grew dark, she brought in glasses and beer. They didn't speak much, but after a while she asked what it had been like in prison. But first, she said, while he was still thinking about how to answer her, she wanted to hear about his night at the Palm Garden. He nodded. The Palm Garden was the best hotel in Grangat, and when they were children, they had sometimes dared to venture into it as far as the lobby. He told her how the steak had tasted and about the feel of the fresh bedclothes and the strangeness of being able to open the door whenever he wanted. She leaned forward, crossing her arms over her knees, just the way she had always listened when he was telling her a story. Later, she made sandwiches and opened a jar of pickles. When she laughed, it made him want to look at her closely—he saw both their childhoods so vividly in that laughter. Later, she opened up the cabinet to reveal the small lighted bar, and they poured themselves cognacs. Elke told him about their mother's death. He nodded and eventually got back around to telling her about the prison and what his daily routine there was like. He attempted to describe the existence he'd led in the cell. She leaned back in her chair.

"So what was the worst thing about it?"

He looked at her. For a while, he said nothing, but finally he dared to ask her the question that had been on his mind the whole day: "Do you really hate me?"

Elke shook her head. She searched for the right words. Eventually, she said quietly, "Your car's doing well."

"The Isabella?"

"Yes. I left it in the care of a farmer after the Salmon was sold."

"That's unbelievable! I was sure it had been sold off years ago. I'll go take a look at it first thing tomorrow!"

Elke laughed. Then she turned serious. A tall, narrow standing lamp gave off a weak light through its shade of rough beige fabric, all covered with knots and loose threads.

"Just so you know, Hans—you're my brother. That's why I didn't send you away. But it's true that I'm not sure what to think of you."

He looked at her intently.

She went on after some hesitation. "Back then, I could hardly believe what everyone was saying and what was written in the newspapers, what you were supposed to have done. I couldn't imagine it. Katrin was with us a lot then, and she told us about visiting you in jail, and then came the trial. You're right about that, you know: I did hate you then. I thought you had destroyed all our lives."

"And now?"

"Now I don't know what to believe."

"That's the way I feel—that was the worst thing for me, too, all those years in the can."

His sister looked at him, waiting for him to go on.

"Not knowing what's real."

Elke nodded. After a while, she told him she had to be at work early the next morning, and he didn't ask about her job. The two brought the dishes into the kitchen together, and she made up his bed on the sofa and gave him a leather wallet containing the keys to the main door and to her apartment. She wished him good night from the doorway of his room, and he waited until he heard her come out of the bathroom and close her bedroom door before going to the toilet. Afterward, he opened up the door to the balcony and poured himself another cognac. The liquid didn't quite have the strangeness of the Dujardin he'd drunk yesterday at the hotel, but still the alcohol flooded his mouth with a taste that seemed to want to drown him, and he gasped briefly for air. It seemed to him that he'd been dancing without cease ever since he'd left the prison and his lawyer had driven him to Grangat, and even if he wanted to, he couldn't have done any differently. I come from a world with a different gravity, he thought. The race for the moon was on. In a movie, he'd seen a backpack-style personal rocket thruster that enabled its wearer to take yard-high strides. He noticed how awfully quiet it was there along the Murg River. This was a place where the people who worked in the city came to sleep. It wasn't very far from Schutterwälderstrasse, the street where he'd grown up and where the Salmon had been. Nor from the railway overpass where he'd met Marie. Tomorrow, he decided, he would go back there, and then he poured himself another cognac.

He was amused at himself for having expected that Elke would still be the twenty-something girl she had been back then. It wasn't just the new fashions that he found strange, the hideous wide lapels of the jackets, the men's long sideburns, the women's short hair and pantsuits. He didn't like the look of all the new houses with naked cement facades that he'd seen on the drive through Grangat. It even seemed to him that people now held their cigarettes differently when they smoked, and there were moments in the interviews he'd given when the journalists had laughed in a manner that was utterly foreign to him. It was as if he didn't belong in his own time. He'd asked Elke if she remembered the time they ran away from home and wanted to go down to the Rhine by themselves, and she just shook her head, not remembering it all. His head was a cell. For him, that expedition had been unforgettable, he told her. He would never forget it.

Next to the couch was his suitcase, and in it, beside the new clothes that Klein had bought him, was the box containing the billiard balls. Without looking, he opened the latch by feel and took out one of the balls. The black one. He had asked Klein when the new trial would begin, and what he ought to do till then. Time was at a standstill, it seemed to him. The black ball was cool against his temple. If it hit him there harder, he'd be dead. He thought of the other two, sleeping in their bed of velvet, and imagined himself whipping the ball with his hand across the green felt of a Brunswick table and the way it would follow its seemingly limitless course, ricocheting from cushion to cushion, following the angles of incidence and reflection, until finally it slowed and stopped like a weary animal. Summer's coming, he thought, and wondered whether the reeds still stood as high as they once had beneath the black swarms of mosquitoes at the railroad overpass. The spring air was fresh and turning cooler, and eventually it washed away the cares of his day and carried Arbogast off to sleep.

45

Summer had passed and fall, too, when at last they got a letter from Ansgar Klein saying that the time had come. The Grangat lower district court had set the trial date for November 24, 1969. Katja Lavans had long since collected all the documents she would need, as well as the reports analyzing her research and the photos and slides. She had everything ready in various file folders to present to the travel office and the assistant dean of the medical faculty. She had applied to the travel office for permission to go to Grangat to testify as an expert witness in the Arbogast case. The request had been quickly approved, with the proviso that she report to the office no later than ten days prior to her date of departure to take care of the remaining formalities. The travel office of Humboldt University was located in two small rooms on an upper story of the main building; looking out past the employees at their desks, she had a view of the clear winter's day outside and a corner of the opera building.

Katja could see the revulsion of the university administrators when they saw the photos of the cadavers—that shudder in the face of death with which she was so familiar but which she hardly experienced herself any longer. She knew the name of every one of the dead bodies she'd used for her experiments in the past months, knew their life stories precisely and, in most cases, thanks to her investigations, knew more about the pain they had suffered and the particularities of their lives than did their own relatives. She firmly believed that each of the corpses had somehow granted her its personal consent to be included in her work. She was also aware that people could sense this connection she had to the dead and that it gave her a certain power over the sort of people who wrongly imagined that death could be bargained with. The older of the two officials pushed her materials away from him onto a narrow plastic-laminated table. Sunlight streamed in through the window at a sharp angle and reflected off the table's surface, producing an unpleasant glare. The man cleared his throat and nodded at Katja.

Then he began to tell her how she was to behave on her trip to the Federal Republic. She would be a representative of her country and, above all, of the superior scientific stature of Humboldt University, which had been acknowledged by the very request for her to come serve as a witness at a West German trial. Katja nodded. She was to be exceedingly cautious in her dealings with the press and to speak only on the topic of her professional expertise. She was not to engage in any sort of comparison of the two systems of government. Katja was not exactly sure what he meant by that, and she was about to inquire further, when the other man, who had remained silent till that point, interrupted the conversation. He was young and very thin, with sharp-angled cheekbones and a prominent Adam's apple protruding from above the collar of his shirt, which was buttoned to the top but so loose on him that it gaped open around his neck.

"Upon your return," he said quietly, "you will prepare in sextuplicate a detailed report describing your journey and turn it in to the president of your college and the other appropriate governmental authorities."

He nodded at her and smiled.

"Which by no means implies any inability on our part to keep track of all that you do while you're abroad in nonsocialist countries."

Katja nodded back at him. "I understand."

After a somewhat threatening silence, the assistant dean once again took control of the conversation, telling her how proud the faculty was of her work. Finally, Katja shook hands all around and took her leave.

The D-218 was scheduled to depart from the Friedrichstrasse station at 11:05 a.m. on Friday, November 21. They had reported Ilse sick at school and she, Mrs. Krawein and Bernhard all went along to the border-control area at the station, which was known as the Tränenpalast—the Palace of Tears—to see Katja off. She savored every detail of the priceless feeling of passing through border control, suitcase in her hand, then following the maze of barrier walls, mirrors and neon lights and coming out onto the nearly empty platform and boarding the train that would take her through no-man's-land. She would certainly return to that memory later. She found the empty compartment where she had reserved a seat, then stood at the window, looking out while the train crept slowly through the city like a wary animal in unfamiliar surroundings—and then it simply crossed the border, just like that. It had been nearly ten years since she'd been in West Berlin, and she was almost surprised to find that everything looked familiar. Shortly before the train pulled into the Zoo Station, she took her seat, smoothed out her beige wool suit and pulled the hem of the skirt down to her knee. Apparently, the heating had only just been switched on, and with the warmth, the stale smell of old cigarette smoke spread itself through the compartment and across the nubby dark green imitation leather of the seats. The lid of the brass ashtray rattled in time with the vibrations of the train until the train finally ground to a halt. Katja Lavans lit a cigarette. She looked out at the facade of the federal court building and down the extension of Hardenbergstrasse. She heard loud voices approaching along the corridor and watched a group of kids go past. One of them was carrying a seabag tucked under his arm and had hair down to his shoulders. Another wore black horn-rims and a suede shirt. From the next compartment down, or the one after that, she heard laughter. No one joined her in her compartment. At 11:28, the train pulled out of the Zoo Station.

For a moment, on that winter morning, Katja Lavans had a view into the open edges of the residential neighborhood of Charlottenburg, onto the balconies that lay in shadow even at midday and seemed near enough to reach out and touch—they were just as grimy as the railway track. She peered into the depths of rooms in the grand old buildings, saw antique chests of drawers and round tables gleaming with polish, so black they trapped all light. Then the tracks took the train out of the city toward the southwest and along the road called the Avus to the train station at Wannsee. Katja Lavans didn't hear anyone get on or off the train—the stop was really just a hesitation before Griebnitzsee, the transit station from which the train would reenter the East. There, they stopped for a long time. Outside the window, right up against the side of the train, there was a waist-high cement wall. There were spotlights mounted on poles all along the wall, as well as megaphones that constantly repeated the following announcement: "Embarkation and disembarkation are strictly forbidden!" The pathologist pulled the seam of her skirt back down over her knees and sat very still. The train groaned forward and then back again repeatedly. She could hear people outside, walking up and down the cars. Metal clanked against metal, and when she looked out, she saw uniformed men inspecting the undercarriage of the train with large mirrors. Then she heard footsteps inside the train car, coming up the corridor, the opening of the compartment doors and dogs.

Katja Lavans sat at the window, facing forward. Her suitcase was on the rack above her. The border-control guard touched his cap with his right index finger in greeting and then silently let his hand fall and hang open in front of her. Her passport and the papers she'd received from the travel office were in her handbag, which lay on the seat beside her. Her passport contained the requisite visa. She handed the pass to the soldier. Behind him, two others passed by, and a wet, panting German shepherd stopped briefly beside the soldier's legs, looked at her and sniffed before he was dragged on by his lead. The soldier wished her a pleasant journey and smiled. She smiled back, and he saluted once again and closed the door to her compartment behind him. It began to rain lightly.

At first, it was just a thin drizzle, but when the train began to pick up speed, the rain slithered in thick snakes across the window. It would take the train over five hours to reach the border at Gerstungen station. It stopped frequently along open stretches of rail, then started up again; at other times, it clattered along the track at a pace no faster than a walk, and she knew that soon she would feel a thunderous rush and a high-speed train would bear down upon them, as if in ambush, then roar past, a deafening intrusion in the quiet landscape. Then it would be still again. Once, she saw a power station far off on the horizon, and she looked down empty roads whose paving stones buckled like the skeletal backbones of half-buried animals and were flanked on either side by rows of barren trees. But mostly what she saw out the window were just endless wet black fields, and eventually night fell over them. Katja Lavans didn't go to the dining car. She had some bread, an apple and a Thermos of tea in her suitcase. It had grown quite warm in her compartment, and when the train stopped, she could hear the ticking sound of the steel as it slowly returned to some inner equilibrium.

The train arrived in Gerstungen at 5:34 p.m. and didn't leave the station again till 5:54. Passport control moved forward slowly, car by car. Katja closed her eyes and waited till the door to her compartment was thrown open. This time, she had to open her suitcase. They changed engines there, then did it again when they got to Bebra, back to an electric one, arriving in Fulda at 7:08 p.m. Despite the darkness, Katja could sense that the landscape grew hilly, then flat again. They passed Hanau and finally arrived in Frankfurt at 8:20, only slightly late. Katja had pulled on her gray wool coat and gone to wait at the door of the train car as soon as the tracks crossed over the Main. She hadn't realized the train would take such a wide swing through the city before reaching the station, which reminded her of the one in Leipzig. Ansgar Klein was waiting for her on the platform, as promised.

He said hello, took her suitcase and escorted her through the north exit to the parking lot. He started up his car—a white Mercedes, she noticed—and asked, "Where to?"

"What do you mean?"

"Where would you like me to take you? What hotel are you staying at?"

"You didn't get a room for me?"

Ansgar Klein turned the ignition key back off and looked at her, at first with astonishment and then contrition.

"Oh God. I hope you will forgive me—I completely forgot."

"Can you tell me how I was supposed to do that from East Berlin?"

"Of course you're right. I'm terribly sorry." He thought for a moment. "What about this? You can stay with me tonight."

"I don't think so."

"Why not? I have an extra bed, and I can make us some dinner. We've got the hotel set up for all of next week in Grangat. Would that be all right?"

Katja nodded and leaned back in the red leather seat. Since his divorce, Klein had been living in a small apartment in a postwar building in Frankfurt's West End. It was nestled between two five-story apartment houses from the nineteenth century, having been put up to fill a hole left by bombing during the war. His place had a large window looking out onto the street, and there were two connected, open rooms with white textured wallpaper and light parquet floors, all of which made it seem spacious and bright. Klein opened up a bottle of French wine, a red, and disappeared into the kitchen for a moment. He returned with a platter decked with pumpernickel and Gouda, cornichons, caviar and salt sticks. In his other hand, he carried two heavy crystal glasses. Then he took a record from the shelf and put it on the record player. He carefully cleaned the vinyl with a small brush and wiped dust from the needle under a small red light before setting it down in the groove.

Katja Lavans sat on the sofa and waited with some suspense. The sound of a big band filled the room, then applause, then silence. Next the strings started back up, quietly, and there was the hesitant tinkling of the piano. "Here's a song that was the favorite song of a great friend of mine," said a woman with a husky voice, and then she began to sing.

"Do you like it?"

"Who is it?"

"Marlene Dietrich at her last concert, five years ago in London."

Katja Lavans nodded.

Soon enough, they were deep in conversation about the case, describing the results of their work to each other. The pile of pictures and diagrams on the glass coffee table mounted, and once again she silently watched another person attempt to come to terms with those images. She showed him the slides she planned to present at trial, and while he was engrossed in them, she had the chance to take a closer look at him. He picked up the images and moved them around with his fine-boned hands, repeatedly tugging on his white cuffs, so the small amber cuff links peeked out from the sleeves of his jacket. Then he would reach up and rub his hand over the gray stubble on the crown of his head and slide it down to the top of his high forehead. He didn't look at her, and she liked that. He had thin lips. In the meantime, she had gotten up and now was sitting on the dark blue carpet, with her back leaning against the sofa. She observed Klein the same way she'd observed so many others in her efforts to come to an understanding of death, though the dead would not reveal their secrets.

"Please don't take this the wrong way, Dr. Lavans, but somehow it looks like they were all just staying with you—and as if they felt quite at home there."

Katja Lavans laughed. She wasn't the least bit offended. And then, when she began to explain how she'd conducted her experiments, she got the feeling that he really did want to hear the stories her corpses had begun to tell, as they did if only one gave them the chance. Eventually, Klein was able to convince Katja Lavans to take his bed for the night—she didn't protest much—for of course there really wasn't a guest bed after all, just the sofa in the living room.

46

In the morning, she got up and went out. Before they headed to Grangat, she absolutely had to get hold of several things she'd promised to take back to Bernhard. When she stepped outside, she was pleased to see that it wasn't raining—she'd forgotten her umbrella in Berlin. At that early hour on a Saturday morning, the streets were nearly deserted in the quiet neighborhood of Frankfurt's West End, but the nearer she got to downtown, the more shops she discovered. With the help of Bernhard and his glossy magazines, she'd made up a shopping list. She had actually planned to go to one of the large department stores, but along the way, she came upon a small boutique that was just opening up for the day. There she found some clothes that were made of a synthetic fabric that flowed across her fingers like silk and was still cool to the touch from the night before. After trying a couple of things on quickly, she decided on a close-cut dress that fell just above her knees. The fabric was light green. As she went to pay for it, she saw in the glass counter that they also carried lingerie of the same lightweight synthetic material, and she decided she had to try on some of that, too. She went into the changing room, where there was a poster of a London bus and numerous models standing in front of it in colorful raincoats, and the salesgirl handed her brassieres and panties. Next, Katja looked for a shoe store and found one that had almost exactly the pair of boots she had imagined for herself: short white vinyl, with zippers at the instep. She inquired at the shoe store about where she could find a perfume shop and was directed to what was clearly a very well established shop in a building whose entire ground level was done in highly polished black tile and brass-rimmed show windows. A white neon sign over the window said PARFUMERIE MAJAN in cursive, and beside it in blue and gold was the emblem for the original 4711 brand of cologne.

Katja Lavans set her shopping bags full of shoes and clothes down by the counter. She was looking for liquid foundation. The blasé salesgirl left Katja alone with a couple of samples and a mirror that she could move around on a telescoping arm. Every day, Katja looked into the faces of strangers far more closely than she ever did into her own. With her pinkie finger, she smoothed away one of the crow's-feet beneath her left eye. Her daughter was twelve now, and in two weeks Katja would be forty-one. She rubbed the makeup carefully onto her cheekbones. This is fabulous, she thought. Much better than powder. As she waved over the salesgirl to ring her up, she looked around the store once more and noticed for the first time the Styrofoam mannequin heads: They were supposed to be women, but really they were just the bewigged heads of girls stuck onto long swan necks.

She stroked one of the wigs and discovered that the hair was just as real as the hair she combed and pushed out of the way and shaved off her body every day. She'd read something in one of Bernhard's magazines about how totally modern it was to wear wigs these days—a woman who wore a wig was always having a good hair day.

"Could I try this one on?" Katja pointed to a wig with long red hair, and the salesgirl came out from behind the counter. She took a comb and used it to pull Katja's hair back tightly, then, without saying a word, slipped a large elastic band over Katja's head, around the hairline. It felt a little tight at first, but then once the wig had been settled on top of it, it contributed to the extremely pleasant feeling of being in costume. She hadn't particularly noticed anyone unusual on the train yesterday or this morning, but she knew someone would be keeping an eye on her during the trial. She smiled, imagining how confused her minder would be when he realized how different she suddenly looked. She liked the feel of flicking a stranger's hair from her face, but then when the salesgirl handed her a mirror, she was startled. Marie's hair was red, thought Katja, staring. She couldn't tear herself away from her own reflection.

"Would you like the wig, too, then?" asked the salesgirl after a while.

Katja Lavans nodded.

Ansgar Klein woke up beside his alarm clock, which he'd set on the coffee table the night before, and found a note from Katja saying that she had gone out to get some things but would be back on time and that she would get breakfast while she was out. He packed his suitcase and was just gathering up the files and papers that he'd brought home from the office the day before when the doorbell rang. It was an elevator building, and Klein had to wait for both the inner and outer doors to open to see who it was. It wasn't so much that he felt he was looking at a stranger, at first—rather more that he seemed to be experiencing an absence. The woman who stepped toward him from the elevator looked very much like Katja Lavans, yet she seemed most definitely to be someone else.

"Would it be possible for you to lend me some cash, Mr. Klein?"

"Yes, of course. But what for?"

"For the wig. Or didn't you notice it?"

"On the contrary, of course I did. It's fabulous."

Katja Lavans had long red hair, parted in the middle. Ansgar Klein closed the apartment door behind them.

"May I ask—just out of curiosity—don't you have any money?"

The woman, who apparently was Katja Lavans—although she now also wore a short green dress she hadn't had on the day before—stood in front of him and scrutinized him.

"Do you really want to know?"

"Yes, if you don't mind."

"Very well: I'm allowed to exchange fifteen marks a day, at a rate of one deutschmark to one East German mark. I'm required to declare the foreign currency I receive for my services as an expert witness when I reenter the East, at which point I must also deposit it with the authorities. Two-thirds will go directly into my bank account, and the remainder will be placed in a foreign-exchange account. Is that clear?"

"Sounds pretty complicated."

"It is. Eventually, I can apply for those funds to be made available to me, and I'll receive the value of the West German marks in the form of Intershop vouchers, which can be used to buy Western goods."

"Oh God."

"Exactly. That's why I figured I'd do better by spending the money right here. And since I just blew my entire savings on the wig, I'd be grateful if I could borrow what I'll need from you in Grangat, just until I'm paid the honorarium."

"I'd be glad to do that."

As they talked, Katja got her things together and put them in her suitcase. Ansgar Klein remained standing in the hall, staring at her.

"Aren't we in a hurry?"

She took one of the file cases with Klein's materials for the trial so they could get everything down to the car in one trip. It wasn't till they were actually sitting in the car that he realized what he'd been wanting to say to her.

"So I take it that we now share a secret?"

Katja Lavans smiled. "I knew I could count on you."

He grinned and started up the car. As they drove off, he looked over at her, at the way she brushed the hair from her face. He was still grinning.

"Tell me about the wig."

"I absolutely had to have it. You can't get anything like this in the East, not in red anyway. But here, I found it at a salon, a specialty shop, practically right around the corner. It's real hair."

"Was it expensive?"

"Very—over four hundred marks. How long till Grangat?" she asked, noticing the way he kept turning to the side to look at her.

"About three hours."

Katja leaned forward slightly, pushed in the cigarette lighter and sat back to wait till the coils glowed hot enough to light the cigarette she held at the ready in her right hand.

"Ansgar really is quite an extravagant name, isn't it?"

"You think so?"

"I do."

"My father said he didn't want to give me a common name, a name that would be too obvious."

"What?"

"Because in the end, he would have to live with the fact that he'd given it to me."

Katja lit her cigarette and took a deep pull. She replaced the lighter in its socket and brushed her hair away from her face. Watching her from the corner of his eye, Ansgar Klein was amazed—it seemed to be a long-accustomed gesture. He could already imagine to himself that he'd never seen Katja Lavans with short hair at all. Sometime later, she asked him why he drove this particular type of car, and he started to talk about the tail fins on the Mercedes 300 series and to describe the power steering.

"Actually, I'm not all that interested in cars."

Ansgar Klein nodded, keeping his eyes on her as she brushed back her hair. At some point, the Kaiserstuhl came into sight, on the right, and then, on the left, the hills of the Black Forest. The trial's scheduled to start the day after tomorrow, thought Ansgar Klein. Just as he was about to point out to Katja Lavans that they would soon be entering Grangat, it started to rain, and he had to turn on the windshield wipers.

47

"To the Chief Editors of the *Frankfurter Allgemeine Zeitung*," began the letter that Dr. Heinrich Maul, the director of the Institute of Forensic Medicine at the University of Münster/Westphalia, had typed at midday on November 25, 1969, on his traveling typewriter.

> Dear Sirs,
>
> With reference to your article, "Arbogast Case Reopened," I would like to provide you with a copy of my deposition. I would ask you to base your opinions of this deposition on the enclosed document. As for the so-called integrity of Arbogast, which is mentioned in the article, I would direct your attention to a closer examination of the files. As far as I am aware, he did not have a clean record, indeed had multiple prior convictions that were relevant to the case in question.
>
> As a condition of releasing these papers to you, I request that you see to it that they are handled by an independent editor who is capable of understanding how things really transpired.

The chief pathologist had brought the letter and the envelope containing the document to which it referred to the reception desk. In his letter, he argued that it was a serious error to reopen the trial merely on the basis of the supposed expertise of Frau Dr. Lavans. He read it through one last time and signed it "Respectfully yours, Professor Maul." But then he hesitated before slipping the sheet of paper in with the rest of the package. He was familiar with the hotel from the first trial against Arbogast—indeed, he remembered that time quite fondly. It was only afterward, when the accusations began, that his memory of the two days he'd spent there had been spoiled, along with his sense of satisfaction at having affected the outcome of a trial with his testimony. As he understood all too well, he'd been at the pinnacle of his influence then. It was senseless to come back here now. He took the cap off his fountain pen and wrote, "P.S. During the trial, I can be reached at the Palm Garden Hotel in Grangat."

The place was very different now. It had been the best hotel on the square even before the war. Then, in the late fifties, it had been thoroughly renovated and now had gleaming polished granite in the entranceway and lobby. The ornate ironwork railings, the vases and the reception desk all matched, as did the pale pink damask wallpaper. The result was harmonious but rather chilly, an effect that was only reinforced by the entirely new dining room. Maul shook his head when he saw the light blue kidney-shaped recessed area that had been set into the ceiling to conceal the indirect lighting. The professor decided not to take his afternoon coffee there after all, considering the ever-increasing number of journalists and photographers whose luggage already threatened to overflow the lobby and perhaps the dining room, too. Of course, the *Spiegel* reports on the case were responsible for the fact that this retrial was going to be covered by the national, not just the local, news. And as Professor Maul well knew, the mood of the pretrial coverage was quite different this time around: There was the general expectation that a profound miscarriage of justice was about to be corrected. It seemed to him that the people coming and going in the lobby were already resolved on that account. He was aware of being openly snubbed.

It was as if someone had drawn a circle of invisibility around him, within which the sounds of strange voices and laughter echoed unpleasantly. Later, he would ask himself why he'd stood around in the reception area for so long, as if he had been waiting for something. Why hadn't he been long gone from the hotel before Ansgar Klein and Katja Lavans showed up in the doorway?

Immediately, flashbulbs started popping. The pictures that appeared in the papers the following day documented the awkward meeting, during which Ansgar Klein and Heinrich Maul had said hello and then the lawyer had introduced the pathologist. What wasn't visible in the pictures was the way Klein and Lavans had briefly been drawn into that zone of invisibility around Maul, or the fact that Katja Lavans had felt she was going to suffocate—that there was no air there. While Klein had exchanged pleasantries with Maul, she had barely been able to manage shaking the professor's hand. She saw very clearly how much he enjoyed her discomfort, but the smile that the photographers captured on Maul's lips at that moment would have been incomprehensible to anyone who hadn't experienced the peculiar atmosphere surrounding him.

48

" 'Grangat is a town of some twenty-four thousand inhabitants, situated in a wine-growing region in the foothills of the Black Forest, just on the edge of the fertile Rhine valley.' " Katja Lavans nodded and lit a cigarette while Ansgar Klein read on from his small mint green 1965 Baedeker. " 'The gateway to the central part of the Black Forest, it now functions as an important rail and highway nexus. The old free city of Grangat was founded by the Zähring family and was first mentioned in recorded text in 1173. The city flourished during the fifteenth and sixteenth centuries. In 1689, it was burnt almost entirely to the ground by the French. From 1701 to 1777, it fell under the control of the Margravate of Baden, after which it enjoyed a period of independence under the protection of the royal house of Austria until 1802, when it once again came into Baden's control. Grangat's major industries are tanning, spinning, weaving and enamel and glass making.' "

They were standing on Langenstrasse, just having come from the old District Superior Court, where Arbogast's first trial had been held. For the past five years, the elegant Baroque building with its enormous double doors had stood empty. The new one must be around here somewhere, Klein thought. It was growing dark and it was bitterly cold out, but instead of looking to the map in his travel guide to figure out where it was, Ansgar Klein read on. " 'The main thoroughfare and shopping street is Hauptstrasse, which runs from north to south. The old part of the city, south of the train station, is surrounded by attractive parks. On the market square, the Town Hall, completed in 1741 by Matthias Fuchs, is of particular note. On its north facade, a statue of Granos, the town's legendary founder, stands in a wall niche ornamented with volutes.' "

"I'm getting kind of hungry. Could we go get some dinner?"

"Yes, of course." Ansgar Klein looked up. "Let's go back."

"But I'd really rather not eat at the hotel."

"Maul?"

Katja Lavans nodded. "Let's find a little place around here. What does your guidebook say about where to eat?"

" 'Also noteworthy is the Neptune fountain by Nepomuk Speckert and the Unicorn Pharmacy, which has existed in this location since the beginning of the eighteenth century.' "

"Enough!" Katja dropped her cigarette and ground it out with her foot.

"There's the Silver Star at Hauptstrasse twenty-nine. That must be pretty close by."

Klein pointed down a small alley and they quickly emerged at the other end onto Hauptstrasse, which led onto the market square some blocks beyond. Just a few steps further found them standing in front of the Neptune fountain mentioned in the guide, and then they reached a large and cozy-looking restaurant, the Silver Star. Light shone from its many small windows. The dining room was furnished with simple wooden tables and a bench that ran all the way around the room, except where it was interrupted by the large green-tiled stove, whose heat could be felt pouring out, even from the doorway. There was dark wood paneling along the walls above the long bench. As usual, the place was busy, and they ended up sitting next to each other on the bench, since they couldn't find a chair that was free, much less a place to put one. The lawyer suggested that at least there was little danger of Professor Maul joining them there unexpectedly, and Katja Lavans smiled.

They drank a bottle of Klingelberger, an aromatic local Riesling, and both ordered bowls of Alsatian onion soup. Then Katja Lavans had the snails and Ansgar Klein a grilled ham and egg sandwich. The lawyer asked her about life in the East, and she told him about Ilse and her divorce, and then quickly moved on to the subject of the institute. He asked her whether she wasn't frightened by working with the cadavers and what it was like to examine them in search of a cause of death. She shrugged off the all-too-familiar question with a smile, took a drag off her cigarette and shook her head. But then she told him how much she had come to care about Marie Gurth, after all that time, and she asked him what he really thought of Hans Arbogast.

"How am I to understand that question?"

Katja Lavans laughed. "It's not a hostile question, Mr. Public Defender—it's really not a hostile question."

Klein could feel himself turning red. He often got himself into such embarrassing positions if he didn't watch what he said.

"I'm sorry." He tried to smile.

She gave him an amused smile and raised her glass to him.

"That's okay, but I'll still stick to my question: What kind of man is Arbogast?"

Ansgar Klein described some of his visits to Bruchsal and told her how he'd gotten the impression over the years that Hans Arbogast was losing touch with reality.

"This is all coming just in the nick of time, you see."

Katja Lavans nodded. "Has he changed physically? He looks so young in the pictures from the first trial."

"Everyone always said he was a handsome man."

"That's not what I mean."

"He hasn't changed all that much—he still looks quite youthful. But he moves incredibly slowly. You get the impression he's guarding against banging his head or his elbows against the walls and ceiling of his tiny cell."

Ansgar Klein didn't raise his eyes from the wineglass as he took the last swallow. The pathologist drained her glass, too. From the corner of his eye, he watched as she flicked the hair from her face with that gesture whose birth he had more or less witnessed.

"There were times, when I was doing my experiments and I had to lay the young women's heads down on those cold stones, that I just couldn't help but think about what it would be like—to be ripped away from a warm embrace by death. As if everything within one had just shattered. But actually, I'm not sure if it's so horrible. The literature contains accounts from patients who describe suffering intense pain but also report a sensation of complete relaxation. Everything opens up. Nothing has a purpose anymore and never will again, for once and all. Isn't that precisely what people are always hoping to find in love?"

Now Ansgar Klein was looking at her again. He had always managed to avoid thinking of love in any connection with Arbogast. He realized how absurd that was, and yet he felt compelled to follow his instinct. Katja Lavans brushed her hair out of her face once again.

"You know," he said slowly, with the dawning realization that he was about to say something he had never been able to acknowledge till that moment, "all these years, I've never been certain what happened that night. But unlike you, I've never really wanted to know. Do you know what I mean?"

Katja Lavans nodded but said nothing.

A short time afterward, they went back to the hotel. When he thought about it again, later that night, Klein wasn't sure if the pathologist had ever answered his question. The city had been completely quiet and the heavy, freezing fog had laid a thin sheet of ice on the sidewalk. It had crackled underfoot as they'd walked. This city was where Arbogast had lived. It almost seemed to Klein that the whole town was waiting for the trial to begin. He also thought it was about to start snowing. They crossed Schillerplatz and passed by the hospital.

The big glass doors of the hotel were already locked for the night, and they had to ring for the night porter, who took a long time to come out from the little room behind the reception desk. As the two of them stood there outside the door, waiting beside one another, he had the idea that they belonged together, and at just that moment, Katja turned to look at him and smiled. Then the porter let them in, and they followed him silently through the lobby to the desk and waited like a pair of lovers for him to give them their keys. The elevator was a Paternoster lift, which had a chain of continuously running open cars, and they took it up to the third floor, watching as the floors slid past the open cabin of their car. Katja Lavans stubbed out her cigarette in the brass ashtray affixed to the wall beneath the control panel. As the gray linoleum of the third floor moved from eye level toward their feet, it became clear to Klein that it had been jealousy that had made him speak of Arbogast that way to Katja Lavans. Their rooms were adjoining, and while he was still considering how they ought best to say good night, Katja Lavans raised her left hand, placed it at the back of his neck and kissed him. Without thinking, he closed his eyes and kissed her back. He didn't put his arms around her, but neither did he stop kissing her until at last her lips disengaged from his and began to speak. She was wishing him good night, her breath hot against his skin. That was when he first took her hand, and she let him have it for just a moment.

49

Ansgar Klein did not sleep especially well that night. Long before morning, he was lying awake, and he went down to the dining room very early. Through the picture windows, the fog was rising up from the park in the dawn light, and he was surprised to discover Fritz Sarrazin already seated at one of the rear tables in the otherwise deserted room, cracking open a soft-boiled egg. Sitting across from him was Hans Arbogast, with whom Klein had arranged to meet that morning. Arbogast jumped up to greet his lawyer. They had been in contact fairly frequently over the past months, but all three of the men saw this meeting as a kind of reward for their long efforts. Arbogast thanked both the lawyer and the writer repeatedly. Eventually, Sarrazin picked up the conversation that had been interrupted, asking Arbogast about Bruchsal and telling his own impressions upon visiting the penitentiary. The lawyer half-listened, staring out into the fog, which didn't seem to be lifting at all. In front of the window was an enormous rhododendron with scraggly branches that stretched down toward the ground and in some places scraped against the glass.

Sarrazin pushed a copy of an open magazine across the table. The familiar image of Marie Gurth lying naked in the blackberry thicket shone out of the darkness of the double-page spread. The headline read THE ARBOGAST CASE: ANALYSIS OF A MISTRIAL, and next to it was a thoughtful-looking portrait of Sarrazin, who was now grinning at him from across the table.

"Well, what do you think of it?"

"Fabulous. Did they print the entire text?"

"Exactly as we discussed it."

Klein began to read. " 'In all the long history of jury trials in Germany, the Arbogast case is unique. From the beginning, it should have been impossible for any objective observer to come to a guilty verdict.' " The waitress came by to take his drink order, and he closed the magazine and handed her an enameled tin teapot that he'd brought with him. Reluctantly, the waitress listened to him explain exactly how the tea must be prepared, and he was glad when she left and he didn't have to try to be polite any longer. Once he'd had the first cup of tea, he'd be able to talk to Arbogast, and then to spend much of the rest of the day with Sarrazin, going over their plan for the opening of the trial the following day. But just then he was still drifting between half sleep and a certain restless nervousness that gave way to wild heart palpitations when he spotted Katja Lavans out of the corner of his eye. She closed the door to the dining room behind her before coming over to them.

"It's a great pleasure to meet you in person at last, Mr. Arbogast."

Arbogast stood up and shook Katja Lavans's hand. Behind him, an impenetrable cloud of fog pressed against the windowpane. Ansgar Klein stood up, too, and introduced Fritz Sarrazin, who was sitting directly across from her. Klein noticed that she was wearing the same cream-colored wool dress she'd had on the day before. It seemed to him she wasn't paying him the least attention. They all sat back down, and he pushed the magazine to the side. On the marble window ledge were cacti, Christmas stars and a rubber plant that was sending out shoots in every direction. Sarrazin asked her how her trip from East Berlin had been and what kind of car she drove.

"I don't even have a driver's license."

Arbogast shook his head in disbelief and said one of the things he had most looked forward to the whole time he was in prison was being able to drive his car again.

"But does it still . . ." said Katja Lavans, and they all noticed how she hesitated before going on. "Does it still exist, that car?"

"Oh yes! It turned out it was sitting in a barn the whole time, well oiled and covered. Actually, it's not far from here."

"And what was it like, driving again?"

"You're really asking that? About *this* car?"

"I don't know much about cars."

"It's an Isabella."

"That's a pretty name." Katja Lavans laughed.

Fritz Sarrazin explained what a remarkable car it was, adding that he thought it was a pity that the maker, Borgward, had gone out of business. Arbogast couldn't stop staring at the pathologist. Ever since he'd read her deposition, he'd been trying to imagine what she looked like. But he'd never imagined that he'd get this whiff of that bygone time from her—a whiff of the time that had been locked up inside of him when they locked him away. The longer he looked at her, the more amazed he was. It was as if the secret of that time were contained in the very way she brushed her hair out of her eyes. He interrupted Sarrazin, who was describing what sort of car an Isabella was, in midsentence.

"I can show it to you, if you like."

"You mean right now?"

"Sure, why not?"

Ansgar Klein could see she was taken aback by the invitation, which he himself thought was rather tasteless. What was Arbogast thinking, suggesting such a thing? Katja hesitated, brushed the hair from her face. She was aware of the fear rising within her. His stare was so rigid. Sarrazin observed how closely the lawyer watched Katja Lavans during the ensuing moment of silence.

"Sure, why not?" she said at last, very slowly.

She looked around at the three men, smiling.

"After all, it's almost like I'm here on vacation. A person ought to be able to do as she pleases on a trip abroad, don't you think?"

50

Arbogast pushed the wide barn door open, letting the milky light of that foggy Sunday morning filter into the barn. The floor was paved with damp blackened bricks, and the air smelled musty. On the right, beneath what had once been the hayloft, which now appeared to be littered with all sorts of junk, one could make out the shape of a car draped in the old green canvas tarpaulin of a U.S. Army tent.

"Can I smoke in here?"

"No, but go ahead and do it anyway."

Arbogast walked over to her, hands jammed into the pockets of his short coat, and smiled. "Okay, are you ready?"

Katja Lavans nodded. It was cold. The car waited beneath the tarp like one of the bodies in her lab. The first thing she saw when Arbogast pulled the canvas away was the dark red door, then the sweeping curve of the door panel and the chrome trim at the roofline of the coupe, the whitewalls. The two headlights with their chrome covers peered out toward the door of the shed. Arbogast dragged the tarp over to the other side, and the pathologist approached the car. The interior was obscured by condensation on the inside of the glass. The body of the car was clean and completely free of dust. The paint shone and felt cold and smooth to the touch. She traced the chrome trim with her fingers, the Borgward logo in script on the front, the chrome wings on the mud flaps. She imagined the car moving under her control. She put one hand on the edge of the car's roof—it felt like muscle under skin—and laid the other on the door handle.

"May I?"

Hans Arbogast looked across the roof at her from the other side of the car and nodded. She opened the door. The air inside didn't smell strange at all. She sat in the passenger seat and carefully pulled the door closed behind her. This was where it had happened. Everything was cool to the touch: the upholstered seats, the metal trim, the black-and-white synthetic material that lined the doors. Even the silence was cold, and Katja Lavans was freezing. She imagined what it would feel like if Arbogast were to take her in his arms. She pressed herself into the seat cushion, held her breath. Had they listened to the radio? In the end, there had been a lifeless body lying on the narrow backseat. She hadn't been a large woman. Katja Lavans hadn't seen any fear in the photographs—you never saw the fear. She remembered placing the head of a young woman on a hard brick. It had been cold then, too. I guess the cold doesn't bother me, she thought. The cold skin of the woman lying on the brick. Nothing bothered her, either. The dead woman had been twenty-three years old, dark-haired and rather thin. She'd gassed herself. The other one was older. The two women had been like sleepers, sunken deep within themselves, each nevertheless aware of the nearness of the other. She wondered what it would be like to be strangled, and she was so lost in her own thoughts that she didn't even notice Hans Arbogast standing there beside the car, clearly uncertain about what he ought to do. Then he opened the driver's door and sat down beside Katja Lavans. Neither spoke.

But at one point, Katja Lavans opened up the ashtray, thinking to tap the ash of her cigarette into it, and she saw the butts—numerous long, yellowed filters of an unfamiliar brand, on which she thought she saw traces of bright red lipstick. Slowly, she pushed the ashtray closed again.

"Mr. Arbogast?"

Hans Arbogast turned to her.

"I'm not sure I understand why the car is still here, in the barn. I thought you had driven it again, since you were released."

Arbogast shook his head no.

"Not at all?"

"No."

"I see."

Katja Lavans nodded, leaned back in the seat and closed her eyes. And she held her cigarette between her thumb and forefinger for so long without taking a drag that eventually the ember at its tip died out on its own.

51

It began raining early the following day, November 24, and every time the train stopped at a station on the way from Freiburg to Grangat, Paul Mohr could hear the hard little drops being pelted against the glass by the gusting wind, each one thwacking distinctly, so that it sounded like a handful of shotgun pellets being poured onto a plate. And although by then it was really only a thin drizzle, it chilled him thoroughly as he made his way from the station to the court building. There was no time for him to go drop his bag off at the Silver Star, where he'd reserved a room for the expected two-week duration of the trial, so he took it with him, switching it from hand to hand as he walked. He thought back to the first trial, which had been held in the old District Superior Court building. The new building, a three-story box situated in a park on Moltkestrasse, contained various other city offices, in addition to the court. The crowd of journalists thronging the narrow cement walk that traversed the well-trodden lawn was even larger than he'd expected. There were numerous cameras set up on tripods in the wet dirt, their lenses focused on the entrance. Beside the doors, there was a slim steel sculpture depicting larger-than-life-size figures surrounded by bands of steel. He hadn't eaten any breakfast and he was cold.

"Paul?"

Paul Mohr wasn't surprised to hear her voice. He had, of course, hoped that he would bump into her here, but now, as he turned back to look at her, his heart was thumping. For a moment, it seemed to him that she looked exactly the same as she had fourteen years before. The journalist hesitated.

"Hello!" he said at last. "Hello, Gesine."

"It's nice that you came," she said quietly.

He took careful note of the signs of aging in her face and imagined that they matched the changes in his own features. They shook each other's hands for a long time. Paul Mohr was so happy to see her again that he found it almost painful to stand so close to her now. He couldn't understand why he'd never tried to get in touch with her. She was wearing a short black vinyl raincoat with wide lapels. The collar was turned up, and the coat was tightly cinched at the waist with a belt. She held her camera with its high-speed telephoto lens the same way she always had, with both hands, keeping it out in front of her body. He smiled, not knowing what else to do.

"God-awful weather."

"Yes."

"I'm staying at the Silver Star again," he said, not knowing why. But she nodded and smiled. Then they stood there silently again.

"So, do you want to go in together?" he asked at last.

"I can't."

"Why can't you?"

"I'm being called as a witness on Tuesday, and witnesses are forbidden from watching the trial prior to their testimony."

"What do they want from you?"

"I think it's about the pictures."

"Oh yes, of course, I see. So maybe we could see each other later?"

"Why don't you come by my place when they finish up for the day."

"I'd love to. Is the shop still where it used to be?"

She laughed. "Yes."

Paul nodded at Gesine, who was still holding her camera firmly in both hands, and the nod became a silent gesture of parting before he pressed forward into the throng of journalists and then into the court building. Gesine stood in place, took a few pictures and waited until Ansgar Klein's white Mercedes pulled up to the parking space reserved for him, a few minutes later. Arbogast and his lawyer stepped out, and all the cameras immediately trained their lenses on them and began shooting. Klein stepped around to the trunk of the car amid a swarm of reporters with popping flashbulbs and microphones. With his black robe over his arm, he took out a stack of files, some of which Arbogast helped him to carry. Then they went into the court together, and those of the onlookers who'd been able to reserve one of the few free seats in Hearing Room II of the Grangat District Superior Court followed them inside.

The eighty seats of the rosewood-paneled courtroom were completely filled by members of the public and representatives of the press, as was the vestibule that opened onto the courtroom. The judge permitted television and still photographers to shoot up until the point when the jurors were sworn in. People entered the room through a side door at the back of the spectators' gallery, and a court officer led Arbogast and Klein forward to the defense table on the left side of the courtroom, directly beneath the band of high windows, through which daylight shone into the room. At the head of the room was the raised judges' bench, and on the right, across from the defense, the prosecution table. Behind that was a podium for additional judges and alternate jurors, who would be called, if necessary, to stand in for any of the regular members of the court. Behind the bench was a large clock face, just a circle delineated by twelve shining brass squares and the hour and minute hands. On either side of the bench were the doors that led to the judge's chambers. Through the high windows, Arbogast could see the bare branches of a row of poplar trees, but when he sat down, they disappeared from view. He was wearing a dark blue suit with a white shirt and a brilliant red tie.

It was 9:30. Although he strove to appear calm, Hans Arbogast was agitated. He hadn't slept well, and he was barely able to endure the quiet manner in which Klein was arranging the files in front on him. Then the lawyer pulled a silver Thermos out of his bag, unscrewed the lid and poured the light brew of tea into the silver lid, which also served as a cup. At the table across from them, two district attorneys had taken their places and were spreading out their files, just like Klein. Sitting in the first row of the gallery, almost within speaking distance, sat Fritz Sarrazin, who smiled and nodded at Arbogast. He was wearing a beige linen suit with a black shirt and a red bow tie, and the whole outfit looked pretty out of place there in Grangat—and not just on account of the weather. Beside the author sat Katja Lavans, the pathologist from East Berlin. Arbogast looked at her in her wool dress with wide shoulder straps and a grass green shirt with a pointy collar beneath it, and she looked back. Slowly, she brushed the hair from her face and nodded at him. Surprised, he looked away and continued glancing around the room.

He thought he recognized some of the journalists. Again and again, he heard his name being called, and when he looked up, flashbulbs popped. Once, when he'd turned around and was still half-blinded by the glare, he saw Father Karges in the halo of white light, sitting off to the side of the room. Arbogast was horrified. The priest noticed that he saw him and nodded at him with a thin smile, as if he were wishing him well. But just then, Arbogast saw that a man was removing a cardboard sign that read RESERVED FOR THE PROSECUTION from an armchair situated on the far side of the room, next to the rows where the spectators were sitting.

Arbogast bent over toward Klein and whispered quietly enough that the journalists couldn't hear him: "There he is. Maul actually came."

Ansgar Klein turned around and spotted the white-haired old man, who was just removing the sign. He fell heavily into the armchair and let the sign fall to the floor. The pathologist's gaze seemed farsighted, unable to fix on anything as he looked around him. Klein thought he noticed a tremor in his left hand, though Maul was holding it down in his lap with his right one. The lawyer was glad to see Henrik Tietz sitting two rows further back. The *Spiegel* writer was wearing a light brown corduroy jacket and an extremely narrow tie.

"Just try not to get too excited, Mr. Arbogast," said Klein quietly. They were still being photographed.

"That's easy for you to say. What I'd really like to do is punch him."

"Have you lost your mind? Pull yourself together. The trial is about to begin, and I'm not going to be happy if tomorrow all the papers have photos of you with a scowl on your face. So please just get yourself under control. I don't even want to think about the editorials we would see if you actually did slug him. Am I clear on that?"

"Quite clear." Arbogast nodded without looking at the lawyer.

Klein leaned back in his chair and closed his eyes. He was outraged at the special treatment that Professor Maul had evidently been extended, and he wondered why the pathologist even wanted to be there. He gripped the satin collar of his black robe, which he had just thrown on over the black suit that he always wore to court. As usual, he had on a white shirt and a white tie beneath it. Ansgar Klein knew that he would be photographed; he knew, too, that he was vain. There was nothing wrong with that. Everything depended on public opinion from now on. It was quite unusual that he hadn't given up after his first petition for retrial was rejected—especially considering that there was no money in it for him. Why, it had taken him an entire year just to get new expert witnesses lined up, convincing them to testify for free and casting doubt on the credibility of the old ones. Now they were about to find out whether all his preparations had been enough. Klein took a sip of his tea. It had gone bitter. Regardless what sort it was, tea simply didn't hold up well in a thermos, a discovery that the lawyer suffered anew every time he went to trial. Ansgar Klein wasn't nervous. He usually drove to court alone. He hated hotel rooms. It was about to begin.

He took a couple of deep breaths in and out and then leaned over to Arbogast without opening his eyes.

"Do you know what makes a trial so remarkable?" he whispered and felt his client shake his head no.

"The trial that's about to begin has two basic principles: It's conducted orally and it's immediate. That means everything that's essential to the case, every piece of evidence and every witness's statement, must to be brought to light here and now. It's like theater, but it's real."

At that moment, the two doors behind the judge's dais swung open and the judge and jury entered the room. Everyone stood, and Arbogast noticed that Klein doffed the black cap that went with his jurist's robe.

"Do you want to know what I've got in there?" Klein whispered as they stood up, pointing at a gray cardboard box sitting on the table among the piles of documents. Arbogast shook his head again.

"A garrote," said the lawyer with a grin on his face.

Arbogast looked at his lawyer with alarm. There were now nine people standing behind the judges' bench: the three judges in their velvet-trimmed robes and three jurors on either side. Next to them, at one edge of the judges' bench, was another young man. The chief judge, who was in the center, waited a moment until the room grew silent. The feeling of expectation was palpable. Arbogast felt anxious.

"The court is now in session. We take up the matter of the retrial of the *People of the Federal Republic of Germany versus Hans Arbogast*, docket number two five/three eight-o nineteen fifty-five. Please be seated." The judge cleared his throat. "Good morning," he added when the scraping of chairs on the floor had ceased. He looked around the room and announced to the journalists that filming and photography would be permitted only until the jury had been sworn in. "I hope you understand the need for this measure."

While this was going on, the lawyer continued whispering to Arbogast. "There are two different kinds of jury trial. In America, the jury alone is responsible for deciding whether the defendant is guilty at the end of the trial. But there the jury has no right to ask questions, and even the judge serves only as a moderator during the proceedings. Almost everything is done by the lawyers for the defense and the prosecution. We do it differently. Here, the entire court, which consists of the judges and the jury, decides together. And all of them are permitted to interrupt with questions throughout the course of the trial."

Arbogast nodded, and they looked on silently while the jurors were sworn in. They were all people from the surrounding area: a cabinetmaker, a farmer, the mayor of a small village, an office worker, a master cooper, the owner of a small business in Grangat. Ansgar Klein looked at them closely, though he knew they wouldn't say a word during the entire trial. Even now, at the beginning of the trial, he had to be thinking ahead to the time when all the members of the court would finally withdraw to the judge's chambers to deliberate. For him, that was always an eerie moment. He had often felt certain of having made his case convincingly, only to hear, in the wake of that dreadful conference that took place behind closed doors, a verdict read out that he previously would have thought impossible.

"Do you know the judges?" asked Arbogast.

Klein leaned toward his client. "The chief judge is District Superior Court Judge Horst Lindner, the second-in-command here in Grangat. Actually, his boss should have been the lead judge on the case, but he ducked out of it, reported himself sick. This trial is Lindner's big chance to make a name for himself. You want to know the big problem with our judicial system?"

Arbogast nodded.

"The problem lies in the conflict between the two roles, asking questions and passing judgment," Klein whispered. "In America, questioning and passing judgment are strictly separated, but with us, the judges have to base their judgment on the very questions they themselves have asked. This can give rise to problems where members of the court introduce their own biases into the proceedings—as your own case revealed."

The chief judge had finished swearing in the jurors, and the journalists left the room. It grew quiet, and when the area between the judge's bench and the prosecution table and the table where he was sitting was finally empty of people, Arbogast suddenly had a view of the chair, surrounded on three sides by a low railing, that sat in the middle of that space. In front of it was a small table with a microphone, a carafe of water and a glass.

"Representing the prosecution are the chief district attorney, Dr. Bernhard Curtius, and Günter Frank, district attorney with the Grangat DA's office. For the defense, the attorney Dr. Ansgar Klein." Horst Lindner paused and then pointed to the chair in front of the judge's bench. "Mr. Arbogast, would you please step forward?"

When Hans Arbogast stood up and went over to the witness box, Katja Lavans could see in his shuffling gait that he was someone who had done time—it was something that the elegant suit this tall man was wearing couldn't hide. She remembered what the lawyer had told her about how much Arbogast had changed in prison, his self-mutilation, how withdrawn he'd become, how his sense of reality had dwindled while he was incarcerated. She watched him closely as he sat down and smoothed his jacket, anxious to hear what he would say.

She was glad it was getting under way. Since breakfast, she'd had to explain to the other pathologists who were there what she was going to state in her testimony, and then she'd had to deal with the press corps's questions about her trip across the Iron Curtain, being very careful not to answer in a way that would get her in trouble when she got back home. And finally, she'd been trying to avoid Professor Maul, a feat that wouldn't have been possible without the help of Sarrazin, who had quite charmingly stuck by her side all morning. She'd seen Arbogast only briefly, and she still wasn't sure if that aura of quiet that she perceived around him was real, or just her own imagination. The judge asked him the usual questions about himself, and Katja Lavans could see him take a deep breath and lick his lips. Over and over again, when she was doing her experiments, touching cold flesh, she'd tried to imagine his hands, his gaze. She watched the way he pushed his hair back across his forehead.

Before he began to speak, Arbogast summoned in all its particulars the memory of how his first trial had opened, fourteen years before, and once again felt a pain in his throat at the thought of how it had changed him irreversibly into another person. And so he began to tell the story of his life, feeling as if he wore his own biography like a prosthetic limb—a feeble replacement for the original, which had been mangled by time. He stated that he'd been born on April 29, 1927, in Grangat, where he had grown up and attended high school.

The judge nodded to the clerk at the side of the dais, and he began taking down Arbogast's dates.

"Please go on."

"My parents hoped that I would go on in school, but I actually wanted to become a chef. In the end, after I passed the college-entrance exam, my father arranged for me to be apprenticed to a butcher."

"This was after the war?"

"Yes."

During the war, Arbogast had run the family restaurant, the Salmon, since his mother was forbidden to work because of her membership in the Women's Association of the Nazi party.

"How active was your mother in the party?"

"Oh, hardly at all. All she did was knit sweaters in the winter." Arbogast fell silent, took a sip of water.

"Please go on."

Because he hadn't been making enough to get by that way, he took on work as a long-haul trucker, and then he ran a quarry for a while, and then he became a traveling salesman. But all of those ventures had resulted in him losing money rather than making it. Eventually, he went back to working at his mother's restaurant and had taken over a dealership to sell Brunswick billiard tables on the side. He got married in October of 1951, and his son, Michael, was born a few weeks later. His wife, Katrin, was the daughter of Mr. Teichel, the math teacher at the Schiller Gymnasium in Grangat.

"You knew your wife from school?"

"Yes. We had been going out since the end of school." He added that his wife had left him while he was in prison.

"When was that?"

"1961."

Then the junior DA, Frank, asked, "What profession are you practicing now?"

Arbogast turned to face the prosecution table. "I haven't worked since I was released. Once, I almost had a job, but when the employer heard that I had been convicted once and was about to go back on trial, he threw up his hands and just told me to move along."

"Are there any other questions?" The judge turned to his fellow members of the court, to Curtius and finally to Ansgar Klein. He nodded at the clerk. "Have you got it all so far? If so, we can proceed with the reading of the indictment. Thank you very much, Mr. Arbogast."

While Hans Arbogast went back to his place, Fritz Sarrazin looked over at Ansgar Klein and saw that the lawyer appeared satisfied with his client's performance. Now all eyes turned to the district attorney, who began to read the indictment: Again the charge was murder. Sarrazin could see that Katja Lavans was uneasy; also, the spectators in the gallery seemed to grow even quieter once the circumstances of the crime were described. The senior DA, Dr. Bernhard Curtius, was a calm man in his mid-fifties who wore large glasses and had a receding hairline. He spoke deliberately, with pregnant pauses that allowed time for listeners to imagine for themselves such things as couldn't be sufficiently described in words. While all the members of the court listened attentively to the indictment, the chief judge appeared to Sarrazin more capable of detaching himself from the prosecutor's recitation of charges than were his colleagues, District Superior Court Associate Judge Severin Manoff and the inconspicuous Phillipp Müller. Sarrazin noticed that Judge Lindner was constantly looking over at Arbogast, as if to see what effect the DA's descriptions of the crime had on him. But the accused man appeared to be working hard to stay calm, and Sarrazin, at least, wasn't able to read anything from his features.

"Would you like to respond to the accusations that have been levied against you, Mr. Arbogast?" asked Lindner when the DA sat down.

"Yes," said Hans Arbogast quietly.

"Then please come forward again and simply tell us what happened on the unfortunate day—I think we can all agree at least that it was a tragedy, if not something more."

Arbogast nodded and returned to the witness chair in the center of the room. Sarrazin noticed the way Katja Lavans leaned forward in her chair, as if she wanted to get closer to the quiet voice with which Arbogast began, hesitatingly at first, to speak.

He said that on September 1, 1953, which was a Tuesday, he had had some business to take care of in Grangat in the morning. Then in the early afternoon, he had set off toward Freiburg to pay a sales call—he had a new shipment of billiard tables to sell. She had been standing by the side of the road—it was route B3, at the old railroad overpass just south of Grangat—and she'd waved him over.

"She was good-looking, very pretty, a nice young girl. And she was wearing an ice blue dress."

"You picked her up and offered to take her on a tour of the Black Forest?"

"Yes, that's right. I drove through Münchweier to Schönwald, and then on the way back we stopped for a meal in Triberg, at the Over the Falls Hotel."

"What did you eat?"

"We both had the soup to start and then roulade of beef with mashed potatoes and cabbage. For dessert, we had ice cream sundaes with whipped cream on top—you know, they came in those tapered silver ice-cream dishes."

The judge nodded. "Did you drink anything?"

"Yes, of course. She had wine, a Trollinger, and I had two beers. And then after dinner, I ordered a cognac, and she said, 'I'll have one, too!' "

Arbogast paused briefly and smiled to himself. Katja Lavans imagined the moment: Marie must have felt that she was living large when she ordered that cognac. Arbogast went on to say that she had already told him she didn't have any money and had offered to sell him her handbag for six marks. She hadn't had a choice, thought the pathologist. Arbogast said that he'd taken her up on the offer.

"That would be the handbag that you later took back to your wife?"

"Yes."

"What happened next? Did you stop again?"

"Yes, in Gutach, at the Angel."

"Why?"

Arbogast smiled and shook his head. "I don't think either of us wanted to go back."

"I see."

The chief judge looked to his left and his right at his fellow judges, and Judge Severin Manoff took up the questioning. "What did you have at the Angel?"

"She had a cola; I had another beer."

Manoff nodded. Paul Mohr had taken a seat pretty close to the back of the gallery, since none of the seats reserved for the press were still open when he got there. He drew lines over the printed rules of his notepad with his ballpoint pen, and the more Arbogast said, the deeper the lines became, till there were grooves in the paper, but otherwise his page was still blank. Marie Gurth had taken his arm when they walked back out to the car, he said, and she had mentioned the good weather by way of quoting an old saying—"When angels go abroad, the heavens smile."

"What do you think she could she have meant by that?" asked Severin Manoff, and Arbogast shrugged.

"Please go on."

He said that when they got back to the car, they had begun fooling around.

"What do you mean by that?"

"Kissing, necking, touching, of course—the way people do," he said.

Then he described pulling off the road halfway between Hausach and Gutach and stopping the car in a field.

"And then?"

"Mrs. Gurth began to take her clothes off."

Up till this point, Arbogast had told his story without any particularly long pauses, though his voice had grown increasing quieter as he went on. Now he fell silent.

"Just a moment, please, Mr. Arbogast."

The chief judge conferred briefly with his two colleagues regarding the imminent depiction of intimate contact between two people, and a moment later, they had decided not to exclude the public from hearing it.

"I am of the opinion that in the year 1969, adults need not leave the room for this testimony, but I do request that any minors present remove themselves from the court."

Two teenagers got up and left the courtroom. Lindner looked around the courtroom once more and then nodded to Arbogast.

"The first time we were together, it was quick. We did it the regular way," he said, then fell silent again.

Klein observed the way his client sat waiting, staring at his hands. He was smiling to himself, as if he were alone, despite the fact that there were well over a hundred people in the room, all of them staring at him, hanging on his every word and gesture. The past surrounded him and seemed to rise up and take shape in the courtroom—something broad and iridescent. For the first time, Klein thought he could understand what it had been like for Arbogast in that cell that was full to overflowing with what had taken place.

"I was thinking we would just put our clothes back on and go home," said Arbogast almost inaudibly.

Ansgar Klein saw from the corner of his eye that Katja Lavans was staring hard at his client. She slowly brushed the hair out of her face. Ansgar Klein liked it that he was the only one in the courtroom who knew she was wearing a wig.

The district attorney cleared his throat. "Mr. Arbogast, may I briefly read to you the account of Professor Dr. Maul, the expert witness from the first trial, describing what he believes happened next?"

Ansgar Klein was startled from his thoughts and looked over at the prosecutor. Curtius pulled out a file and fixed his gaze on the accused man, whose body suddenly squirmed with motion. Klein considered raising an objection to this text being read aloud, but he decided against it.

" 'The accused may then have hit Mrs. Gurth about the nose and face, at which point she presumably attempted to run away. Apparently, the accused then ran after her and struck her on the head. After these blows, she collapsed, at which point he put a length of cord or twine around her neck and powerfully cinched it tight. The accused then turned her over and removed all her clothes. He bit into her breast and her belly. Finally, during the three-to-eight-minute period during which she struggled for her life, he had sex with her, possibly also continuing after she was dead.' "

The spectators in the gallery were no longer silent. People were whispering, chairs were scraping against the floor, and it seemed to Ansgar Klein as if all the noise was somehow the direct result of the uneasiness Arbogast showed as he sat on the stand. He squirmed and fidgeted in his chair and tried to hold himself still. There was no doubt that he was suffering. This was it—the fabricated past that had been the source of so much pain. Sarrazin could tell from where he sat that Klein, too, was intensely anxious, and then Klein leapt to his feet at the same instant that Arbogast turned and jumped up from the witness box.

Arbogast wheeled around to face Professor Maul in the gallery, almost as if he'd felt his eyes on his back the whole time, and shouted, "Why don't you just come out and admit it!" Over and over, he shouted that Maul should own up to the fact that there were errors in his testimony. Arbogast leaned forward, his fists balled. Only with great difficulty was Klein able to calm him down. Finally, he fell silent, but he was still trembling, and Klein put his arm around his shoulder.

"Look at me," said Arbogast to Professor Maul, who sat motionless in his armchair. He spoke more quietly now. "I've spent sixteen years in prison because of your testimony. You have destroyed my life!"

"Please sit back down, Mr. Arbogast." The judge spoke calmly to him. "Mr. Arbogast, please do not think that we are trying to make a fool of you here." He threw a look at the prosecutor and added, "It is certainly understandable that he would feel the need to defend himself against such a statement."

Ansgar Klein voiced his agreement and requested that his client be allowed to present his version of the events in full before he was confronted with this testimony.

"Please continue, Mr. Arbogast. You were telling us that you and the deceased had had intimate relations and that you had then expected to drive back home."

Arbogast took a sip of water and a deep breath before he went on.

"All right. We went back to the car and smoked a cigarette. But then Mrs. Gurth started getting affectionate again, and we got back out of the car. She turned around, and what happened then was that we had sex from behind."

"You mean anally?"

Arbogast shook his head reluctantly.

The prosecution jumped in to assist the judge. "The autopsy report refers to injuries that were likely to have been caused by anal sex."

"No!" Arbogast shook his head vehemently. "We just did it the regular way."

"And so how do you explain those injuries?"

"Maybe that happened later, in the car, when I was cleaning her up."

"Just a moment," said the judge. "Right now, we're still out in the field. What happened there?"

"We made love, very intensely."

"What should the court understand when you say 'intensely'?"

Arbogast paused, and at that instant Katja Lavans suddenly saw all the details of the autopsy report before her. She felt she was experiencing every motion, every gesture, that she tasted every kiss, and she knew the pain of every desperate attempt that the two of them made to hold the other. The pathologist closed her eyes and therefore couldn't see that Ansgar Klein was looking at her from out of the corner of his eye, without turning his head. He saw her face and had to confess to himself that he resented the sympathy she extended to his client. He'd already been troubled by the interest she'd taken in Arbogast's car the day before. He found her curiosity repellent. She was waiting with her eyes closed for him to go on, and Klein watched Arbogast slowly brush his hair off his forehead. Arbogast was considering what words could possibly be sufficient to describe this event that had happened so many years before and had guided all his memories since.

"Marie was much more active than the first time. She put her breast to my mouth and told me to suck, and then she asked me to bite her."

"And you did as she asked?" asked Ansgar Klein.

"Yes, and meanwhile she was kissing me all over. She bit my neck and scratched my back."

"You're saying that what you did together was undertaken with mutual consent?" asked the lawyer.

"Yes, of course."

"What happened next?" asked Lindner.

"Then Marie turned over on her stomach, and I pushed into her. But I could barely hold on to her like that."

"But eventually you did succeed in getting hold of her?"

"Yes. I had one hand on her hip and the other was at her neck."

"Did you strangle her?"

"No, I was only holding her because she was moving so wildly, and then she suddenly collapsed in my arms."

"What do you mean when you say 'collapsed'?"

"I mean she literally collapsed beneath me. I didn't think anything of it at first and waited for her to go on. But then I suddenly realized something had happened to her."

"And then?"

"She wasn't moving at all, and I put my ear to her chest. But I couldn't hear a heartbeat." Then he had tried to resuscitate her, he said. He had used his hands to press on her chest numerous times. The chief judge called for a law clerk to come forward from the gallery and lie on the floor so that Arbogast could demonstrate what he had done. Arbogast knelt on the floor by the young man.

"I thought she was dead. I know it was a mistake not to go for the police or to a doctor."

"You can return to your seat," said the judge to the law clerk, who rose and slapped the dust from his trousers before returning to his place. Arbogast's eyes were riveted on Lindner.

"But I just lost my head. I think I'm a reasonably intelligent man, but how could any person know how to react in a situation like that?"

"What exactly did you do next?"

"First, I carried Mrs. Gurth to the car and put her in the passenger seat. Then I gathered up all the clothes, got dressed myself and moved her body to the backseat. I covered it with her slip. Then I drove toward Grangat. I threw the rest of her clothes out the window a few hundred yards down the road. The only thing I forgot to get rid of was her purse, which I had put under the seat. When I was near Gengenback, I got the idea of leaving her body between Kaltenweier and Hohrod, because I knew the body of a woman had already been found there. But then shortly before I got to Grangat, it suddenly began to smell powerfully of feces in the car, so I pulled over. Marie had wet herself and soiled herself, too, if you understand what I mean, Your Honor."

Lindner nodded. "We understand you. Go on."

"I ripped off part of her slip and cleaned her up, using it as a rag. And then I drove on past Kaltenweier on route B-Fifteen, in the direction of Hohrod. Where the road branches off to go to Duren, I pulled over. I pulled Marie out of the car and let her slide down the embankment."

Arbogast nodded at his own words and said nothing for some time, then added in a low voice that he'd gone back toward Grangat by way of Kaltenweier. He'd filled up at the Kühn gas station and then he'd just sat for a couple of hours at the parking area for the mill.

"I was completely exhausted. I must have sat there for three or four hours."

"Did you sleep?"

"No!"

The judge waited to see if Arbogast would say anything more. "Well then, tell me what you did do, so we're not left with the idea you were able to sleep soundly that night."

Arbogast shook his head. He said he'd returned home sometime between 2:00 and 3:00 a.m. He left Mrs. Gurth's handbag on his wife's bedside table as a gift, and then he finally went to sleep himself.

"Why in the name of God did you do that?"

Arbogast shook his head. "I don't know."

Lindner nodded. "What happened next?"

"On Saturday, I read the report in the paper. On Monday, I went to the police."

"Why was that?" asked Curtius.

"I thought it would be better if I helped."

"Isn't it true, Mr. Arbogast, that you were afraid the handbag could implicate you somehow?"

"No, I wanted to help clear up what had happened."

That was all Arbogast said. The judge nodded and looked around to see if anyone had questions. Finally, the prosecutor spoke up.

"I find it a little strange to hear you say you wanted to help clear up what had happened. The transcripts of your statement at the time give quite a different impression. In the first interview, you admitted only that you'd picked up Mrs. Gurth on the road and that you'd bought her handbag from her. In the second round of questioning, you insisted that you'd had no contact whatsoever with Mrs. Gurth, but then in the third session, you admitted to the DA that Marie Gurth had died suddenly in your presence. Finally, you said that you had caused her death, though unintentionally. Then later, you recanted this confession, saying it had been coerced. How does all of that fit together with what you're telling us today—that you just wanted to be helpful?"

"From the very first, everyone thought I was the murderer! Every word I said was twisted just as soon as it was out of my mouth."

"Even the interrogation transcripts? Those were your words."

"I didn't say it the way it came out." He said that Mr. Oesterle, the DA, had never let him speak freely or say what he wanted to. "That man wore me down to the point that I didn't even know what was true anymore, or what was false."

"Any further questions?" asked the judge. "Mr. Prosecutor? Dr. Klein?" They both shook their heads.

"Thank you. Tomorrow at eight-thirty, we will continue with the introduction of evidence. The court is adjourned."

52

By the time Ansgar Klein had packed up his files and was ready to leave the courtroom, most of the spectators and journalists were already gone. The courtroom was located on the second floor of the courthouse, and the brightly lit stairwell, which earlier that morning had been so packed that it was impossible to get through, now stood almost empty. Klein was glad to see that Professor Maul was gone, and Karges didn't seem to be around either. Downstairs, by the entrance, Sarrazin, Katja Lavans and Arbogast stood waiting for him. As he was coming down the stairs, Klein saw that the pathologist was engaged in an intense conversation with Arbogast, and he decided he'd rather eat alone at the hotel. He stood there beside the others for a moment and then said good night. They were all surprised, especially Katja Lavans, who looked at him with some confusion, but he left them, explaining that he still had work to do. Paul Mohr happened to be leaving the courthouse at the same moment and held the door open for Ansgar Klein. The journalist introduced himself as a writer for the *Badische Zeitung* and told him the initials he used to sign his articles—initials the lawyer was sure to recognize from the yellowed clippings in his press file on the first Arbogast trial. Then Mohr asked him if he'd be willing to share his impressions of the first day of the trial.

Ansgar Klein nodded and stepped out in front of the courthouse. He told Mohr that this case ought to serve as a reminder of how serious the need for a reform of the Penal Code had become in Germany, adding that he was 100 percent certain that that reform would come eventually. Times had changed, thank God! His client was a symbol of all that could go wrong in the hands of an inflexible justice system, and he certainly hoped that Hans Arbogast would now, after so many years, be granted a just outcome.

"One more question, Mr. Counselor. What did you think of the way the prosecution team was paying court to Professor Maul today?"

"I found it extremely inappropriate, but I'd rather not say anything more on the subject, which I'm sure you will understand."

Ansgar Klein nodded good-bye to Paul Mohr, who thanked him for his time. Then, lost in thought, Klein followed the journalist for some distance—he seemed to be going the same way. It was only when Paul Mohr turned off down Kreuzgasse that Klein stopped for a moment to consider where he was and what the best way back to the hotel might be. He saw the journalist push open a door and disappear into a shop with an illuminated Kodak sign.

It was the same bell. Paul stood waiting at the glass counter and looked around him. Then the red light at the upper right corner of the doorway to the darkroom went out, the heavy curtain was pushed aside, and Gesine Hofmann emerged from the lab.

"I'm so glad you came!"

"Thanks for asking me. Fourteen years later! I can't believe we haven't seen each other in all that time."

"Yes, I know."

"Everything's just the same."

Gesine smiled and looked around the little shop as if for the first time.

"I've got some lunch ready. Come on."

Gesine waved for him to follow her and then went through a small door behind the counter. On the other side, shelves lined an already narrow hallway. They were stacked to the ceiling with all sorts of photographic equipment. At the end of the hall was a set of stairs leading up to the second floor. Upstairs, off the small entryway, whose wooden floor sagged ominously in one corner, there were several white paneled doors, and the one that opened onto the kitchen stood open. Paul followed the photographer inside and watched as she turned the gas on under two large pots on the stove. Against one wall was a stove and an old-fashioned kitchen sink; on the other, a large kitchen cabinet with glass-fronted doors that were hung with crochet work in all shapes and colors. Over the table was an embroidered sampler that read, *Five were invited, ten came to call. Pour water in the soup and welcome them all.* On the windowsill, there was a wooden coffee grinder. The room smelled of onions. It was clear to Paul that nothing had changed here in many years.

"How's your mother?" he asked.

"She passed away."

Paul nodded.

"Well, why don't you sit down," said Gesine, looking over her shoulder while she stirred a pot and tasted its contents. "The food's almost ready."

Paul Mohr nodded and remained standing.

53

At that very moment, there was a knock on the lawyer's door. Room service brought in his order: a sandwich and a large glass of water. Ansgar Klein set the tray down on the unused side of his bed, where it slowly sank deep into the puffy down comforter while he continued going though the list of witnesses he planned to call in the following days. He had the necessary files laid out on the small table by the window. The room was drafty and the gray linoleum underfoot was cold. There were several thin rugs on the floor, but they slid about underfoot with every step. Beside the large gray file folder, there was a pad of unlined white letter-sized paper with Ansgar Klein's name printed in the upper left corner. The pad had numerous pages filled with his notes, and lying open beside it was the old English fountain pen with the shellac case that his father had given him. Ansgar Klein was chilly and went to draw himself a hot bath. On his way to the bathroom, he noticed the sandwich, which he'd entirely forgotten, and then when he stepped back out of the bathroom, leaving the water rushing loudly into the tub, there was another knock on the door.

The lawyer was startled to see Fritz Sarrazin standing in the hallway. Without even saying hello, he came into Klein's room and began offering his impressions of the day's proceedings in the courtroom. When Klein went to the bathroom to turn off the tap, Sarrazin followed him and after briefly inspecting the toothbrush glass and finding it clean, he filled it with water. Then he stepped back out into the bedroom and sat down at the small desk. He raised his glass to Klein.

"Enjoy your meal. *Bon appétit!*"

He slowly took a sip of water and then waited a moment before changing the subject.

"A person could have gotten the impression today," he began, "that you were avoiding Frau Lavans. Or am I imagining it?"

There was a long pause. Sarrazin drank down half the glass of water in a series of small rhythmic sips.

"No, you're not wrong."

Klein had sat down on the bed, since there was only the one chair in his small room. Again, he took his glass from the room-service tray and drank from it. "I'm sorry. I know it's ridiculous."

"We're relying on Katja Lavans."

"Yes, I know."

"But in addition to that, I think she's an extremely intelligent woman."

"Yes."

"And charming."

"Yes."

"Are you jealous?"

"No, of course not."

"Forgive me, but I don't believe you." Sarrazin laughed rather gaily.

"I'm just worried about her."

"Because of Arbogast?"

Ansgar Klein was slow responding to that one. Arbogast hadn't been able to take his eyes off her since the first moment he'd seen the pathologist, and Klein was feeling uneasy about it. Perhaps it did force him to admit his fascination with her, but it seemed to Klein that his anxiety had to do with more than just that. He took another sip, set his glass carefully back down on the tray and slowly turned it in place between his thumb and forefinger without looking up.

"Arbogast is innocent." Sarrazin had grown serious again.

"Right." The lawyer's voice was at once toneless and doubtful. He could feel Sarrazin looking at him and he avoided meeting the writer's gaze.

"So, all right, then—you're jealous," insisted Sarrazin, and Klein nodded, though reluctantly.

54

"The court will now resume its proceedings in the case of the *Federal Republic of Germany versus Hans Arbogast*, docket number two five/three eight-o nineteen fifty-five. Today we will commence with the introduction of evidence. The court calls Katrin Teichel as a witness."

A court officer who was waiting by the door stepped out to summon Arbogast's ex-wife. Katrin Teichel came forward slowly, her steps barely audible. She was wearing a dark blue suit and a white blouse. She had gained weight and seemed puffy. She wasn't wearing lipstick but had on a light, shimmery eyeshadow. She wore her hair up. Almost as soon as she had sat down, she said that she wanted to claim her right not to testify and she declined to make any statement. Judge Lindner nodded and asked her to simply state her name, age, place of residence and her professional and marital status, which she did. Arbogast stared at her intently, but she avoided his gaze.

"In that case, I will release you, Mrs. Teichel. You may go. Did you have any expenses? Here's a voucher. You can take it to the cashier's desk in order to be reimbursed."

As he spoke, Lindner was filling out a form, which he handed down to Arbogast's ex-wife from the judge's bench.

"Your Honor?"

"Yes, what is it?"

"May I remain here and listen to the proceedings?"

"Of course you may, Mrs. Teichel. Find a seat in the gallery. As its next witness, the court calls Jochen Gurth."

Hans Arbogast watched intently to see where Katrin would find a seat. He noticed that the armchair that had been set out for Professor Maul the day before was no longer there. His eyes quickly scanned the gallery to see if the man who had testified against him back then was still present at the trial, and he spotted him at the very back of the room. When their eyes met, he quickly looked away and turned back to the front of the room, where the husband of the deceased had now taken the stand and begun to answer the basic questions about his identity. Jochen Gurth was forty-five and worked as an engineer in Braunschweig. He had remarried. At the request of the court, he described the circumstances of his and Marie's 1952 flight to the West. They had been married five years at the time and had two children, ages three and four, whom they had left with their grandmother. At the time of her death, they had been living at the refugee camp in Ringsheim for a year. He said his wife had been depressed by the existence they led at the camp and had been considering going back to her children. No, he answered when Ansgar Klein inquired of him, she had not had any substantial household duties. Yes, she had had a zest for life. "She was a passionate lover, relatively speaking," he said.

"Did you have the impression, then, that your wife was less than completely faithful?"

"Yes, of course." He went on to say that she was always going off on expeditions through the Black Forest with men who picked her up as a hitchhiker. He hadn't, however, known that she was pregnant in September 1953.

"On September first, 1953, Marie came to see me at my job in Grangat during the lunch break. As I was going over to the canteen, I saw her getting out of an unfamiliar car and saying good-bye to the driver. We had lunch together and I suggested to her that she wait around till the end of the day so we could take the train back to Ringsheim together. But Marie didn't feel like waiting. She said she'd rather try to hitch her way back to the camp. I gave her a couple of marks so she could get a coffee. And I never saw my wife again."

"Why did you wait four days before going to the police?"

"I figured Marie must have gone to Stuttgart to look for work."

"What gave you that idea?"

"A while before that, a man from Stuttgart had been at the camp, and he had offered her a job."

The judge pondered how the questioning ought to proceed from there. The prosecutor, too, just stared at the witness. Jochen Gurth was a slight man and not very tall. He was wearing a dark suit and had his hands folded in his lap. He added quietly that he'd also considered it possible at the time that his wife had returned to Berlin or had simply run off. But then on September 5, a Saturday, he'd happened to look at the newspaper and seen the article reporting the discovery of the body of an unidentified woman. While reading the description of the victim, he'd started to think it might be his wife.

Ansgar Klein took note of the intensity with which Hans Arbogast watched his onetime lover's husband. All Arbogast would ever know about Marie's life was what Jochen Gurth was saying right now. The lawyer slowly let his gaze rove across the courtroom. It didn't matter what court was in session—every trial he'd ever seen had the same deadly intensity. And although every word spoken was rooted in the past, together they would forge a reality that had never before existed. No, said Ansgar Klein, he had no questions for Mr. Gurth.

Judge Lindner called witness after witness to the stand: those who had found the body and those who had recovered it, starting with Mechling, the gamekeeper, a skinny old man, who used almost exactly the same words, Klein noticed, as he had at the first trial. He spoke in the local dialect, and the melody of his sentences always rose at the end, as if he were surprised or indignant. After Mechling came Rudolf Hinrichs, the former chief of the Freiburg Homicide Division, now retired with the rank of captain. By the time he arrived at the scene, he said, a doctor had already examined the body. He wasn't able to rule out the possibility that the body had been moved. The photographs were not taken until later. Hinrichs described a broken branch that had been lying beside the woman. He couldn't say, however, if it might have been the actual cause of the strangulation marks that Professor Maul had discovered. The last witness in the morning session was Chief Commissioner Willi Fritsch, who had interrogated

Arbogast when he first turned himself in. He testified that the accused had initially admitted only to having picked up a hitchhiker and bought her handbag from her.

In the afternoon, Judge Lindner called to the stand the district attorney of Heidelberg, Ferdinand Oesterle, who had been the first prosecutor in the case. This time, it was Ansgar Klein who began the questioning, as soon as the formalities were taken care of.

"Is it true that on the occasion of your sixtieth-birthday celebration you told a journalist that you were 'just as convinced now as ever that Arbogast committed the murder'?"

Oesterle was a tall, bony man. He wore large horn-rimmed spectacles and looked to be nearing seventy. His white hair had turned yellow, the way it does with heavy smokers. He was wearing a thin black tie and had one thumb hooked in the pocket of his vest. His breathing was shallow and his voice was low and raspy.

He didn't linger over the question. "Yes, that's right. And I still feel the same way."

Ansgar Klein was genuinely surprised by this response. So much had happened since then that he had found it difficult to imagine the original trial while he was preparing for this one, but now suddenly he felt the atmosphere of the 1950s present in the room. He could see how suspicious people must have been of Arbogast's story. They had been reluctant to follow where it led. The repulsion was unavoidable. Klein could understand that people had been only too eager to hear what Professor Maul had to say. Arbogast was growing restless. Until this point, he had followed the questioning attentively, almost completely without stirring. Now he began to turn around and peer out into the gallery. He avoided looking at Oesterle.

"Isn't it true that once you saw the autopsy report," said Ansgar Klein in a placating tone, "you ought simply to have closed the case?"

Ferdinand Oesterle just shook his head. He described how one pathologist had told him, after the autopsy, that he'd never seen a woman's body with such a large number of injuries. Throughout his investigation, he hadn't been able to get that vision of the victim out of his head.

"Maybe that was the case during the interrogation, as well. Is it true that you said the following to Hans Arbogast: 'You're not getting out of here till you've confessed, I don't care how long it takes'?"

"No! I absolutely deny having coerced the accused into saying anything. The interrogation was conducted in a calm fashion. And by the way, the accused never admitted to anything beyond what we were already able to hang on him."

Arbogast couldn't contain himself any longer. "You made me confess!" He was gripping the edge of the table with both hands.

"That's absolutely false," said Oesterle calmly, not looking at him.

"If you swear to that, you're perjuring yourself!" shouted Arbogast, standing up from the table. The judge admonished him to be silent, and Klein spoke to him until he finally sat back down.

"You're out of order, Mr. Arbogast," said the judge. "If you can't control your outbursts, I will have to conduct this trial without you. I would suggest that you leave it to your lawyer to present your objections to the way you were interrogated. You were given the chance to make your point yesterday. Can you agree to that?"

Arbogast nodded and strove to quiet his breathing. His hands were back in his lap, intertwined.

Ansgar Klein began again. "Times have changed," he said. "Don't you think that back then everyone was a little too quick to jump to the conclusion that this incident had to be the work of a pervert?"

Oesterle shook his head with certainty. "No, I wouldn't say that at all."

Without turning to look at him, Klein could tell that Arbogast was becoming agitated again; he could hear his client quietly muttering to himself. He laid his hand on Arbogast's arm until he quieted down.

"Mr. Oesterle, my client has said that during the trial, Professor Maul displayed a bloody shirt. Is that correct?"

"That is not correct. The first time I ever heard about a shirt was in an article by Mr. Sarrazin that appeared in the magazine *Bunten*," said Oesterle, and nodded in the direction of the gallery, where Sarrazin was sitting.

"The case files contain a shirt that was tested for traces of blood by the Federal Office of Criminal Investigation."

"I have no recollection of that."

"And the 1955 indictment refers to a shirt as one of the critical pieces of evidence," added Judge Lindner.

"That may be so, but I have only a vague memory of this shirt."

"Are you absolutely certain that this shirt did not come up at the trial?"

"I'm certain that this shirt was never introduced in the courtroom."

"You're no longer acting as the district attorney here; you're a witness, whose duty is to present the bare facts," responded Ansgar Klein gruffly.

"The prosecutor is aware of that," said Lindner. "He knows the code of procedure."

"He's not following it."

"What I just said is what I believe I know, and as a witness, I'm allowed to state that."

"No further questions." Klein threw himself back into his chair, clearly annoyed.

The judge nodded to the prosecutor.

"Would you tell us how you arrived at the idea that the murderer of Marie Gurth might be the same person who was responsible for the other body found by the side of the same road?"

"Well, it's a simple fact of psychology, well known to all, that the criminal always returns to the scene of the crime."

"Oh yes, then why don't we do away with the Homicide Division entirely and just go out with nets and capture the criminals when they show up at the scene—it would be cheaper!" Klein muttered this, but he did it loudly enough for the public to hear him. People in the gallery laughed.

"I must warn you to restrain your comments to the matter at hand, Mr. Counselor!"

"Please understand me. I have been fighting for nearly four years, entirely without recompense, just to help this poor man get released from prison. I've let my legal practice go. All this because of the wretched quality of the original investigation, and the reliance on such meaningless truisms as that one."

"That's a malicious characterization! The man was highly suspicious." Oesterle turned to face the defense lawyer for the first time. "Even if Arbogast denied any intent to kill, he admitted that he had grabbed her by the back of her neck. He told me then that he had done the same thing to other women before because it made them livelier."

"The witness is out of order!"

Klein just shook his head, and the prosecutor, too, waived further questioning when the judge looked over at him. Ferdinand Oesterle was told he could step down.

The last witness called was Gesine Hofmann, who was asked to describe the circumstances under which she took the photographs. She told them how her mother had awakened her in the wee hours, saying the police needed a photographer, and described how they had come to pick her up, driven her out to the highway and led her out to the spot by the roadside where the white body lay, immediately recognizable against the dark thorn patch.

"Was the sight shocking to you?"

"No, not at all." Gesine seemed amazed to be asked that.

"Tell us a little more about your impressions."

"She was so beautiful."

As if she was unsure she had a right to state this opinion, Gesine shot a quick glance in Arbogast's direction. She saw that his gaze appeared calm and approving. He knew how Marie had been, after all.

"What exactly do you mean by that?" asked Judge Lindner cautiously.

Gesine Hofmann looked at him for a moment with her bright green eyes before responding that she wasn't quite sure. It had been cold and wet, and yet Marie had lain there so peacefully, as if none of it mattered to her. "Time had no power over her," she said.

"You were seventeen at the time?"

"Yes, that's right. I had just celebrated my birthday."

She nodded seriously. Arbogast watched her with greater alertness and interest than he'd had for anyone else. He was captivated by her expressive mouth, which continually seemed on the verge of a smile and then shifted to some other expression. He could see the fine downy hairs on her cheek.

"It seems rather odd to me that a young woman was permitted to take these photographs," said the prosecutor, twirling a pencil between his index and middle fingers.

"For the previous thirty years, my father had done everything that had to do with photography in Grangat, but he had died a short time before. That's why they called for me that morning."

"Because of your father's reputation?"

Gesine nodded again.

The judge dismissed her and announced that the trial was in recess until the following day. Arbogast followed her with his eyes until she disappeared through the door of the courtroom. Out in front of the courthouse, Paul Mohr caught up with her and suggested that they go to the Silver Star for dinner. She told him she'd prefer to go home that night, but she did walk him back to his hotel. Paul Mohr worked on his story about the day's proceedings until the early evening, then called the piece in to the editorial desk and went downstairs to the restaurant, where he sat down at a table with some of the other journalists. Meanwhile, at a quarter to ten, Gesine Hofmann was in her kitchen, making tea and setting out a plate of bread and sausage, as a result of which she missed the opening of a television drama based on a Françoise Sagan novel that she'd been planning to watch for some time. She heard the music of the title sequence playing as she laid a couple of sliced pickles on her plate. Gesine had bought her mother the television cabinet, which was set up across from the sofa in the living room, shortly before she'd died. After the daytime programming, Willy Brandt's national policy address came on. Since her mother had died, Gesine found she watched a lot of television. The television movie was called *In a Month, in a Year*. Gesine was especially impressed with the young Hannelore Elsner, whose dark brows and eye makeup contrasted rather dramatically with her dyed blond hair. Gesine's favorite scene was the one in which Elsner sat on an Oriental rug in the middle of the floor and smoked without moving her lips. Gesine herself did not smoke.

55

"The physical conditions in which the autopsy was conducted were dismal."

"What do you mean by that?"

"The autopsy was conducted in a side room of the mortuary. We had very poor light, no assistant to take down the report and were not equipped with the instruments and investigative tools that a forensic pathologist would take for granted today." Professor Bärlach paused briefly. "It was really a punishment for the pathologist to have to work under those conditions."

Bärlach, who had been a research assistant in Freiburg when he'd conducted the autopsy with Dr. Dallmer, explained that at the time, they hadn't really been certain what the cause of Mrs. Gurth's death was. They hadn't found any hemorrhaging in the tissues around the eyes, which is generally considered the definitive sign of death by strangulation. There were just the bruised areas on the neck.

"What do you think of Professor Maul's testimony?"

"I think his determination that there were rope marks and signs of strangulation was an error."

Bärlach was the first witness that morning. Next, the court called Dr. Dallmer to the witness stand. He described how surprised the entire community of forensic pathologists had been at the sudden and dramatic turn of events brought on by Professor Maul's assertion that there was proof of strangulation.

"What do you mean when you say you were surprised?"

"Quite simply that it practically knocked us off our chairs when we heard about this garrote theory of Professor Maul's."

"Thank you for your statement. You may step down."

That afternoon came the much-anticipated testimony of the two Swiss experts. The first, Dr. Max Wyss, was the chief of Forensic Science Service of the Zurich Police Department and one of the most famous criminologists in all of Europe. He had analyzed the photographs of Marie Gurth, using special equipment developed at the technical college.

"The whole discussion could have been avoided if only a strip of tape had been applied to the dead woman's neck and then removed for analysis. We could even have determined whether it was a cord made of hemp or sisal. But that wasn't done."

"Is this method you describe in common use?" asked the prosecutor.

"Today, it's standard practice. I first published a description of my technique for using tape strips to collect this sort of evidence some five years before the incident took place."

"I see."

"In a just society, we cannot hold the accused responsible in the absence of proof."

"Could you speak to the question of the photographs?"

He explained how easy it would be to misinterpret the information conveyed by the photographs. One had to be very careful to be certain whether any possible artifacts might have given rise to defects in the print. "Let me speak clearly here: I'm talking about things like flyspecks."

He had determined, for example, that the negative for the photographs of Mrs. Gurth's back had several scratches that had produced darkened areas on the prints. It was important to exclude such marks, for which reason he had analyzed the images with a special machine that had been developed by the technical college.

"We're talking about an absolutely reliable electronic device that we're able to use to eliminate all subjective factors. It's called an isodensitracer, and it can be used to bring previously undetected levels of detail out in a photograph. I used this device to investigate whether the pattern of a rope mark was detectable in the range of gray tones on the photograph."

Dr. Wyss projected his results on a screen that had been set up in the courtroom and compared them to images of rope marks that were taken from an undisputed case of strangulation—a suicide.

"And what conclusions have you reached?"

"I have not been able to prove the existence of any hidden pattern indicative of strangulation, either by a fibrous cord or a metal wire."

"And how do you interpret the marks on the throat that can be seen on the photograph?"

"It's conceivable that a tree branch could have made the impression on Mrs. Gurth's throat. My equipment doesn't suggest anything to the contrary, but I can't make any sort of definitive statement about that."

"Thank you very much, Dr. Wyss. I now call Professor Dr. Kaser to the witness stand."

Kaser, a professor of geodesy and photogrammetrics at the Confederate Technical College in Zurich, agreed with Wyss. "The photos of the body don't show even the slightest indication that Marie Gurth was strangled with a garrote or other ropelike implement," he said.

He further pointed out that there was no connection between the mark on the dead woman's chin and the other mark in the region of her ear. One scientific interpretation of the Y-shaped mark visible on the left side of her neck, he suggested, was that it might have been caused by the position of the deceased on the incline.

"But for a rope to have caused that mark—the way it would have had to have been positioned—well, all I can say is that that would have to have been some rope trick."

Kaser confronted Maul directly. The pictures taken in 1953 were thoroughly amateurish. The exposures were poor, the prints were poor, and they were poorly enlarged. First of all, no expert should have been allowed to use these images as the basis for stating an expert opinion, but on top of that, Maul had manipulated the photographs before distributing them. He had used a sticker to cover a spot that showed editing and had drawn numerous arrows to emphasize the bruise marks on the neck.

"This is abominable. It's what we would technically refer to as 'camouflage,' and from the point of view of scientific interpretation of photographic evidence, it's simply unconscionable."

After Professor Kaser, there were two further expert witnesses still to testify that day. Dr. Kantuczyk from the technical college in Karlesruhe had been asked by the Grangat district attorney's office to use a new method to analyze the photos. He told the court that the pictures were of such poor quality that he had been able to draw conclusions about only one of the images. In 1953, no one had taken images that focused just on the throat of the woman. But studying the pictures that did show marks on Mrs. Gurth's throat, he had been able to discern within those marks microscopic structures that ran in several different directions. He was unable to interpret what these structures might mean, however, saying he would leave that work to the forensic experts. Finally, Dr. Peter Schäfer, a university lecturer from Grevenbroich, who had also evaluated the photos, was unable to draw any certain conclusions about the changes to the deceased's neck, but he suggested that the marks might have originated from the branches of the shrubbery in which Mrs. Gurth's body had been placed.

The very last witness of the day was Otto Junker, the seventy-odd-year-old retired police department employee who had recorded the transcripts of Arbogast's interrogations in the fall of 1953. With every question, it seemed Junker had to struggle to remember what had happened, and his answers came slowly. Eyes blinking, the haggard, almost completely bald old man stared vacantly into the space in front of him. Yes, he said, the DA had repeatedly insisted that Arbogast must confess to having killed Mrs. Gurth, but Arbogast had never done it. He couldn't say with any certainty whether Oesterle had refused to strike specific passages that Arbogast wanted removed from his stenographer's transcript, since Oesterle had dictated what went into the transcript himself, on the basis of Arbogast's statements.

"It was a harsh interrogation." Junker cleared his throat. "At any rate, Oesterle was determined to get him to confess that he'd had the intent to kill."

It was growing dark, and the longer it took for Otto Junker to deliver his testimony in his low, halting voice, the quieter it grew in the courtroom. The lights hadn't been turned on yet, but the defense table where Hans Arbogast sat beneath the high windows already lay in the shadow of the early evening. Suddenly, Katja Lavans noticed that the dim, diffuse light began to glow again. At the same moment, Hans Arbogast turned toward the windows and saw the late-afternoon sky, which had been dark with rain clouds just moments before, turn as white as a sheet of paper. The tender birch branches were quickly lined in white and flakes of snow etched the brightness back into the clouds.

"Should we go for a ride in the Isabella?" asked Hans Arbogast quietly as they were leaving the building. The chief judge had adjourned the court for the day. Katja Lavans turned back to give him a friendly nod over her shoulder, when suddenly Father Karges appeared before them, grinning. For a moment, Arbogast was frozen with horror and stood stock-still in the midst of the throng. The priest's white collar glowed brightly above his black cassock. "Don't think that I'm not watching over you," said Karges—that was his job as a shepherd after all, and he told Arbogast he still considered him part of his flock. The priest looked at him with obvious satisfaction.

"But have a good time nonetheless," he said with a nod. "Have a very good time."

56

They had hardly gotten out of Grangat before the thin layer of snow grew heavy enough to blanket the street. The slopes of the vineyards were crusted with the first frost of the year, and where the B33 crossed over the Murg River, the valley spread out white before them in the early-evening light. Then the snow stopped again, and the sky was almost clear. Katja Lavans lit a cigarette. She didn't have to ask where they were going. The engine of the Isabella had started out with a couple of backfires and been a little shaky at first, but now it was running smoothly. Arbogast drove the car as carefully as if each shift of the gears and each turn of the wheel were a part of some choreography that he'd rehearsed countless times in his mind. Night finally darkened the snowy landscape, and the only whiteness was that caught in the milky vials of light cast by the car's headlights. Katja Lavans looked over at him, watching the way he threw his whole shoulder into the gearshift and the large motions with which he adjusted his grip on the steering wheel whenever he navigated a tight corner in one of the small towns they drove through.

He was wearing the same thing he had been for the past few days: a single-breasted black suit, a white shirt and a tightly knotted red tie that glimmered in the headlights of every car that went past them, moving in the opposite direction. And as had been the case for her the past few days in the courtroom, she couldn't stop staring at him. She watched his rather coarse, long face, his strong chin, his slightly thick lips and the way his jaw muscles played beneath the skin of his cheeks, making it seem like he was constantly grinding his teeth.

When he blinked, his lids slid closed so slowly over his eyeballs that his eyes seemed to be smiling. They didn't speak, and the radio was off. It was quiet except for the sounds of the car. Katja was enjoying the nighttime drive through the empty snow-covered countryside and she lost track of time. When they passed through towns, Arbogast downshifted, and she tried to get a glimpse inside the lit windows of the houses, into courtyards, down narrow lanes. She peered up at a church tower once, without even thinking to notice the time announced by its clock. Once, Arbogast reached up and touched his own hair, then held his hand to the base of his neck—it was something he'd done numerous times in the preceding days, whenever an idea became clear to him. His hands are enormous, she thought, just as they were crossing a small bridge, and realized that they had just passed the place where it had happened.

A short distance down the road, they came upon a cluster of houses. Arbogast took his foot off the gas, put on the blinker and turned off the road into the parking lot of a restaurant. She followed him out of the car. It was cold, and she snuggled into the collar of her coat, which she was wearing over a red wool sweater and a dark blue pantsuit, both of which she'd bought the day before. She was thinking about how much she liked the suit's big gold-tone buttons when Arbogast spoke, startling her out of her thoughts. He was still standing by the car. She hadn't been able to make out what he'd said. His breath was like a cloud of smoke. But when she saw the neon sign, she knew where they were: the Angel.

"You did want to come here, didn't you?"

He had suddenly switched over to using the familiar form of the word *you*, and she couldn't make sense of the aggressive tone in his voice. The outing had been his idea. She wondered now whether it would have been better for her to have broken the silence during the drive. But then again, she thought, I did want to come, didn't I?

"Yes."

She brushed the hair away from her face. It was windy, and she was cold. She lit a cigarette. There had never been a description of the neon sign in any of the files.

"Why?"

Actually, she did know why, but she just shrugged. She had finally realized what she was after: For once in her life, she wanted to take part in a story that she would otherwise only have gotten to know from the other side—death. After all she'd done for Marie, she thought she had a right to that.

And so Katja Lavans asked him, "Have you been with a woman since then?"

It was the first time he'd felt that the gravitational force exerted by the past was increasing, beginning to pull the present closer. He leaned toward her, came very close, and for a moment it seemed he was about to strike her.

She took his arm, trying to calm him. "I'm cold."

She flicked her cigarette into the darkness.

"Then let's keep driving," he said, and they went back to the car.

He bent over slightly as he turned the key in the ignition, then turned to look at her. "The first time we kissed each other, right here, everything else seemed to vanish. I had never experienced anything like that before."

Katja Lavans nodded, glad that the threatening moment had passed. She settled herself into the seat, and Hans Arbogast pulled back out onto the road.

"I understand," she said.

He looked at her with puzzlement.

"Keep your eyes on the road!" She laughed. "I saw the pictures of her. I know that she was happy. And I've seen a lot of dead women."

"Does that mean you believe I didn't kill her?"

Katja Lavans looked out the passenger window without answering him, and it was some time before the awkwardness of her silence was swallowed up by the sound of the car's engine. The valley got narrower there, and the nearly full moon rose above the horizon and into the clear night sky. The forest grew right up to the edge of the roadway, and Arbogast had to downshift where the road curved. In places, the asphalt glittered. At one point, where the road was straight for a while, he let his right hand fall from the gearshift and brush against her upper thigh. It lay there pressed against her leg, almost as if it were unintentional, merely a habit. Katja Lavans didn't return the light pressure of his hand, nor did she shrink from it. They passed any number of enormous Black Forest farmsteads that loomed out threateningly from the side of the road, and the few lighted windows that glimmered out from under their gigantic rooftops resembled the running lights of clipper ships crossing the sea, hulls shining in the moonlight.

She thought about the careful way she had laid the cold waxen flesh against the damp bricks. The following day, she would explain to the judges and jury why Arbogast was innocent, and with that act she would write herself into his life like a passage of her own diary, and yet he would never be able to comprehend what she had discovered in her experiments. The skin of the dead is as cold as the past. Had she really ever liked her work? Was she afraid? She tapped a cigarette free from the pack and lit it.

She closed her eyes. When she opened them again, Arbogast was steering the car though a small town. The road led along a stream that cut deeply into the hillside and then turned steeply up toward the top of the mountain. At a sharp curve about halfway there, Arbogast pulled over.

"Was that Triberg, where the two of you had dinner back then?" she asked.

"Yes. That's the hotel up there."

Katja Lavans rolled down her window and blew smoke out into the night. It was very dark there, and you could hear the stream rushing over the rocks and down the mountain, but the waterfall itself was out of range of hearing. They could make out lights from the hotel on the slope above them, coming through the trees.

" 'Its flowing streams / are too frigid to bear . . .' Do you know that one?"

"No. What is it?"

"A poem about the Black Forest."

"About this place?"

"Yes, up there." She looked out into the night and then closed her eyes for a moment, taking in the scent of the snow and the damp forest floor.

"How does it go on?"

" 'But here down below / our beds are yet colder."

Katja struggled to remember the rest of the verse, which she had memorized as a schoolgirl.

"Who's it by?"

"Brecht."

"The Communist?"

"Yes. He was born in the Black Forest."

"Really? And didn't he go over to the East after the war?"

"Yes."

"And what about you? Are you going back?"

She tossed her cigarette out the window and shrugged. Everyone asked the same thing, and she didn't know how to answer it anymore. Of course she would go back—there was Ilse.

"I have a young daughter."

"How old is she?"

"Ilse's twelve."

Arbogast nodded, as if he understood what she was thinking. Everyone thought they understood her when they asked that. Of course she would go back to her daughter. That was the only reason they'd let her travel out of the country—they were certain of her return. But there were times when she felt there were far too many dead bodies back there, waiting for her. Arbogast let his eyes roam across the road and then peered into the woods. She only wished she were able to dissect his memories the same way she could have done with any other tissue.

"But Brecht is dead."

"Yes, he's dead."

"It's a nice poem, though."

"It goes on, but I've forgotten the end."

As usual, Katja Lavans was reluctant to think about going back. She suggested that they have dinner up at the hotel—maybe it would remind her of the poem.

"I don't think so."

"But didn't you go there with Marie?"

Arbogast nodded, and both of them looked up at the row of illuminated windows on the first floor of the hotel.

"You're not hungry?"

"I am, but everyone would stare at us."

"You're right."

She turned to face the driver's seat and leaned her arm against the backrest. There was a wide smile on her face.

"You're my most famous case, you know," she said, brushing the hair from her face and letting him kiss her.

And when she closed her eyes, it seemed to her that she was somehow, oddly, his sworn ally, that she shared his secret. His lips played slowly with hers. He kissed the way she had hoped he would—like someone who had the potential for violence within him. She breathed in his breath. She knew this much: Even if he had killed Marie, he was unlikely to kill again. Surely he hadn't even noticed when the back of her neck had stiffened unexpectedly, just for that briefest of moments. She hadn't defended herself. Quite the contrary, she thought, her breath catching in her throat. His lips hesitated, then pulled away from hers. The past is catching up to the present, he thought, and grew afraid. He held her face. He ran the flat of his hand across her closed eyelids, and a moment passed before she exhaled.

Then he started up the car. He faced forward, and they drove back. Again, they hardly spoke, and it seemed to her that the journey home took much longer than the journey out. She smoked a cigarette, slowly, and afterward, when she tossed the butt out the window, he saw sparks scatter across the now dry road. A little later on, without taking his eyes from the road, Arbogast told her that this was where it had happened. They were just past the spot where the road crossed the small bridge. Outside the rear window, trees and shrubs grew alongside a small river, which never came into view from the road. Fields in the moonlight, the frozen pavement, no one out on the road but them.

Once again, his hand fell from the gearshift to the edge of her seat and pressed against her thigh. Katja Lavans brushed the hair from her face and closed her eyes. At some point, the back of his hand began tracing the side seam of her pants, up and down, as if he were restlessly following a trail. When he had to shift, he left off doing it just for that moment when the clutch released the drivetrain from the engine, and then he would begin to fondle her again with the same calmness with which he drove. After a while she had the pleasant feeling she, too, was harnessed to the engine, a part of what drove the Borgward forward. Eventually, the motion of the car slowed, it rolled forward in neutral and then finally stood still. Katja still had her eyes closed. What she felt reminded her of the sensation she got when she was playing the theremin—that every motion of her hands connected her to the instrument invisibly, though she never touched it. It was as if the air took on a living form that gave rise to sound. If only, just for once, she could be on the side of the living. Then her face was in his hands again, and once again she let him kiss her. It was the first time she had noticed his smell.

"You can open your eyes now. We're here," he said quietly.

He whispered close up against her ear, and she imagined his smile and, trusting him, opened her eyes. It took her a little while to figure our that they were back at the barn. A couple of rafters cast dark shadows in the moonlight that penetrated the barn through the cracks between the wooden shingles. His body was above her and it covered her in blackness. They wrapped their arms around each other and kissed, his hands everywhere, under her sweater and down her pants, and she held him fast, but soon the space in the car was too tight and they got out.

The damp brick floor of the barn was black and glistening. It was musty and cold. But cold was not the sort of thing that could have stopped them. She couldn't wait to be naked at last, and she closed her eyes and leaned against the hood of the car while he undressed her. Then she leaned forward and laid her cheek against the warm, dry metal. She pushed against him so powerfully with her hips that she kept breaking out of rhythm with him. Finally, he reached out his hand to her neck and forced her to keep in time. She felt him inside her like some beautiful animal, and for a moment, she was still. She saw the rafters and the shadows in the barn clearly, smelled the mustiness all around her, breathed the cold air deep into her lungs. Then his hand cut off all her air. She was on the verge of coming, almost. Just this once, she thought, death is irrelevant. She had turned the dead woman very gently onto her side. She'd had lovely shoulders, Katja Lavans remembered. She had stroked her short hair. With one hand, she had carefully lifted up her head and with the other she'd slid the brick beneath her neck. The pain was in her throat. Just this once, death is irrelevant, she thought, and her lust only grew. Marie, she thought, and grabbed at the hand around her throat. I can't breathe, she thought, and closed her eyes and came. She came and didn't stop coming, and for a moment everything was simple. The painted metal had cooled down in just seconds, and its chill spread to her throbbing temple as quickly as her arousal dwindled to a glowing, tingling pain. And then even that began to fade. Even that was dying. It lingered for just another moment within her; then it was over. Weakly, she struggled against the hand that was wrapped around her throat. She saw blurrily, as if from a great distance, that Arbogast was still thrusting into her, and she tried to push him away.

She didn't know then, nor would she understand afterward, exactly why she suddenly thrashed, ripped his hand from her throat and tried to scream. She couldn't get a sound out at first, but she rolled away from him, until he finally slid out of her. Just a moment of air, she thought, just a moment. He grabbed at her shoulder, but she dodged his grasp again and again. Finally, he tried to get her by the hair, and in so doing, he ripped the wig from her head. He froze for a moment, surprised, and stared at her. She looks like an angel, he thought. She took a deep breath, despite the pain in her throat, and felt the cold air in her lungs, then gagged and brought up some bile and a bit of vomit. She didn't let him out of her sight as she gasped for breath, but he didn't move.

"You pig," she barked at last. "You fucking pig."

"Now I understand why you wear red," he said, as if in a dream. "Marie said that redheads never wear red clothes."

He was still holding the wig in his hands, as if it were her, and blinking into the darkness. She could see his jaws working, but he said nothing more. She endured looking at him for just another moment or two, until her breath had calmed down enough for her to put her clothes back on, and then she left. He didn't react when she pulled the wig from his hand.

57

Over the sink in the bathroom, there was a small porcelain shelf where she kept her toothbrush, standing in its glass, her toothpaste and the cosmetics she had bought in Frankfurt. Above the shelf was a mirror almost a yard wide. When she looked at herself, she could see in her pupils the tiny reflection of the fluorescent tube that was mounted above the mirror, a cold, meager bar of light. And in that cold light, the bathroom echoed like some far-off hell with the constant low gurgling sound of dripping water from the leaky toilet bowl. She had washed her face long and hard with soap and water and then turned off the spigot—that was when she first heard the drip.

The first thing she had done when she got back to her room was to pick up the telephone and ask for a connection to East Berlin. She wanted to talk to Bernhard. Then she'd sat smoking in bed for half an hour, tapping her ashes into the glass ashtray that she set on the pillow beside her. When the phone finally rang, she'd grabbed up the receiver, but it was only the voice of a young woman from the Hamburg long-distance-operator service, who told her that all lines were busy and there was no chance of getting through to East Berlin that night. Katja Lavans had wound the telephone cord around her hand, said thank you and hung up.

It would have been a great help to hear Bernhard's voice. She wasn't sure if she would have told him what had happened, but just to hear his voice would have done her good, and maybe she would have been able to bring herself to talk about the dead women. Bernhard knew what had happened to Marie, and he was familiar with the experiments that Katja had been conducting at the Charité for the past six months, as well as the pictures she'd taken of them. She looked at herself in the mirror and tried to decide if Arbogast had injured her. She licked her lips and brushed her hair off her forehead, tucked it behind her ear. She was ashamed that she had trusted him—she knew Marie too well. That was why she was here. But whereas he had known Marie's beauty in life, she had only seen pictures of her in death. Slowly, she ran her fingers through her hair, tugging on her bangs and pulling the pieces above her ears into place and generally setting straight the hair that she had hidden under the wig for the past several days. The thought of her long red hair in his hands was repulsive to her. What she saw before her was strange as well, however. She was too familiar with this sort of humming fluorescent light to be shocked by the face that looked back at her in the mirror, and yet the cold fear she saw in her own eyes was something new to her.

58

It was still dim in the courtroom at eight o'clock on Thursday, a damp, cold morning. The snow had let up. Ansgar Klein had picked up his client early, and they waited at the defense table, undisturbed by the members of the press, who were only just now arriving. The room filled slowly. Klein had wanted to get to the court early that morning because he had to get the slide projector set up on the table in front of him. Arbogast had stretched the extension cord all the way across the room to plug it in at the one single outlet, beside the judge's bench. Now Klein was looking through his notes. Arbogast straightened his tie and stared blankly ahead of him. After a while, the lawyer got out his Thermos bottle, as he did every day. He unscrewed it, turned over the lid and poured himself a cup of the light green tea that the hotel staff had finally learned to prepare to his satisfaction. It was only when the proceedings were about to begin that he began to be concerned about Katja Lavans—he didn't see her anywhere. In a few minutes, the judges would be coming into the courtroom, but she still hadn't shown up. He asked Arbogast if he knew where the pathologist could be, but Arbogast just shook his head.

"Didn't you go for a drive with her last night?"

"That's right."

Arbogast looked at him with a blank expression, and Klein began to worry about what could possibly have happened to prevent Katja Lavans from showing up on time on the day she was scheduled to deliver her testimony. It was a mistake not to have arranged to meet at the hotel, the way they had done the preceding few days, and drive to the courthouse together. He should have gone and knocked on her door when she didn't show up at breakfast. But then, just as the judges and jury entered the room and everyone rose to their feet, Klein spotted Katja Lavans coming in through the rows of chairs reserved for the general public. She sneaked in hesitantly, and he was surprised to see her real hair, rather than the red wig she'd been wearing the past several days. Their eyes met, and Klein was disturbed by the utterly unfamiliar appearance of her face. From the corner of her his eye, he could see that Fritz Sarrazin had held a place for the pathologist beside him, just as he'd done every other day of the trial so far. Sarrazin appeared to notice the surprise on Klein's face and turned around to look for its source.

Klein reassured himself that it was inconceivable Katja Lavans wouldn't have shown up, but he kept his eyes on his expert witness as everyone took their seats. Although there were no places free in the gallery, apparently she didn't feel confident about going forward to join Sarrazin, choosing instead to crouch down and lean against the arm of a chair in one of the back rows. She tugged at her hair repeatedly. He couldn't imagine what might have caused this sudden nervousness to come over her, and he only hoped it didn't have anything to do with the testimony she was about to deliver. Then the judge declared the court in session.

"We now resume the proceedings in the case of the *People of the Federal Republic of Germany versus Hans Arbogast*, docket number two five/three eight-o nineteen fifty-five. I see that all members of the defense and prosecution are present. The court calls Frau Dr. Lavans to the stand as an expert witness."

Ansgar Klein held his breath—for a moment, it seemed almost as if she were considering leaving the courtroom instead of coming forward. Despite the distance from which he was watching her, Klein thought he saw her take a deep breath before finally standing up and stepping to the front of the courtroom. Meanwhile, the prosecuting attorney had risen and was addressing the court. "I would like to inform the court that Professor Maul has sent a document he prepared to various parties involved in this trial."

The chief judge was alarmed. "What, today?"

"Yesterday. All of the scientific experts have assured me, however, that they did not review this document, and in some cases, they returned it directly to Professor Maul."

"Did you receive a copy of this document, Frau Dr. Lavans?" Lindner was angry.

Katja Lavans, who had remained standing, appeared to pause for a moment to consider the question, almost as if she hadn't been listening and didn't know what they were talking about. Then she said quietly, "No, Your Honor, I did not," and stared at her hands.

Ansgar Klein stood up. "I would like to state for the record that I strongly protest this attempt by Professor Maul to influence the expert witnesses at this trial."

Judge Lindner directed the clerk, who was recording the proceedings, to note this objection in the record, then turned back to the pathologist.

"Please state your name."

She turned back to look at Arbogast.

"My name is Dr. Katja Lavans. I am a forensic pathologist at Humboldt University in East Berlin."

"Your age?"

"Forty-one. I was born on September ninth, 1928."

"In Berlin?"

"Yes."

"Your marital status?"

"Divorced." Katja Lavans's right hand lifted up, as if she wanted to brush the hair out of her face, then hesitated, and finally it slid across her right temple to the back of her neck, where she let it remain. "I have a twelve-year-old daughter."

Her eyes raced across the parquet floor, as if they wanted to make an escape. Then she looked at Arbogast. Ansgar Klein saw the look she gave him, and he turned to watch his client's reaction. He held his hand to the corner of his mouth in puzzlement. He could see in Katja Lavans's eyes that she didn't find whatever she was looking for from Arbogast, any more than he had. Arbogast didn't move a muscle. Katja Lavans was still holding the back of her neck with her left hand. From where he sat, Fritz Sarrazin could see only her back, but he'd noticed the lawyer's uneasiness and sensed the anxiety in the way she held her hand fast to her neck—something wasn't right.

"Is everything all right, Frau Dr. Lavans?" asked the judge when she didn't stop staring at Arbogast. Then she shifted her gaze to the front of the room and nodded.

"Good." The judge smiled at her. "Today will be our day for pathology. Frau Dr. Lavans, I must make you aware that you are about to testify before a court of law. Expert testimony has the same weight and bears the same obligations as that of any eyewitness. You must speak the truth, and if the court judges it necessary, you may be obligated to testify under oath. Making misleading statements of a scientific nature is punishable by law."

"I understand."

Katja Lavans nodded and paused a moment before she began to speak. "First, I would like to make it clear that I take no pleasure in the testimony I am about to deliver. I have come to conclusions that are very different from those of a widely respected colleague." As she spoke, her voice gradually acquired confidence.

"On the other hand, I feel an absolutely essential responsibility to help reverse a verdict that resulted from a dubious piece of expert testimony. There is no question that the entire Arbogast case seemed to be an extremely dramatic situation back when it happened. A short time prior to the discovery of Marie Gurth's body, another body had been found in the same area, and then this second body appeared, with bite marks on the woman's right breast no less. All of these circumstances must necessarily have worked to the disadvantage of a defendant with prior convictions. But did the bite marks even come from the defendant? No one attempted to determine this fact scientifically. Even if they did come from the defendant, the question of their severity remains. Were they, in fact, merely superficial? Was there sufficient evidence of brutality to suggest that base motives were at work? None of these things is certain from the start. Biting is certainly not uncommon in the context of consensual sex—indeed, it can be considered normal—but it may also be done in rage or out of hatred. Then again, it's not just sexual partners who bite one another—there are cases of mothers who have bitten their children, a phenomenon that is also well known to behavioral scientists studying animal behavior. And of course, we are all familiar with the expression 'I'm going to eat you up!' "

Katja Lavans paused and took a sip of water. Her voice was clearly audible. She avoided looking at Arbogast, focusing her gaze on the judges and the jurors instead. In front of her on the table, she had a pad, and once she had finished this preamble, she opened it. From the side, Klein could see that she had written out a list of points to make.

"The judgment passed in 1955 was based on forensic findings that were, in part, simply incorrect and were, furthermore, misinterpreted on the basis of misleading expert testimony. A particularly cautious approach should have been taken by the forensic experts in this case, given the fact that no forensic pathologist was present at either the discovery site or during the autopsy. As a result of this oversight, certain crucial errors were made.

"For example, it was overlooked that certain hemorrhages, regardless of whether they were sustained pre- or postmortem, would have appeared larger and more serious because the cadaver lay for some time on an incline, with its head lower than its body. This position resulted in the bruises appearing darker than they otherwise would have—that is, if the body had lain horizontally. It was furthermore absolutely essential to the autopsy findings that any dissection of the tissues of the throat be conducted such that blood could not drain into those tissues from the surrounding areas of the head and chest. This importance of this technique is described in Professor Maul's own textbook, by the way. And yet the autopsy report reveals that in Marie Gurth's case, the correct procedure was not followed. Another error in the autopsy report is the determination of anal sex. Traces of feces were identified by the presence of shreds of meat, starch, plant oils and so on. Well, I'm sure that if the tests had been run on a pot of goulash, the results would have been similar. And yet special emphasis was laid on this finding.

"Finally, it is well known that in cases of strangulation, and in particular the use of a garotte, as described in the original verdict, hemorrhaging is always seen in the connective tissues of the neck. This was established by the work of Dr. Bschorr in 1967. The 1955 verdict, written under advisement of the expert witness, Dr. Maul, attempts to explain, in contradiction of this basic tenet, that the absence of any hemorrhaging in the connective tissue was nevertheless consistent with strangulation because the garotte was tightened so swiftly that the blood flow was stopped before it could collect there. And yet a finding of bruised and abraded tissue encircling the neck is absolutely to be expected in such cases of swift compression of the throat or when the force used is great enough to stop the flow of blood to the brain. No such marks were found. Additionally, the verdict draws attention to the edema of the lungs and cites the bloody mucus found in the airways as evidence that the deceased had suffered a blow to the nose. This conclusion is not acceptable. On the contrary—the finding is an extremely common one in cadavers and has no forensic significance."

The pathologist had picked up her copy of the autopsy report and now began to page through it. "The reason such speculations were ventured may be traced to item nine of the autopsy report. I quote: 'Uncoagulated blood was drained from the right outer ear.' " She paused and looked at the judge.

"As we heard yesterday from one of the police officials who was called at the first trial, bloody fluid drained from the nose of the cadaver when it was turned over and transported. Now, where would this fluid come to rest if the body was subsequently laid on its back? The ears! Subsequently, the body was cleaned up and photographed, and later, during the autopsy, it was noticed that this same blood was pooled in the outer ears." Katja Lavans shook her head. "These are rudimentary errors!"

She threw the autopsy report onto the table with her notes, and for a moment Ansgar Klein was afraid it was going to knock over the carafe.

"Furthermore, it is fully incomprehensible to me why the coroners and the district attorney's experts would have concluded that the deceased's injuries were sustained vitally, meaning prior to death."

Katja Lavans paused, and the chief judge used this break just as she had intended him to: to ask a question. "Just a moment now. Are you saying bruising can be caused even after death?"

"Yes, naturally. It's been part of the classic forensics literature since the work of Dr. Shultz in 1896 and is universally accepted as a fact of forensic medicine. That the blood of a cadaver remains uncoagulated for a matter of hours after death was established by Theo Steinburg in his 1937 University of Rostock dissertation, entitled 'The Creation of a Furrow by Rope Compression During the Transportation of a Cadaver,' and was subsequently confirmed by Schleyer in his postdoctoral thesis, *Clotting Factors in the Blood of Cadavers*, which was published by Schmorl and Seefeld in Hanover in 1950—and should therefore have been well known at the time of the first trial."

"So, then, how can injuries sustained prior to death be distinguished from postmortem ones?"

"They can't. If force is exerted upon a cadaver in the hours immediately following death, it cannot later be forensically determined whether it was pre- or postmortem. Furthermore, for precisely that reason, it's questionable whether the finding of dried skin in the neck region can be used to support a conclusion that strangulation occurred—the injuries might have been sustained entirely postmortem. Indeed, in this case, the body was subjected to extensive handling: resuscitation attempts, transportation in a car. And one also has to consider the roll down the embankment, landing in the brambles, and then the time the body lay there, exposed to the weather."

"Could you please explain further what you mean when you refer to dried skin?" asked Ansgar Klein.

"Patches of dried skin on a cadaver arise primarily from the abrasions that naturally occur in the process of strangulation. But it's important to note that even relatively minor rubbing can cause such dry patches, as is described in Johann Ludwig Casper's *Atlas to the Handbook of Forensic Medicine*, first published by the Berlin firm Hirschwald in 1860. In it, he demonstrates that even rubbing the skin of a cadaver with a coarse flannel can give rise to such dry patches."

"That's not a very current source," remarked the judge.

"Indeed not," replied Katja Lavans with some agitation. "Everything I'm telling you could have been said thirty years ago. But rather than casting any doubt on my analysis, I would suggest that this calls into question the conclusions drawn from the facts of the case back in 1955."

"Please go on, Frau Dr. Lavans."

"When the body of the deceased was rolled from the roadway down into the blackberry thicket, it would have been in the earliest stages of rigor mortis, and as the relevant photographs clearly establish, it came to rest on fallen branches. The Y-shaped mark on the neck may well have been the impression of a forked tree branch, from where the body lay against the ground. Furthermore, during early rigor mortis, minor articulations of the limbs and shifts in body position often take place. The weather on the day of the body's discovery would have encouraged the development of the resulting abrasions into the dry patches we're discussing. Dampness and immersion accelerate this process, and the weather service's reports for the area on that day called for heavy dew and light precipitation."

"But all these are speculations."

"No. Anyone who has studied forensics at a good school knows these things. But in order to illustrate for the court exactly how the dry patches are caused when a cadaver rests on a sharp edge or a forked surface, I have conducted a series of experiments using bodies of cadavers already at the morgue of the Charité Hospital. I have photographed the results and would like to present them to the court."

The chief judge looked around at his fellow judges and at the prosecution, and when they nodded their assent, he invited the witness to present her photographs. The lights were dimmed. Ansgar Klein turned on the machine and projected the first of the pathologist's slides onto the side wall of the courtroom, behind the table where the prosecutor sat. Everyone in the room turned their heads to see. Katja Lavans thought back to the recent evening in Frankfurt when she'd shown her work to the lawyer, and it seemed like it had happened an awfully long time ago. He won't be interested in me anymore, she thought bitterly, then began her presentation.

"Here you see the first in an ongoing series of experiments designed to demonstrate the causation of the dry, abraded areas on cadavers. Please note that these bodies were left lying for between twelve and fourteen hours, whereas Marie Gurth herself lay out in the open for some forty-eight hours. What you see in this slide is the body of a twenty-three-year-old woman. The cadaver had been refrigerated at ten degrees Celsius for five days before it was taken out and laid in such a position that the neck pressed against the edge of a brick; it was left in this position for twelve hours. After three hours, photographs were taken using both thirteen-by-eighteen large-format black-and-white film and six-by-six color film. The image shows a peaked, Y-shaped abrasion, with the fork of the Y lying just behind the ear."

Ansgar Klein watched the pathologist closely, and when she nodded, he advanced the button on the slide carousel and the second image was projected on the wall.

"This experiment was conducted in the following manner: The cadavers were positioned so that the left sides of their necks rested on bricks wrapped in damp fabric, and they remained in the same position for approximately seven to eight hours—after death. Then the bodies were turned onto their backs and a photo lamp with a two-hundred-watt bulb was set up at a distance of one meter from the body. This served to speed up the process of drying out. The heat from the lamp was applied for thirty minutes. This slide shows the results. Here, too, you can see that there are gaps in the dried patch on each body. I believe that this experiment can explain the diverse array of abrasions found on the body, including those with and without such gaps. Here you see several other experiments."

Ansgar Klein showed the remaining slides. Afterward, the judge had the blinds reopened and Katja Lavans went on.

"Now, in the case of Marie Gurth, the deceased had a particular medical history that is relevant to these considerations. According to the records of a Berlin social service agency where we made inquiries, Frau Gurth contracted syphilis in 1948 and had undergone therapy consisting of six rounds of alternating Salvarsan and bismuth treatments. In addition, at autopsy it was determined that the uterus contained a placenta the size of a five-mark piece and that the patient had suffered an incomplete abortion."

"An abortion?"

"Yes, at the end of the second month."

"The second month?"

Katja Lavans nodded.

"These factors are far from irrelevant when it comes to assessing cardiac and circulatory function. We must therefore refer to the pathologist's report on microscopic examination of the heart tissues. There were signs of prior myocarditis as well as a current inflammation. Furthermore, it would have been advisable for the doctors who conducted the autopsy to consider the possibility of an air embolus, as one always should when investigating the sudden death of any woman of childbearing age. In this case, all the conditions that could allow an air embolus to enter into the abdominal cavity were present: dilated cervix, retained products of the conceptus, including fetal and placental remains, and above all the position of Mrs. Gurth on all fours, which, according to Amreich, 1924, is a particular risk factor for this event, because it brings about venous dilation."

The pathologist paused briefly to see if there were any questions before going on.

"The defendant has repeatedly stated that Marie Gurth died suddenly in the middle of their second act of sexual intercourse, which was performed *a tergo*. The question of anal sex that arises here begs particular consideration. This possibility is addressed in items eight and thirty of the autopsy report, which reads 'Upon the separation of the buttocks, the anus is dilated.' This finding is not in the least surprising, but the hypothesis that the absence of feces in the rectum might have been caused by compression from the penetration of the penis is grotesque—it suggests a fundamental ignorance of both anatomy and physiology. Quite to the contrary, the absence of feces in the rectum strongly suggests that the cause of death was something other than suffocation, which is commonly accompanied by a release of urine and stool into the rectum. It is quite possible that the actions the defendant described having taken to clean the deceased could have given rise to the defects in the mucous membranes found on autopsy. To this extent, there are no autopsy findings that contradict the defendant's statement.

"To this, we must also add consideration of the possibility that sudden death resulted from acute cardiac arrest due to sympathetic overstimulation, and, above all, the Valsalva maneuver, in which increased abdominal pressure can trigger a sudden drop in blood pressure. With her slight build and short stature, the deceased had all the characteristics of the asthenic type that is predisposed to this condition. We have reports of cases of sudden death during sexual intercourse dating back to the seventeenth century. The frequency with which it has been reported at different periods in history is discussed in the work of Ueno, *On the So-Called Coition Death*, Nihon University Press, 1965."

Katja Lavans studied her notes briefly.

"This manner of death occurs more commonly during extramarital sex than it does between husband and wife, by the way."

She nodded at the judge and put her notebook back down beside the carafe. Then she drank half a glass of water and refilled the glass.

During this pause, Ansgar Klein stood up, walked around from the defense table and removed a small box from the stacks of files that he'd brought with him to the courthouse every day of the trial.

"Do you know what this is, Frau Dr. Lavans?" The lawyer opened the box, took out a length of silk and held it up so everyone could see. Katja Lavans shook her head.

"It's a garotte."

There was murmuing in the gallery. Both the jurors and Hans Arbogast alike leaned forward to see it better. Klein handed the length of silk to the pathologist, who examined it closely.

"Do you believe that Marie Gurth was strangled with an implement of this sort?"

"No."

Katja Lavans handed the length of silk back to him, and the lawyer returned to his seat.

"What, then, in your opinion, was the actual cause of death, Frau Dr. Lavans?" asked the judge.

"In my opinion, death ensued from sudden failure of the already weakened heart muscle, meaning that the heart was prone to this sort of failure, and this condition was probably exacerbated by myocarditis. Add to that the circulatory stress associated with the sexual act."

"You're saying that according to you, there are no findings that suggest a violent attack on the woman while she was alive?"

"No, none."

"And all the signs that have previously been understood to suggest violent treatment of the deceased are actually just artifacts of the handling of her body after death, such as hiding her in the bushes."

"Yes. It's like this: Not everything dies at death."

"And the cause of death is heart failure?"

"Yes."

"Can the possibility of a violent death be ruled out?"

"Yes. I would say there is no possibility that a violent assault on Mrs. Gurth, in particular on her neck, was the cause of death."

The judge nodded and thanked Katja Lavans for her remarks. He then called Dr. Günther Monsberg, the director of the Institute of Forensic Medicine in Cologne, to the stand. Monsberg, a witness for the prosecution, confined his statement largely to discussing the inadequacies of the autopsy.

"They really left us in the lurch here."

"What do you mean by that?"

"I mean that, first of all, I can't even imagine that a licensed pathologist dictated such an autopsy report." It was imprecise in both its methods and its language, he said.

Monsberg also confirmed the fact that there was nothing new about the idea that the blood could flow, even after death—that was basic science—and he agreed with Katja Lavans's opinion that there were no indications that any violence had occurred while the deceased was still alive. In such cases, he said, it was essential that a forensic specialist be called to the scene immediately and that nothing be moved or changed until that person had had a chance to inspect the body.

"I fully endorse every word of what Frau Dr. Lavans told the court."

After that, court was recessed until the afternoon, when the final witness of the day, Professor Schmidt-Wulfen, who had collaborated with Professor Maul on his original written deposition, testified that even back then he had thought it possible that the injuries were sustained postmortem. He, too, said he was aware that postmortem hemorrhaging was possible, but he did feel "something may have happened to Mrs. Gurth while she was still alive."

"What do you mean by that?" Ansgar Klein asked. Schmidt-Wulfen, the dean of forensic medicine at the University of Freiburg, was a heavy man and nearly bald. He wore a dark tweed suit, the lapels of which he jammed to the side so he could hook his thumbs in the armholes of his vest.

"I think it entirely possible that force was used on the neck. It's just that there's no sign of it."

The public responded to this statement with murmuring, and for just a moment Arbogast looked up and caught the eye of the pathologist on the stand. Schmidt-Wulfen maintained the eye contact with some puzzlement, until eventually Arbogast looked away. Then the judge told the pathologist he could step down. He thanked all the expert witnesses who had testified that day for their cooperation and informed the prosecution of his decision: "Given the situation, I no longer consider it necessary to investigate further the personality of Hans Arbogast, by which I mean to say that we will dispense with any further discussion of the defendant's prior convictions."

Dr. Ansgar Klein offered his approval of this decision and then turned to address the experts. “On behalf of my client, I would like to thank you all for offering your expertise without remuneration.”

The members of the public applauded, and Judge Lindner called for order, saying that such behavior would not be tolerated in his courtroom. “This brings the presentation of evidence to a close. Tomorrow, we will proceed with closing statements.”

59

On Friday, Fritz Sarrazin had the newspapers delivered from the well-stocked newsstand at the train station, and as far as he could tell from what he read, the recognition for Katja Lavans's expert testimony was universal. He was particularly amused by the item in the *Grangater Tageblatt* and he took it with him to the courtroom to show to the pathologist while they were waiting for members of the court to arrive.

"For a Swiss, it's always somewhat annoying to hear one's country constantly described as being small."

"But it is small!"

"Oh, come on! Please don't you start. Yours isn't all that much larger. Why don't you just listen to how people praise you: 'On this day of forensic-expert testimony, court-watchers witnessed an embarrassing development: The criminologists from the diminutive nation of Switzerland were celebrating victory in the Grangat courtroom, and the Federal Republic of Germany, despite all its federal and local offices of Criminal Investigation, had very little to offer in its own right. Regardless of what effect such testimony has on the outcome of the Arbogast case, it was an important day for the science of forensic medicine in Germany—both parts of Germany.' "

"Here they come! Let me see the whole thing, will you?"

Sarrazin passed Katja Lavans the paper, and the pathologist read until the judges and jury had entered the courtroom.

"I recommence the proceedings and invite the district attorney to make his closing statement."

The chief district attorney, Dr. Curtius, stood up and began his statement with a general remark. In his opinion, he said, press reports such as those appearing in the newsmagazine *Bunten* constituted a dangerous assault on the justice system, as they were capable of infringing on the impartiality of the members of the court. But then he conceded that he had not been able to refute the claims of the forensic experts for the defense or their conclusion that Arbogast had not hurt Marie Gurth.

"I would nonetheless like to convey to you my firm belief that the verdict handed down in the year 1955 was the result of a serious attempt to do what was right and that no one then involved should be reproached as having treated the matter casually, much less maliciously. That said, there is no way for us to prove that Marie Gurth might have been strangled to death."

He said he wanted to speak freely: "I do not now believe myself capable of securing a verdict against the defendant on any point of law."

The judge nodded to Dr. Curtius.

"Thank you, Mr. Prosecutor. And now I would ask the defense attorney to make his closing statement."

Ansgar Klein opened his speech by thanking Horst Lindner, the associate judge of the Grangat District Superior Court, for the fair and appropriate manner in which he had conducted the proceedings, which, he said, had originated out of a desire to learn the truth and to permit Hans Arbogast finally to experience justice. There was no longer any reproach against his client. He said that the Arbogast case should be seen as an early warning against the dangers of the death penalty and that the case would make it into legal history because it had raised the essential questions that had to be raised if the justice system was ever to be reformed.

The Arbogast case would also be important for the field of forensic medicine, he said. He deplored the fact that the expert witness from the first trial, Professor Dr. Heinrich Maul, had not possessed sufficient personal resources to admit that he had made an error. Given that, he was all the more eager to thank the other scientists, who had served the causes of justice and truth and done credit to their discipline. He requested that the guilty verdict levied against Hans Arbogast on January 17, 1955, for the crime of murder be overturned and that the costs of the trial be reimbursed by the state, at which point a determination should also be made with regard to a settlement of damages resulting from Arbogast's wrongful incarceration.

Ansgar Klein sat down. The judge thanked him and then gave the accused himself the final word. Hans Arbogast stood up, and it briefly seemed like he was striving to call up from memory the sentence that he'd prepared for the occasion. A smile hovered around his lips as he spoke.

"I ask the court to return to me the justice that I have awaited for the past sixteen years. And I would like to thank my lawyer for his selfless efforts on my behalf."

"This closes the proceedings. The members of the court will withdraw for deliberation. The reading of the verdict is scheduled for nine a.m. on Monday."

The instant the courtroom doors were opened, photographers and cameramen poured inside and surrounded the defense table. They kept asking Arbogast to thank his lawyer for them all over again, and finally he just shook his head and sat back down. The glare of flashbulbs swept across the walls. Arbogast waited for Klein to gather up his files, and then they went downstairs to the small entryway where Sarrazin and Katja Lavans would be waiting for them, as they had waited for them every day that week. But first Paul Mohr stopped him and asked Arbogast if he would consent to give him a brief interview. Standing next to him was the photographer who had taken the pictures of Marie. Gesine told Arbogast that she wanted to apologize for the part her pictures had played in sending him to prison for so many years.

"You know, it was just dreadful taking those pictures."

Yes, he said, he understood.

"Really?"

But the truth was, she had fully expected him to understand her—after all, they both shared the memory of Marie Gurth. Arbogast nodded. Meanwhile, Klein had gotten his files together, and now they wound their way out of the courtroom together. The room was emptying out fast, since most of the journalists were in a hurry to get back to the train station or to their cars so they could spend the weekend at home before returning to Grangat for the verdict on Monday. Arbogast asked Gesine if perhaps they could meet sometime, away from court, perhaps the following day. Gesine nodded and shook his hand. "Till tomorrow, then," she said, and just as she disappeared, Arbogast saw Paul Mohr in conversation with Father Karges, who looked over and gave him a friendly nod.

"Mr. Arbogast!" Paul Mohr turned to him. "Father Karges was just telling me that he counseled you while you were in prison."

Arbogast shrugged his shoulders as if to say he didn't know what Mohr was talking about, but then Karges laughed loudly and pressed his head in close to Arbogast. "My congratulations, Arbogast. It seems to me that you may really be on your way back to innocence after all."

Paul Mohr was surprised by the wrathful way Arbogast looked at the priest, but then again, he'd been aware of Karges all week long, and he'd heard from his colleagues that the priest had vehemently defended the opinion of the original district attorney and insisted that Arbogast must not be allowed to go free. When asked a direct question, though, all he would do was remark that all the prisoners at Bruchsal opened their hearts to him, sooner or later—no one was without guilt. Paul Mohr had never taken any of that stuff seriously, but now for the first time he saw a certain hardness in Arbogast's eyes that others had described while they were sitting around at the Silver Star but which had never shown itself during the trial.

And even now, Hans Arbogast just looked at the priest for a long time without speaking and then quickly followed his lawyer out of the room.

Every day that week, and every time the trial came closer to reaching its hoped-for goal, Klein had felt a new level of exhaustion. It was as if something were being drained away from him that had heretofore been a necessary part of his life. He set the heavy files down on the grooved pavement, which was damp with snow, and stretched. Sarrazin nodded to him with a smile.

"Do you want get some dinner at the hotel?" Sarrazin asked.

Klein rubbed his temples. "Yes, gladly."

"I don't think it would be out of order to celebrate a little, do you?"

Katja Lavans stamped her white patent-leather boots and fastened the neck of her jacket, which was of the same material, tightly around her throat. She was freezing. Ansgar Klein looked over at her inquiringly. He seemed to have something he wanted to say.

"Are you coming, too, Hans?" asked Sarrazin.

Arbogast nodded, and the four of them turned right, heading down Moltkestrasse in the direction of the Palm Garden Hotel.

The dining room was almost empty, just two other tables—a married couple and a family with three children, all in blue sweaters. Ansgar Klein called for a bottle of red wine and they all ordered the daily special, venison stew with dumplings. Sarrazin and the lawyer discussed the day in court and the closing statements. Katja Lavans, who was sitting by the window, looked out the corner of her eye at the branches of the rhododendron that were being tossed by the wind and repeatedly hurled against the glass along with a thin spray of snow. She was relieved that Arbogast continued to avoid looking at her, just as she did with him, and she tried to engage herself in conversation with Ansgar Klein instead. Since Sunday, she had been paying Arbogast only just enough attention so as not to be impolite.

Fritz Sarrazin seemed to notice this attempt, and as soon as the plates had been cleared away, he struck up a conversation with Arbogast. He ordered cognac, offered Arbogast a cigar and leaned so far back in his chair that the white table seemed to be a vast snowy landscape that separated him and Arbogast from the pathologist and the lawyer. Katja Lavans smoked, looked out the window and tried to think of something to say. She could feel the time racing by. Klein drank his cognac. He had pictured things differently, she thought, remembering that evening in Frankfurt. It had been just a week, but that night now seemed to have happened much longer ago, separated as it was from the present by the thing she didn't want to talk about. Because I'm just not certain of it, she thought, that's why. She'd told herself that over and over again the past few days: You're not sure. But it didn't help. Beginning with that one tiny moment of time when it had happened, it had gone on ceaselessly to devour time, threatening to eat its way through everything that had ever happened or ever might.

Katja Lavans stubbed out her cigarette. Fritz Sarrazin allowed himself to lean forward into the silence and reach for the ashtray just as Katja Lavans was pushing it toward the middle of the table. He tapped the long gray ash from his cigarette.

"But don't you think," he was asking Arbogast, "that this experience might somehow be useful to you? You did complete a course of study."

"Yeah, maybe."

Lavans and Klein looked over at Arbogast almost involuntarily to see what else he'd have to say, but he said nothing.

"So, do you think you'll ever remarry?"

To ask that question, Katja Lavans had had to remove the still-unlit cigarette from between her lips. Arbogast shrugged. A short time later, Sarrazin announced that he wanted to treat everyone, and he called over the waitress—or, as he called her, "the girl."

60

Gesine was watching television again that night. She had made herself some potato soup, which she ate while watching a program called *The Sale of Nature* on Channel 3, but the images were so shocking to her that she kept having to put her plate down, and she was considering turning it off entirely. Then she closed her eyes and thought about the date she had made. She hadn't told Paul who it was she was planning to meet on Saturday evening, and now she tried to imagine talking to Arbogast. The small room over the shop was dark except for the blue light, which shimmered with images of dead fish, until she finally turned the television off.

At the same point in time, Fritz Sarrazin was peering out at the glistening snow in the park from the window of his hotel room. He had ordered another whiskey, and he picked up the glass from the small tray, pulled off his shoes, sat down on the bed and placed a call home. It wasn't particularly late. It took five rings for Sue to pick up.

While it rang, Katja Lavans heard the distant ringing of another phone in the quiet of the hotel and then a knock at her door. She stepped out of the bathroom in her pajamas and went to the door with some trepidation to see who it was.

She didn't dare speak, and at first Ansgar Klein, too, just stood there in the doorway. Then he took a careful step toward her, and it seemed he was about to take her face in his hands. The memory surged up so threateningly before her for a moment that she had to struggle not to slap his hands away. But she held still and let it happen. At some point, she asked him to come in, although in retrospect she couldn't say they had ever separated from their embrace. He silently undressed and they slipped into bed.

When she awoke the following morning, she was lying just the same way she had been when they'd fallen asleep. She'd spent the whole night in a state of light sleep, just on the edge of dreaming, never forgetting he held her in his arms. She had been aware that it was getting colder in the room and then eventually that it was growing light outside the window, but she'd never quite awakened entirely. But when she did, the mere fluttering of her lashes against his skin was enough to waken him, and he stretched. She drank in his scent. The morning air was cold on the pillows. His mouth was so close against her ear that she could feel the warmth of his breath, the vibrations of his voice when he spoke. She closed her eyes against the bright daylight.

"Do you know any poems by heart?" she asked quietly.

"Yes, just one."

"Recite it for me."

"I don't want to."

"Why not?"

He shrugged.

"Come on, do it."

He took a deep breath and cleared his throat. Then whispered:

"*Animula vagula blandula,*
hospes comesque corporis,
que nunc abibis in loca
pallidula rigida nudula
nec ut soles dabis iocos."

She couldn't help but think of the Brecht poem she had so recently recited from memory and she felt the shame rise up in her cheeks at the thought that someone knew her in that particular, unbearable manner. When she spoke, she wasn't able to make her voice sound as calm or as quiet as she wanted it to.

"Does that word *animula* come from *anima*—the soul?"

"Yes. It's an endearment."

"An endearment for the soul?"

He detected a strange metallic tone in her voice.

"What's wrong?"

"What do you mean?" She stared at his shoulder.

"I wish I knew what you were afraid of."

She freed herself from their embrace and turned to look at him, as if he might be able to tell her something, but he just looked at her expectantly.

"No," she said. "It's nothing. I'm just sad, that's all. Maybe because I have to go back soon."

He nodded but continued to look at her searchingly. She had seen that look before. But never before had anyone guessed a secret Katja Lavans didn't want to reveal. She knew her fear was too great. It's a pity, she thought, but she knew she would never speak of what had happened to her. Unless he really could see it—just by looking at her? No, he had already given up trying.

"What do you think? Shall we spend the day in bed?"

She laughed, and it sounded almost innocent.

"Yes, definitely. But first things first: I'd like to get the full translation of that poem. You say *animula* is an endearment. So it starts out with something like 'My sweet little soul'?

"Yes. 'My sweet little soul' is nice. 'My wandering sweet little soul, vessel of my love, go you now to that ashen, barren place, my small naked one, you will not play with me again.' "

"Death," she said, forgetting herself.

She knew now what she realized she had always known: It would never stop. Not for me, she thought. Sometimes, when she had turned a cadaver onto its side, it would groan quietly. Of course it was just the air being expressed from the lungs. Her face, as if she were only sleeping on that brick. The short hair. But as soon as she stroked the cold skin, her fear always went away.

"*Nec ut soles dabis iocos.*"

"Who's the author?"

"The Roman emperor Hadrian. A.D. 138."

" 'And the sky was empty.' "

Her voice had taken on that metallic sound again, but this time she knew he would misunderstand it; he wouldn't ask her about it again. And then perhaps someday the memory would fade.

"Yes."

61

Late on Saturday afternoon, Fritz Sarrazin rang the doorbell at Arbogast's sister's house on Lupinenstrasse. At first, she didn't recognize him. But then, when he introduced himself, she gave him a friendly welcome and invited him to go right upstairs to the living room on the second floor. Hans Arbogast rose from the sofa in surprise when he came in. They shook hands and stood there in front of each other awkwardly for a moment. Then Sarrazin took a seat in one of the two armchairs and Arbogast sat back down on the sofa, where a newspaper was lying open. There was a pot of coffee and a cup on the table. Arbogast was unshaven and wore a blue jogging suit with the zipper almost all the way undone, revealing the white undershirt he had on beneath it. He was barefoot. Just as he was explaining that he was having his breakfast rather later that day than usual, there were footsteps in the hall and in came Elke Arbogast with another cup.

"Would you like a cup of coffee?" asked Arbogast.

"Yes, thank you."

The sister poured it for him, then gave a nod as if to say, *Bon appétit*, and left. Sarrazin could hear the stairs creaking.

"Milk and sugar?" asked Arbogast.

"Thanks."

Arbogast smiled. "Is that 'No thanks' or 'Yes, thanks'?"

"I'll take it black."

On the coffee table, there was a thin pamphlet made of letter-sized paper. It was old and much worn. Sarrazin picked it up as he took a sip of the hot coffee. The picture on the cover showed the head of a majestic African elephant beneath the words *Krämer Ernst Wilh, Manufacturers of Ivory Goods*. Underneath, in smaller type, it said "Catalogue of Fine Ivory Goods and Billiard Equipment." Sarrazin flipped through the pages and looked at the pictures of chess sets, billiard balls, napkin rings, small figurines, shoehorns.

"You were really interested in the billiard-table dealership, weren't you?"

Arbogast nodded. "Oh believe me, the billiard tables I had were the very best. They were Brunswicks, named after a young Swiss cabinetmaker who emigrated to America, where he took the name John Moses Brunswick. He made his first billiard table in 1845. Today, Brunswick is the largest manufacturer of billiard tables in the world, and their tables set the international standard."

"How did you get involved with them?"

"At the end of the war, the company celebrated its first hundred years in business by introducing a model they called the Anniversary, which they continued to produce through the end of the 1950s. They were brought over to Europe by the Americans, and the first time I saw one, I knew I wanted to take on a dealership. Do you play?"

Sarrazin shook his head and took another sip of coffee.

"The Anniversary is an amazing nine-foot table," gushed Arbogast, pulling another thin brochure out from a stack of magazines beside the sofa. He flipped through the pages till he found a picture of the table. "Take a look at that!"

Sarrazin looked at the picture.

"Would you like to do that again?"

"It's over with."

"But why?"

"It just is."

"So what now, then?"

"I'm not sure. I took those correspondence classes in business management in prison. Maybe that will turn into something."

"Have you actually gotten used to it yet—being out?"

Arbogast stared at Sarrazin, who blinked in the sunlight now shining into the room. "I don't think I understand what you mean."

Sarrazin nodded. The door to the balcony was bright with the winter sun. On the windowsill, beneath the curtains, there were two small cacti. The wallpaper had a pattern of lines in small boxes on a yellow ground. On the bookshelf, there were a dozen copies of *Reader's Digest* and a multivolume set of a reference work published by Bertelsmann.

"I know it's only thanks to you that I'm free today," whispered Arbogast, "and I'll never forget what you've done for me."

Sarrazin smiled and squinted in the sunlight that was now streaming through the window, which had lain in shadow when he first sat down.

He raised his hand to shield his eyes so he could see Arbogast's face in the blinding sunlight.

"Do you know how they used to make billiard balls?" Arbogast asked.

Sarrazin shook his head. "No, I don't."

Arbogast pulled a small wooden case out from under the couch. It was fastened with a brass latch. He set it on the table without opening it.

"Ivory grows in rings, like trees," he began, and his low, whispering voice took on a pleasant singsong tone. "Right at the center of every tusk lies the blood vessel that feeds it. And so there's a black vein at the core of every severed tusk. In the manufacturing, that spot where the vein comes out marks the exact center of the ball. That's where the ball is fixed, during the grinding. It's essential that the ball be made perfectly round, or it won't roll straight."

Arbogast spoke so quietly that every sound in the small house was audible, especially in the kitchen, where Elke Arbogast could be heard at work. Sarrazin watched as Arbogast opened the case. Three balls lay nestled in the blue velvet—one black, the other two of such a creamy whiteness that, looking at them, Sarrazin could hardly help but think of very pale skin. Arbogast ran his index finger lightly over the shining balls.

"But because ivory is a natural material, it varies in density." He looked straight into Sarrazin's eyes.

"You can't see that from the outside, though, and you can't tell it when you're cutting through the tusk. Only once the ball has been ground and polished can you tell if the point where the vein runs through the center actually lies at the center of its mass—and only if it does will the ball roll perfectly straight."

Sarrazin nodded. He saw what Arbogast was getting at. From below, there came the sound of a bath being run. The rushing of water pouring into the tub, the sound of the pipes in the walls. Arbogast's gaze was empty. He wasn't there.

"There are only a very few perfectly balanced ivory billiard balls in the whole world," whispered Arbogast. "Just once, I'd like to roll such a ball across the felt, feel its perfect motion in my hand. I imagine the line it would follow as a moment of unbearable beauty. Do you understand, Mr. Sarrazin? You would be able to see the divine harmony that's hidden within the bone."

Sarrazin nodded again. He understood all too well that Arbogast was talking about death.

62

They had breakfast in bed. When they heard a knock at the door, Katja pulled the covers up to her neck and Klein went to open it. The waiter rolled the serving cart to the side of their bed. The carnations quivered in their narrow silver vase, the coffee gave off its aroma, and the morning passed away while they fell back asleep, her head on his chest. She was awakened by the sensation of his hand stroking her back. It was bright in the room, and even with her eyes closed, she could see the afternoon light dancing across her lids. His hand stroked up and down her back in large, slow sweeps. His breathing was so slow and regular, it was almost as if he were still asleep, and for a short while her fear had no chance against the harmony of his breathing and the motion of his arm. Her lids fluttered open and she opened her thighs a little, allowing his fingers to touch her sex. But then the fear slowly rose up in her again like a stagnant tide, and she closed her legs and turned onto her side.

"Please don't. I can't."

She could feel him nod. His hand lay on her hip. She fell back into a half dream, imagining that she was on a beach with the warm light on her face. It seemed to last for only a moment. She turned toward the light as if she were sunning herself, and in so doing, she burrowed against his shoulder. Sleep must have been waiting for her there, because it took her back again, unequivocally, until eventually he spoke again.

"Can I have a kiss?" he asked.

The sand vanished out from under his quiet voice, and she had no idea how long she'd been dreaming. She shook her head, which was buried deep in the crook of his arm.

"Kiss me," he whispered, and his lips grazed her ear.

But again she shook her head and nestled deeper between his shoulder and the pillow. Then he carefully pulled his arm out from under her. She heard him going into the bathroom, and suddenly she was wide awake. She looked over at the remains of their breakfast on the room-service cart—its white tablecloth lay in shadow now, as did the wallpaper with the bright pink garlands—and realized that the brightness of midday was long past. She listened to him pissing, lit a cigarette, got out of bed and went over to the window. The room looked out over the park and its white fields of untouched snow. A path that was black with footprints circumscribed the snow-covered lawns, and the gigantic old rhododendron stood directly beneath their window, its waxy leaves shining with the afternoon light. I'm safe here, thought Katja Lavans, and blew smoke against the glass, leaving a faint gray haze. She heard the bathroom door open, and when she turned around, he was standing in the doorway in a towel, smiling at her.

She turned back to the window and said she was going to take a bath.

"Okay," he said, nodding.

When she had heard him sit down on the bed, she walked across the room to the bathroom. He watched her. She nearly laughed, then quickly closed the bathroom door and turned on the hot-water tap. There was a bottle of green bath salts sitting on the edge of the tub, and she poured a small amount into the water. She stood in front of the mirror and looked at herself while the bath filled, until eventually the mirror was clouded with steam. Then she slid into the hot water and closed her eyes. She could feel undissolved crystals of the bath salts between her buttocks and the enamel, scratching her. She'd never bathed in such a large tub before. She submerged herself to the tip of her nose and found herself in the realm of plumbing—from all sides there came humming and splashing sounds, as if it were an underwater echo chamber, and it seemed to her she was connected to all bathrooms everywhere. She lost herself for a long time in the watery noises of the hotel, and once again she forgot her fear. The heat set her face to throbbing and stabbed at her skin.

When she reemerged from the bathroom with a white towel wound in a turban around her head and another wrapped around her breasts, Ansgar Klein was sitting at the white-and-gold Empire writing table, making a phone call. He had a pad beside him on the table and was taking notes. The table lamp and the small wall sconce by the bed were on. Katja lay down on the bed, within the glow of the light, and picked up one of the newspaper reports on the trial. Sarrazin was always giving them to Klein, and now there was a stack of them in a pile beside the bed. She continued reading long after his phone call had ended, and it was sometime later before she realized he was now sitting at the desk, writing. She read on, hardly noticing the text, and more than once she left her cigarette burning, forgotten, in the ashtray. Once, he stood up and opened the window a little. She never looked up from the papers—just as if they had known each other for a long time. That was how the afternoon passed, with her thinking of nothing but avoiding looking at pictures of Arbogast. Then it was night outside the window. She cleared her throat.

"What are you writing?"

"Letters." He didn't turn to look at her.

"To whom?"

"Clients. The law office in Frankfurt is busy."

Katja nodded and thought of Ilse.

"Are you afraid to go back?" he asked, and she was completely stunned. It was as if he had read her mind. Now he was looking over his shoulder at her with interest.

"When you put it like that, no. After all, Ilse's there."

"But . . ."

She shrugged. "The time here was so short. I'm not quite sure what I would be trading it all in for."

He smiled. "Freedom?"

"That's ridiculous." She had to laugh.

"Me?" Suddenly, Ansgar Klein was serious.

The laughter fell from her face and she looked away, lit a cigarette, took a deep drag.

He said her name quietly.

"I'd really like to see you again," he said very slowly.

Now she was the one who smiled. "I'm hungry."

He nodded. "Shall we eat here?"

She laughed. What a good idea. "Yes. I don't care what we have."

He nodded again and picked up the telephone. As he dialed, she went back to reading an article. But by the time the knock on the door came, she had no idea what she'd read. He told her to make room on the bed, then set the enormous tray down among the covers. There was liver and onions, as well as potato pancakes.

"Katja?"

"Yes?"

"What actually happened?"

She shrugged and kept eating.

"Arbogast?"

"It's nothing."

"Maybe it would be better if I knew."

"I don't want to talk about it."

"I'm still his lawyer."

"No!" She threw her fork at the plate and went over to the window.

Wait for time to pass, she thought. She looked out at the snow. Now it was illuminated by the lights from the dining room. Time was a prison. She knew Klein was staring at her, but she couldn't have cared less that she was standing there naked in the hotel window.

"Would you put the wig on again, please?"

"You must be insane," she said without turning around.

"Please, just once. For me."

She looked out, but she could feel his eyes on her. Then she heard his fork clink against the plate, and she was annoyed by the fact that he had gone on eating. She went into the bathroom abruptly.

She tried to put on the wig, which was lying in a bag beneath the sink, without looking at herself in the mirror. It had gotten easier to do as the week had gone on, and when she once again felt the netting snug against her scalp, she felt nostalgic for a brief moment—she had enjoyed the luxurious feeling of the long hair. But then the revulsion of her memory overwhelmed her, and she suddenly felt claustrophobic. It was suffocating in the bathroom. She threw open the door.

"What now?"

She was surprised to find it dark in the room. The first thing she saw was her own reflection in the full-length mirror on the wardrobe door: standing there in the illuminated bathroom doorway with long red hair. She brushed the hair from her face. Then she noticed Ansgar Klein, whose face lay in the shaft of light that shone from the bathroom door. He looked silently at her silhouette in the doorway for a while, then asked her to brush the hair out of her face again. When she didn't respond, he stood up and did it himself. She didn't move as he very carefully reached up to her temples, took the wig in both hands and pushed it backward off her head. He removed hairpin after hairpin and then the band that held her own hair back. Then he gently laid the elastic band, the hairpins and the wig on the gold-and-white table by the door to the bath, and they went to bed.

Ansgar Klein fell asleep quickly, and, oddly enough, as the lawyer's breathing grew calmer and deeper, her thoughts turned to Max, his laugh. With her eyes closed, she wrinkled her brow and nestled down in the pillows. Again and again, Max's laugh entered her dreams, and later she had the impression that the laughter had gone on without cease all night—that was how lightly and restlessly she'd slept. Finally, she woke, freezing and drenched with sweat. She bent over the lawyer to get a look at his travel alarm clock, a small leather case that snapped open to reveal a clock face that could be raised up to prop the whole thing open like a triangular tent. It was just five thirty.

She tried to go back to sleep, but the dawn crept in, and the blue light made her even more wide awake. She stood at the window for a while, watching the snow gradually go from blue to white, and eventually she decided she couldn't stand it any longer. Maybe I'm just not used to sleeping beside a man, she thought, and threw on one of the robes that was hanging in the bathroom. She put on Klein's dark red leather slippers and slipped quietly through the sleeping hotel to the dining room. Everything was quiet and dark except for a subdued clattering that came from the kitchen and a single doorway through which she saw a light on. The night porter looked up tiredly when she asked him for a cup of coffee.

"If it's not too much trouble. I'll be in the dining room."

He nodded, and she thanked him and pulled the collar of the bathrobe snugly across her throat. The lights in the dining room were still turned off, and she had her hand on the switch by the door when she spotted a figure silhouetted against the snowy blue light at the window. She saw immediately that it was Fritz Sarrazin in his light suit, which gleamed in the diffuse glow from the window. He had a small pad of paper in front of him and was making notes. Beside that was a glass containing a small bunch of fresh peppermint. He didn't look up or notice her until she'd sat down beside him at the table. Then he wished her a rather surprised good morning.

"Do you always get up this early?"

"No, actually not."

He looked at her.

"You must come to visit me in Tessin sometime. You know, on the far side of my garden there's an old stone wall with a table and chairs in front of it. It's somewhat off to the side of the house, but that's where we get the most sunlight. If we were sitting there right now, we'd be a lot warmer."

"Sounds nice. And do you work there so early in the morning, too?"

"Sometimes, yes. It's a good time, when you can't sleep. It happens more and more with age. I'm sure you'd like it there, Frau Lavans. There's a pomegranate tree and a fig tree. And two old grapevines. Muscatel, oddly enough. Are you familiar with muscatels?"

Katja Lavans shook her head. "Did you see the moon landing?"

"No." Sarrazin shook his head. "We don't have a television."

"Too bad. I would have been curious to hear what you thought of it."

"Shall I tell you what I'd really like to know?"

She looked at him.

"How you're doing."

As she was thinking about what to say in response, she looked up and saw Ansgar Klein in the doorway, also in a bathrobe, though he was in just his stocking feet. He stood before them for a moment, and all three were grinning.

"I have just invited Frau Lavans to come see my pomegranate tree. Do you remember the spot by the stone wall?" asked Fritz Sarrazin in greeting.

"I certainly do. And I would by all means suggest you take him up on the offer, Katja."

"If only it were that easy!"

"Perhaps the two of you will come together. I would very much like to see both of you again."

They nodded, smiled. All of them were thinking that their sojourn in Grangat would soon be over. The night porter brought Katja her coffee and promised to give their breakfast order to the kitchen.

"Well," said the lawyer to Sarrazin quietly, "what do you think now of our long and selfless campaign for a good cause?"

Sarrazin raised his eyebrows. "What, did he do something?"

Klein didn't respond.

Sarrazin nodded and looked at the other two as if all three of them were conspirators.

"All right now," said Sarrazin, and it seemed to Katja that after every word he spoke, he paused a long time. "It may be we are dealing here with a murder of a sort that can no longer be considered a murder. Do you get what I'm saying?"

He took the pad and opened it to a new page. "I went to see Arbogast yesterday, and I do think that what happened back then was some sort of accident. But also an eruption, a sort of blown circuit, a storm, a vestige from the war that suddenly discharged."

"What's the war got to do with it?"

"He's got it in him."

"So?"

"I think everyone felt that back then. People knew the scent of it all too well. The jurors, the judges, the press, all of them knew one thing: That had to go. It mustn't be allowed. The fear was too great. Then people got civilized—and now the fear is gone. People have actually forgotten it was ever there."

Katja looked out at the snow that covered the lawns and drank her coffee. Even the waxy leaves of the rhododendrons were decked with a thin layer of white. It had gradually gotten louder in the hotel. They'd heard voices filtering in from the lobby for a little while, and now the first guests entered the dining room for breakfast. Their food was brought to the table, and they ate. Sarrazin and Klein went on talking quietly while the day broke around them. She couldn't listen to what they were saying anymore. Her fear was nearly gone.

63

Just as he had done every morning, Professor Maul had ordered a pot of coffee from room service, and afterward he checked out of the hotel. At that hour on Sunday, the train station was deserted, and he was sure he wouldn't meet anyone other than the clerk at the ticket counter, who silently pulled a lever and spun the rotating tray, delivering the brown card-stock tickets to his side of the safety glass. But then when Professor Maul stepped onto the platform, one side of which was covered with a thin layer of powdery windblown snow, Father Karges stepped out from behind the shelter of an advertising pillar, almost as if he'd been waiting for him. He'd noticed the Catholic priest in the courtroom on the last day of the trial. Karges greeted him with a slight bow, and Maul gladly went over to him.

"You're leaving today, then, Professor?"

The pathologist was slightly annoyed that the man didn't introduce himself, but he set down his suitcase and gave a small nod.

"Quite a reasonable decision," said Karges. "It looks hopeless now."

"When you're right, you're right," agreed the professor. The priest smiled.

"Shall we travel together then, Professor? You can't imagine how much I admire your work. I have so many questions."

64

Hans Arbogast carefully pushed the door of the barn shut and locked it behind him. Under his arm, he had the red license plates that he'd gotten a couple days before, making it legal for him to drive the Isabella once again. Now that it had started snowing, the Isabella would stay in the barn. Dirty snow was piled up at the edge of the footpath. The sky hung low over the town that day, holding the smoke of the coal ovens close, and there was soot on the roads. All week long, journalists had repeatedly asked him what sort of job he planned to pursue now, and Ansgar Klein had done the answering, saying that his client's future professional life was assured. He'd had to promise his sister to sell the car in the spring. Without a job, he couldn't afford a car.

Hans Arbogast stopped for a moment beneath the neon sign that read KODAK and inspected the camera equipment and photo albums in the window display. There were wedding pictures, formal portraits and a large-format winter landscape depicting a Black Forest farmstead. He wondered where the picture had been taken as he pulled the door open and entered the shop to the sound of the jingling bell on the door. In the corner, there was a woodstove, whose chimney pipe rose up above the glass pane in the door. He could hear a moped buzzing past outside and then footsteps coming downstairs. The door behind the sales counter opened and Gesine emerged.

"Am I early?"

Gesine shook her head. "No, not at all. I was just tidying up a bit upstairs."

"Thank you again for offering to show me the pictures of Marie. It really means a lot to me."

"Yes," said Gesine, pausing to consider that for a moment. "I think I know what you mean. Come on around."

She went to the heavy curtain that separated the lab from the shop and held it open. She had already gotten out the file, and it was lying on a table beside the developer. Now she pulled out the negatives. Arbogast, who had never seen a photo lab before, looked around with curiosity while she put on her white lab coat. The thing that most interested him wasn't the shallow developing pans, the machinery or the shelves stocked with supplies, but a mask that was hanging on the wall above the fixer bath. It was an old Black Forest mask made of polished, painted wood, the kind he remembered being worn with costumes at carnival when he was a boy. It was a female face, with the typical high forehead and black wig with red ribbons woven into it. The eyebrows were expressive, shiny stripes, and the nose was beautifully shaped. The eye sockets were empty and the mouth smiled faintly at nothing.

"She looks like an angel," said Arbogast.

Gesine turned back to look at him, surprised. "My little mascot there?" She laughed. "When I spend the whole day standing in here, sometimes I wish I couldn't see anything either."

Arbogast nodded and leaned toward the mask. Its shiny wooden skin had a waxy pallor and was somewhat dinged up in places. Each cheek had a pink spot, and near the outer corner of each eye, a small red ornament had been painted. It looked like a half-moon with a stylized flower, and the points faced inward. Gesine turned off the lights.

"I've got all the negatives together."

It was dark for a long moment, and Arbogast remained stock-still. Then a red glow began to cut through the darkness, and gradually he was able to make out the contours of the table, the shelves. Gesine, whose white coat glowed red, was busy with the developer.

"I've never shown anyone all of the pictures before. You know, I was really moved by the way you told the story in the courtroom. It made me so sad for you. You know, somehow I have the feeling that I was there, too." Then she added very quietly, "In those days, I just couldn't stop pressing the shutter."

A square of light flashed before them. Gesine focused it and stepped aside. Hans Arbogast looked eagerly at the projection of the negative. Framed by the white light of the shrubbery, Marie's face was so black that it seemed time had withered it. It was almost just an outline, yet he recognized her features within it, in some ghostly way. Silently, Gesine slid negative after negative into the slot of the enlarger, relieved to be sharing the impact of these images with someone after so long. The incline by the side of the road. The forester pointing down the slope. Police. Marie, asleep in the blackberry thicket.

He had gone back there one evening not long before, but there was nothing that reminded him of her. Except in his own imagination, there was no picture of how he'd dragged her from the car and embraced her one last time before she slowly slid away in the dark grass. Never in all those years in the cell had he imagined that once restored to freedom, he would still have to go looking for her. The touch of her slightly too cool, somehow sour skin. Her voice so close against his ear. *You found me once, now come back and take me with you.* Marie on a stretcher. The naked Marie.

Arbogast watched as Gesine inserted picture after picture into the enlarger. She would briefly vanish in the darkness; then she would appear again, illuminated by Marie's light. At some point, she felt his breath on her neck. At first just a wisp, then the warmth very near, and then she heard him breathing in and out. And just then, the bell on the shop door jingled. She was annoyed to recognize the voice that called her name.

"Gesine?" called Paul Mohr.

65

On Monday, the courtroom was so overfilled it had to be closed to further spectators. The court officers had to push the crowd that had spilled from the hearing room back down the stairs and all the way out to the entrance of the courthouse before they were able to shut the doors. Microphone booms, handheld flashes and cameras being held overhead all hovered in quiet anticipation as the doors were pushed closed in front of them. While Ansgar Klein watched him closely from the side, Arbogast laid his left hand in the cupped palm of his right one. Finally, the two doors on either side of the judge's bench opened, all rose, and the members of the court entered the room. Horst Lindner nodded to the courtroom at large and then opened a file.

"In the name of the people, the following verdict had been reached. The defendant has been acquitted on all charges. The relevant verdict of the Grangat District Superior Court, dated January seventeenth, 1955, is overturned. The defendant will enjoy the restoration of his civil rights. As for the question of monetary compensation for time served in pretrial detention as well as in fulfillment of the original sentence, an award will be granted. You may be seated."

Lindner waited till it was quiet in the courtroom again.

"This court is of the opinion that there are no further grounds for suspecting that Hans Arbogast intentionally murdered or abused Mrs. Gurth."

Lindner paused and then went on to say that it didn't fall within the jurisdiction of the District Superior Court to make rulings on such questions as whether the current laws governing appeals and compensation for wrongful imprisonment were just. Such a task far exceeded the competence of this court. But, he said, the trial against Hans Arbogast certainly had revealed some obvious holes in the criminal justice system. He personally expressed his sympathy for the injustice Hans Arbogast had suffered.

"The court deliberated for seven hours. Its job here was solely to consider questions of criminal justice, not questions of morality or propriety. This is not an occasion to praise Hans Arbogast for his behavior on September the first, 1953. In the initial questioning, he was not always truthful and was apparently too cowardly to give a full account of what had happened. And while the court is convinced that District Attorney Oesterle questioned Arbogast in a manner less gentlemanly than it was severe and intense, we must also ask ourselves where we would be in the fight against crime if it were not permitted to speak harshly to those under suspicion of having committed serious crimes."

Arbogast grew increasingly restless during these explanations, and Ansgar Klein finally clasped him on the arm and quietly admonished him not to interrupt the judge.

On the other hand, Lindner continued, Arbogast had always denied having committed the crime, even in the face of energetic interrogation. All the expert witnesses called were in agreement that there was no way to prove whether the injuries discovered on Mrs. Gurth's body had occurred while she was still alive. In this respect, he said, it was also noteworthy that no artifacts of self-defense had been found—for example, under the fingernails. This, too, supported Arbogast's version of the events.

He added, however, that the court remained convinced that Arbogast had engaged in unnatural intercourse with the woman, quite possibly without her consent.

Arbogast looked at the floor, and Lindner paused for a moment. Then he looked out at the members of the public in the gallery. In recent days, he said, the court had received numerous letters of concern about the case. All he could say was that they had attempted to make a well-informed decision and done their work in good conscience.

"Only Hans Arbogast knows if we have made a mistake."

Lindner let his gaze roam around the room and then finally come to rest upon Hans Arbogast. With a nod, he thanked his fellow judges and the jurors and declared the trial over.

The doors opened immediately, and the journalists who had been forced to wait outside now stormed into the courtroom and surrounded the lawyer and his client. With some difficulty, Klein managed to arrange with Katja Lavans that they would meet back at his car. The onslaught of microphones and flashbulbs wasn't directed at her, but Klein would have to make his way through it to escort Arbogast outside the court building. He took the opportunity along the way to inform the press that Frau Dr. Lavans of the Institute of Forensic Medicine at Humboldt University in East Berlin had retained his services to bring a slander suit against Professor Maul, who on Friday, after the closing statements, had told a Münster newspaper editor that Dr. Lavans's testimony had been bought in exchange for favors. The slander suit would be withdrawn only if Professor Maul offered a written apology.

"How long will the pathologist remain in the West?" Klein was asked. He said that she would remain in the Federal Republic until the weekend. Klein and Arbogast had reached the bottom of the stairs. A reporter asked what lessons Klein thought should be drawn from the Arbogast case, and the lawyer called for a reform of the appeals law, which was over a hundred years old.

"And then there's the fact that the maximum compensation that can be awarded to a person who has been wrongly imprisoned is still determined by a law that dates from the year 1898, and the figure is set at seventy-five thousand DM. That sum is laughable in exchange for sixteen lost years!"

"Herr Dr. Klein, just one more question, please. UPI news agency. What conclusions do you personally draw from this case?"

"I have received a flood of inquiries from prisoners in German penal institutions. If a mere fraction of their claims are well founded, we shouldn't be able to sleep at night. It's that horrible."

The crowd quickly thinned out at the entrance to the courthouse, and as they emerged onto the street, Klein saw Katja, who was already waiting by the car. Sarrazin was with her, just taking his leave. He raised his hand to the lawyer over the crowd, laughing and gesturing that he would call him. Ansgar Klein waved back and watched Sarrazin give Katja a hug. Then he turned to take his leave of Hans Arbogast, who still hadn't left his side. The flashbulbs popped once again as Klein extended his hand to Hans Arbogast, but he wasn't able to summon up the warmth he had meant to. Just a quick press of the hand and the expression of a wish that things would go better for him from here on out.

Paul Mohr had left the court a little more quickly than the others and stood off to the side, watching as Klein turned and went over to the white Mercedes where Katja Lavans was waiting by the passenger door. Photographs were taken as the lawyer unlocked the doors, and then the two of them got in and drove off without looking back. In his narrow dark blue coat and shiny new black shoes, Hans Arbogast watched them go. He stayed there, standing out in front of the courthouse for a while. And whatever direction he turned, he was caught by a flash of light.

66

Katja Lavans and Ansgar Klein left Grangat, crossed over the Murg River and got onto the Autobahn. The Dog's Head disappeared from the rearview mirror. On the right, the foothills of the Black Forest lined up in neat rows toward the north. It was snowing, and the windshield wipers danced under the countless vanishing points of the snowflakes that were driven against the glass. In Frankfurt, the snow lay beneath yellow light. The headlights of the other cars on the road had long since disappeared beneath its white crust.

The pathologist stayed till the end of the week. As if it were something they were long since accustomed to doing, they hardly left the apartment. Katja Lavans spoke a good deal about her daughter, Ilse. Sometimes, if Ansgar Klein touched her in a particular way, it seemed to him that she would stiffen briefly. Then she would relax again, but sometimes she would laugh in a way that didn't sound happy. They went out shopping together a couple of times, mostly for presents for Ilse and the items on the list that Bernhard had given her. They also got her a winter coat and some perfume. Her train, the D201, left at 10:34 p.m. on Saturday. It was cold and drafty under the fluorescent lights at the station that night. Rain kept blowing in under the great arched glass roof. Here and there, a pigeon took off with flapping wings and then landed again. Both of them avoided discussing whether they would see each other again, but they kissed for a long time before Katja got on board.

From Bebra on, there was a sleeping car that went all the way to Berlin, and she was glad to get the compartment to herself. At 1:10

a.m., they reached the border at Gerstungen, where the train stood still for an hour and a half. She couldn't sleep, so she listened to the dogs and the men rapping on the wheels with sticks. Border guards thundered up and down the corridors, and her luggage was inspected the first time they came in. They thoroughly searched through her suitcase and all her new things. Then the train slowly lurched back into motion. Katja held her breath as it began to move. But it didn't take long, and they were at the Zoo by twenty past seven the next morning. At 9:05, the train stopped at Friedrichstrasse. Her luggage was searched again.

As she left the border-control area, Katja Lavans was on the verge of tears—it seemed to have been not just her belongings but also her memories that were run through the sluice gate at the border, and it had stripped them irrevocably of the scent that had made them so priceless to her. But then Ilse ran toward her, followed more slowly by the waving figure of Frau Krawein, her neighbor, with whom Ilse had been staying for the past two weeks.

67

Fritz Sarrazin looked up at the mountains for a moment. Down in the valley, the sun was glittering on the lake. His eyes skimmed across the breakfast table and then stopped to linger on his wife, her hair, the open front of her bathrobe. Letting the newspaper fall with a rustling sound onto his knees, he wondered how Ansgar Klein was doing. At Christmas, he'd gotten a card from Katja Lavans. Fritz Sarrazin closed his eyes. The warm sunlight beat lightly, calmly on his face, and from the mountains there came a tranquil sound of silence that wouldn't last long. At dusk, they would go down to Bissone, as they did every day, to get the mail and have drinks at the Albergo Palms. When death found him, he thought, he would be ready. He picked up the *Frankfurter Allgemeine* from his lap, spread it out wide before him in both hands, and reread the article he'd just come across in the section called "Germany and the World."

> The ex-convict Hans Arbogast has taken up with the wife of a Munich cabaret actor. The forty-two-year-old Arbogast, who was exonerated of murder charges and released from prison last year, after wrongfully having served sixteen years in prison, had recently spent several weeks in Munich, where he served as an adviser to the Munich Rational Theater's production of *Slammer* at the request of its director, Rainer Uttmann. The situation culminated in Arbogast's running off with the wife of Jürgen Froehmer, an actor with the company of the political cabaret. Froehmer has apparently declared that his marriage is

over, while Uttmann has described the events as an example of the successful reintegration of an ex-convict into society.

"Sue! I've got to read this to you."

Fritz Sarrazin cleared his throat and smoothed out the newspaper before he began reading. For a long moment, he thought about the picture of Marie Gurth and the way she had lain in the blackberry thicket by the side of the road on that cold night.